The Cape Light Titles

CAPE LIGHT

HOME SONG

A GATHERING PLACE

A NEW LEAF

A CHRISTMAS PROMISE

THE CHRISTMAS ANGEL

A CHRISTMAS TO REMEMBER

A CHRISTMAS VISITOR

A CHRISTMAS STAR

A WISH FOR CHRISTMAS

ON CHRISTMAS EVE

CHRISTMAS TREASURES

The Angel Island Novels

THE INN AT ANGEL ISLAND

THE WEDDING PROMISE

On Christmas Eve

On Christmas Eve

A Cape Light Novel

THOMAS KINKADE

& KATHERINE SPENCER

BERKLEY BOOKS, NEW YORK
A Parachute Press Book

THE BERKLEY PUBLISHING GROUP
Published by the Penguin Group
Penguin Group (USA) Inc.
375 Hudson Street, New York, New York 10014, USA
Penguin Group (Canada), 90 Eglinton Avenue East, Suite 700, Toronto, Ontario M4P 2Y3, Canada
(a division of Pearson Penguin Canada Inc.)
Penguin Books Ltd., 80 Strand, London WC2R 0RL, England
Penguin Group Ireland, 25 St. Stephen's Green, Dublin 2, Ireland (a division of Penguin Books Ltd.)
Penguin Group (Australia), 250 Camberwell Road, Camberwell, Victoria 3124, Australia
(a division of Pearson Australia Group Pty. Ltd.)
Penguin Books India Pvt. Ltd., 11 Community Centre, Panchsheel Park, New Delhi—110 017, India
Penguin Group (NZ), 67 Apollo Drive, Rosedale, Auckland 0632, New Zealand
(a division of Pearson New Zealand Ltd.)
Penguin Books (South Africa) (Pty.) Ltd., 24 Sturdee Avenue, Rosebank, Johannesburg 2196,
South Africa

Penguin Books Ltd., Registered Offices: 80 Strand, London WC2R 0RL, England

PRINTING HISTORY
Berkley hardcover edition / November 2010
Berkley trade paperback edition / November 2011

Berkley trade paperback ISBN: 978-0-425-24326-8

The Library of Congress has catalogued the Berkley hardcover edition of this text as follows:

Kinkade, Thomas, (date)
    On Christmas eve : a Cape Light novel / Thomas Kinkade and Katherine Spencer. —1st ed.
        p. cm.
    ISBN 978-0-425-23692-5
    1. Cape Light (Imaginary place)—Fiction.   2. City and town life—New England—Fiction.
3. New England—Fiction.   4. Christmas stories.   I. Spencer, Katherine, (date)   II. Title.
PS3561.I534O6 2010
813'.54—dc22

2010017355

PRINTED IN THE UNITED STATES OF AMERICA

10 9 8 7 6 5 4 3 2 1

DEAR READERS

Giving a title to a book is like naming a child. You mull over ideas. You speak the names out loud. You find one you like. You change your mind. You want to make sure that the name you give will fit and will somehow fulfill the promise of this new creation. This Cape Light book is called, very simply, *On Christmas Eve.* It's a simple title, but those three words evoke so many feelings.

On Christmas Eve, our homes are filled with color, light, and song.

On Christmas Eve, we gather with those we love.

On Christmas Eve, we count our blessings and face our challenges with hope and faith.

And so it is for our friends in Cape Light. Lucy and Charlie Bates have been through several hard patches in their long marriage. Now Lucy's powerful connection with a teenage runaway threatens to tear them apart . . . Unless, of course, this difficult young girl is actually the angel in disguise who will bring them closer together.

Meanwhile, solid, practical Betty Bowman has fallen in love—with Santa Claus. Well, not *the* Santa, but a department store Santa. The situation would be funny, except that under his fake white beard, this Santa carries a genuine hole in his heart. A hole that may be too deep for Betty to fill.

On Christmas Eve is filled with challenges but also with successes. The people of Cape Light never forget those less fortunate than themselves. The whole town comes together to help neighbors in trouble, as they always do when there is an emergency. But on Christmas Eve their efforts fill them with a special satisfaction. What better way can there be to celebrate the birth of the Lord than to share his greatest gifts: faith, love, and charity?

I hope you enjoy this visit to our little town. And I wish you peace and happiness all year long—especially on Christmas Eve.

Share the Light,
Thomas Kinkade

CHAPTER ONE

*B*ETTY BOWMAN CHECKED THE ORDER SHEET, READING the list out loud. Her partner, Molly Willoughby, was crouched inside the catering van, making sure all the food and equipment they needed was present and accounted for.

". . . eight boxes of mini quiche, six pigs in a blanket, two trays of chicken wings . . ."

"And a partridge in a pear tree?" Molly asked.

"It's hard to find a partridge this time of year. They'll have to settle for chicken."

"Settle? Our wings are legendary," Molly reminded her. Betty watched her hop down and close the van door. Painted letters across the side read *Willoughby Fine Foods* in plum-colored script, outlined in gold. Betty had joined the business as a partner years ago, but Molly was the company's founder, and they had decided to keep the name the same.

"This one's going to be a no-brainer. Just a big Sunday afternoon buffet," Molly said. "Mostly kid food."

Betty knew what she meant. The party order suited a palate somewhere between the ages of five and fifteen. But that's what she loved about catering. The variety of venues and foods always kept it interesting. They'd serve pâté de foie gras at a mansion one night and pizza puffs in a school gym the next.

Betty slipped the file under her arm and checked the time. "I'd rather kick off the season with an easy one. We have about a hundred more booked before Christmas."

"Not quite, but close. Not that I'm complaining," Molly quickly added. "Not in this economy."

Betty felt the same. Business had slowed down considerably in the fall, after the spring and summer rush of graduation parties and company picnics. But the phone had started ringing again as the holidays approached, and Betty knew they had to count their blessings.

Betty hated it when business was slow. It wasn't just the financial side. She liked to keep busy and feel productive. It was just her personality. Okay, maybe she did have some workaholic tendencies, but was that always a bad thing? She enjoyed her job—her two jobs, actually. She still kept a hand in at Bowman Realty, which she had run successfully for nearly twenty years until catering had caught her fancy.

She had started out helping Molly in a pinch, when Molly was pregnant with her third child. By the time Molly was ready to admit she was overwhelmed and needed real help, Betty was hooked and ready to jump in. She was no cook, but she was so good at managing the staff and the books and smoothing over ruffled clients—areas that were not Molly's strong points—that Molly had welcomed her partnership. Betty had been ready for a change and decided to follow her bliss. She and her closest friend had been building the business and having loads of fun ever since.

"How about a quick cup of coffee?" Betty said, heading back inside the shop. "I could use a little caffeine to keep me moving."

"Me, too," Molly admitted, following her inside. "Thanksgiving wiped me out. We were at Jessica and Sam's house this year, but I still brought over most of the food. It's hard for Jessica with the new baby." Molly came from a large family, and most of her siblings, like her older brother Sam Morgan, still lived in the area. "Then I stopped by the Kavanaghs' anniversary party last night just to check on things. Two of the waitstaff hadn't shown up, and Sonia was in over her head. So I ended up staying until the last waltz."

Betty glanced at her pal as she poured two mugs of coffee. "You should have called. I would have come to help."

"It wasn't a big deal. But you know Cynthia Kavanagh. If anything went wrong, our good name would be trashed all over town." Molly sat on a high stool at the counter and doctored her coffee with a dollop of milk.

Cynthia Kavanagh did have a wide network, and Betty knew that much of their success depended on personal recommendations. But Betty thought Molly was sometimes too anxious about that. Still, she knew where her friend was coming from. Molly had only recently become successful and accepted into certain circles in town. Years back, as a struggling single mother, Molly had cleaned houses for women like Cynthia Kavanagh. But Molly had transformed herself with hard work and a real vision for her future. Betty always admired that about her. It was one of the reasons she put up with Molly's bossy streak.

"I wouldn't have interrupted you last night if this shop had burned down," Molly said flatly. "How was your date with Alex Becker? I'm dying to hear. You haven't said a word."

Betty smiled and shrugged. "There's not that much to tell. It was just a first date."

"*Just* a first date? That's the most important one," Molly insisted.

"It's absolutely crucial. Especially a blind date. Do you know most people make up their mind about a stranger within twelve seconds of setting eyes on him? It's some chemical thing that goes on in your brain."

Betty took a sip of her coffee. "You're always coming up with these pseudoscientific facts about relationships, Molly. If you ever want to give up catering, you could be a . . . a relationship scientist. If there is such a thing."

"If there were, I'd be pretty darn good at it."

"A Nobel Prize winner," Betty conceded. "Let's see . . . the first twelve seconds. Well, that part went pretty well," she reported, thinking back. "He was punctual. A few minutes early, in fact. I opened the door and I thought, 'Hey, not bad. He's very attractive. Tall, in good shape. Has most of his hair and a very nice smile.'"

Molly nodded approvingly.

"He was well-dressed. A suit and tie, very polished and well groomed."

"Alex can afford to look good. He's a doctor, a very successful one, too," Molly reminded her. "It sounds as if he wanted to make a good impression."

"I thought so. He even brought me some flowers, which was a nice touch. I mean, it wasn't as if I was making dinner and he had to bring a hostess gift."

"See? A lot can happen in twelve seconds. Sounds like you guys were getting along great. And he had barely walked in the door."

"It was fine. It can be really awkward when you've never met the person before," Betty confessed. "You know how I feel about blind dates."

"Don't remind me. I'm just glad you broke your rule for this one."

Since her divorce more than ten years ago, Betty had been on her share of first dates—blind and otherwise. More than she wanted to remember. She had basically sworn off them altogether. But

Molly had insisted on introducing her to Alex Becker, a friend and colleague of Molly's husband, Dr. Matthew Harding. Matt had a family practice in Cape Light, and Alex, a cardiologist, had a practice in Newburyport, a town about ten miles north.

Betty had gently avoided the matchup, but Molly had been relentless. Betty rarely minded being single. She was fine with being on her own most of the time, but the holidays always made her feel a little lonely. So finally, after much coaxing and pestering, she had given Molly permission to give her number to Alex.

"Where did you go for dinner?" Molly continued.

"Water's Edge, in Newburyport," Betty reported. She could have predicted the look on Molly's face. Shock, awe, and envy.

"I knew it." Molly set down her mug with a thump. "The reviews for that place are over the top. How was it?"

"Quite a Saturday night date scene," Betty admitted. "I'm glad I wore my little black dress and good jewelry. They seemed to know Alex pretty well. We were whisked off to a table right away."

"Nice. I love that celebrity treatment." Molly grinned and glanced at her watch. "We have time for some highlights. Let's skip the meal for now. What did you guys talk about?"

Betty smiled. She wasn't sure what Molly liked talking about more, men or food. Sometimes, it was definitely a draw.

"Just the usual. His job, my job. Kids. Hobbies. Ex-spouses. Sometimes I wish I could just fill out a questionnaire and mail it in." Betty laughed at her own joke, but Molly didn't look quite as amused.

"But not with Alex? I mean, you enjoyed getting to know him, right?"

"Oh, sure. He's very easy to talk to. Good social skills. We have a lot in common. He's been divorced for a long time, too, and also has grown children. He likes to travel, play golf, go sailing. We talked about movies and books. We seem to have similar tastes . . . It was nice."

Betty took another sip of coffee, glancing at Molly over the rim of her mug.

Molly waited, staring at her expectantly. "*Nice? That's it?*"

Betty shrugged. "I'd like to say sparks were flying or I was struck by lightning. But I don't think he felt like that either. Really, Molly. It's just not like that at this stage of the game. Very nice is good," she tried to explain. "Really good. Better than average."

"Okay, okay." Molly held up her hands. "I'm sorry. I'm being way too nosey, even for me."

"Yes, you are," Betty agreed. "But I've gotten used to that by now." She paused and met Molly's eye for a moment. "I know you're dying to ask me, so, yes, he kissed me good night—a quick, friendly sort of peck. And he said that he would call."

"Terrific. That's a good sign. I'm sure he will."

Spoken like a happily married woman, Betty thought. Molly had obviously forgotten how perfectly nice men often made that promise—and then you never ever heard from them and never had a clue why.

"I hope so," Betty said finally. She gulped down the rest of her coffee and set down her empty mug. "Sonia and the crew should be there by now. I think we should go."

"On with the show," Molly agreed. She slipped off the stool and grabbed her jacket from a hook near the door. Betty locked up the shop, and the two women got in the van.

Betty took the driver's seat. "So where are we headed again?"

"The old Elks Lodge on Tinker Lane. The Rotary Club always has their charity party there. I guess they get to use the space for free."

"The party is for a charity?" Betty asked. "I thought it was just for the club and their families."

"The Rotary finds families who can use a little boost and some cheering up. It's mainly for the kids, but the parents enjoy it, too.

There seem to be a lot of folks in that category this year," Molly observed.

"How true," Betty said quietly. She sometimes felt sorry for herself because she was alone, but so many others had it so much worse. Betty knew she had to be thankful this year and do her best to help some people who were not as fortunate.

"It would be nice if our company did something for charity this Christmas, Molly. Don't you think?"

"Sure. We do give this group a big discount. They're getting everything practically at cost."

Betty meant something more than that but didn't want to pursue the issue at that moment. Molly was less openhanded than Betty tended to be. More practical minded. Betty knew that Molly had seen some lean years and had a tougher time working her way up. *She'll come around,* Betty thought. *I just have to find the right situation.*

The Elks Lodge was located a few miles out of town. It had formerly been a huge old house and was still surrounded by a vacant tract of land, though a portion had been paved as a parking lot on one side of the house and in back.

Back in the days when she worked in real estate, Betty would have called the place a fixer-upper. But someone had draped pine garlands and red bows on the porch rail and a big wreath on the door, which made the old house look inviting and cheerful today.

And Christmasy, Betty thought with a jolt. It was the Sunday after Thanksgiving, and the TV was already flooded with Christmas commercials; the car radio was playing nothing but Christmas music. But Betty still found the approach of the holidays to be a shock. She hoped this first party would get her more in the mood.

As she steered the van into the lot, she noticed that it was already crowded. "Look at all these cars. We're not late, are we?"

"Must be club members," Molly said. "I hope they don't get in our way when we set up."

"Maybe they'll be helpful," Betty said optimistically. Though clients rarely were. They usually slowed you down with a lot of questions and reminders that you'd already heard a hundred times before.

Betty pulled the van into a spot near the back door, the entrance nearest to the kitchen. The company's other van was parked nearby. Their helpers, Sonia and Joyce, had left the shop earlier with chairs and tables and had already carted that load inside. Now Sonia and Joyce met them at the back door and helped carry a load of food to the kitchen. The first load of many, Betty knew.

The first floor of the house had been gutted and was now an open space, perfect for a meeting or a party. Betty saw swarms of people hanging lights and putting up decorations, including a big Christmas tree. The tables for guests were set up on one side of the room, and the buffet was set up near a passageway closer to the kitchen. All the tables had been covered with bright red cloths and decorated with centerpieces of fresh greenery.

While Molly looked over the arrangement and gave Sonia and Joyce additional instructions, Betty returned to the van. She climbed inside and grabbed as much as she could carry. The trays of frozen hors d'oeuvres were not heavy but a bit unwieldy. Some were covered with plastic wrap and didn't stack on top of each other evenly. Betty knew carrying them would be tricky, but she didn't feel like walking back and forth to the kitchen a hundred times, so she piled up as much as she could and headed for the back door.

She couldn't quite see over the top of the pile but didn't think that would be a problem. Until she reached the door. She quickly discovered that she couldn't reach out and open it, or even knock, without tipping so far to one side that she risked an appetizer avalanche.

She tried to knock with her foot and then her shoulder. But the effort was useless. Nobody heard her with all the action going on inside. She considered setting the load down, but that was risky, too. As soon as she started to bend her knees, the weight shifted and the trays threatened to avalanche in the other direction.

"Gravity. Sometimes I could really do without it," she muttered.

She took a breath, tilted back, and balanced as she made a grab for the doorknob.

Miraculously, it swung open, pulled from the inside.

Betty was relieved for a moment. Then she shrieked as the trays began to sway, threatening to tumble out of her grasp. She had been so surprised by the door opening that she had unconsciously jumped backward. Not a good move.

"Wait a second. . . . I've got it. . . . Just stay right where you are. . . ."

She heard a man's voice call out to her. Then it felt as if the trays were suddenly stuck between her body and a wall. But she knew it was not a wall when two strong arms encircled her, appetizers and all.

Betty stood with one cheek plastered against the pile. She was glad the food hadn't fallen, but this was definitely awkward. She tried to get a look at her helper. He was quite a bit taller than she was, his head visible above the stack of trays. She realized that if she budged even an inch in the wrong direction, all would be lost.

"Are you okay back there?" a deep voice asked.

"I'm fine . . . I guess. What do we do now?"

"Good question. Do you have a video camera handy? I think we could get some good money for this one." She heard his quiet laughter and felt it, too, the pile between them gently shaking.

She nearly started laughing herself, partly out of sheer embarrassment. "Don't make me laugh. I'll totally lose it. All this humiliation will be for naught."

"Yes, you're right. We can laugh later. Right now, I think we should just both grab hold of the bottom of the pile and lower it down very slowly. . . . What do you think?"

He was actually asking her opinion? Not the usual masculine approach to problem solving, Betty noticed.

"Sounds good to me. On the count of three," she said quickly. "One . . . two . . ."

"Three," he finished.

Betty gripped the bottom of the pile, held the trays steady with her body, and slowly lowered them down to the ground while her partner did the same.

Finally, the pile of hors d'oeuvres was safely settled and she slowly straightened. She felt so relieved she nearly started laughing again.

"Wow . . . success. That was tricky. Thank you so much. That would have been such a horrible mess." She looked up, chattering away, to find the bluest eyes she had ever seen.

"Not at all. It was my fault for bumping into you like that."

Betty hardly heard a word he'd said. She took a breath and stepped back. "I was just trying to carry too much at once," she said. "It was just . . . dumb." She looked down at the trays and took a few off the top, a safe number to carry.

"Here, let me help you." He smiled and stepped over to help. Before she could reply, he leaned over and picked up the rest of the pile, lifting it easily. "Lead the way."

Betty maneuvered her trays through the open door and into the kitchen.

"You can just put them down on the table. That would be great," she told him.

He set them down and stepped back. "Do you have anything left to bring inside?"

Betty shook her head. "That was it. Thanks again for rescuing me."

"No problem." He smiled at her again. Now she noticed dimples, too. Along with those eyes, they were a potent combination.

She quickly looked away, pretending to check the fine print on a box of ravioli.

"Looks like you're busy in here. See you later," he said.

"Right, see you." Betty glanced at him an instant, forcing a polite smile. She felt flustered and hoped he hadn't noticed. It had to be the stunt with the trays. Definitely embarrassing, she thought as she watched him go.

He was just about her age with thick, straight hair, dark brown with touches of gray. He wore a gray-blue sweater, faded jeans, and a pair of well-worn running shoes.

If you had to be knocked over by someone, he had not been a bad choice, she thought.

Molly was working at a big commercial stove with Sonia. She had barely noticed Betty's arrival. "The oven is loaded, but I think you can squeeze a few more pans in there. I'd better go and see if the DJ got here yet."

Betty nodded and set to work. She slipped off her jacket, washed her hands, and put on gloves. Then she grabbed her Willoughby Fine Foods apron and tied it around her waist.

No sense standing around flirting all afternoon. *But I forgot to ask his name,* she suddenly realized. *Just as well. You don't want to seem too eager,* she told herself.

He was attractive. And seemed nice. And there was definitely chemistry. Sparks even. The kind she had felt very little of last night with the intelligent, social Dr. Becker.

Slow down, Betty. You don't even know if he's single.

Yet something about him did seem single, she decided as she tore open a box of mini pizzas and placed them on cookie sheets. Next time she ran into him, she would have to check for a ring.

With that plan in mind, Betty focused on the job at hand. There were going to be a lot of people here, she realized. The party was going to be more work than she had expected. But keeping an eye out for the mystery man was bound to make it all a little more interesting.

While Betty worked in the kitchen, the party in the rest of the house quickly picked up speed. In the time it took to heat a few trays of appetizers, the Elks Lodge had filled with families, laughter, and music. On one side of the room, the parents and volunteers worked with the children at different tables, making ornaments to decorate the tree. There were also games going on—Pin the Red Nose on Rudolph—and a few of the older kids gathered around the DJ, who was teaching them new dance moves.

Betty scurried in and out of the kitchen with trays of food. The music was blasting, and she could barely hear herself think. Each time she dashed outside to deliver more food and clear away the empty trays and dishes, she looked around for the man who had helped her. At one point, she thought she had spotted him, on the far side of the room near the Christmas tree. But a few minutes later, he had disappeared into the crowd again.

It was early, Betty reminded herself. They hadn't even served dinner yet. Everyone turns up for dinner, she told herself, and she was working behind the buffet. She would surely see him pass by.

When it was finally time to serve dinner, Betty kept a careful watch, stationed between the salad and the pasta. As she dished out the food, she kept glancing down the line. No mystery man in sight. Maybe he had only volunteered to set up? Maybe he was on a diet?

She scanned the room again once everyone had sat down. Either he had left early or had vanished into thin air.

Just my luck, Betty thought. She retreated to the kitchen and poured herself some ice water. No matter what the weather, catering was hard, hot work.

Molly came in, her face flushed. "Dinner's almost done. They're just coming up for seconds. Have you checked the coffee? I didn't mean to pack that percolator. It's a little iffy."

Betty had already automatically checked the progress of the coffee on her last visit to the kitchen, but looked again. "It's bubbling away. No problem."

"Great. We'll clear the food in a few minutes, but we're not supposed to serve dessert yet."

Betty wasn't really happy to hear that news. Now that the mystery guest had left, the party seemed to be dragging on. She was ready to wrap it up and go home.

"What's next on the agenda?" she asked Molly.

"Let's see . . ." Molly picked up some notes from the table. But before she could reply, Betty's question was answered.

The unmistakable sound of brass bells filled the air. The sound seemed to be coming from just outside the house, at the front of the building. The party guests grew very quiet as Molly and Betty rushed to the kitchen doorway to see what was going on.

The DJ took up a microphone. "What was that? Who's out there?" he asked the children.

"Santa Claus!" they yelled back.

"Santa Claus? Do you really think he's out there?"

"*Yes! Yes!*" they shouted.

"Should we let him in?"

Betty quickly covered her ears. The response was nearly deafening.

The DJ started across the room at a brisk pace, urged on by the screaming children. A few of the more precocious guests had escaped their parents and run over to the front door to take matters into their own hands.

But before anyone could reach the knob, the door swung open, and there he stood, in all his red-suited glory. Santa nodded and smiled, a silky white beard flowing down over a big belly, a huge black sack slung over one broad shoulder. He smiled down at the children, and they jumped back in awe. Even Betty felt her breath catch. She'd seen a lot of Santas at these holiday parties and in the shopping malls, of course, but this guy had to be the best. The most convincing and genuine-looking. He strolled in, beaming down at the kids, patting their shoulders and gently touching their heads in a warm, reassuring way.

His costume was stunning, a rich red velvet with a thick white trim. A real leather belt and heavy black leather boots with wood soles. Just the way you imagined Santa's boots would be. It was top-of-the-line, a theatrical-quality outfit. No question.

But it wasn't just his costume, Betty realized. It was something more. Something about him, a certain energy of pure benevolence, generosity, warmth . . . and a hint of mischief. From the tip of his fur-trimmed hat down to his knee-high boots, he was the very embodiment of Christmas.

"Well, now . . . who's been good this year?" Of course all the children answered at once, claiming perfect behavior. They circled him excitedly as he strode into the room.

"Sit here, Santa. We have your chair all ready for you." The DJ stepped forward and guided Santa to a large armchair near the Christmas tree at the far side of the room.

Any of the children who still remained at the tables quickly jumped out of their seats and ran over to the tree. They surrounded him, mostly sitting on the floor. A few hung around the chair, practically climbing on top of him. But he didn't seem to mind. He hardly appeared to notice. He was like a huge, solid mountain in the midst of a storm, solid and serene. Unshakable. His blue eyes roamed the upturned faces, and he looked at each child in turn, as if he recognized every one and was truly happy to see them all.

"I have a present here for each of you. And later, you can tell me what you want me to bring you on Christmas."

"I'd like a new exhaust fan for the shop," Molly murmured. "Think he'd bring that for me?"

"If any party Santa could deliver, I think he's the one."

"He is good," Molly replied. "I'm going to get his card. The Santas we have on file don't even come close."

While Santa entertained the children, Betty, Molly, and their crew cleared away the dinner and set out dessert, coffee, and tea on the long tables. There were platters of cookies and brownies, pecan pies, and an extra-large chocolate-frosted Christmas cake.

For once, the kids hardly noticed the sweets coming out. Santa had them mesmerized. There was no lag of attention after they got their gifts, either. He did some magic tricks and then read them a story.

When it was time for him to go, some of the little ones clung to his leg as if hanging on to a giant red trunk before their parents came forward and pried them loose.

"I'd love to stay longer, but I have to get back to the North Pole and make more toys," Santa explained. "Christmas is coming. I have to be ready to pack the sleigh."

He waved his big gloved hand as he headed toward the door, the empty sack draping across a broad shoulder. The adults gently held the children back, so they couldn't follow.

Or get close enough to a window to see Santa slip into some mundane hatchback or pickup truck, Betty realized. Unless he was so well equipped, he'd even rented some reindeer.

"'Bye for now. Next time I see you guys, you'll be fast asleep. It won't be long. Merry Christmas! Merry Christmas!" he called out in a booming voice as he slipped out the front door.

"Good-bye, Santa!" the younger children called back, many of them sounding genuinely sad to see him go. Betty almost called good-bye, too, but caught herself just in time.

She heard the sound of bells coming from the front porch. Then, suddenly, it was silent. She felt a little sad. But also as if something magical had just happened.

Funny how she had never noticed the costumed Santas at these parties before. But this one was different. Somehow, despite her preholiday funk, his appearance had made her smile and remember what the holidays were all about. The good part, she amended. His visit had made her heart a little lighter, and she felt better about Christmas coming now.

Molly walked past with a pyramid of brownies neatly arranged on a tray and garnished with candy canes. "He's a hard act to follow. But at least we have plenty of sweets to console them."

"Good strategy," Betty agreed with a grin.

The abundant dessert platters were soon emptied, with barely a cookie or slice of cake left over. Some families had left early, and the rest packed up to go as the buffet tables were cleared. Luckily, Betty thought, since all the sugar had revved up the kids. A few were quite wild, chasing each other around the big room. But they would all sleep well tonight.

While visions of sugarplums dance in their heads, she thought with a grin.

Many of the Rotary Club members stayed to help Molly and the crew clean and pack up their equipment. This was Betty's least favorite part of the job, but it usually didn't take that long. They efficiently kept up with the mess in the kitchen and even the party area as the event went on. They did like to leave a space as clean as they had found it. Sometimes, even cleaner, Betty thought as she sprayed the kitchen counter and wiped it down with a paper towel.

Molly came into the kitchen, her coat pulled over one arm and her phone in the other hand. "Betty, I nearly forgot. I promised Matt and the girls that we would go to the tree lighting in the village tonight. Matt just called. He's on his way to pick me up. Do you mind if I run?"

Each year on the Sunday after Thanksgiving, the town of Cape

Light held a tree lighting event on the village green. Betty never missed it when her son was young but hadn't been to one now in years. Molly and Matt had four girls altogether, two from Molly's first marriage, one from Matt's first, and little Betty, who was three. Betty thought it was nice that the older girls still wanted to see the tree and sing carols, but they probably all enjoyed watching their little sister take in the sights—especially when Santa showed up on the back of a fire engine.

"No problem. You go ahead," Betty told her. "We're almost done in here." She yanked off her plastic gloves and tossed them in the wastebasket.

"Great, thanks." Molly leaned over and gave her a quick hug. "I'll see you tomorrow."

Betty took a last look at the kitchen. Everything seemed to be in order. She grabbed her coat and bag and headed out as well.

A few lingering Rotary Club members were still in the lodge, talking over club business, but Betty didn't want to interrupt. She knew they would shut off the lights and lock the door, so she didn't worry about that final detail.

She strolled out to the van and took out her keys. It was a clear night with a few bright stars twinkling in the darkness. It had been so warm in the kitchen that the cold, brisk air was like a slap across the cheek.

She hopped into the driver's seat and turned the key in the ignition. She could hardly wait to get the heater going. Where were her gloves? Her fingers already felt like ice.

She turned the key once and heard an annoying whine. But the van was old and often temperamental. "Come on now. Stop fooling around. I'm tired. I want to go home," Betty said out loud.

She took a breath, then turned the key again, this time more focused on the outcome. "Come on. . . . You're kidding, right?" she said quietly.

Another noisy whine, this time louder and more ominous-sounding.

"Oh, blast!"

Betty stared out the windshield, fuming. Car trouble. Just what she needed. She got out and lifted up the hood, not even knowing what she was supposed to be looking at.

Unless there was something really obvious going on, like a wild animal stuck in the motor, she wasn't going to be able to diagnose this situation, she realized. Nothing to do but call roadside service and wait here for them to come, she thought glumly.

"Having trouble with your van?"

She turned at the sound of a man's voice. A vaguely familiar voice, she realized.

It was him. The mystery man. The one who had prevented the appetizer avalanche. She stared at him and blinked, as if he had fallen out of the sky.

Where have you been all night? she nearly asked him.

"The engine won't turn over," she said instead. She turned and glanced down at the motor, taking a minute to regain her inner balance.

"Could be anything. Let me take a look." He walked over and peered under the hood. He stood close to her, their shoulders nearly touching.

For a moment, she thought she had imagined him. But here he was again, real enough. And really attractive, too. She hadn't imagined that, either.

"There's some corrosion on the battery terminals, see?" He pointed to the metal bolts on top of the battery. Betty nodded. She did know what that part was. "I'll try to scrape it off. You get in the car, and I'll tell you when to try it again."

"Okay." Betty got back in the driver's seat and waited for his direction. She saw him take out a big key ring then heard metallic sounds as he scraped the powdery material from the bolts on the battery.

"Okay, try it," he called out to her.

She put the key in the ignition, but the engine didn't catch. There was only the whining sound, and finally she gave up.

"What now?" she asked, getting out of the van. "I can call roadside service. Maybe it needs to be towed."

"Let's try to jump it first. I'll just pull my truck up and see if we can get it started."

Before Betty could comment one way or the other, he had walked away, headed for a nearby pickup truck.

He quickly pulled up beside the van. He got out a set of cables, then opened the hood of his vehicle. "Okay, stand back a bit. I'm not really sure how this goes."

"You're not?" Betty stared at him.

He glanced at her. She could tell from the laughter in his eyes that he'd been teasing.

"Don't worry, I remember. Nothing to it."

He attached the red and black clips to the terminals and then brought the other ends of the cable to his truck and did the same.

Then he climbed into the van and tried to start it. The engine sputtered a bit but soon caught and started running smoothly.

"Success." He jumped down from the van. "We'd better leave it running awhile so it charges up. Do you have far to go?"

"I'm just going home. I live in the village."

"I'll follow you, just in case," he said. "I'm headed that way myself."

Betty nodded. "Okay. By the way, I'm Betty. Betty Bowman. I don't think I caught your name."

"Oh . . . right. Nathan Daley." He smiled and extended his hand. "Nice to meet you," he said politely.

Betty took his hand a moment. His grip was strong and warm,

despite the cold. She knew her own fingers must feel like ice cubes, and she quickly put her hand back in her pocket.

"Do you live in Cape Light, Nathan?" she asked curiously. *He must be new in town. I can't see how I missed him,* Betty thought.

"Not in the village. Out near the old Warwick Estate. But I'm going into town for the tree lighting."

He looked at her hopefully. Was he going to ask her to join him?

"I'm just headed home. It's been a long day."

"I'm sure. You were working hard at the party," he noted. "It was great. Your company does a terrific job."

Betty felt a bit confused. She thought he had left the party. She'd certainly been watching for him and hadn't seen him all night.

"We do our best. It was a nice group," she added. She glanced at him curiously. "I'm a little surprised to hear you say that, though," she admitted. "I didn't see you there. I thought you left after everything was set up."

"I did leave for a while. But I came back." He paused, and Betty thought he was working hard to hold back a smile. "You didn't recognize me? I did change my clothes."

"You did?" Betty was pretty sure she would have recognized him in any outfit, from a scuba suit to a tuxedo.

"A red suit . . . and a beard?"

Her eyes widened. "You were Santa Claus?"

"That's right." He nodded, smiling widely now. He caught her glance, and she stared into his eyes a moment. Those sky blue eyes, sparkling above the snowy beard. She remembered now.

"I didn't guess. Obviously." She smiled at him, still surprised. "You were very good. Molly—my partner," she explained, "and I, we've seen a lot of Santas. You were top notch. We both agreed."

"Thank you. I appreciate that." He nodded, accepting the compliment. "Meeting Santa means a lot to children. I think most adults forget that. I do take it seriously. I work at it."

That much was obvious. The question was, what else did he work at? As a *real* job. "That's great," Betty said. "What an interesting hobby." She looked up at him, wondering if he would take the bait.

"It's more than a hobby. I mean, it's pretty much the way I earn my living during the Christmas season."

"Really? How interesting." Betty hoped her disappointment didn't show. *Just my luck. The first man I'm genuinely attracted to in who knows how long. And he turns out to be a professional fake Santa?*

She searched around her pockets for her gloves. He really was a nice man, and it had been refreshing to meet him. In fact, it had reminded her of what a person was supposed to feel on a first date. On any kind of date.

"You look a little cold," he noticed. "Why don't you get in the van and put the heat on?"

"I'd love to," she said honestly. He opened the door for her, and she climbed in then leaned over and turned on the heater full blast. She closed the door and rolled down the window so they could continue talking.

"You just need to run it another minute or two. Do you feel better now?"

"Much better, thank you." *Most men wouldn't have noticed if I'd turned into an ice statue out there.* He was considerate, too. What a waste, Betty thought with a sigh.

"So you must get a lot of work. You're very good at what you do," she said after a moment.

"I'm pretty well booked for the season." He took out a pair of black wool gloves and pulled them on. He wore only a down vest over the gray-blue sweater but didn't seem to be affected by the cold. "I work at the mall a few hours a week, but I prefer charity events, like this one. I'm actually double-booked tonight. I'm the Santa at the tree lighting, too."

"You are? I'm impressed. That's an important job. I hope I'm not making you late?"

"Not at all. I have plenty of time. I don't arrive until the end, for the grand finale."

"Yes, I remember. On a fire truck, right?"

"That's right. That part is fun," he admitted.

"I'll bet," she said sincerely. She smiled back at him, feeling wistful.

They didn't speak for a moment. Then he said, "Your battery is probably charged enough now to get you home. But you'd better bring it to a shop tomorrow. You don't want to get stuck again."

"No . . . I don't." *Not unless you're around to help me,* she silently amended.

For a brief moment, she had the oddest feeling he knew what she was thinking. Betty quickly turned away, suddenly fascinated by the cup holder on the dashboard.

He disconnected the cables, slammed down the van's hood, then got into his truck. "You go ahead, I'll follow," he called out the window.

Betty nodded. She pulled out of the lot and turned onto Tinker's Lane. She was used to being on her own, driving everywhere at any hour, doing what she had to do. If she had gotten stuck on the road on the way home, she would have pulled over and called for roadside service. But it was a good feeling to see the headlights of Nathan's truck following behind her in the darkness tonight. An uncommonly nice feeling.

They soon arrived at Betty's house. She stopped in front and waved to him. He pulled up and opened the window. "Good night, Betty. It was nice to meet you," he called out.

"It was work. Admit it," she teased him. "But thanks again for rescuing me. That was twice in one day."

"My pleasure. Next time, I'll give you a lift with the reindeer."

His reply made her laugh. She waved as he drove away and laughed again when she caught sight of the bumper sticker on his truck's tailgate: MY OTHER CAR IS A SLEIGH.

The bright feeling quickly faded. There would not be a next time. Unless she ran into him at another party. She wondered why he hadn't asked for her phone number. He seemed to like her. She could tell that much by now.

Perhaps her disappointment about his career track—or lack of one—had been obvious. Or maybe he was in a relationship—even though he hadn't been wearing a ring. It was hard to see how an attractive guy like that could be unattached. What was the point of even thinking about it?

Betty sat in the van a moment and stared at her house and then at the others nearby.

Quite a few of her neighbors had been busy today, decorating outside with lights and wreaths and pine garlands. Her next-door neighbor had set candles in each of the front windows, which looked warm and inviting.

Her house, a classic colonial that was way too big for her now, looked a bit bare and empty. Which was how she suddenly felt, deep inside. The spark of Christmas spirit she'd felt at the party had faded, and Betty walked up to the front door feeling lonely and tired. No two ways about it, it was hard to face the holidays all alone.

CHAPTER TWO

~

*C*APE LIGHT'S ANNUAL CHRISTMAS TREE LIGHTING CERE-
mony on the green was a time-honored village tradition and
always attracted a crowd of families. This year had been no different, Lucy Bates observed. In fact, it seemed that an even bigger
crowd had turned out, happily braving the chilly breezes off the
harbor to sing carols together and sigh aloud when the tree lights
were turned on.

The good folks of Cape Light seemed eager this year to celebrate the simple pleasures of the holidays, she noticed. Including
the traditional visit to the Clam Box diner right after the lighting,
for a cup of hot cocoa and a donut or a slice of pie and coffee.

When she passed by the diner on her way home from work, the
place was jammed. She knew her husband, Charlie, was short on
waitstaff, as usual, and could use her help. Even though she was
dog tired after an eight-hour nursing shift, she parked and went
inside. Her guess had been correct. The only person working the

floor was Trudy, Charlie's most reliable employee. Charlie himself was running between the tables and the kitchen, not at all in the Christmas spirit.

Lucy didn't even bother to announce herself. She just pulled on an apron and found a pencil and an order pad.

For all her education, certifications, and experience these past few years, it sometimes seemed to Lucy that very little in her life had changed. On the outside, maybe. She spent most of her days nursing now, not waiting tables. But in a deeper place, she often felt as if some larger part of her was still stuck back here, in the diner. But maybe that had more to do with her marriage.

Of course there had been some changes since she became a nurse. But only the bare minimum, she had come to see. Like repairs you make on an old car—just enough to keep it running. No great investments or overhauls. Not on Charlie's part anyway.

Lucy twisted her apron strings into a quick knot. She was still slim as the day she had gotten married and could wind the strings around her waist twice.

"Lucy, where did you come from?" Trudy greeted her with a look of relief.

"Santa sent me. He got your note." Lucy patted Trudy's shoulder as she raced by, a burger deluxe platter in each hand. "I'll cover the front, you take the back."

Lucy swept the room with an experienced glance, quickly determining which customers were waiting for food, which were still studying the menu, and which were about to call for the check. She headed to a booth near the window, a family with four fidgety children who were squirming out of jackets and gloves. She grabbed some menus, and a bucket of crayons and "Smiling Clam" place mats, printed with riddles and word games, then sallied forth on autopilot.

The demands of the busy diner quickly pulled Lucy away from

her troubled thoughts. She and Trudy raced from the kitchen to the tables, serving and clearing away as fast as they could. Charlie had no reason to complain, though, of course, he managed to find something.

"Who's got the pie a la mode? It's starting to look like apple soup," he groused.

Trudy ran up to the serving station and whisked away the offending dessert. Lucy followed. "Cool down, Charlie. The rush is over. They've all gone home or asked for the check."

He stared at her, about to argue, then looked out at the dining area. It was true; only one or two families lingered, finishing up their treats. There was also a teenage girl, Lucy's customer. She sat alone near the window, paging through a magazine. She would occasionally look up and stare out the window at Main Street and the snow that had just begun to fall. She had eaten the middle of a grilled-cheese sandwich and drunk several cups of tea using the same bag.

Charlie leaned over the counter and pointed with a spoon at the girl. "What about that one? Did you drop a check?"

"Not yet. She didn't ask," Lucy said.

The girl didn't seem in any hurry. Maybe she thought the Clam Box stayed open past midnight, like one of those coffee places with jazz playing in the background and free Wi-Fi. Lucy grinned at the thought. That would be the day.

"She must think we stay open late," Lucy said.

"Well, we don't. Better tell her we close at ten." He turned and wiped down the counter with a damp cloth that smelled of chlorine, the "closing time" smell, which was usually strong enough to drive customers out without any further reminder. The girl didn't even seem to notice.

As Lucy headed toward the table, Trudy met her halfway. "Lucy, could I head out a little early? I've got to pick up my son at the movies. His ride fell through and I don't want him walking home in the cold. It just started snowing, too."

"Yeah, I noticed. I hope it doesn't get too messy out there. You go on, Trudy. I'll help Charlie close up."

"Thanks, Lucy. I just have the one table in the back left, and they have their check." She pulled on her coat, grabbed her handbag from under the counter, then cast a grateful smile in Lucy's direction as she headed out the door.

Trudy's remaining customers were leaving. Lucy took the check and made change at the register. Charlie was still in the kitchen, and she could hear the familiar sounds as he performed his usual cleaning routine. He would soon come clanking through the swinging doors, pushing the rolling mop bucket. Lucy knew it was time to find the broom and sweep up what she could.

When she passed by the girl, she stopped at the table, waiting for her to look up from her magazine. Lucy had the distinct feeling she wasn't reading. Just staring at the page, willing Lucy to go away. The girl turned the page, revealing a blue tattoo around her wrist that looked like a bracelet of twisted vines. Then she broke out into a harsh cough, covering her mouth with her hand.

It didn't sound good, Lucy thought. She knew a lot about coughs by now and could practically diagnose the cause by the sound. This girl's cough came from deep in her lungs, and she seemed to be shivering.

She was wearing a khaki army-style jacket, which couldn't be very warm. Her jeans were tight with a few, fashionable tears. Her hair was long and dark, but pushed up into some sort of disheveled twist, with strands falling down in all directions. A few streaks of iridescent blue and red glistened against natural, lustrous brown. A long row of piercings decorated one ear, and there was a small gold ring in one nostril. Her skin was very pale, especially in contrast to her heavy black eye makeup.

She looked about the same age as Lucy's oldest son, C.J.—and just the type of girl she hoped her son would avoid. Definitely not a cheerleader on a study break.

"We close in a few minutes," Lucy said. "Would you like anything else?"

The girl looked up briefly, then shook her head. "I'm good. Thanks."

"Okay. I'll leave the check. You can pay at the register when you're ready."

The girl stared down at the magazine and nodded.

Lucy had already totaled the bill. She set the slip facedown on the table, then headed for the utility closet near the restrooms to find the broom and dustpan.

Lucy had just opened the closet when she heard Charlie shouting in the dining room. She spun around just in time to see him spring out from behind the counter and grab at the girl's pack as she headed for the door.

"Not so fast! Where do you think you're going?"

"Hey, jerk . . . let me go!" the girl shouted back at him, yanking hard on the strap to shake off his grip. "Who do you think you are?"

"I own this place, and I just caught you skipping out on your bill. That's who."

The girl gave Charlie an angry, indignant stare. As if he were a particularly repulsive bug. "Just chill, would you? It's not exactly the end of the world." She rolled her eyes. "As if you're going to go bankrupt or something."

Charlie let go of the strap, but took a stand between the girl and the door. He crossed his sinewy arms over his chest. "You're not leaving without paying, young lady. This isn't a soup kitchen."

The girl took a step back, her eyes scanning the diner. Would she try to dodge around him—or break down in tears?

Lucy stepped toward them quickly. "What's going on here, Charlie?" she asked, though she already knew.

"This one was trying to sneak out on her check," Charlie said. "I was crouched under the counter, putting away the ketchup bottles. She must have thought I was still in the kitchen."

The look on the girl's face told Lucy his account was true. But she managed to sound outraged. "What is the big deal? I just forgot, that's all."

"Hah! That's a good one." Charlie made a snorting sound.

Lucy picked up the check from the table. "It's seven dollars and fifteen cents."

She glanced at the girl and waited, wondering if the girl would finally take out her wallet and pay. Maybe she didn't have the money, or had so little, she was trying to conserve her resources.

"You heard the lady. We don't have all night," Charlie reminded the girl. "Seven dollars. You can skip the change."

He had hardly raised his voice but his tone was harsh. The girl looked scared. Her chin trembled. Then she looked up at him, her eyes hard. "I don't have any money. Sorry." She shrugged, not looking sorry in the least.

"What do you mean you don't have it?" Charlie's temper was rising, Lucy could tell. "You don't have it, or you don't want to pay? That's just plain dishonest. That's stealing. You came in here, ate the food. Now you have to pay for it."

"I just told you, mister. I made a mistake. I thought I had more money in my wallet. But I don't. What are you going to do? Lock me in here overnight and make me wash dishes?"

Charlie's mouth hung open for a moment, then snapped shut. This little girl had a smart mouth. Lucy and Charlie didn't allow their kids to talk like that. Charlie hated to be disrespected. It got under his skin in the worst way.

"Now you're smart-mouthing me, on top of everything? I'll tell you what I can do, Missy. I can call the police. They'll take you back to the station and lock you up. You'll be sitting there until your parents come to get you. Now what do you have to say?"

The girl didn't say anything. She stared at Charlie with an angry expression, her arms crossed over her chest. Her defiant look would have wilted most anyone, Lucy thought. Anyone but her husband, Charlie. It only made him madder.

This was getting out of hand. The girl was brazen and rude. But she was just a kid, after all, and it was late, Lucy reasoned. Maybe a token amount would satisfy Charlie, and they could send the girl home. She didn't look like she had much to spare. They didn't have to browbeat her over seven dollars.

"Slow down, Charlie. Let's just talk a minute and try to figure this out."

Charlie met her glance. "I just did. Seven dollars—or I make a call to Tucker. That's the choice, clear and simple."

It wasn't so clear and simple to Lucy. Did this girl even have parents who would come running after that sort of phone call? Looking at her, Lucy had to wonder.

The girl stood with her head bowed, chewing on her cuticle.

"Look at her, Charlie," Lucy implored in a hushed voice. "She's a kid. She must be about sixteen, or even younger. I bet she's telling the truth, and she has no money."

"It's the principle of the thing, Lucy. This girl needs to be taught a lesson. Maybe she'll think twice before trying to swindle someone else."

"I'd hardly call a check for a grilled-cheese grand larceny."

He glared at her. "Now you're smart-mouthing me, too?"

Lucy didn't answer. She turned to the girl, who was coughing again and wiping her nose with a wad of tissues. While Lucy and Charlie had been arguing, the girl had sat down in a spare chair near the door. Her forehead and hairline looked damp with sweat. Either nerves or a fever, Lucy thought.

"Where are you headed to tonight?" Lucy said kindly.

The girl looked surprised by Lucy's tone—surprised and suspicious.

She shrugged. "I'm going to my aunt's house. She lives around here."

"Really? Maybe I know her. What's her name?"

"I don't think you know her. She just moved here," the girl said quickly.

"What street does she live on?" Lucy knew she was pressing now, but she could already guess the answer.

"I'm not sure. . . . I have it written down somewhere," the girl said vaguely.

Lucy didn't answer, just nodded.

"So, can I go, or what? My aunt is waiting for me. She'll be worried."

The girl rose and took a step toward the door, and Charlie took a step toward the girl. "Hey, not so fast. We still have some business to settle, miss."

"That's right, we don't want you to go yet. Just sit down over here for a minute, please." Lucy led the girl away from the door and sat her at a nearby table. "My husband and I have to talk. You can leave soon, I promise."

The girl twisted her mouth with a frustrated look but did as she was told. Another coughing fit took hold, and Lucy thought it was a good thing the girl was seated. She looked so pale and weak, she might have fallen down.

Charlie stared at the girl like a hound that had cornered its prey. Lucy had to pull him aside to talk privately. "Just leave her a minute. She's not going anywhere."

"You're so gullible, Lucy. That one will run as soon as we turn our backs."

"That's just the problem, Charlie. I think she's a runaway, out on the road. She's got all the signs. No money and doesn't seem to have a place to stay." Lucy glanced back at the girl and sighed. "I know it's a pain in the neck, but we can't just let her go."

"Who said anything about letting her go? We'll call Tucker. Let him handle it." Tucker Tulley was Charlie's closest friend. A sergeant with the Cape Light police department, Tucker was Charlie's go-to guy for any legal questions. "She tried to walk out on a check. That's grounds enough to lock her up for the night," he insisted.

"Lock her up? Are you crazy? Tucker will never arrest her over a seven-dollar check." Lucy knew their softhearted police officer friend too well.

"Okay, maybe he won't charge her. But he'll let her sleep in the station. They let vagrants sleep in the lockup if they have no place else to go." When Lucy didn't answer right away, he added, "Come on, Lucy. What else can we do? Let's not stand around arguing about this kid all night. It's snowing out there. I want to get home."

Lucy was tired, too. And frustrated and annoyed at having this problem dumped in her lap at this hour. She didn't want to feel responsible for this teenage girl—a surly, rude, and not entirely truthful one at that. But she did feel responsible, and leaving the girl in the town lockup for the night was no solution. The sheer idea of it was outrageous.

"She's barely sixteen. She can't sleep in any smelly old lockup. Look at her," Lucy urged her husband. "She's sick. She needs help."

Charlie practically gritted his teeth, but he did turn to look at the girl. Under the makeup, punked-out hair, and trashy clothes, Lucy saw a glimmer of vulnerability. Or maybe she just looked even sicker now. Still sitting in the chair, she shivered and pulled her jacket tighter around her slim body.

"Don't tell me you're thinking of taking her to the hospital, Lucy. That drive is over an hour and will take two in the snow. And I know you don't want to do that on your own at this hour."

Lucy knew very well how long it took to get to the Southport Hospital. She made the trip back and forth nearly every day. She had already considered that solution and rejected it. Charlie was right. It was too long, too late, and too cold outside.

"No, not the hospital. You're right. It's too late to take her there." She paused and met his glance but didn't say anything more.

"Give it to me straight, Lucy. But I hope you're not thinking what I think you're thinking," he warned.

Lucy knew she probably was. "Please, Charlie. We have to take her home with us."

There, she'd said it. It wasn't the solution either of them wanted, but what else could be done?

Charlie's eyes rolled back in his head. "Are you out of your mind? Look at her, Lucy. Does that look like a 'nice' girl? She'll rob us in our sleep. We'll be out more than seven dollars and fifteen cents before she's through—"

He would have gone on longer, but Lucy quickly cut in. "Stop that. You're just talking off the top of your head. You don't know anything about her."

"Neither do you," he shot back. "That's just my point. All we know is she skips out on checks. Great recommendation."

Lucy couldn't deny what he said was true. Yet she felt it was just one part of the picture. The girl had no money, probably no place to go tonight, and she was sick. She was certainly no Girl Scout, and her fashion sense was horrific. But they couldn't just send her back out on the street. Maybe taking her home wasn't an ideal solution, but there didn't seem to be a better one. They had to help her. It was the responsible thing to do—the right thing.

Lucy knew that if she didn't take charge of this kid tonight, she wouldn't be able to sleep a wink, wondering what had happened to her. While Charlie was certainly not heartless, she knew that he would not lose much sleep over it. The girl was a stranger, not a friend or family, and she had tried to cheat him on top of it all. But Lucy saw it differently. As she often did. She knew it was no use trying to convince him.

"Charlie, I'm too tired to argue with you. There's no place else to bring her—unless you have a better idea?"

"You've heard my idea," he grumbled. "You can't just bring strangers off the street home to our house, Lucy. It isn't safe."

Under most circumstances, Lucy would be inclined to agree with him. But this girl . . . well, she obviously tried hard to look dangerous, but Lucy doubted there was any threat. Not tonight anyway.

"She's sick, Charlie. It's just the decent thing to do. If you won't let me bring her back to our house, I'll bring her someplace else. I'll call Vera Plante," Lucy added, mentioning a woman who rented rooms in her big old house to boarders. "Maybe she has a room or two."

"Maybe she does," Charlie shouted back at her. "Maybe you can find some other homeless bums around town and bring them all over there, Lucy."

Lucy didn't say anything. She took a deep breath then checked her watch. "I'm going to call Vera. It's not too late. She's probably still up watching TV."

Charlie stared at her, as if he didn't believe she would go through with her threat. She turned and headed toward the phone near the cash register. She picked it up and dialed information.

When the operator came on, Lucy said, "It's Plante. P-l-a-n-t-e. Initial V . . ."

Charlie waved his hand at her. "Okay. You win. No need to call in Vera Plante. That old busybody will tell the whole town you've moved out on me."

Lucy wanted to grin but forced a serious expression as she hung up the phone. It was true. Vera was a nice woman but an incurable gossip. Vera would have broadcasted her own assumptions, no matter what reason Lucy gave for taking a room.

He let out a long sigh and shook his head. "She's all yours." He glanced over at the girl, who now sat with her head resting on her folded arms. "It's just for tonight. Understand?"

"Of course it's just for tonight," Lucy assured him. She felt obliged to help the child at this late hour, but she wasn't a social worker. Nor did she want to be. She would make some calls tomorrow and find someone who was.

Charlie shook his head but didn't answer. He swung around and grabbed the mop, which was propped up against the counter. "Guess I'm stuck finishing up here alone. See you later."

Lucy walked toward the girl and gently touched her shoulder. She had dozed off. She probably had a fever, Lucy thought. The girl lifted her head slowly and blinked, seeming disoriented.

"How are you doing?" Lucy asked quietly. "Not feeling so good?"

"I'm all right," the girl insisted in a raspy voice. "So, what's the verdict? Am I going to jail?" She sat up and yanked down her jacket, then wiped her nose with the back of her hand.

"We've decided not to call the police. Even though you shouldn't have tried to sneak out without paying," Lucy added. "That wasn't right."

The girl glanced away, but didn't say anything. Then she looked back at Lucy, her gaze hard again. "So, what's the story? You want me to write you an IOU or something?"

Lucy nearly laughed out loud. "Let's just skip it. I'm going to drive you to your aunt's or someplace safe. Maybe to a friend's, where there's an adult at home? Or, if you want, you can come home with me and stay at our house."

Lucy had a feeling there was no aunt in town. No relation or friend of any kind. But she also had a sense that this child would react badly if confronted. The situation had to be handled carefully, Lucy decided, or the girl would just take off again.

The girl stared at her a moment, then pulled out her scarf and wound it around her neck. A gauzy material, black with pink polka dots. Lots of fringe, little warmth, Lucy guessed.

The girl seemed confused, biding time. Lucy could almost hear the wheels turning and knew she was weighing her choices.

"I never told you my name," Lucy said, sitting down next to her at the table. "It's Lucy. Lucy Bates. What's yours?"

"Zoey . . . Zoey Jones."

Lucy doubted that. But she tried not to let on. "That's a pretty name. Very unusual."

The girl looked up, about to reply, but was interrupted by a coughing fit. The worst so far. Lucy rested a hand on her shoulder. "You're sick, honey. You need to get into a nice, warm bed and have some hot tea, with plenty of lemon and honey. I'll drive you to your aunt's house tomorrow," she added, playing along with the story. "How does that sound?"

The girl had gotten her breath again. "Okay. It is sort of late. My aunt might be sleeping by now. She isn't really expecting me. I was going to surprise her."

Lucy nodded. "Better not wake her then. Let me grab my coat and we'll go."

They settled into Lucy's car, and she headed for her house on the other side of town. The girl sat in the passenger seat, staring out the passenger window. She occasionally coughed but otherwise didn't say a word. Lucy knew how teenagers were. Her older son sat in the car like a stone lion. When he did communicate, it was a mixture of grunts and monosyllables.

They rode along in silence for a while. When Lucy finally

glanced over at Zoey, she found the girl fast asleep, her head settled back and her eyes closed.

Ten minutes later, Lucy pulled into the driveway and turned off the engine. Then she softly roused the girl and led her inside. They stood in the foyer a moment while Lucy hung up her coat. "Can I take your jacket?"

Zoey shook her head. "That's okay. I'll keep it with me."

Just in case you need to make a fast getaway, Lucy thought. But she guessed this whole situation was awkward for the girl. She didn't want to make it any harder.

She shut the closet door and turned back to Zoey, who was gazing around curiously. It was a comfortable house, Lucy knew, though by no means grand. But the way the girl was looking around, you would think she had stepped into the Ritz-Carlton.

"Come on upstairs. You'll be in the guest room on the third floor. Lots of privacy. We hardly ever have guests, but Charlie's mother usually stays there when she comes up from Florida to visit."

When they reached the second-floor landing, Lucy noticed the door to her younger son Jamie's room was closed. C.J.'s door was open a crack. He was still up but so engrossed in his computer that he didn't even notice them pass by. Just as well, Lucy thought. She would explain the situation to her boys privately.

"I have two sons. Jamie is eleven and C.J. is sixteen," Lucy told her. "You'll get to meet them tomorrow, I guess."

Zoey didn't answer or show any response to her one-sided conversation. But she was sick, Lucy reminded herself. She had to get the girl in bed and take her temperature right away.

When they reached the third floor, Lucy showed Zoey the room and the adjoining bathroom. She took out some towels and a new toothbrush from the linen closet. "Do you need to borrow a nightgown or anything?" she asked.

Zoey sat on the edge of the bed and shook her head. "I have my own stuff."

"Okay, then. You make yourself comfortable. I'm going to fix you that tea I promised. It will make your throat feel better." Lucy reached out and pressed her palm to the girl's forehead. Zoey shrank back a bit, barely enduring the touch. Like a stray cat that's been treated badly and lost trust, Lucy thought.

"You definitely have a fever," Lucy told her. "Do you have a sore throat or a headache?"

"Yeah . . . I guess. A little. I don't feel that great," Zoey finally admitted.

Lucy's heart went out to her. She'd lost her tough edge for a moment and looked so forlorn, lonely, and defenseless.

"You get cleaned up and get in bed. I'll be right back." Then Lucy left the room, giving Zoey her privacy.

When she returned a short time later, Lucy knocked on the door. She waited, but Zoey didn't answer. Lucy peeked in and saw that the girl was in bed with the covers up to her chin. Her backpack sat right next to her on the quilt, as if it were a security blanket. Or as if Zoey was afraid someone might steal it during the night. The pack looked dirty and Lucy didn't think it should be up on the bed, but she didn't dare touch it.

Zoey seemed to be wearing a black T-shirt for a nightgown. Lucy could only see the edge of the shirt but imagined the name of a rock band on the front. The girl's thick, shaggy hair was in a ponytail that stood up on the top of her head. The black eye makeup—most of it—had been washed off her face and she looked much younger, Lucy thought. More like a little girl. Her eyes were closed but she was visibly shivering.

"Do you have the chills? I'll get you another blanket." Lucy crossed the room and took another thick blanket from a quilt rack near the window. She spread it over Zoey and tucked it tight. "How's that? Any better?" Zoey met her glance and nodded.

"Okay, let's see what's going on with you." Lucy set the button on the electronic thermometer. "Put this under your tongue and hold it there until it beeps."

Zoey took the thermometer and did as she was told. A few seconds later, the beep sounded. Lucy took it out and checked the reading. One hundred three . . . and a half?

Good heavens, that was high for a grown girl. She glanced back at the girl with concern.

"You have a high fever," Lucy said quietly. "We've got to get that down. Can you take ibuprofen? You're not allergic or anything?"

"I've had that before. It's okay," Zoey said.

"Good. This works well on a fever." Lucy measured out the dose and gave it to Zoey with a glass of water.

"Now sit up and have some tea," Lucy encouraged her. "I put plenty of honey in it for your throat." Lucy took the water glass and carefully handed over a mug of hot tea. She also set a box of tissues and some throat lozenges on the bedside table.

She watched Zoey sip the tea. She seemed to like it.

"I'm going to leave this water for you. Try to drink some during the night. You shouldn't get dehydrated."

Zoey set the mug down on the table. "What are you, a doctor or something?"

Lucy couldn't tell if she was being snide or not. "I'm a nurse."

"A nurse? Gee, I thought you were just a waitress."

"That's just my hobby," Lucy said, knowing she wouldn't get the joke. "Do you need anything else? Would you like to look at a magazine or a book before you go to sleep?"

"I have my tunes." The girl showed Lucy her compact music

device. Lucy couldn't tell the difference between an MP3 and an iPod—or a pea pod, for that matter. But when the girl plugged the buds in her ears and got that certain, spacey expression, Lucy knew she was off in music land.

And will be off in dreamland in about five minutes, Lucy predicted.

"I'm just down one flight if you need anything. Last room on the right," Lucy explained as she headed for the door. "I'm going to look in on you later to make sure your fever is down. Don't be scared if you see me come into the room."

Zoey nodded. Or maybe she was just nodding to the beat of her music? Then she slipped down under the covers again and closed her eyes.

Lucy went down to her own bedroom and began to undress, guessing that Zoey was already out like a light. Just as well. The best thing for a fever is sleep. If the girl was still this ill tomorrow, she would have to see a doctor.

Lucy knew that she would also have to make some calls to the local social service agency and see what they had to say about the situation. If the girl was really sick, she might need to stay another day. Unless there was someplace else for her to go.

Someplace besides that imaginary aunt. Lucy doubted there was any truth to that story at all.

When Lucy came out of the shower, she heard Charlie downstairs, rattling around the kitchen. He would soon come up and drop into bed, then fall asleep like a stone. Then get up tomorrow at the crack of dawn and start all over again.

He did work so hard. Lucy had to grant him that.

Charlie would not like the idea of Zoey staying a minute longer than Lucy had promised. But Lucy decided she wouldn't bring it up tonight. She'd had enough arguing for today. It was best to just take it one step at a time.

She found the thriller she was reading. It would come in handy tonight. She needed to stay up to check on Zoey and make her drink more water.

Why fuss so much over a complete stranger? That's what Charlie was going to say, and Lucy had to wonder herself. She didn't know why. Maybe this girl had been in trouble or was on her way to more. But sitting here now, Lucy did feel sure that she had made the right choice. She had done the kind and decent thing.

"What wisdom can you find that is greater than kindness?" She remembered that quote from a college course she took a few years back. Some French philosopher—Jean-Jacques Rousseau? Lucy thought that was the one.

Well, whoever said that had been right. There was no greater wisdom. She felt sure of that.

CHAPTER THREE

◝

*L*UCY WOKE WITH A KNOT IN HER NECK. SHE OPENED HER eyes as she rubbed the spot and realized she had fallen asleep in a living room chair. The book she'd been reading had slid off her lap and the lamp beside her was still on, though early-morning light filtered through the curtains.

She checked her watch; half past six. Time to wake the boys. Jamie didn't leave for school until eight, but C.J. had to catch the bus at seven fifteen. She knew that Charlie was already gone and was surprised he hadn't woken her up when he left the house. He was probably so mad at her for staying up to take care of Zoey, he wasn't talking to her right now.

Or he wouldn't be by this evening, Lucy reasoned, when she told him Zoey had to stay. Lucy had tried to get Zoey's fever down all night with little success. The girl was quite sick. It was more than just a cold, and Lucy knew that Zoey would have to see a doctor.

She went upstairs and woke the boys, knocking on each of

their doors. "Jamie, hon? Time to get up," she called into the first bedroom. "C.J., are you up yet? You'd better get moving. You're going to miss the bus again."

If C.J. was late one more time, he was going to get detention. She couldn't figure out what took him so long in the morning. He certainly didn't torture himself over his outfits; a T-shirt and jeans were all he needed. Maybe it was the shaving, she thought with a secret grin. A painstaking, manly ritual, though he hardly needed to bother.

She went up the next flight to the guest room and peeked in the half-closed door. Zoey was sound asleep. At some point during the night, Lucy had propped her up on extra pillows and set up a vaporizer to aid her breathing. Zoey had slipped off the pillows and now lay curled on her side, one hand gripping the edge of the blanket and tucked under her chin.

Her skin looked pale as paper in contrast to her dark hair. Lucy touched the girl's forehead. She still felt feverish. Zoey couldn't have another dose of ibuprofen until at least nine, so sleep was the best thing for now.

Her backpack was still on the bed, pushed to the bottom of the mattress. The zipper was open and most of the contents had spilled out. Lucy didn't mean to be nosy, but she couldn't help noticing a long, shiny purple leather wallet. It had a small window in the front for ID. Lucy picked it up and saw Zoey's photo on what looked like a school ID. The name below the picture read Elizabeth Dugan. Elizabeth? Lucy nearly laughed out loud. That was a long way in the alphabet from Zoey. And the last name Zoey had given her—Jones—that was obviously an alias, too.

Lucy glanced at the address. Gloucester. Zoey had come quite a ways on her own. Lucy wondered why. There had to be someone in Gloucester wondering about the girl, worrying where she was. The ID didn't give a phone number, but Lucy would try to find that on her own.

Zoey rolled onto her back and coughed in her sleep, gasping a little for air. Lucy put the wallet back in the bag and waited until the girl settled down again. Then she left to fix the boys' breakfast.

Lucy had packed up both lunches and given Jamie his cereal, toast, and juice by the time C.J. came clomping downstairs in his huge sneakers. He swept into the room, poured himself a tall glass of juice, and gulped it down.

"How about breakfast? Have some cereal at least," Lucy coaxed him.

"No time." C.J. took a bite from Jamie's toast, and Jamie punched him in the ribs, which C.J. ignored. "Can you give me a cereal bar?"

Lucy found the box and gave him two. She tried to buy the healthy kind with less sugar and a little protein. But it still wasn't real food. "I wish you would leave yourself time to eat some healthy food in the morning. It's the most important meal of the day."

"So I've heard, Mom." He rolled his eyes while tugging on his jacket and shoving books into his backpack.

"Listen . . . before you go, I need to tell you something. We have a houseguest. She was only going to stay the night but she might still be here when you get back from school."

"A houseguest? Up in Nanny's room? Who is it? Do we know her?" Jamie asked.

"Her name is Zoey. I just met her last night—at the diner. She's a teenager, about your age, C.J. She's sick and she didn't have a place to stay."

"Where are her parents?" Jamie asked.

"I don't know," Lucy said honestly. "I don't know if she even has any."

"So you just . . . brought her home? Like a stray cat or something?" C.J. asked her.

Just like his father. Well, almost.

"It wasn't like that. And don't be so smart," she scolded him.

She thought it best not to explain the skipped check incident. "Your father and I could see she needed help, so we offered to let her come here. I hope to heaven that some responsible adult would do the same for you if you ever needed help," she told her son. "Kids get themselves into trouble. They don't mean to. They don't know any better. They're just kids."

"Good point, Mom." C.J.'s mouth was full of cereal bar. "I'm going to remember you said that next time I screw up and you and Dad freak out on me."

Lucy shook her head and kissed his cheek. She practically had to get up on her tiptoes, he was so tall now. "You'd better go, mister. You'll miss the bus."

C.J. grabbed a banana and headed out the back door.

Jamie took one last spoonful of cereal and got up from the table. "How long is Zoey going to be here, Mom?"

"I'm not sure," Lucy said. "I'm going to bring her to Dr. Harding today. She has a fever and a cough. I guess she might stay a day or so."

"Can I say hello to her?"

"She's still sleeping, honey. You can meet her later, when you get home from school."

Jamie nodded. "It's all right if she wants to try my video games. I don't mind. She might get bored sitting around all day."

Lucy smiled at him. "I'll tell her you said that."

While Jamie went upstairs to dress Lucy found the phone and dialed information. She asked for a listing for the Dugan residence on Anderson Street in Gloucester, the address she had seen on the ID. The operator said there was no listing for that name at that address. There was one listing for that last name at a different address, but when Lucy dialed the number, she heard a recording that said the phone had been disconnected.

So much for catching up with the girl's family. That probably wasn't going to happen unless Zoey—or Elizabeth—gave her the phone number.

After Jamie left for school, she went upstairs and got dressed. Then she headed up to the guest room again. At first Lucy thought the girl was still asleep, but as she walked closer, Zoey's eyes flickered open.

"What time is it?" she asked in a croaky voice.

"Let's see . . . getting close to nine," Lucy answered, glancing at her watch. "How are you feeling?"

"I'm okay. I feel better," Zoey insisted. She pushed herself up in the bed and then began coughing so hard, she nearly doubled over.

"That cough sounds bad. You need to see a doctor. You could have pneumonia," Lucy said. She had spotted all the textbook symptoms—a loose, hacking cough, fever, chills, and last night, Zoey had complained of shortness of breath and pains in her chest. Lucy wouldn't have been surprised if the girl was too weak to make it to the bathroom on her own.

Zoey shrugged and swung her feet to the floor, then squeezed her eyes shut. Feeling a little dizzy, Lucy suspected. The girl grabbed her pack by one of the straps. "I don't have pneumonia, and I don't need to see a doctor. It's just a stupid cold."

"Yeah, a really stupid one," Lucy agreed. She couldn't force Zoey to visit Dr. Harding if she didn't want to. "Are you hungry? I'll bring you something to eat. How about some tea and toast? Or a poached egg?"

"A poached egg? Gross!" Zoey made a face. Lucy nearly laughed at her.

"Okay, how about hard-boiled then?"

"I hate eggs. They're . . . yucky. Some toast would be good. I guess I am a little hungry."

A good sign, Lucy thought. "Coming right up. You stay up here. I'll bring a tray."

"Okay. I'm just going to use the bathroom."

Zoey rose and glanced at Lucy over her shoulder. The long, baggy T-shirt came down practically to her knees, making her legs look like long white stalks. With her ponytail flopping plumelike to one side, she seemed delicate and birdlike.

"I left you a robe. It's on the back of the bathroom door," Lucy told her. "I'll be right back."

The bathroom door snapped shut, and Lucy headed for the kitchen. She could have predicted Zoey would refuse to visit Dr. Harding. Lucy decided she had brought it up too soon; she would try again, after breakfast.

Lucy had just set up the tray with tea and toast when she heard a crash in the hallway, near the front door. She ran to the foyer to find Zoey, fully clothed in jacket, jeans, and boots, crumpled in a heap on the floor. A side table that held a big ceramic bowl had toppled over, and the bowl had broken into several pieces.

Lucy ran to the girl's side, nearly stumbling over the ever-present backpack, which had fallen nearby. She knelt down and lifted Zoey's head. The girl's eyes were closed.

Lucy lightly slapped her cheek. "Zoey, can you hear me? Wake up. Open your eyes." Lucy's tone was firm and clear. She was trying hard not to sound hysterical. That was one of the first things they taught you in nursing school.

Zoey's eyelids fluttered, then finally opened. She raised her hand and touched her head. "What the . . . what happened to me?"

"Looks like you fainted. What's the last thing you remember?"

"I was coming down the stairs . . . and I felt sort of dizzy and hot all over. Everything started spinning, so I grabbed on to that table . . . and then I don't remember."

"You blacked out. It's the fever. You're probably sicker than you think, young lady." Lucy sighed. "Come on, I'll help you back to bed. You aren't going anywhere—except to the doctor."

She thought Zoey would argue again, but the girl either felt too weak or had finally given in. Lucy led her back upstairs and helped her undress and get into bed. Zoey was quiet, almost docile, the fire gone from her dark eyes. For now, Lucy thought.

Lucy sat on the edge of the bed and handed her a glass of water. "You need to drink more fluids." Zoey took a sip of water. "So, where were you headed? Sneaking out without saying good-bye?" Lucy asked bluntly.

Zoey met her glance, then looked away. "I didn't want to bother you. . . . I have to get going. I was going to write you a note or something," she added. "Honest."

"Yeah, sure. So is the Queen of England—when she gets around to it." Lucy paused, watching her. Zoey looked so sick, it was difficult to be too tough on her. But the girl obviously considered her a complete pushover.

"Listen, sweetie, I don't know you and you don't know me. All you know about me is that I'm softhearted, taking in a kid like you for no apparent reason, no questions asked. So you probably think I'm a real sucker. But waiting tables for years and working in a big hospital, I've seen a thing or two. Now, let's get the truth. Your name isn't Zoey Jones. It's Elizabeth Dugan, right?"

The teenager looked shocked—then indignant. "Great. You were snooping through my stuff while I was sleeping. It doesn't take the FBI to figure that out. Did you empty my wallet, too? Guess I have to check everything."

She leaned down to grab her pack off the floor, but Lucy stopped her.

"Calm down. Of course I didn't steal your money. Do you have any? Last night you said you didn't even have seven dollars, remember?"

Zoey sat back against the pillows and crossed her arms over her chest. Her expression was hard and infuriated. Lucy could tell she felt cornered. But maybe that meant they were getting somewhere.

"Hey, kid, I stuck my neck out for you. My husband didn't really want you here. But here you are, and plenty sick, too. So it looks as if you need to stay for a few days—unless your parents or some other adult guardians somewhere are looking for you. What's the real story?"

Zoey stared straight ahead and let out a long breath. She was stonewalling, pretending Lucy was invisible. Lucy held her ground. "You ought to just tell me. I can go downstairs and get on the phone and find out, one way or the other. Someone must have called the police by now if you ran away from home."

Zoey nervously picked at some threads on the edge of the blanket. "Not home . . . a foster home. There's a big difference," she said finally. "I hate that place. It's horrible. I bet those jerks didn't even notice I'm missing. Please don't send me back there."

"Where's the foster home—in Gloucester?" Lucy asked.

"No. In Beverly. I used to live in Gloucester, a long time ago. Before my real family split up."

"Oh." Lucy didn't know what else to say. Zoey sounded angry but also fearful, and Lucy didn't want to send her back to a place that scared her. Still, Lucy knew she was going to have to call someone—some county office, social services? She would ask Dr. Harding. He'd probably know what to do.

"What are you going to do now?" Zoey looked up at her. "Send me back?"

She might have to go back, Lucy realized, once they reported the situation. But Lucy didn't want to tell Zoey that. It might send her running out the door again.

"I really don't know what's going to happen. Once I find out, I'll be honest with you. But you've got to start being honest with me. Can you do that?"

Zoey met her glance then gave a reluctant nod.

"Okay, then. I think you have an upper respiratory infection. Maybe even pneumonia. You need to see the doctor today and get some antibiotics. Be honest, don't you feel awful?"

Zoey lifted her chin, getting ready to deny it, but a coughing fit doubled her over. "I . . . I feel like something stuck to the bottom of a shoe," she admitted when the coughing let up.

"I'm not surprised," Lucy said sympathetically. "I'll bring you something to eat. Then I'm calling the doctor's office. We'll figure the rest out later." Lucy got up from the bed and headed for the door. "And I'd better not catch you sneaking out again."

"No problem. I feel like I'm half-dead. I can hardly move."

Lucy believed her. The girl was weak. "Fine. Just so we understand each other."

Lucy left the room feeling they had made some progress. At least she got some answers to her questions. But now there were even more. Wasn't that the way these things always seemed to go?

CHARLIE CAME HOME IN THE LATE AFTERNOON, BETWEEN THE lunch rush and dinner hour. Lucy was in the kitchen, lining up Zoey's pill bottles on the counter and double-checking the times and dosage. She noted them all on a list and made a schedule so Zoey wouldn't miss any medication.

"What's going on here? Are you opening a pharmacy, Lucy?"

"This is all Zoey's medicine. We had a visit with Dr. Harding today. Just what I thought—she has an upper respiratory infection. It's not pneumonia yet, but it could be if she's not careful."

"That bad, huh? Sounds contagious . . . Is she still upstairs?"

Trust Charlie to think first of his own skin, and then kin, in that order.

"What the heck is she still doing here, Lucy? You promised me it was only for one night. *One night.* And then she'd go. Isn't that what you promised me?"

"I did," Lucy agreed. No use denying it. "But I didn't realize how sick she is, Charlie. We can't just toss her out in the cold."

"No, of course not. But you can send her back to wherever she came from. Did you even ask her the real story?"

"She told me she was in a foster home and she ran away. She said it was horrible, and she was never going back."

"Oh, all teenagers think their families are horrible."

"Well, maybe this one really is. Matt Harding gave me some phone numbers. I've been calling around all afternoon. I did catch up with a social worker who knows Zoey."

"And? What did she say? Doesn't she want the kid back? Aren't there some rules and regulations about this sort of thing?"

"Of course there are rules." Lucy finished her list and sat down at the table with her husband. "But it seems that Zoey's foster family never even reported her missing. So they broke that rule and they're in trouble now. They can't have her back."

Charlie took a breath. She could see he was trying to control his temper. "Okay, I get it. But she's got to go somewhere. Doesn't the county have a place to keep these kids when they don't have a family to live with?"

"Yes, but since she's so sick, that wouldn't be the best solution either. The social worker said so herself," Lucy hastened to add.

"Right. Don't tell me. You offered to keep her until she gets well?"

"I didn't see any other choice, Charlie. She can't go anywhere. She'll end up in the hospital."

"Great. Now we'll all get sick and end up in the hospital. Ever think of that?"

Lucy had thought of that. She was around sick people all day, and her immunity had built up. But she didn't want the boys to get sick, miss school, and play havoc with her work schedule. There was a certain risk in keeping Zoey here when she was so ill. But before she could say anything more, Charlie continued to make his point.

"I can't afford to miss work, Lucy. Who's going to run that diner? Can you fit it in between your real job and nursing perfect strangers?"

"Calm down, Charlie." She stood up and stepped over to the counter and handed him a bottle of vitamin C and another of hand sanitizer. "That should help. Besides, Zoey's on antibiotics. She won't be contagious after twenty-four hours."

"Great. What am I supposed to do, hold my breath until then?"

"Well, that might help if you could manage it," she joked. She gave him a quick smile, and when he refused to return it she went on, "A social worker is coming here tomorrow. She needs to do a home visit and ask us both a few questions. And talk to Zoey, of course. It's pretty easy to be cleared as temporary guardians. Then Zoey can stay with us until—"

"Absolutely not," Charlie answered before Lucy had even finished talking. "She's not a nice girl, Lucy. Just look at her. I'll bet she's been in plenty of trouble at school and maybe even with the law. Did the social worker tell you anything about that?"

Actually, Lucy had been wondering about Zoey's background and even the kind of trouble she might have gotten into. She would have admitted these concerns to Charlie if he wasn't so . . . combative all the time. He put her on the defensive and made it so hard to talk things out.

"We've worked too hard to keep our boys away from kids like that," he went on. "Why invite trouble right into our house? Does that make any sense?"

"Because she needs help, that's why," Lucy insisted. "And if you had just let me finish before, I would have told you that it's only for a few days. I think our kids can survive her influence that long."

He didn't answer, just looked at her with an angry expression.

"I know she's not a Girl Scout, or anything close," Lucy

continued. "But she's had no guidance, no one looking out for her, for years. This last foster family didn't even report her missing. It was probably an awful environment. She practically begged me not to send her back there. She's sick and she has no place to go other than some sort of shelter or group house. . . ." Lucy heard her voice getting shaky and emotional. She took a deep breath and got to her feet. "I know you don't like the idea, but I can't see what else we can do. If you think about it and search your heart and conscience, you'll realize that, Charlie. At least, I hope so," she added quietly.

Lucy meant it. Charlie's hot temper could flare up in a second, like a match hitting kerosene. But deep inside he had a good heart, she thought. Or, at least, he used to when she married him. Had he changed so much over the years?

Charlie let out a long, ragged breath and looked up at her. "All right, she can stay. You got around me. This time. Meanwhile, tell that social worker to get on the job and figure out where she's going next. I'm not signing on to take care of a wild, runaway teenage girl. I'm telling you right now."

Lucy didn't answer. She had won round two at least. But she wondered what Charlie would say in his interview tomorrow. He didn't seem to realize Zoey couldn't stay if they weren't approved to be temporary guardians. Both of them.

But before she could ask him about that sticky wicket, she heard the back door fly open and the sounds of C.J. coming in, dumping his basketball and book bag on the floor.

"Hey, everybody, I'm home," he announced. He strolled into the kitchen and patted Charlie on the head, like a pet dog. "Hey, Pop. What's up?"

Charlie gazed up at him without a word of objection. C.J. was the only one who could ever take such liberties with Charlie. Lucy didn't know how he got away with it. Firstborn son and namesake. Charlie was so proud of him, especially now that C.J. was almost a man.

"What's up with you, buddy? How was the game? Score any points?" Charlie grilled him eagerly.

"It was just a scrimmage. I sunk a few."

"Good boy. Make it more than a few next time," Charlie advised.

"Are you coming to my game on Wednesday? We're home against Newburyport."

"Sure, I can make it," Charlie promised. "Tell the coach to play you in the first half. I might have to leave early."

"Okay, Dad. I'll tell him you said so." C.J.'s tone was sarcastic, as usual. Typical for his age, Lucy knew. Still she knew how much C.J. appreciated Charlie's interest. She had to give her husband some credit. Attending the boys' school or sports events was important to him and practically the only time he allowed himself to leave the diner.

"Guess what? Your mother opened up an infirmary in the guest room," Charlie told C.J. as he gazed into the refrigerator. "Better drink some orange juice," Charlie coaxed him in a serious tone. "Better drink that whole carton."

C.J. took the juice out and turned around to look at him. "What are you talking about? That girl upstairs that Mom brought home?"

"Yeah, that's the one." Charlie rose from his seat and cocked his head in Lucy's direction. "Go ahead, ask your mother. I don't know much about it. Even though I pay all the bills around here," he added, directing the remark at Lucy.

That wasn't true. Lucy paid plenty of them now that she was earning a good salary. But she let him vent. He had a right, she reasoned, watching him stalk off to the family room to watch the news.

It wasn't that her husband's objections were unfounded or even unreasonable. But there was more to figuring out life's problems than just looking at the facts. Well, at least she had persuaded him to let Zoey stay a day or two more. The girl would get well quickly now that she was on antibiotics. In a day or so, she would be well enough to go.

Good deed done. End of story, Lucy thought.

C.J. pulled open the cupboards, looking for something to eat. "So what's the story with this girl, Mom?"

"She was in a foster home, but they weren't treating her right. So she ran away. She has a bad upper respiratory infection, and she has to stay here awhile—until she feels better and until another home is found for her."

"Great. Can we catch it? I have a big game coming up. I don't want to get sick."

"You won't if you're careful. Just keep washing your hands and put all the cups and glasses in the dishwasher. And take some extra vitamin C," she added. "We all had our flu shots. I think we'll be okay."

She sent up a little prayer just in case. All she needed was Charlie or one of the kids coming down with something. He'd never let her forget it.

Lucy turned to C.J., who had the refrigerator open again and was staring into it like a hungry wolf. "Do you have any other questions you want to ask me about her?" Lucy knew it was important to be straightforward with the boys. She didn't want them to think there was something mysterious or secret going on.

"Yeah. When's dinner and what are we having?"

"Six o'clock. Roast chicken and potatoes," she answered succinctly.

"Great. I'm going up to do my homework," he said.

That went well, she thought. Now if only Charlie Senior were as easily satisfied with her answers.

EVER SINCE SHE HAD GOTTEN INVOLVED IN THE CATERING BUSIness, Tuesday had become Betty's favorite day of the week. On Monday, she was usually pooped from supervising parties all weekend. And by Wednesday they were already gearing up for the next round. But on Tuesday, she and Molly had time to work at their own pace, experiment with recipes or table settings. Sometimes they would just talk and cook all day.

It had turned out to be one of those days as they tried out a new hors d'oeuvre, a marinated goat cheese served in little pockets of radic-chio. Molly was explaining how she had seen a celebrity cook fixing the dish on TV while she was walking on the treadmill at the gym.

"I love to watch the cooking shows while I work out. Even though it makes me hungry," she confessed with a sigh. "It's the only way I can speed walk a few miles a week—with a chocolate cake or some barbequed ribs dangling in front of my face."

"Or some goat cheese," Betty added. She taste-tested the cheese with a teaspoon. "Mmm . . . creamy. Where did you get it?"

"At the Gilroy Goat Farm, on Angel Island. You'll have to come with me the next time I go out there. They've done wonders with the place. It's really lovely."

Angel Island was just across the harbor from the village, con-nected to the mainland by a land bridge. There wasn't much out there except for a few cottages and an old inn that someone was trying to renovate. It was a beautiful and wild place.

"I used to love driving to Angel Island whenever I had a house to show out there," Betty said wistfully. "It's such a romantic spot."

"Matt and I used to go there a lot before we were married. Per-fect for a date," Molly said knowingly. "Speaking of dates, has Alex called you yet?"

"He did. Just last night. We're going out on Friday. We're going to play tennis at his health club, then go to dinner."

"That sounds like fun. I didn't know you played tennis." Molly had started the marinade and measured out a cup of olive oil.

"Well, I don't really. Not anymore. But I mentioned that I used to play a lot of tennis and golf with Ted," she explained, mentioning her first husband. "I told Alex I wanted to get back to it again someday. I meant some far-off time, when I'm retired and have nothing to do. But he got all excited and wants to help me brush up. Apparently, he's a big tennis player."

"I didn't know that. Well, there's something else you have in common," Molly said happily. "Sounds like he's looking for a new mixed-doubles partner."

Betty had the same feeling. "I hope this isn't the tryout. I won't make the cut."

Molly handed her a bunch of scallions, and Betty started dicing with a long, sharp knife. Cooking was so calming. She wasn't a great cook but did enjoy the therapeutic benefits.

"Don't look at it like a contest," Molly advised. "Men like to be helpful and feel they're teaching you something. Especially a sport. He'll probably have a much better time giving you a few pointers than if you trot out there and wipe the court with him, like Serena Williams."

"So I play the helpless damsel, who doesn't know which way to point the racket? Is that it?" Betty's tone was sarcastic but Molly didn't even notice.

"You're catching on." She winked and pulsed the food processor, now filled with a mixture of parsley, basil, scallions, and garlic.

Betty sighed. "I know he just wanted to plan something fun for us to do together. But now I've got to dress up in a tennis outfit and swing a racket for at least an hour before I can eat."

"Now, now. Get a grip, Betty. You're a good sport."

"I am. But the truth is, I would have rather seen a movie," she confessed. "Come to think of it, I would have rather he asked me first before he reserved the court time and all that. Next time, I'll suggest a movie. In fact, maybe I'll plan the date and ask him out."

"That sounds like a good plan. In the meantime, suit up and try to have fun. You've been on worse dates, I'm sure." Molly's words were meant to be comforting, but they only reminded Betty of how many bad dates she had endured. Now it was hard to tell if she was actually having a good time on a date—or if it was just slightly better than complete boredom.

Molly placed the chopped herbs into the olive mixture, and Betty turned everything with a long metal spoon. "Do you remember that guy at the Rotary Club party who helped me carry in the appetizers?"

Molly's brow crinkled. "Sort of. I didn't really get a good look."

"Well, he was cute, take my word for it. He has these awesome blue eyes," Betty recalled. "After you left, I had trouble with the van, remember? He was the guy who helped me and jumped the battery."

She had told Molly on Monday that the battery in the van had died and the vehicle needed to go into the shop. But she hadn't gone into details about how Nathan had helped her.

Molly put the goat cheese on a cutting board and cut thin, even slices. "Did he ask for your number?"

Betty shook her head. "No, he didn't. He was very sweet and followed me home, to make sure the van didn't die again. The thing is, when he told me what he does for a living, I guess I reacted . . . badly."

"What does he do? Is he a garbageman? No, wait . . . Does he work in a funeral parlor?"

"It's not that bad." Betty had to laugh. "Remember the party Santa? Well, that was him. I didn't recognize him all the way across the room. He was disguised really well."

"The costume was great," Molly agreed. "Was he a volunteer there, part of the Rotary?"

"Nope. He does it for pay. Well, maybe not that party. He says he likes to do parties for good causes. But he is a professional Santa. No way around it. He had another appearance right after, at the tree lighting in town."

"You're kidding, right?" Molly laughed. Betty could see she found it all very amusing. "That was him?"

Betty nodded, wishing she *were* kidding. "Yep. He's obviously good at what he does and very much in demand." Was she trying too hard to put a positive spin on this situation? Well, maybe a little.

Betty had tried to put the attractive party Santa out of her mind, but over the last few days she realized how much she had liked him. She had enjoyed talking to him. There had just been something very easy about their rapport. And that was rare.

"Too bad. He seemed like a nice guy." Molly was sympathetic. She had also totally dismissed the idea of Betty getting to know Nathan better. The Santa thing definitely disqualified him from Molly's list.

"He is nice," Betty assured her. "But I sort of blew it. I must have made a face or something when he told me," she confessed. "But it does seem . . . odd. I wonder why anyone would be a professional Santa. I mean, what does he do the rest of the year?"

"There are other holidays," Molly said thoughtfully. "On Easter, he can dress up as the Easter Bunny, Uncle Sam for the Fourth of July, a patriot on Founders Day. Maybe a warlock or vampire on Halloween?"

"Yes, very true." Betty acted amused but secretly felt a bit embarrassed.

And Molly wasn't through. "—Then there's probably a big demand for dancing cheesesteak sandwiches at the mall. . . . Or friendly baked potatoes?"

"Okay, Molly. You made your point." It was just what she expected. If she ever got involved with Nathan, this was what she would have to put up with. It was just as well he hadn't asked for her number. But why did that thought make her feel a little sad?

* * *

CHARLIE GLANCED AT HIS WATCH AND DECIDED TO IGNORE IT. The watch was a cheap one and had never been accurate. If he really wanted to know the time, he had to check the clock in the kitchen, the official standard for employee time sheets.

Charlie knew that he should probably check the clock back there right now. Instead, he decided to clean off the grill. The breakfast rush was over, and his watch read half past ten, give or take ten minutes either way. Charlie knew he was due home soon. Lucy had some social worker coming to the house to fill out papers about the girl. But he was in no hurry for that appointment.

As he mulled over his wife's possible reactions, Charlie saw his friend Tucker Tulley come through the door. Tucker usually came in earlier and Charlie had been wondering if he would drop by today at all. Here was the perfect excuse to linger behind the counter.

"Hey, Tucker. Where you been? Taking your business across the street?"

They both knew what Charlie meant. The Beanery had opened up on Main Street about seven years ago, becoming the only real competition to the venerable Clam Box. Charlie still considered the place a passing fancy, predicting people would soon get bored with the bohemian atmosphere and strange menu. And what the heck was a "Curry Hummus Vegetable Wrap" anyway?

"I've got a real thing for those caramel cappuccinos," Tucker answered. "It's hard to go back to your muddy old coffee, Charlie."

"Real men don't drink foamed-up coffee, pal. Haven't you heard?" Charlie poured Tucker a mug of coffee and pushed it toward him. "Here you go. The real thing. This will get you straightened out again."

Tucker sipped the coffee and grinned. "So what's happening on the home front? Still have that girl at your house?"

Charlie had told Tucker all about Zoey, how she tried to skip out on her check Sunday night and how Lucy had insisted on taking her home.

"Lucy took her over to Dr. Harding yesterday. The kid has a chest cold or something. Lucy called social services. Seems the kid didn't even give us her real name. She ran away from a foster family, so the social services won't send her back there, and she's too sick to go into a shelter. Or so they tell Lucy."

"So you and Lucy are taking her in for a while," Tucker surmised.

Charlie didn't like the sound of that. "Just for a day or so. Until the medicine kicks in."

"I see. Temporary guardianship," Tucker clarified. He'd seen a number of homeless kids and runaways. He knew how the system worked.

"Well . . . it will be. If I go home in time for the appointment," Charlie admitted. He checked his watch again, not sure if the minute hand was working today. "What time do you have, Tucker?"

Tucker checked his watch, a big silver Timex. "Quarter to eleven. What time is your meeting?"

"Oh, I don't know. I think Lucy said to get home by half past ten, but she knows that I'm stuck in here, working."

Tucker glanced around. He was just about the only customer in the place, and the very capable Trudy was on today, covering the tables. "Did you say working hard—or hardly working?"

Charlie glared at him. They had been friends since grade school, and it had always been the same between them: Tucker was Charlie's own Jiminy Cricket, always reminding him of what was right and what was wrong, just like Pinocchio's friendly little conscience in a top hat.

"Come on, Tucker. Give me a break. You know how I feel about this. Let Lucy deal with the woman. She's the one who really wants the girl there. If that social worker needs to talk to me so badly, let her come down here and ask me questions."

Tucker frowned as he stirred his coffee. "This stuff really is bad. I don't know how you stay in business."

"That girl has tattoos, Tucker," Charlie went on. "And streaks in her hair—and about a thousand holes in her ears and her nose."

"Yeah. You told me about that," Tucker replied evenly.

"It would be different if she was a nice girl. A lot different," Charlie insisted. "But she's got a smart mouth and she always looks like she might be up to something. Anyone can see she's not a nice kid."

"It would be different. But nice girls usually don't run away. They have nice families to help them figure things out when they get in a jam," Tucker pointed out.

Charlie stared at him a moment, then gave him a mock-thoughtful expression. "Really? Well, thank you, Oprah. I didn't know that."

Tucker just shook his head. He had an easygoing nature, but Charlie knew his friend didn't back down easily when he thought he was right. Charlie looked at his watch again. It seemed like the hands had hardly moved, and he knew that couldn't be right.

"You want to know what time it is, Charlie? It's time to go home," Tucker told him. "If you promised Lucy, then you ought to just do it. Tell her face-to-face what you're trying to tell me. But don't hide behind that lunch counter."

Tucker's blunt reply made Charlie's blood rise. Tucker always had to be the know-it-all. But he wasn't the one with some punked-out, tattooed teen camped out in his guest room, was he?

Before Charlie could come up with a good retort, the diner's phone rang. Charlie quickly checked the number. Lucy, at home. Calling to see why he was late, he guessed. He didn't pick it up. He gave his friend one last, dark look and yanked off his apron.

"Was that Lucy?" Tucker asked.

"You know it was," Charlie said. He reached under the counter and grabbed his baseball cap and down vest. "Guess I'll go home and do the right thing. Are you proud of me?"

"Always, my friend." Tucker laughed and shook his head. "Let me know how it turns out."

"Thanks, Jiminy. I will." Charlie slipped out from behind the counter and caught Trudy's eye, giving her the signal that he was going out for a while.

"What did you just call me?" Tucker asked, swinging around on his counter stool.

"Jiminy Cricket. That's my new name for you. I'll explain it to you sometime," Charlie promised. Then he headed out the door.

LUCY WASN'T WORRIED ABOUT THE SOCIAL WORKER'S HOME VISIT. The woman handling Zoey's case, Mrs. Schuman, had been very easy to deal with over the phone. Lucy was curious about Zoey's story and hoped to get answers to some of her questions. The social worker would be asking questions, too, of course. But she had assured Lucy that the screening for temporary guardians was a simple process, and Lucy thought it would be.

Except for Charlie. He had been dragged, kicking and screaming, into this situation. He said that he would be home for the meeting. Now Lucy wondered if he would keep his promise. She hoped he didn't just hide out at the diner and pretend he had forgotten.

She could understand Charlie's reservations about taking even this small step. It did seem so . . . official. But these were the rules of the system, even if Zoey was only staying one more night. Lucy understood that. Meanwhile, Charlie acted as if Lucy wanted to take the girl in permanently. And that was not the case at all. Lucy felt sorry for her, but she had enough on her plate right now, with the boys and her job. And Charlie. Zoey wasn't a bad kid. Not the way Charlie made her out to be, Lucy thought. But there were families out there ready, willing, and able to take in troubled kids like Zoey. Lucy had her own children to take care of and worry about. This situation was just for a few days, a good deed sort of thing.

Lucy looked out at the street through the living room window but she didn't see any cars approaching the house, not Charlie's or the social worker's. The boys were at school and Zoey was in bed, resting comfortably. Lucy had told her what was happening and though Zoey never showed much reaction either way about things, Lucy sensed the girl liked the idea of staying longer.

Just as she considered calling Charlie again, she spotted a small black sedan pull up and park in front of the house. A woman got out, a leather briefcase and purse slung over her shoulder, and headed up the walk. Lucy knew it had to be Mrs. Schuman. Lucy fixed a friendly smile on her face, then pulled open the door.

"Sorry I'm late," Mrs. Schuman said as the two women shook hands.

"I'm just glad you're here," Lucy said, leading her into the living room.

Mrs. Schuman gazed around. "You have a lovely home, Mrs. Bates."

"Thanks. I'd love to keep the place neater, but with two boys and my job, all I can really shoot for is comfortable."

"Believe me, I know what you mean." The social worker smiled, then slipped a binder from her briefcase and opened it on her lap. She looked to be in her midforties, Lucy guessed, maybe a little younger. She was just as Lucy had pictured her, with curly brown hair and warm, dark eyes.

"I just need to ask a few questions, Mrs. Bates. You may have already told me some of this information over the phone. I'm sorry to make you repeat yourself."

"That's all right. Ask away—and please, call me Lucy."

"Great, I will. Please call me Rita."

The questionnaire went quickly. It was all fairly basic information. Then Rita Schuman asked Lucy about her family. "How do your boys feel about having Elizabeth here?"

"We call her Zoey. I guess she likes that name. Anyway, my boys don't seem to mind her. She's been so sick, the kids really haven't had too much to do with her yet. C.J. is very busy with school and sports. We hardly speak to him. Jamie offered to let her use his video games. That was a good sign, I thought," Lucy said.

Rita smiled. "Yes, I think it is. And how about your husband? Wasn't he going to be here this morning?"

Lucy felt her cheeks color. She hated when that happened. Still blushing at her age. It was embarrassing.

"He did plan on coming home to meet you. But something must have come up at the diner," Lucy began. Rita already knew that they owned the Clam Box. "Charlie's the type who's afraid the place will fall down without him. It's hard for him to get away, even for a few minutes."

Lucy couldn't tell how the social worker was interpreting Charlie's "no show." She made a note on the application and glanced at her watch. "Maybe he's just running late," she said. "Let's continue."

Lucy showed her the rest of the house. "Would you like to see Zoey now?" she asked, after showing Rita the second floor. "She's upstairs, in the guest room, but she's probably sleeping. The medication really knocks her out."

Rita considered for a moment. "Why don't I visit with Zoey later? You and I can talk some more."

"That would be good," Lucy agreed. "I have a few questions for you. I'd like to know more about Zoey."

"I'm happy to fill you in," Rita said when they were back in the living room. "I know that you have great sympathy for her and wonderful intentions. But with children like Zoey, that's not always enough."

Lucy nodded but didn't really understand what the woman was trying to tell her.

"Zoey has some heavy issues. Her parents split up when she was about seven. Her mother was an alcoholic, and Zoey and her brother moved around between their relatives."

"Zoey has a brother?" Lucy was surprised. The girl had not mentioned any family. "Is he in the same foster home she ran away from?"

"No, he was placed with another family," Rita said. "I'm checking with them now to see if they want to take Zoey."

"That would make sense." Lucy nodded. "At least she would be with her brother."

"It would make sense, but things don't always work out sensibly," Rita said with a sigh. "I told you Zoey's mother was an alcoholic. She wasn't capable of caring for her children, so they went to live with her mother. Unfortunately, the grandmother wasn't in good health. She passed a while ago. So their aunt took them. But Zoey wasn't happy at her aunt's house. She didn't feel welcome, and her aunt couldn't control her. Zoey did poorly in school and kept running away. When her aunt told us she felt overwhelmed, the two kids were put into the foster care system, in the hope that their mother might eventually resume custody. But she died in a car accident, about three years ago."

"Oh, how awful." Lucy shook her head. "Zoey's really had a tough life, hasn't she?"

"She's had a lot to cope with. I had hoped her last placement would help stabilize her and build her sense of trust and security. But that was unfortunately not the case."

"Sounds like it was just the opposite," Lucy said.

"The thing is, Lucy, while we may understand and sympathize with Zoey's problems, we still have to face the fact that she can be a difficult and very challenging kid. She was in a lot of trouble at school and cut out more than she came to class. She seems to like art the best of all her school subjects, but we couldn't even get her interested in a vocational program. She dropped out this year and doesn't seem to have any intention of going back. And she was picked up for shoplifting twice."

Lucy was suddenly glad that Charlie was not around to hear this part. She could practically hear him saying, "I told you so. I could have told you that the second I saw her."

"All right. She has problems. She acts out and behaves badly. That's no great surprise," Lucy said honestly. "Is that what you're trying to tell me?"

"Partly. She can also be very manipulative and take advantage of your sympathy for her."

"Meaning?"

"Meaning, she lies. She can't be trusted. When things get tough for her, she runs away—and might steal your wallet as she's heading out the door." Rita looked at her gravely. "We all want to help Zoey. But we need to be realistic and not approach her with some rescue fantasy."

Rescue fantasy? The words hit a nerve. *Is that what I'm doing?* Lucy wondered. *I was just trying to do a good deed here, to reach out to a stranger.*

"It's important," Rita went on, "that when we look at Zoey, we don't just see what we want to see."

"I understand that," Lucy said. "I'll tell you what I told Zoey the other day—when she tried to sneak out of the house and fainted in the foyer. I told her that we had to be straight with each other. I might look like a pushover, I might even act like one, but I'm not. I have a pretty clear eye about people. I see Zoey, and I can handle her," she promised. "And I've already hidden my good jewelry, credit cards, and any cash."

Rita laughed out loud at the last line of Lucy's little speech. "Okay, Lucy. It sounds as if you do understand what I'm trying to say. But what about your husband? Does he share your commitment to Zoey?"

Lucy knew that the answer she gave to this question would make all the difference. It was her nature to be honest. Charlie called her an open book. She also knew that in this situation total honesty might disqualify them. But she couldn't paint too rosy a picture of Charlie's attitude. Sooner or later, Rita was bound to speak to him face-to-face.

"Well . . . I have to say that it was my idea to let Zoey stay with us," Lucy began slowly.

Rita nodded. "Yes, I think you mentioned that."

"My husband has been . . . accommodating," she added, trying not to stretch the truth too far.

"By that you mean, in favor of the idea?"

"Um, yes. We talked about Zoey staying and he agreed to it," Lucy said, purposely misinterpreting the question.

"All right." Rita looked puzzled and made a quick note. Lucy hoped she was done. Since Zoey would only be staying for a day or two, maybe they could squeak by without Rita ever talking to Charlie in person?

But just as Lucy thought the interview might be wrapping up, Charlie walked in. He was wearing a down vest over his cooking whites and his worn-out Red Sox baseball cap, which he didn't bother to remove.

"Well . . . well, here he is now," Lucy said with false cheer. She jumped up from her seat to greet her husband. "Hi, honey. This is Mrs. Schuman, the social worker handling Zoey's case. She's here to interview us today. Didn't you remember?"

"I'm here, Lucy, aren't I?" Charlie said in a testy tone.

He shook Rita's outstretched hand. "Nice to meet you," he said curtly. He sat on the couch next to Lucy. "So, what do you want to know? I haven't got much time. I've got to get right back to work."

Rita gave Charlie a tight smile. "Well, your wife has already answered the basic questions. What I'm interested in now are your feelings about the situation—taking Zoey into your home and acting as her guardian."

Charlie shrugged and threw his hands in the air. "I think it's fine. The kid is sick. She has no place to go. You've got to find a new family to take her in, so I guess we're sort of stuck with her for now, right? What can you do?"

Lucy winced. "I think my husband is trying to say that circumstances have led Zoey to our door, and we both feel very strongly obliged to help her, ethically and morally. . . ." Her voice trailed off. She wasn't sure Rita was buying it.

"Mr. Bates, is that how you feel? Is that what you think, too?"

Charlie laughed nervously. He looked at Lucy, who focused her entire body on giving him a look that said, *Blow this, buddy, and you'll regret it forever.*

"Hey, I'm just the dad around here. Lucy says the girl is sick, we have to help her. So that's what we're trying to do. I guess it's the right thing. What they teach you in church." Lucy let out a breath she didn't know she'd been holding. That answer wasn't so bad, she thought.

"I know the kid's sick," Charlie went on. "She can't go anywhere right now. So she can stay a few days until the medicine kicks in. Meanwhile, you work on finding her a new place with folks who take in kids like this on purpose. Not by accident, the way it happened here."

Lucy glanced at him then at the social worker, wondering how this was all going over. Charlie did not exactly sound positive, concerned, and committed. More like cynical, confused, and conflicted.

"All right, Mr. Bates. I think I understand your position." Rita made a few more notes and closed her binder.

"Great. Are we done here? Because I have to get back to the diner."

"Yes, that's all. Thank you for meeting with me," Rita said politely.

"That's okay. Nice to meet you, too." Charlie stood up and took his car keys out of his pocket. "See you tonight, Lucy. I'll be home late. I have to stay and close up. Jimmy isn't coming in." Jimmy was the cook who mainly worked the dinner shift. When he was out, Charlie had to man the grill, then clean and close the place.

"Okay, see you," Lucy said. She tried not to sound too forlorn but couldn't hide her feelings. She was sure Charlie had blown this interview and ruined their chances for approval, even as temporary guardians.

Lucy hadn't thought that much about it beforehand. She had almost felt as if she were doing the social services agency a favor by taking care of Zoey while Rita Schuman looked for a new family for her. But now it seemed all turned around—and important that she and Charlie pass some . . . some test.

Charlie left quickly through the front door and when it closed behind him, Lucy let out a long sigh. She glanced up at Rita Schuman, who was writing something more in her binder.

"My husband works very hard," Lucy said finally.

"I can see that," Rita replied.

"He feels a lot of pressure running his business. He doesn't have a lot of patience for small talk. Or big talk either," she added honestly.

Rita glanced over with a slight smile. "I can see that, too."

"I hope what he said didn't ruin everything," Lucy went on. "But he was telling the truth, more or less. This wasn't his idea. But he's going along with it. For my sake, mainly."

"You don't intend to apply as permanent foster parents for Zoey, is that correct?"

"No, we don't," Lucy said quietly. "That's just not a possibility for us right now."

She would have liked some time to think about it and get to know Zoey better, but she knew Charlie would never agree in a million years. It would be a major responsibility and commitment. Lucy honestly wasn't sure if she was willing to take it on either.

Rita stood up and closed the binder, then slipped it into her briefcase. "I'd like to go up and visit with Zoey for a while now."

"Right. Of course. It's the third floor, the only room up there besides the bath. I think I'll fix her something to eat. It's almost time for her pills."

"Good idea. Come on up whenever you're ready," the social worker said as she climbed the stairs.

Lucy went to the kitchen and heated some chicken soup she had cooked the day before.

The benefits of chicken soup weren't just an old wives' tale. Scientists had proven that there was a compound in the soup that fought viral infections and helped clear congestion.

When the tray of food was ready, Lucy carried it carefully up the two flights of stairs. She found Rita sitting in a chair near Zoey's bed, chatting quietly. The social worker turned and smiled when Lucy walked in. Zoey just stared at her with big, dark eyes.

Lucy could tell the girl felt self-conscious, being the subject of so much attention. Maybe she even felt a little apprehensive, wondering what was going to happen and if she was going to be sent away. Lucy felt the same way.

"Here's some soup and crackers, Zoey." Lucy set the tray on the bedside table. "Careful, it's still hot." Lucy helped Zoey sit up and fixed the pillows behind her. "There we are. The pills are in that cup. You need to take them after you eat."

"That looks good, Zoey," Rita said. "It looks homemade."

"Would you like some? I can fix you a bowl downstairs," Lucy offered.

Rita got to her feet. "Thank you. But I have to get back to the office. Zoey, I hope you feel better soon. Call me if you want to talk about anything."

The women went downstairs, and Lucy retrieved Rita's coat from the closet. "She seems to be doing a little better every day," she told Rita. "But this bug really knocks you off your feet."

"I can see she's getting excellent care, Lucy. There's no question about it."

"Well, I am a nurse. That helps."

Rita shrugged into her overcoat and slipped her briefcase strap over her shoulder. "You're a very good-hearted person. That helps even more."

Lucy didn't know what to say. Did that mean they'd been approved? Or was the social worker just trying to be nice to her, knowing it wasn't going to work out?

"I need to make a recommendation to my supervisor. But it won't be long. I should call back by tonight," Rita said.

"Call anytime. We'll be home," Lucy told her. "And thanks for your time," she added politely, hoping her gratitude wasn't misplaced.

For the next few hours, Lucy distracted herself with housework. Then Jamie came home from school, and she helped him make a poster for his social studies class. He was gluing on pictures that he had cut from a magazine when Zoey called out and asked if she could take a shower and wash her hair. "Are you okay on your own for a while?" Lucy asked her son.

"Totally," Jamie told her.

Lucy convinced Zoey to take a bath. All she needed was to have

Zoey get a dizzy spell and fall in the shower. The girl was still weak and feverish and felt light-headed every time she got out of bed.

After the bath, Lucy washed Zoey's hair in the kitchen sink. This was something she had missed, having a girl to fuss over. The boys had long since outgrown her help and fussing. The truth was, she adored her sons but she'd hoped for a daughter, too. Although Lucy had put away that wish long ago, now it came back to her. A mother's relationship with a daughter was just . . . different.

"You have beautiful hair, Zoey," Lucy told her. "It's so thick and pretty."

Zoey rolled her eyes. "I hate my hair. It's totally gross. Sometimes I want to just cut it all off and shave my head."

Lucy feared she might not be exaggerating. Zoey was the type of kid who *would* shave her head.

"Oh no . . . don't do that. Your hair is really beautiful," Lucy said. She meant it, too, discounting the red and blue streaks. "When I was your age, I didn't like my hair either. I hated standing out with this carrot top. I used to get teased a lot, too. Kids can be so mean if they see anything different about another kid."

"Tell me about it," Zoey said knowingly. Lucy guessed that she had been teased a lot, moving to different schools, coming from a foster family. "I like your hair," the girl went on. "I think it's cool. I didn't think that was your real color, though. I thought you dyed it."

"There's a little gray in there now if you look closely. It's all for real."

"I'd like hair that color. I might try it someday," Zoey said casually.

Lucy stood behind her, combing out her wet hair and rubbing it with a towel so she wouldn't get a chill again. "That doesn't hurt, does it?" she asked when she hit a small tangle.

"I'm okay. It feels good. My grandmother used to comb out my hair like this for me. Then she would make a braid."

"I bet you looked really cute."

Zoey shrugged. "It was just neater that way, easier for her. My brother and I lived with her for a while, in Gloucester. But she got sick, so we had to go live with my aunt."

Lucy felt a wave of sadness, hearing Zoey tell her story. It was different from hearing it from the social worker. "Yes, Mrs. Schuman told me about your grandmother . . . and your aunt." *And your mother, too,* she wanted to add. But that seemed too private and sad somehow.

"What's your brother's name?" Lucy asked.

"Kevin. He's five years younger than me. He's a cool kid. But I haven't seen him in a while."

Lucy couldn't imagine her two boys living separately, falling out of touch. Even though they fought like cats and dogs at times, they were still close and always would be, she believed.

Kids love their siblings in a different way than they love friends. It was a pity that Zoey and her brother had been split up that way.

The phone rang, interrupting her thoughts. Lucy froze and she saw Zoey stiffen. They were both wondering if it was Rita Schuman with the verdict; Lucy was sure of it.

Jamie picked up the extension and called down to her. "It's for you, Mom. Someone named Mrs. Schuman?"

"I've got it, honey," Lucy said, grabbing the phone in the kitchen.

"I handed in my report on the home visit and spoke to my supervisor," Rita began. "We've approved you and your husband as Zoey's temporary guardians."

Lucy felt relieved—and happy. "That's great news. I'm very pleased. Thank you."

"I know your husband has reservations, but he seemed more or less neutral to me. And your positive, caring attitude, I thought, more than compensates."

Lucy could have laughed out loud. Wasn't that her life story? Or rather, the story of her marriage? "Charlie has a good heart. He just has a hard time showing it."

The social worker didn't comment. "There are some papers you both need to sign. I'll bring them by later. And we'll speak on a regular basis. I need to know how Zoey's coming along with her recovery, of course, and adjusting to your household. If you have any questions about dealing with her, or if anything unexpected comes up, please call anytime."

"I will. Thanks," Lucy said again.

"Thank you," Mrs. Schuman replied. "And good luck. May I speak with Zoey now?"

"She's right here." Lucy handed the phone to Zoey, who had obviously overheard the news. It was hard to tell what she was thinking, but Lucy sensed she was pleased—or maybe just relieved to know she didn't have to start all over someplace new.

"Yeah. . . . I'm okay with that. It's cool." Zoey looked up and met Lucy's glance. She didn't exactly smile, but did look as if some of the heavy burden had been lifted from her shoulders. And Lucy remembered again why she was going to all this trouble for a stranger.

CHAPTER FOUR

⌒⌒

"GOOD SHOT! TRY TO BRING YOUR RACKET BACK A LITTLE more. You'll get more power." Alex returned Betty's mid-court volley with a smooth, effortless backhand. He was an excellent tennis player. He could have sent the ball smoking over the net, into a deep, unreachable corner. But he was trying very hard to be considerate of her rusty form, keeping the ball in play and giving her every chance to reach it.

Betty ran from one side of the court to the other, trying her best not to look foolish or out of shape. Which, under the circumstances, was a real challenge. She couldn't understand it. She worked out at her gym several times a week and hadn't put on any extra weight, even with her catering work. But tennis was more demanding than it looked. All that starting and stopping.

It didn't help that she was also dealing with Alex's helpful—but relentless—instructions.

"Back to the baseline," he reminded her. "It's always easier to run up to the ball than to try to chase it behind you."

She forced a smile and moved to the back of the court. She knew he was just trying to be helpful. And her game was rusty. But his tips would have been more palatable if she didn't already know how to play and had not taken lessons for years at the country club where she and her ex-husband, Ted, had once belonged.

You brought this on yourself, a little voice reminded her. *You told him you wanted to start playing tennis again. He's just trying to accommodate you.*

Definitely a case of "be careful what you wish for," Betty decided. And how was she supposed to know that he enjoyed being a tennis coach so much?

They had the court for an hour, and Betty had a feeling Alex would keep them playing until the next duo stood waiting on the sidelines. She watched the big clock at the other end of the courts. The minute hand moved painfully slowly. But after they volleyed awhile, she felt herself warming up, her old form coming back. She surprised Alex with a passing shot that zipped by him before he could even react, bouncing an inch or so before the baseline.

"Nice one . . ." He stared at the ball and then over at her, looking quite surprised. "That had a lot of topspin."

Betty smiled and picked up a stray ball. She was sure he thought it had been beginner's luck. Little did he realize, that had been her money shot when she played in the annual doubles elimination tournaments. And rose to the top of the ladder.

"Feel ready to keep score?" he asked politely.

"Sure. Why not? Don't worry, I'll be easy on you," she joked.

"I appreciate that," he joked back. "You serve first," he suggested, giving her the advantage. He tossed a few balls over to her side of the court before she could reply.

Betty picked up two and pushed the others aside. Then she took a position behind the baseline, in the middle of the court.

"Want to take a few to warm up?" he asked.

She shook her head, bouncing the ball near her right foot to get her rhythm. "I'm okay. I'm better when I don't think too much about it."

And in a sneak attack, Betty added silently.

He smiled at her warmly and got ready to receive the serve. He liked her sense of humor, she could tell. And that made her like him a bit, too.

Betty tossed the ball up and took her swing. The serve went wildly out of bounds, and she felt embarrassed. It had been a while, she realized. She should have taken those practice shots, after all.

Alex smiled encouragingly. "Just relax and take your time."

Betty kept her game face and didn't show she was rattled. "Second serve," she called out. She tossed the ball up again, focusing more and thinking less, and then came down with full force.

The ball zipped over the net, hit the court just inside the line, and smoked right by the good doctor. Alex lunged, swinging his racket in an awkward motion and missing the ball by a mile. He'd been totally caught off guard.

"Fifteen, love," Betty called out, moving to the other side of the court to serve again.

She couldn't help swinging her hips a little under her short blue skirt.

Beginner's luck? I don't think so, pal, she said to herself. *I'm back.*

They played on, with Betty winning most of the games she served and even taking one game that Alex served. She could tell she was playing well when he finally stopped giving her instructions and looked as if he was really trying.

Finally, the bell sounded to mark the hour. Another couple stood nearby, waiting to take the court. Betty felt relieved but realized she'd had a good time—a much better time than she had expected.

"That was fun, Betty. Good match," Alex said as they walked off the court. "You had me fooled there for a while. I thought you said you hadn't played in years."

"I haven't. But it started to come back once you gave me a few tips," she said, trying to be a good sport.

"I can see that. You'd be dangerous if you played every week," he predicted.

"I doubt it. But I had a really good time."

"We'll have to play again soon. Would you like to?"

"Absolutely." She nodded, feeling as though she had made it through the tryouts. It had been nice to get out and play again—after the initial embarrassing moments. Betty had forgotten how much fun tennis could be and how good you felt afterward. It was a different kind of workout from jogging mindlessly on the treadmill at the gym.

They changed and met in the lobby of the tennis club. Alex had made reservations at a new French restaurant in Hamilton.

The restaurant looked like a country house inside, decorated with Provençal fabrics and traditional yellow and blue patterned pottery. It was casual yet elegant and a romantic spot, too. It made Betty wonder if perhaps Alex liked her more than she thought, taking her to a place like this on just their second date.

They were seated at a table in the corner, a quiet spot where they could talk easily. Alex took out his glasses and then examined the menu. "Hmm, all my favorites."

"Mine, too. The specials sound delicious," Betty said.

The waiter came by and took their orders and then brought a bottle of wine Alex had selected.

"So, how is your business doing these days?" Alex asked. "I guess you've been affected by the recession."

"It's fallen off a bit. But it's definitely not as bad as it could be.

Luckily, we have a low overhead. It's just me and Molly and a few hourly employees. The shop is small, and we don't pay much rent so . . ."

Alex sat listening with interest. But suddenly his phone sounded, and he pulled it from his jacket pocket. "I'm sorry. I have to take this," he apologized. He listened intently to the caller then answered a few questions. Finally, he wound up the call. "I'm so sorry. I have a few patients in the ICU right now," he explained. "I have to be available for any situations that come up."

"It's okay, I understand," Betty said. She did, too. He was a doctor. He didn't have a nine-to-five job. She'd been around Matt and Molly enough to know how demanding the medical profession could be.

"So . . . you were saying . . . you have a low overhead?"

"Yes, we try to keep costs down. That's where I come in. Molly is a genius in the kitchen, but she was never the best manager or great at figuring out her profits. But I had all that experience from the real estate brokerage. So we make a good—"

The phone rang again. Alex rolled his eyes and sighed. He reached over and patted Betty's hand. "Just another minute . . . my daughter. I guess she doesn't realize I have a life, too."

Betty smiled at the joke and sat back on the banquette, watching discreetly as he spoke to his daughter. He was high-energy, very animated and expressive. She liked that in a person. It showed that they weren't cut off from their emotions. Though in Alex's case she was starting to feel as if he were a bit of a moving target. It was like trying to watch TV when someone kept switching the channels.

Betty, just stop. You're being too critical. What are you griping about? He's a smart, successful, charming guy who likes you. And he's good-looking, too. She did like his beard, clipped close to his face but dense. He had straight white teeth and hazel eyes. He was bald on top but that didn't bother Betty. If she had to eliminate suitors for that reason, she would never leave the house at this age, she thought with a secret grin.

She could do worse. A lot worse. Dr. Alex Becker was very attractive. A dedicated doctor, intelligent, warm, and fun to be around. Practically any woman she knew would agree.

It just takes me a while to get to know someone and feel relaxed, she reminded herself. She had to stop being so picky. *Just relax and give the guy a chance,* she told herself.

For the rest of the evening, Betty followed her own advice. There were a few more phone calls, but Alex kept them short and always apologized. He was concerned about his patients; she couldn't find fault with that. He also had a real talent for remembering where their conversations had broken off, which showed he was really listening.

After dinner, Alex drove her back to her house. He parked in front and turned off the engine. "I had a great time tonight, Betty. I hope you did, too. I really enjoyed the tennis . . . and talking with you. Though I'm sorry about all the calls. Next time I'll get some other doc to cover for me, promise."

"No problem, I understand," Betty assured him. "I hope the next time I need a doctor, I can find someone as dedicated as you are."

Alex laughed and smiled at her. "Just try me. I'd definitely pick up for you."

Betty smiled, feeling self-conscious and very aware of the way he was looking at her now. "I had a great time," she assured him. "Thank you."

He looked pleased by her answer. "It's still early. Mind if I come in?"

"I'd love to talk some more, but I have to work tomorrow. I really need to turn in early." She tried to sound regretful when, in fact, she was surprised that he had been so forward; this was only their second date. Well, Alex was an assertive guy. He went after what he wanted, and Betty didn't mind that . . . most of the time.

"How about getting together again this week?" he asked.

"That would be great," she said. "Would you like to see a movie?"

"Sure. That would be fun. I'll call you and we'll make plans."

He leaned over and kissed her, slipping his arm around her waist. Betty leaned toward him and put her hand on his chest. His beard tickled her face a little. The kiss was brief but definitely sent a message. The doctor had an agenda.

"Let me walk you to the door," he said.

"That's okay. I can let myself in." Betty grabbed her purse and got out of the car. "I'll see you soon. Thanks again."

He was probably just trying to be polite, but Betty wasn't ready for more good night embraces on her doorstep, or requests to come in for coffee. She liked Alex. She liked him a lot. But he seemed to like her more and was moving along a little quickly for her. She just needed some time to catch up.

She opened her door and glanced back. Alex was waiting in the driveway, making sure she got inside safely. Betty saw him drive off as she closed her front door. This could be good, she thought happily. This could turn into something.

While Molly might find that a tepid, timid prediction, Betty knew that at her stage of the game, it was saying a lot.

BETTY CAME INTO THE SHOP EARLY THE NEXT DAY. THE PARTY they were catering didn't start until the evening, but it was going to be a very fancy affair and there was still plenty to do. Molly was already at work, grilling shrimp for a spicy noodle dish.

"Morning," Betty said, as she slipped on her apron. She poured a mug of coffee and quickly went to work, sorting and washing a pile of vegetables and fruit that had just been delivered by their produce man.

She wondered how long it would take Molly to ask her about the date. Just for fun, she silently counted. *One . . . two . . . three . . . four . . . five . . .*

"So, how was the tennis match? I could make some corny pun here about a love match," Molly teased, "but—"

"Don't even go there, Mol. Please?"

"All right, I'll skip it. But only if you start talking. So—?"

"We had a really good time. The tennis went fine. Much better than I expected once I got warmed up. We had dinner at that new French bistro in Hamilton. It was really lovely." *Very romantic,* Betty was about to add, then decided to skip that particular detail. Molly didn't need any encouragement.

"Great. I'm glad to hear it. So you're going out again, I assume?"

"Yes, this week. We're going to the movies."

"Sounds like things are progressing," Molly said happily.

"We're getting to know each other. So far, so good," Betty agreed. "He did have this situation with his cell phone going off all the time while we were eating dinner. But he is a doctor and said there were some patients of his in the ICU."

"Tell me about it. Matt's always getting calls from the hospital. You'll get used to it," Molly promised.

Molly did have high hopes for their future, didn't she? She had made the match and now seemed to be invested in it working out. Betty felt a little wary about that but pushed her worries aside.

"It wasn't just the hospital. There were other calls, but . . . it was okay," Betty added quickly. "I mean, it didn't ruin the evening for me or anything like that. So how did your night go? Was there a big turnout?"

Molly had been working at a party last night—another family-oriented Christmas party, this one at the firehouse. She had agreed to manage it on her own, so that Betty could go out with Alex again. But she did look a little tired, Betty thought.

"It was fun. You know the firefighters—they're happy with whatever you give them. Oh . . . that Santa guy was there. You know, the one who jumped the van for you last week?"

"I remember," Betty said blandly. As if her memory needed any major jogging to remember Nathan. "Did you talk to him?" she asked curiously.

"I don't think he remembered me from last Sunday. But I thanked him again for helping you out. He definitely remembered you," Molly added.

Betty felt a little ping in her chest. "He did? What did he say?"

Molly shrugged. She was mixing the spicy peanut sauce for the noodles. "I'm not sure. I think he asked where you were or something like that."

"What did you tell him?"

Molly stirred up the bowl of sauce, took a taste, and added a dash more curry powder. "I said you had the night off and were probably out on a date somewhere."

"You did? What did he say when you said that?" Betty didn't mean to make a big deal out of this small, careless remark, but why did Molly have to put it that way?

Molly shrugged again and added some chopped green onion. "I'm sorry. Am I missing something here? I mean, it's not like you're worried about what Santa Claus thinks, are you?"

Molly sounded so certain, Betty couldn't say what she was thinking. *Yes, I do like Nathan and probably would go out with him if he asked me. Card-carrying Santa and all.*

"It's nothing. Forget it," Betty said. "Nathan's a really nice guy. I might even go out with him if he asked. Maybe just once, out of curiosity," she added. "But I bet he's already involved with someone."

"And you're involved with someone, too. Or practically," Molly pointed out. "I'm just so excited that you've finally met someone you like and really click with. A guy who's a real catch. I have a good feeling about this, Betty. I really do."

Maybe Molly was right, Betty thought. Maybe her relationship with Alex was going to evolve into something serious. Sometimes friends could sense these things more clearly than the people involved.

Besides, what was the difference if Nathan Daley thought she had a boyfriend? No difference at all. She might be curious about a professional Santa, but she definitely needed to be with a more motivated, professional-track sort of man. He didn't have to be a millionaire or the CEO of a huge corporation, but he had to possess a certain amount of polish and maturity. Nathan was clearly lacking in all those categories. Which was very unfortunate, she thought with a sigh.

But it was interesting to learn that he had asked Molly about her. Betty couldn't deny that.

THE CHURCH ALWAYS BECAME MORE CROWDED AROUND THE holidays, Lucy noticed. She and the boys were only a few minutes late to Sunday morning service, but it was already hard to find a seat. Tucker, who was serving as a deacon, met her at the back of the sanctuary and showed them to a row where they found three seats. Emily Warwick; her husband, Dan Forbes; and their little girl, Jane moved over to make room. Emily gave Lucy a big smile hello. Emily was pretty down-to-earth, Lucy thought. She had been mayor of the town for over ten years now, and the only real opposition to her reign had been Charlie. She could have been snootier or held a grudge, but Emily still ate in the Clam Box several times a week and always stopped Lucy to have a chat whenever they ran into each other.

Charlie was at the diner this morning, working. Lucy wished he would come to church with her more often. She thought Reverend

Ben's sermons offered a lot to think about, ideas that might influence her husband's negative attitudes for the better. She sometimes tried to recap the sermons for him, but the only recaps that interested Charlie were for his favorite sports teams.

It was the second Sunday of Advent, and they had arrived in time to see the lighting of the Advent candles. The four large blue Advent candles were arranged on the altar in a pine wreath. Each Sunday in Advent, in preparation for Christmas, another candle was lit and special scripture was read aloud. Reverend Ben would invite a family in the congregation to come up and perform the ceremony. This week the Sawyer family was on the altar. Jack and Julie Sawyer ran the Christmas tree farm just outside of town. Julie had just had a baby, a little girl they had named Madeline, and they also had two other children: Julie's daughter from her first marriage, Kate, who was about six now, Lucy guessed; and Jack's grown son, David, who had served in the Middle East and was now attending college. It was nice to see David doing so well. He had come home from the army in bad shape. That was last Christmas. But now, here he was, standing tall beside his fiancée, Christine.

Jack and Julie couldn't have looked prouder or more grateful for their many blessings. Lucy watched as Jack lifted Kate and let her light the large blue candle with a long, thin taper.

Lucy wasn't sure why, but this was one tradition that touched her and helped her anticipate the holidays. Not with the dread of shopping and cooking and all the other chores. But with a warm, peaceful outlook and appreciation of the better side of Christmas, the warmth of family ties, the promise of spiritual renewal, and goodwill toward all.

She knew she had so much to be grateful for, but sometimes she did feel a yawning lack in her life, in her marriage mainly. It seemed different when the kids were younger. Or maybe their needs had always distracted her from the truth: she and Charlie were just so different. Mostly, she just accepted that challenge as part of their relationship. No marriage was perfect or without challenges. But sometimes it seemed as if that single flaw was all she could see.

Lucy quickly turned her thoughts away from such dangerous ground and, instead, tried to focus on the service. Reverend Ben was making announcements about upcoming events. The annual Christmas Fair still needed volunteers. Lucy usually helped out but didn't think she would have the time this year, not with Zoey in the house.

The service continued. Lucy's mind wandered a bit, but she did enjoy Reverend Ben's sermon, which was about keeping holiday madness to a minimum.

"Have you noticed how the trend these days is to have fewer and fewer ingredients in things?" he began. "I was in the supermarket the other day, and it seemed that all my favorite foods—soups and ice cream and breakfast cereal—all had new labels, boasting about how few ingredients they now contained. 'Only five ingredients!' the soup can shouted at me. But the ice cream carton topped that one. 'Only three here, my friend. Try to beat that one.'"

Lucy chuckled along with the rest of the congregation. Reverend Ben always mixed a little humor in his message.

"Seriously, it seems we're all interested in keeping it simple these days. In getting back to basics, whole foods and natural ingredients, from pet food to perfume. I'd like to propose that this year, we all approach Christmas with the same agenda. A five—or even three—ingredient Christmas. Just the basic, most meaningful and spiritually nutritious elements of the holiday. And toss out all the fillers and additives," he advised.

Lucy liked that idea. It not only made her smile, it made sense to her, too.

Reverend Ben went on to describe just what he meant, and Lucy found herself agreeing with him. It was true that you could get caught up in all the extras and miss the most important parts of Christmas. She was going to try hard to keep her focus this year and follow her minister's advice.

Taking in Zoey might seem like a burden Lucy didn't need at this time of year, but it was really one of the most important ingredients of the season, Lucy realized. Reaching out and helping someone who was less fortunate. That's what Christmas was all about, wasn't it?

Soon after the sermon, it was time for "Joys and Concerns," a chance for the congregation to share the happy moments in their lives as well as their challenges. There were the usual announcements about grandchildren being born and anniversaries and birthdays, as well as prayer requests for family members and friends who were ill.

Lucy raised her hand, deciding to talk about Zoey. When Reverend Ben recognized her, she said, "I'd like you to keep a young girl named Zoey in your prayers. She's having a difficult time right now. She's lost touch with her family and is in between foster homes. She's also been very sick. Please pray for her health and ask that she be placed with a loving family who will take care of her."

Reverend Ben cast Lucy a sympathetic glance. "Yes, we will remember her, Lucy. Thank you."

He turned away and called on someone in the back of the church. Lucy recognized Sam Morgan, who was a builder and carpenter in town. Sam didn't get along with Charlie very well, but Lucy still liked him.

"I just heard this morning that the Three Village Food Pantry had a big flood last night. A pipe broke in the basement, and a lot of their supplies and practically everything they had stored for a Christmas charity project was lost. Not just food but gifts they collected to give to needy families. So they're going to need a lot of donations to keep running during the holidays, and I hope our church can help out in some way."

"Thanks for letting us know about that, Sam. I hadn't heard that news yet," Reverend Ben said. "The deaconate should take this up at their next meeting and see what we can do to help."

Lucy knew that charity. She often brought donations there, from her house and from the diner. She would ask Charlie if he had anything extra in the kitchen that she could bring over. There might be a case of soup or chili. It sounded as if any donation would be helpful.

When the service ended, Lucy wanted to join the line of people who were filing out through the center doors of the sanctuary, waiting to greet Reverend Ben. But she glanced at her watch and decided to get back home to Zoey, who was probably awake by now.

BETTY WAS THE FIRST TO ARRIVE AT THE SHOP ON MONDAY morning. She was surprised that she'd beat Molly in but then saw the message light on the phone and hit the button.

Molly reported that she would be in late. She needed to run up to Newburyport to meet with a client who was planning a big wedding for this coming spring. There was some sudden crisis that had to be worked out. "I must have been a psychotherapist in a past life to end up with this job," Molly complained.

Betty had to laugh. She knew Molly was only venting. Molly was usually wonderful with their clients, satisfying all their whims and going to the limit to understand and create their personal vision of the event. She really was a "catering therapist," if anyone could claim the title.

Sonia and their other part-time helpers wouldn't be in today at all. Betty didn't mind. She liked having the shop to herself at times. She had been a full partner ever since joining the business four years back, but in some ways, the shop still felt like Molly's domain, especially since she was the star of the kitchen.

But Betty liked to putter around in the kitchen, too, when she had the chance. Molly had printed out an interesting new chili recipe, getting a jump start on the Super Bowl party orders that would hopefully save them from the postholiday, winter wasteland.

The recipe called for ground turkey and red kidney beans. They had the ingredients on hand but not enough beans. Well, they had some black beans, Betty noticed. She actually liked black beans better than the red and decided she would do a little variation.

Live large, Betty. You have the kitchen to yourself today.

Betty decided to try a small batch as a taste test. Molly would be back around noon, and she could try it then. Betty's son, Brian, had always loved chili when he was little, and now she wondered if he still liked it. If this recipe turned out well, she would make a batch for him. They saw each other so infrequently now, she didn't even know what he liked to eat. That made Betty a little sad. But he would be here soon, flying into Boston before Christmas, and would be visiting with her for at least a week. Plenty of time to get reacquainted with his preferences again.

As much as she looked forward to having Brian with her, the plan made her nervous, too. It had been so long since they had spent that much time together, just the two of them. And he was a grown man now, about to be engaged. He and Tina had met in college, in Chicago, but Tina's family lived in Concord, about two hours from Cape Light. So now Betty was going to meet her son's future bride. Another milestone in her life. As if facing her fiftieth birthday in February wasn't enough.

"Life just keeps happening," Betty murmured to herself as she began working on the chili. Cooking was a calming activity for her, and her worries were soon replaced by her need to focus on chopping onions and measuring ingredients.

Once the chili was assembled, she left it to simmer and went into the small office, turning to her main role at Willoughby Fine Foods.

She answered some phone calls, checked over the staff schedules, opened the mail, and checked their cash flow.

Their bank account was starting to fatten up again, like the proverbial Christmas goose, and they weren't even halfway through the season. Maybe they could give their helpers a Christmas bonus this year, Betty thought. Everyone worked so hard, and they were a loyal crew. She heard the shop door open and thought it must be Molly coming in.

"Hello? Anybody here?" a man's voice called out to her.

A customer. Whoops. She should have realized one of those might stroll in at some point during the day. Betty slipped out of the desk chair and ran out to the shop. She still had on her apron, and her blond hair was twisted in a knot at the back of her head.

The man stood with his back to the counter as he gazed around the shop. He was wearing a worn leather jacket and had dark brown hair, flecked with gray. She felt frozen in her tracks for a moment. Her eyes were playing tricks on her. It couldn't be . . . Santa standing right there? Could it?

Then he turned and smiled. His blue eyes flashed with surprise. And happiness, too, she thought.

"Hi, Betty. I almost didn't recognize you with your hair like that."

"Oh . . . right." She lifted her hands to the back of her head and undid the clip. He seemed fascinated by the movement, his eyes carefully following the gesture. "I just wear it like that when I'm cooking, to keep it out of the way."

"It looks very nice. Very . . . elegant."

She felt self-conscious from the way he was looking at her and took a breath, getting her bearings. She just never expected to see him here . . . and now, here he was.

But you don't have to act like a silly teenager, Betty. Get a grip, woman. You're too old for this.

"What brings you to Willoughby Fine Foods this morning? Are you planning a party?" she asked politely.

Had he just come to track her down? Maybe to ask her out on a date? The idea made her heart beat a little faster.

"I'm here to ask a favor, actually. Since I fixed your van, I figured you owe me one," he added with a grin.

"I guess I do," she agreed, her curiosity growing.

He pulled out a few pages of the village newspaper, the *Cape Light Messenger*, which he had folded and stuck in his jacket pocket.

"Have you seen today's paper?" he asked as he smoothed out the sheets.

"There's a copy around here somewhere. But I haven't had a chance." So it wasn't about a date. She felt a bit let down.

"The Three Village Food Pantry had a big plumbing problem this weekend. A pipe burst in the basement, and it wasn't discovered for hours. The basement was totally flooded. Tons of stuff has been ruined."

He showed her the article, complete with pictures. Cartons of boxed foods—cereal, rice, crackers, and pasta—floating in water that was knee-high. There were other boxes, too, some of them gift-wrapped. Volunteers in high rubber boots stood holding buckets, trying to bail out the place.

"Oh, dear . . . . what a mess. And right before Christmas. So many people depend on that place for their groceries. More and more each week, I hear."

"Exactly. The organization was planning a big party, like the one the Rotary Club did."

Where I met you? I remember that, Betty wanted to answer. Instead she said, "That was a nice event."

"It was great—and a great help to a lot of families. The food pantry does a party like that, too, and gives out lots of gifts to children. They've been collecting donations for months and had most of the stuff gift-wrapped and ready to go. Unfortunately, it was all stored in the basement."

"And now it's been ruined by the flood," Betty finished for him. She skimmed the news article, then glanced up at him. "Were you going to be Santa at that party, too?"

"Every year since they started it. I'm good friends with the couple who runs the pantry, Michael and Eve Piper. They're amazing people. They work so hard at that place. It's been a real nightmare for them. They didn't have good insurance. It won't cover much."

"Oh, that's awful," Betty said. "Are you going around town, asking for donations to help them?"

"Sort of. The Pipers need to restock the pantry, and they'd really love to give that party. They know it will practically take a miracle to make it all work out, but they won't give up on the idea. I promised I would try to help them."

"They asked the right guy. If anyone could fill that tall order, it would have to be Santa, don't you think?" She smiled at him, catching his eye.

He smiled back in a way that made her feel as if something inside her had just lit up. "It's going to be a tough one, even for me," he confessed. But he didn't look daunted in the least, Betty thought. He looked excited, energized by the challenge.

"So, you're here to ask for a donation. Is that it?"

"To tell you the truth, I'm not really sure what I'm doing—or the best way to go about this." He paused. "To tell you the complete and *total* truth, this is my first stop." He gave her a sheepish smile. "I was going to try the Clam Box first but . . . Charlie Bates scares me."

Betty almost laughed. "He scares most people. You need to polish your act before you take on Charlie Bates."

Nathan didn't say anything. He just looked at her as if he'd found some miraculous key to a door that had always been locked.

She could almost tell what he was thinking: *I've come to the right place. This woman is going to help me.*

She knew she would, too. The opportunity was absolutely irresistible.

Something about Nathan was so sincere. He was so open with his feelings. He didn't seem to have a million levels of defenses like most of the men she met. She felt thrown off balance a bit by his sheer honesty.

"Would you like a cup of coffee or something?" Then she suddenly remembered the chili still cooking. "Oh, blast . . . I left something on the stove. Just a sec. I'd better check it . . ."

She dashed to the back of the shop, and Nathan followed. She lifted the lid on the pot. It had definitely cooked down and looked a little thick. She hoped it hadn't burned.

"That smells great. What are you making?"

"It's a new chili recipe . . . or it's supposed to be. Turkey and two kinds of beans." Betty stirred the chili around with a long spoon. "It doesn't look too bad, does it?"

"Now there's an overwhelming recommendation. I thought this place turned out gourmet food."

She laughed and looked up at him. "That's Molly's department. I'm mainly the office brains." She spooned up a bit of chili and offered it to him. "Here, you be the judge. I'm not great at taste-testing either."

Nathan happily stepped forward and bent closer to sample her efforts.He closed his eyes a bit, concentrating on the flavor. She studied his looks again. His hair was in need of a trim, and his black sweater and jeans looked almost as worn as the leather jacket he wore on top. He wasn't handsome in a conventional way, but something about him drew her.

If I were still selling real estate and this man were a house, I would describe him as "great condition, loads of charm, just needs some TLC. A real fixer-upper for a motivated buyer."

Somehow it all suited him. Rough around the edges but one hundred percent real.

Quite ironic considering his alter ego, Santa Claus, was the very definition of an unreal, fantasy figure.

Nathan nodded in approval. "That is good. I like the two kinds of beans. Black and kidney?"

"That was my idea," Betty confessed. "We didn't have enough kidney beans so I just tossed in the other kind. Is it really okay?"

"It's better than okay. It's excellent. Try it," he urged her.

Her cooking was not typically so well received. She took a new spoon and warily tasted a mouthful. "Hmm . . . That is pretty good. Needs a little more chili powder maybe?"

"It's fine for me. I don't need my mouth burning up to enjoy spicy food."

"Me either. Would you like to stay for lunch? I've made plenty, and it will help my case with Molly if I offer her an objective, unbiased opinion."

"I'd love to. But I'm not so sure I'm that objective about the chef."

Betty glanced at him and felt a little jolt. She decided it was best to ignore the comment.

He was just trying to be nice, she decided.

Betty set two places at the counter and served the chili with iced tea and some cornbread that was left over from a weekend event. "So, tell me more about this food pantry party that your friends planned," she began. "How many guests did they invite? Where is it going to be held?"

Nathan filled her in on the details of what they had planned to do and what they needed now, as much as he knew so far.

"Of course we need a lot of food. But we also need all the gifts for the kids and the families. That's going to be the hard part. People have already made their donations. They probably won't donate to the place twice."

Betty could see his point but didn't believe that hurdle was impassable. "Come on, Santa. You have to be more optimistic than that. Let's think outside the big bag a minute." She was rewarded with another great smile. "There are a lot of places you can try. You don't need to go back to the same supporters. Try the variety store in town, the big toy store in the mall. I know a lot of people. I can make some calls. I can help you get this together," she offered finally.

"That would be great. But only if you really want to and have the time. You guys must be crazy now, with the holidays. I really just came in here to ask for a donation of food for the party." He shrugged. "Maybe you should see how this would fit into your schedule and get back to me?"

Betty glanced at him. She could tell he really wanted her help but was trying to be considerate, allowing her a polite out just in case she had jumped in too impulsively—swept up by the moment, the newspaper article . . . and those startling blue eyes.

He did have a point. Her business was crazy busy right now, though the quiet in the shop today belied that. She was just jumping in impulsively. But she had also been thinking of doing a good deed for Christmas, helping people less fortunate than herself. Here was the perfect chance to do that and really make a difference. Not just write out a check and stick it in an envelope.

"We are very busy for the next few weeks. No question. It's this season and the spring, with all the weddings and graduation parties," she explained. "We more or less live or die by those two seasons."

Nathan listened with an unreadable expression, as if expecting her to back out.

"But ever since that Rotary party, I've been thinking that I'd like to do something this year to help other people. I mean, something more than just writing a check for a worthy cause. I have so much to be thankful for." *Even though I'm alone and think about that too much,* she added silently. "I know a lot of people have it hard this year. But I wasn't sure what to do or even how to figure that out. So this is perfect. I think I could do a good job helping you pull this together. I really want to do it," she said honestly.

Nathan looked surprised and very pleased by her answer. "You don't have to convince me. You've had more ideas in the last ten minutes than I was likely to come up with in a week."

She doubted that was so, but it was nice of him to say. He wasn't afraid to follow a woman's lead, was he? She liked that.

The phone rang and Betty tilted her head to listen to the answering machine. "Excuse me a minute, I have to take this."

While Betty spoke to the client, Nathan got up and carried their dishes to the sink. Betty soon returned and met him in the kitchen.

"It wasn't important. I'll call them back later," she explained. "Would you like some coffee or dessert? We're really stocked today. Brownies, carrot cake, tiramisu—"

"That all sounds delicious. But I'd better go. I'm sure you have work to do. And if I eat any more good food, I'll just want to go home and take a nap."

Betty laughed. She was starting to feel the same way.

"Let me give you my e-mail and phone number," he said, patting his pockets for a pen.

Betty quickly handed him the pad and pencil that were on the stainless steel countertop. Then she found one of her cards. She wrote her home phone number and personal e-mail on the back and gave it to him. Nathan looked at it a moment then slipped it in his wallet.

"I'll try to visit some other stores in town today and see if they're interested in helping. Can I call you tonight?"

"I should be home around seven or so," she said.

"Okay. I'll call with a full report," he promised.

He seemed about to say something else. His gaze was fixed on her, making her feel as if she had already saved the day.

The back door to the shop flew open, and Molly bustled in. She didn't even notice at first that Betty had a guest. "The ride down from Newburyport was torturous. I was stuck behind this dumb old truck that was going about twenty miles an hour. I wanted to scream."

Molly was not the calmest driver in the world, under any circumstance. When she encountered any kind of challenge on the highway, her blood pressure rose to dangerous levels.

She had dumped her briefcase, a sample book of linen swatches, and a big photo album of party setups on the counter. She suddenly noticed Nathan and paused as she pulled off her coat.

"Oh . . . hello. Haven't we met somewhere? You seem familiar." Molly glanced at Betty, then surveyed the scene in the kitchen. Betty knew she had quickly figured out Nathan had been hanging out for a while.

"This is Nathan Daley, Molly. The man who helped me get the van started after the party?" Betty had purposely avoided introducing him as Santa.

"Oh, right. I remember. I'm sorry I didn't recognize you out of uniform," Molly said quickly.

The clever comeback made him laugh. "You know how it is being a celebrity. I'm incognito today."

Very incognito, Betty thought.

"I was just leaving. I'm sure you ladies need to get to work," he said politely. "Nice to see you again, Molly."

"Good-bye, Nathan. Nice to see you, too." Molly's tone was bright but curious.

Betty walked him to the back door. "Thanks again for lunch," he said. "It was super. I'm glad I stopped here first."

"So am I," Betty said honestly. "See you."

She stood by the door as he walked out, then closed it behind him. She felt a bit elated by the visit and guessed it must show. She knew Molly would be full of questions. The best strategy, Betty decided, would be to tell her just the bare minimum—then distract her with the chili.

Molly would be sympathetic to the cause, of course. Betty had no doubt she would offer to donate food and maybe even holiday dinners for the families. But Betty didn't want to get into a conversation about Nathan. She was more in the mood for her partner's cooking tips right now than her advice about men.

CHAPTER FIVE

❧

ZOEY LOVED HER ROOM IN LUCY'S HOUSE. SHE HAD NEVER had her own room before, not even when her family was still together and she lived with her mother. This room was more like a little studio apartment, tucked in the attic, far from everyone. The kind of place Zoey daydreamed about having when she had a job and lived on her own. She even had a TV and a bathroom all to herself. If it was hers for real, she would hang up some posters or the collages she made. And she would paint the walls dark purple or something interesting and get a cooler-looking quilt. The pastel blue walls and flowered, lace-edged quilt made her a little crazy. She felt as if she was trapped in an air-freshener commercial. But the decor was perfect for an old lady, Zoey thought. Which made sense when you thought about it.

Lucy had told her that the room was really for Charlie's mother, who lived in Florida and came up to visit in the summer and sometimes on holidays. But she wasn't coming to New England for

Christmas this year. Zoey had overheard Lucy talking about it with Charlie one night, as they were coming upstairs. It turned out that this year Charlie's mother was going to visit with his sister's family, who lived out in Arizona. Charlie had sounded unhappy about that, pouting like a little boy who missed his mommy. That had definitely surprised Zoey. She couldn't imagine Charlie getting all mushy over anyone. But she could imagine his mother. Any woman who had raised Charlie had to be a tough old bird, Zoey thought. No wonder they had made her such a nice room, one she hardly even used. She was probably really picky and complained a lot, keeping Lucy hopping.

Zoey tried not to complain or ask Lucy for anything special. She mainly tried to just blend into the woodwork, hoping they would all forget she was even there. She would have gladly stayed up in the room forever and never set a foot downstairs, even for food. But she was feeling better, and Lucy said she had to get up and walk around the house as much as she could. Lying in bed too much was bad for her lungs, Lucy told her. She could get even sicker. Lucy had been so nice to her, Zoey tried to cooperate. At least whenever she was around.

When Lucy was home from work during the day, she made Zoey come down and sit in the kitchen or family room with her. Zoey would watch Lucy do housework, or just sit and talk. One day she helped Lucy fold laundry. She was just bored out of her skull. Lucy made a big deal about it and kept thanking her. Zoey could see nobody helped her around here. Lucy did it all and went to work at a hospital, too. And she had that Charlie squawking at her every minute when he got home.

Luckily, he wasn't around much, Zoey thought. Sick or not, she wouldn't have lasted here very long if she had to see too much of that guy. She would have figured out some way to run away. She was surprised she had been here this long. Sunday had been a week and now it was Tuesday, nine days total. Over a week and she had only checked her e-mail once.

Her cell phone had died last Tuesday, a real bummer. The card had run out on her pay-as-you-go plan, and, being stuck here, she couldn't get another one. She couldn't even check her messages. She had snuck down to the second floor and used the house phone once or twice. There was an extension in Lucy's room. She had also found a cell phone in one of the boys' rooms—the younger one, she guessed. But it had a password and she couldn't figure it out.

Using the landline was tricky. She knew Lucy wouldn't mind if she called people, but she didn't want anyone to know her business. Not Lucy Bates. Not even Rita. So she had to sneak calls when no one was around and hope they wouldn't come barging in. She often just had to leave messages for friends who couldn't even call her back. The real problem was not being able to text anymore. That was the way she and her friends really communicated, and you couldn't do that with a dumb old landline.

She didn't mind coming downstairs if Lucy was home. Or if she was alone in the house. But she didn't like it if they were all here. A few times, Lucy had asked her to have supper with them. But Zoey pretended she was too tired or felt sick. She wasn't part of this family. The two boys stared at her as if she had landed from another planet. She had barely said two words to either of them. The little guy was okay. But the older kid didn't seem to like her, on sight. Like his father, Zoey thought.

It didn't matter. She would be leaving here any day now. As soon as Rita found another foster home to dump her in. She couldn't wait until she was old enough to live by herself. She was going to take off and get as far from this part of the country as she could. She would have done it long ago if it wasn't for her little brother. She hated to leave him without even saying good-bye. But she wasn't even sure where he was living now.

Lucy had left a while ago for work, and the boys weren't home yet from school. Zoey decided to go down to the kitchen for a bite of food. She was starting to get her appetite back. The real trick was finding anything good to eat around here. It was all so disgustingly healthy. She felt like she would kill for a potato chip or a french fry.

Zoey reached the second floor and was about to turn on the landing, but the open door to Lucy and Charlie's bedroom caught her eye. Why not use the phone and call her best friend, Caitlin?

She walked over and pushed the door open all the way. It was a pretty room, she thought. The walls were a pale yellow color with a wallpaper border, and the quilt on the bed was the same shade of yellow, with pale blue flowers. The bed was made up neatly, with tons of pillows on top. The rest of the room was neat, too. No dirty clothes or wet towels hanging around. She could have predicted that. Lucy was very organized. The house was as clean as a hospital, Zoey thought; a lot cleaner than most of the places she had lived in.

As Zoey walked to the side of the bed with the phone, she passed Lucy's dresser. There was a large wood-framed mirror above it and a crystal dish that held jewelry and rings. It seemed to be all costume jewelry, no good stuff. She tried on a large silver ring with a blue stone in the middle. It wasn't worth much, but it was pretty. And it fit pretty good, too.

But if she walked off with it, Lucy was sure to notice and realize who had taken it. It wasn't really worth it, Zoey thought. She didn't like it that much.

She slipped the ring off, sifted through a few necklaces, and then looked over the perfume selection. She picked up a large red bottle with a big gold ball on top and sniffed. It had a strong, spicy scent. She knew it was pretty good stuff, because she had tried some once in a department store. She lifted her chin and gave herself a good spray—then had to cough.

The smell was too strong and seemed to go straight to her lungs, screwing up her breathing. Zoey held on to the dresser, coughing her head off, trying to catch her breath.

"Hey, what are you doing in here?"

Zoey spun around and the perfume bottle flew out of her hands and hit the carpet. "Oh no!" She quickly bent down to see if it had broken. Then she turned to glare at Jamie, who now stood right behind her.

"Why did you shout at me like that? See what you made me do?" Zoey coughed again, trying to show him how sick she was, but he didn't look very sympathetic.

"What are you doing messing around in my mom's room? You shouldn't be in here."

"Just chill," she said, catching her breath. "I wasn't doing anything."

Zoey found the bottle and picked it up. It wasn't broken or even chipped, thank goodness. She put it back on the dresser right where she found it, then turned to Jamie.

"Don't worry. Your mom doesn't care if I come in here."

Jamie stared at her with narrowed eyes. "Okay, so then it doesn't matter if I tell her when she comes home that you were in here, going through her stuff."

Zoey stared at him. This kid was a pain.

"She won't care. I'll tell her you were bothering me," she countered. Zoey acted fearless but still didn't want the kid to tell on her. "How old are you anyway?"

"I'm eleven." He announced the number loudly. "How old are you?"

"Fifteen," she told him, then thought she should have exaggerated a little and said she was older. He wouldn't have known the difference.

He looked at her curiously. "Why don't you go to school? Because you're sick?"

Zoey shook her head. "I wouldn't go anyway. I'm finished with school. I already know everything."

"Yeah, right," Jamie scoffed.

"What's so great about school? The stuff they teach you is totally useless. It doesn't help at all in real life," she told him. "But you wouldn't know about that."

He was a little baby, protected in this nice, little house by his nice, little family. Like a little puppy dog, she thought. His older brother was not much further along. Just bigger, louder, and bossier.

Jamie stared at her a moment. "I'm going down to make some popcorn. You want some?"

Zoey was surprised. "I can get some food for myself. Your mom said it was okay."

"I know. She told me to help you when I got home. I'm just trying to do what she said."

Zoey didn't answer him. She ducked her head and jammed her hands in her bathrobe—partly to keep from walking off with the silver ring. It still looked pretty tempting to her.

"Yeah, I'd like popcorn. I am a little hungry."

A short time later they were sitting in the kitchen that adjoined a large family room.

Jamie had made microwave popcorn, and they divided it between two large bowls. Jamie started eating his right away, but Zoey added extras—melted butter and Parmesan cheese.

"Ugh. That's gross." Jamie made a face. "I can't believe you put cheese on it. It smells like baby puke."

"Are you kidding? I think it tastes gross, just dry like that. That's like eating foam."

Jamie walked over to the TV and set up his video game. "Do you mind if I play without the earphones? I can't find them."

"Knock yourself out." Zoey shrugged and ate her popcorn,

watching from the stool at the counter. The game was a little noisy but cool to watch on the big-screen TV.

She'd bet her brother would love one of those things. She wondered if he had one where he was living now. Probably not. Foster families didn't have a lot of extras for the kids. If they had anything good, everyone fought over it so much, it was either taken away or got broken pretty quickly.

"You're pretty good at that," she observed, wiping her fingers on a napkin.

"Thanks. It takes a certain skill," he said in a surprisingly grown-up tone. "Want to try it?"

"Me?"

"It's not rocket science. Girls can probably do this . . . a little."

"Of course girls can do it. They just don't want to." Zoey slipped off the stool and sat next to him. "What the heck. Let me at it."

She didn't have anything better to do except go back upstairs. *Maybe if I play this stupid game with him, he won't say anything to his mother about finding me in her room,* she thought.

Working the controls was harder than it looked. She wasn't very good with eye-hand things, and she usually had to hear instructions for something new over and over again before anything sank in. But Jamie was a patient teacher. He never acted like he thought she was dumb, which Zoey appreciated.

She knew that she was dumb. A real dolt. Everybody said so. All her teachers and her mother and her foster parents, too, though most of them never said it right to her face. They just treated her like some idiot child. That was why she had hated school and couldn't wait to get out. She got tired of feeling as if everyone was talking to her in a foreign language, then laughing behind her back at how slow she was to catch on. Or giving her those big pitiful stares. She hated that the most.

"Oh, man . . . you got that guy good. Did you see the way his pod exploded? Awesome." Jamie leaned so far to one side, laughing, that he almost tipped over.

Zoey had made a good shot. The points showed on the screen along with some wild space sounds.

They played a full game and Jamie cranked it up a level. "Ready for the next dimension? This level is freaking wild. It goes even faster."

"Sure, I'll try it." Zoey hoped she would be able to keep up.

They were sitting on the floor side by side, holding their controls. Jamie turned on the next level of the game. "I hope it doesn't give you nightmares. It's definitely scarier. They go through this time warp, and there are all these space zombies."

She laughed at him. "I won't get nightmares, don't worry."

"That's what you say now. Even C.J. gets creeped out," he said very seriously. "Don't tell him I told you," he added.

Zoey laughed at him again. "You remind me of my brother, Kevin," she said impulsively. "You're just about the same age."

"Where is he?" Jamie asked. "Does he still live in the place you ran away from?"

"He never went there with me. He had to go live with another family."

Jamie gave her a puzzled look. He missed a good shot, and a monster bit his character's head off. "That's weird. Why couldn't you live together? He's your brother."

"It doesn't work like that once your family falls apart. My mom . . . My mom got sick," she said simply. "And she couldn't take care of us anymore. So first we lived with my grandmother and then with my aunt. When that didn't work out we had to go to separate places." She paused and took a breath. "It's complicated."

"It sounds complicated," Jamie said, focusing on the game again. "Sometimes I get really mad at my dad and think about running away. That would show him. But I probably wouldn't do it. My mom would worry too much, even if I was just fooling around."

"That's smart. Don't do it. You could really get hurt," Zoey warned him. "Your father is sort of a jerk. But your mom is nice. You and your brother have it pretty good here. Nice house, your own room with all your own stuff. Lots of good food, you can eat all day if you want. Nobody is yelling at you, either. You've got video games and a computer and a cell phone. You don't have it too bad, believe me."

Before Jamie could answer, they heard the back door open. Lucy called out, "I'm home. Anybody around?" She walked into the kitchen and set some grocery bags on the counter.

"Hello, Zoey. I'm glad to see you up and around. How do you feel?"

"I'm doing okay." Zoey put down the controls from the video game and walked over to Lucy. "Jamie was teaching me how to play his game."

"How did it go? Did you find a new partner, Jamie?" Lucy asked her son.

He kept working the controls on his own and barely looked up at her. "She's not so bad. She has some potential. For a female."

Zoey laughed, then looked back at Lucy. "It sort of gave me a headache. I don't know how he sits there that long."

"Neither do I. But he loves it."

"I'm feeling a little tired again. I think I'll go back upstairs for a while."

"Sure, hon. You have a rest. I'm going to start dinner. Would you like to eat with us, or should I bring you up a tray?"

Zoey wasn't sure what to say. She was obviously feeling better and didn't want to hurt Lucy's feelings. But she still didn't like the idea of sitting down at the Bateses' table and being stuck there with all of them. Especially, being stuck listening to Charlie, who either acted as if she were invisible or just gave her nasty looks.

"I'm not sure," she answered. "Can I tell you later?"

"Of course. See how you feel." Lucy had already begun emptying the dishwasher. Zoey felt an impulse to help her. She always had jobs to do in the places she used to live. As far as she could see, the boys got off pretty easy around here. Lucy would ask them to help her with housework, but they usually weaseled out of it and Lucy ended up doing it all on her own. They didn't seem to notice. But Zoey did. Lucy turned to give Zoey a brief smile. "We're having roast chicken. You like that, right?"

Zoey nodded. She did like it but was still surprised when Lucy asked her preferences.

"Okay, I'll call you when it's ready," Lucy said brightly.

Zoey nodded again, then headed back upstairs.

"Jamie, you need to shut down the game now and start your homework," Lucy called to her son.

Zoey passed Jamie and paused. "Thanks for the popcorn and teaching me your game."

He shrugged. "No big deal." Then he gave her a look, and Zoey knew he wasn't going to tell Lucy on her. She felt relieved. He did remind her of her brother. She hadn't said that just to get on his good side.

A SHORT TIME LATER, LUCY CAME DOWNSTAIRS AGAIN AFTER bringing Zoey a tray. Charlie and the boys were at the table, ready and waiting for their dinner. "Zoey's asleep," Lucy reported. "She probably got tired staying up so much this afternoon with Jamie. But it's a good sign. She must be feeling much better."

Lucy took a platter of roast chicken out of the oven, along with bowls of green beans and roasted potatoes. The boys passed the bowls of food around while Charlie carved the chicken.

"I guess she's over her flu or whatever it was," Charlie said loudly. "Now what? Don't we call the social worker and send her on her way?"

That was more or less what she had agreed to, Lucy knew. But she still didn't like the idea.

"There's some improvement, Charlie. That doesn't mean she's fully recovered and ready to go. She's been very sick. She could relapse in a day."

"Oh, baloney." Charlie filled his dish with food. "We had an agreement, Lucy. And you have to stick to it. We'd be asking for trouble, letting that girl stay. What will she do—sit around the house all day and watch TV? Fool around on the computer? Get into trouble with no one home to watch her? We're darn lucky we've gotten this far with no problems, and that's only because she's been so sick, she could hardly get out of bed."

Lucy knew that her husband had a point. She just didn't like the way he put it. Any teenager left home alone for hours on end was bound to get into some mischief. Lucy had shifted her schedule around so that she could spend time at home during the day to be with Zoey. But she couldn't do that forever.

Lucy helped herself to some chicken. "I've been thinking about it, Charlie, and I have an idea. But Zoey would have to agree to it."

"Oh, here we go," Charlie appealed to the kitchen ceiling. "Lucy has another idea. Can't a guy get a break around here?"

"If you'll stop carrying on," Lucy said calmly, "I'll tell you what it is. Why don't you just listen a minute before you start complaining? My idea will help you, too."

"That will be the day. Okay, shoot. What's the latest scheme, Lucy?"

"What if she gets a job—even a little part-time job that would get her out of the house for a few hours? She would have more structure to her day and some responsibility. Would that satisfy you, Charlie? Would you let her stay longer if she had a job somewhere?"

"A job? I never thought of that," Charlie admitted. He picked up a drumstick with his fork and dropped it on his plate. "A job would be good for her. She ought to be earning her way if she doesn't want to finish school. But who's going to hire her? Did you figure that out?"

"You could," Lucy said brightly. "You're always shorthanded at the diner, and it's always busy around the holidays. You need an extra waitress."

"I'm going to hire her?" Charlie laughed. "I should have guessed that."

"It doesn't have to be the diner," Lucy continued. "A lot of places in the village need help for the holidays. I could go around and talk to some of the shopkeepers—Grace Hegman, maybe, or the Beans. The Beanery is always busy."

Felicity and Jonathan Bean, who ran the Beanery, were Charlie's archrivals. Lucy knew the mere mention of their names pushed all of his buttons.

"I didn't say she couldn't work at the diner," he said gruffly. "But does she even want to? I don't want to feel like I'm forcing it on her. She'll just give me that look and be a slacker."

Lucy didn't want to force Zoey into the idea either or make her feel she had to work for her room and board. "I know what you mean, Charlie. I totally agree."

"Oh, you do, do you?" Charlie couldn't hide his surprise. "Well . . . that's a first."

"She said that once she felt better, she wanted to make some money," Lucy explained.

In order to hit the road again, Lucy had no doubt. But they didn't really have any say over what Zoey did with her life. She would only be with them a short time. All Lucy could do was try to give the girl the kindness and unconditional acceptance that she so desperately needed.

It would be difficult, if not impossible, to explain these things to Charlie, Lucy knew. But at least he was warming up to the waitressing idea.

"Won't you just try her out, Charlie? I mean, if she's willing. This means a lot to me, to help this girl. I really need you to do this."

She watched his expression. Charlie did love her; she knew that. He also resisted any kind of change to his routine or household. She could see him wrestling with the idea. He looked at her and then back at his food again.

He sighed. "Okay. I'll try it. If she wants to. But if it doesn't work out, no more arguments or schemes to keep her here, understand? What if my mother changes her mind and decides to come up here for Christmas after all? That's her room. Where will she stay?"

The room did not belong to Charlie's mother. She had not paid a cent toward the renovation, and there was no brass plaque with her name on the door. Lucy considered pointing out these facts to her husband but instead said, "Your mother sounded pretty set on her plans. And you know how she is once she decides on something." Just like her son, Lucy nearly added. "Besides, the social worker is looking for a new foster home. Zoey will be gone soon anyway."

"Let's hope so," Charlie said. "I don't get it. You seemed fixated on this girl for some reason, Lucy. I know you have a soft heart for every stray animal and lost soul that comes your way. But this is different. I don't understand it," he confessed.

Lucy couldn't deny it. What Charlie said was true. She didn't quite understand it herself. This girl had touched her heart in a deep place, hit some hidden buttons. Maybe it really was a rescue fantasy, as Rita said. Or maybe she just enjoyed having another female in the house—having a girl that would be about the same age as a daughter?

"I know what you mean. I don't quite get it either," she admitted. "I just want to help her. And why does the reason matter so much after all? She's not going to be here very long—a week or so maybe. Let's just try to do the right thing. That's enough of a reason for me," she added.

Charlie sighed but didn't say anything more. The boys had left the table, and Charlie started talking about Christmas, asking Lucy when she thought they should put up their tree and wondering what the boys wanted this year for their gifts. There was so much to do before Christmas. Lucy didn't know how she would get it all done in time. But every year, somehow, she did.

After she cleaned up the kitchen, Lucy went upstairs to see Zoey. The girl was sitting cross-legged on her bed and the TV was on, but she seemed to be doing some sort of art project. Lucy saw a pile of pages torn out of magazines and cut into little pieces.

Zoey was arranging a few of the cut-out bits on a sheet of paper, securing them in place with pieces of tape. She looked up suddenly when Lucy came into the room, as if she had been caught doing something wrong.

"Hey, there. You woke up. Did you eat dinner?" Lucy glanced at the tray on the bedside table. Most of the food was gone.

"Yeah, it was good."

"I'm glad to see you're feeling better." Lucy sat in a chair near the bed. "What are you making? An art project?"

Zoey shrugged and looked away. "It's just something I do when I'm bored. I make these collage things. My grandma was really into crafts and scrapbooks. She sort of taught me."

"That's neat. I can follow a pattern for sewing, but it takes real talent to do something right out of your head." Lucy leaned over to get a better look at Zoey's creation. "Can I see?"

Zoey glanced at her curiously then turned the collage so Lucy could get a better look. It really was interesting, Lucy thought.

There was a mixture of photos from ads—women's faces and bodies, as well as things like flowers, food, and animals. And in between the cutouts, Zoey had done interesting drawings, pulling it all together. A woman's body with a cupcake instead of a head. Another face with flowers in the place of the eyes.

"Wow . . . this is pretty amazing," Lucy said. "What do you do with these things when you're done? Put them in a book or something?"

"A book?" Zoey grinned, as if she found that idea pretty funny. "I don't save them. Most of the time. I just toss them out or they get lost."

"Really? I think you should save them. Gee . . . I would frame this and hang it somewhere."

"Yeah, right." Zoey clearly didn't believe her.

"I would," Lucy insisted. "It's really beautiful. I'd hang it in the living room."

"Okay, when I'm done, you can have it," Zoey said, sounding as though she were practically daring Lucy to keep her word.

"Great. I'm going to remind you, if you forget," Lucy promised. She paused, gathering her thoughts as she remembered what she had really come to say. "I guess if you feel good enough to do artwork, you're on the mend," she began. "It's going to take a while longer to get your full strength back. But Charlie and I were talking. We thought that once you do feel one hundred percent, it would be good if you had something to do. Someplace to go every day. . . . You told me that you didn't want to go back to school. Do you still feel that way?"

Zoey's body grew tense, her eyes hard. "I'm not going to any kind of school. Just forget it. Did Mrs. Schuman tell you to ask me that?"

"No, not at all. That was my own crazy idea," Lucy said, trying to get a smile out of her.

She almost succeeded, but not quite.

"Well, you told me once you wanted to make some money. Do you want to get a job? Just a few hours a week. Just something to keep you busy?"

"A job? Like where?"

"The diner always needs help. I wondered if you wanted to try waitressing. You could earn some decent tips, especially during the holidays."

Zoey shook her head. "No way. I don't want to do that."

Lucy didn't want to push it. "That's okay, I understand. What about some other type of job? Maybe one of the shops in town needs Christmas help."

Zoey looked a bit more interested in that idea, Lucy thought. Maybe she was afraid to work for Charlie. They had definitely gotten off on the wrong foot, and he hadn't been very welcoming to her.

Zoey twisted her mouth, thinking. "I don't know . . . I'm not really the salesgirl type." She held up a blue strand of hair. "Who's going to hire me?"

"Plenty of people—if you have a good attitude and do your best." *And dress a little more conventionally*, Lucy wanted to add. But she thought she ought to save the fashion tips for later.

Zoey considered for a moment, then shook her head again. "I don't think so."

Lucy waited, hoping the girl would change her mind. Finally, she said, "Then I'll have to call Mrs. Schuman tomorrow and tell her that you feel better and are ready for a permanent placement. Is that what you really want—to move somewhere else? To a different family?"

Zoey didn't answer. She looked down at her hands and examined the chipped polish on her stubby fingernails. "I'm always moving to a different place. That's no big deal for me," she told Lucy. "What's the difference? Call Mrs. Schuman. I don't care."

Lucy didn't believe that for a minute, but she didn't know what to say. "All right, Zoey. I'll call her. You ought to turn off the light soon. You still need your rest."

Zoey glanced at her, her expression softening. "Good night, Lucy . . . I'm sorry I'm such a slug. I know you're just trying to help me."

Her simple words and sad tone touched Lucy's heart. She wanted to step over to the bed and wrap the child in a hug, but she knew that would be too much.

Lucy sent her a warm smile instead. "I do want to help you, sweetie. I just wish I knew how. And you're not a slug. Don't ever say that, okay?"

Zoey just sighed and studied her nails again.

It was only a little past nine. Lucy knew she could call Rita Schuman if she wanted. The social worker had told her to call anytime. Rita might have found a placement by now and might just be waiting for the girl to be healthy enough to go. But Lucy knew that once she called, that might be it. Zoey would be gone from her life. And Lucy couldn't quite face that.

AT THE HOSPITAL THE NEXT MORNING LUCY WAS SO BUSY SHE had a temporary reprieve from dealing with Zoey's situation—until her morning break rolled around. Then Lucy knew she couldn't put it off any longer. She had to call Rita Schuman. Her supervisor kindly let Lucy borrow her office for privacy, and Lucy slowly dialed Rita's number.

Rita picked up right away. "Hi, Lucy. How's everything? How is Zoey doing?"

"Much better than the last time we spoke." Rita had called to check on Zoey over the weekend. "She's really coming along," Lucy reported. "She's a lot more energetic, and the congestion is all cleared up. You know how kids are. Give them a little medicine and they spring right back."

"They are resilient," Rita agreed. "I'm glad to hear she's recovering. I've been working on her placement. I may have something for her."

"Oh, really? When will you know? Should I tell Zoey?" Lucy tried to sound calm but couldn't totally hide the distress in her voice.

"I'd rather not say anything until we're certain," Mrs. Schuman said. "But it should all be confirmed in a few days."

That was quick. Zoey might leave by the weekend, Lucy realized. She had known there was a chance of it happening like that, but to hear it said aloud was still a shock.

They hung up, and Lucy gazed out the window into the hospital courtyard. It had benches and pathways for walking. Small flowering trees bloomed there in the spring. But today it looked dreary and empty, reflecting the feelings in her heart. Lucy couldn't wait for the day to pass so she could go home again. Any time left with Zoey now seemed precious to her. She wasn't sure how she had come to feel so attached to the girl in such a short time—but she did.

She was on an early shift again today and would be home by four. She and Charlie had decided it would be a good night to set up their Christmas tree. Charlie had picked out the tree with Jamie on Sunday, over at Sawyer's tree farm. It was ready and waiting in a bucket of water out on the porch.

Decorating the tree was one part of Christmas that Lucy always enjoyed. But it would be a bittersweet night for her this year, with Zoey there, Lucy realized. Still, she had to be grateful for what she had. At least Zoey could share in this little part of the holidays with them.

*   *   *

TAKEOUT FOR DINNER WAS PART OF THE TREE-TRIMMING RITUAL. Lucy loved not having to cook. When she got home with two boxes of pizza, Charlie already had the boys bringing the decorations up from the basement. Some living room furniture had been moved aside, and the tree set in its stand, with the usual old sheet underneath and the tree robe over that.

"So far, so good," Lucy said, surveying the scene. Jamie was working on the lights, untangling a strand and testing them out in the circuit box. "Where's Zoey?" she asked him.

Jamie shrugged. "She's up in her room, I guess. I haven't seen her."

Lucy went up to the third floor. Zoey's door was partly closed, and she could hear the TV on inside. She knocked lightly and then walked in. "Hi, Zoey. How are you doing?"

"Okay." She turned to Lucy and smiled. "A little better, I guess."

"We're having pizza for dinner and decorating the Christmas tree. Would you like to come down and join us?"

Lucy didn't want to sound too eager, but she did want Zoey to spend at least one evening with the family. This seemed like the perfect time.

"Is your tree real? I mean like, totally? Or the fake kind?"

"It's totally real," Lucy assured her. "Charlie just put it in the stand and it's making the whole house smell like pine. I'm surprised you didn't smell it all the way up here. Come on down and see," Lucy coaxed her. "There won't be any pizza left if we hang out here much longer." She had bought two, but she knew that C.J. could practically inhale a whole pie on his own.

"Um . . . okay. I'll come down. For a little while." Zoey turned off the TV and slipped off the bed. She was wearing a sweatshirt and sweatpants Lucy had loaned her. The set was a little baggy, but she looked cute.

Back downstairs in the kitchen, Charlie and the boys had already started on the pizza.

"Hey, guys, leave some for me and Zoey," Lucy called out. "It's not a race."

Charlie nodded at Zoey, a slice dangling from his hand. "Hi, Zoey. Feeling better? You look pretty good," he said. "Your color is better."

That was true, but Lucy couldn't help but think the compliment came from Charlie's relief that the girl would soon be gone. She had called him during the day and told him about her conversation with Rita. It was easy to be nice to her under those circumstances.

Jamie's greeting was more sincere. He quickly calculated that they were short a seat and jumped up from his chair. "Here, Zoey. You sit here. I'll get the stool."

Zoey sat between Lucy and Jamie. The boys talked about school, but Zoey picked at her slice and didn't say a word. She felt awkward, Lucy realized. She hoped the girl wouldn't run upstairs again.

"Okay, let's get to it. It's getting late," Charlie said, rising from his chair.

"I fixed all the lights, Dad," Jamie said, running ahead. "Come and see."

C.J. followed his brother. Lucy gathered up a few of the paper plates and dumped them in the trash. Zoey picked up the dirty glasses and brought them to the sink.

"Thanks, honey. Let's just leave this stuff," Lucy said. "I'll do it later. Come inside, help us with the tree."

Zoey allowed herself to be led along by Lucy's light touch on her arm, but she stopped as soon as they reached the living room doorway. "I don't think so," she said. "I think I need to go back upstairs."

"Just for a minute or two. You shouldn't lie down with a full stomach," Lucy advised her in a nurselike tone.

"Zoey, check this out." Jamie ran over to her with one of his favorite ornaments. It looked like a chocolate-glazed donut. "Doesn't that look real? I bet if I put this on a plate, C.J. would try to take a bite," he teased his brother. C.J. grunted at him but ignored the jibe. Lucy thought he seemed pretty quiet tonight. She guessed he was feeling self-conscious around a real, live girl his own age. He was acting a little more mature and self-restrained, she noticed. This could definitely be a good thing.

Zoey took the donut ornament and looked it over. "Pretty cool. It does look real."

"Wait . . . this is another good one." Jamie ran back to one of the boxes and took out another of his favorites, a shiny red baseball with *Red Sox 2004* written in gold.

"It's from the World Series, when the Sox broke the curse," he explained in a knowing tone.

"You were only four, dweeb. You don't even remember," C.J. cut in.

"I remember," Jamie insisted. He turned to Zoey. "I do."

"I believe you," she said quietly. She glanced at Lucy with a he's-really-cute look.

"Let's sit over here, Zoey, on the couch. There's plenty of room." To Lucy's surprise, Zoey didn't protest but sat down beside her on the couch. "I like to watch more than I like to hang," Lucy confessed, "though there are a few ornaments that are definitely mine. I have a really nice angel collection," she told Zoey. "We didn't unpack that box yet."

After Charlie hung the lights, C.J. and Jamie hung most of the ornaments. Then Jamie found Lucy's box of angels and brought it to her.

She opened it carefully and checked to see that none were broken this year. She always packed them well, but you never knew. "Here they are," she said to Zoey. "Take a look. They're all different, but I like to find a nice spot and put them up together. Like a flock of angels, watching over us," she explained.

"Oh, geez, here we go with those angels," Charlie mumbled to himself. Lucy just laughed. "Where's my Celtics stuff?" Charlie asked. "Anybody see Kevin Garnett? And that big cheeseburger and fries?" Charlie stood in the midst of the boxes, trying to find his own favorites, which mainly consisted of sports symbols and diner food.

Zoey dutifully peered inside the box Lucy held out. Then Lucy saw the expression on Zoey's face change. "Wow, those are pretty," she said.

Lucy took one out and let it dangle from the tree hook. "Here, you help me hang them. Pick a spot."

Zoey sat back, seeming unwilling to take the ornament from her. But Lucy insisted. "Go on. I see a few good places toward the top."

Finally, Zoey took the angel and walked to the tree. She took a few moments choosing the right branch then fastened the hook. The blue and gold ornament dangled from the pine bough, looking very pretty, Lucy thought.

"Good choice. I'll do one now. And you take another," Lucy said, passing the box back.

A short time later, Lucy's collection hung in an attractive arrangement. While the boys finished hanging the rest of the ornaments and Jamie set up the crèche below the bottom branches, Lucy made hot chocolate and brought it in along with some chocolate-chip cookies.

"Not bad," Charlie said, sitting back in the armchair. "I like all those white lights. That was a good idea," he added.

"My idea," Jamie piped up.

Charlie picked up his chocolate and reached for the cookies. Then he lifted the plate and offered them to Zoey. "Have a cookie. They're really good. I made them myself," he teased her.

Zoey looked at him strangely then realized he was joking. She smiled a little. "Okay, I'll try one."

She sat back and munched on the cookie, glancing around as if she expected someone to notice her at any minute and ask her to leave. Lucy hoped she was having a good time with them.

LATER THAT EVENING, WHEN THE BOYS WERE DOING THEIR homework and Zoey was in her room, Lucy grabbed a shopping bag that she had stashed in her bedroom closet.

She went up to the next floor. "Hey, Zoey. I just wanted to say good night. I'm glad you helped us trim the tree. I hope you had fun."

"I did," Zoey said. "I don't remember doing stuff like that with my real family," she confided.

At least we could give her that before she leaves, Lucy thought.

"I saw this in a shop in town and thought you might like it. It's nothing really," Lucy added, offering Zoey the shopping bag. "I mean, my feelings won't be hurt if it's not right. But it looked cute in the window. Sort of reminded me of you."

Zoey took the bag, looking very surprised. She opened it quickly and took out a sweater top with a hood that Lucy had picked out for her. It was purple with thin gray stripes. Lucy wasn't sure about the color, but Zoey seemed to have a lot of things that were purple.

Zoey's eyes widened as she held up the sweater. "This is nice. . . .

I really like the color." She looked up at Lucy with a big smile. "Looks like the right size, too. How did you guess?"

Lucy shrugged, feeling pleased. "Oh, I don't know. You're a little smaller than me. I just figured it out that way. Do you really like it? You can exchange it if you want. I saved the receipt."

"No. . . . I mean, yes. I really like it. Thanks, Lucy." Zoey seemed genuinely pleased and practically hugged the sweater to her chest.

In all the days she'd been with them, Zoey had rarely said thank you and never that wholeheartedly. It was too bad that she was finally starting to relax and she would soon have to go.

"You know, Zoey, something is on my mind. I just want to make sure you know that when I spoke to you about the waitressing job the other night, it was only because I thought you might want something to do. Something productive, outside of the house. It wasn't because we were trying to get some work out of you in exchange for staying here. I really hope you don't think that," Lucy said. "I'd be upset if you had that impression."

"I know you didn't mean it that way," Zoey said. "I'm sorry that I sort of blew you off." Then she swallowed hard and looked down. Lucy had the feeling she wanted to say something more but felt nervous. Finally Zoey said, "I didn't want to try the job because I was afraid I'd screw it up, that's all. I'm sort of a screwup. Everything I touch turns to crap. Can't help it. I was just born that way." She shrugged. "I would have been a total disaster. Believe me, you're lucky I didn't say yes."

Lucy was so upset and moved by Zoey's admission, she couldn't speak at first. She could tell that Zoey was just repeating all the toxic, critical tapes she had heard from the adults in her life. She had been programmed to have a poor self-image and no self-love.

Lucy sat down on the edge of the bed. "Of course you could do that sort of job if you really wanted to. I'm sure of it. You're a smart girl, Zoey. Anyone can see that. And there's not that much to it, once you know the routine."

Zoey glanced at her, her head bowed. "I'm not smart. But thanks for saying that."

"Everyone feels anxious at their first job. I was scared to death," Lucy told her. "You should have seen me when I started my nursing training and they actually let me loose with real patients. I was terrified. . . . And once, I did make a very big mistake and I nearly gave it all up."

Zoey looked at her in disbelief. "You did? What happened . . . ? Did you kill somebody?"

Lucy sighed. It was an episode in her life she would never forget, but it was still hard to talk about. Even after all these years.

"The patient didn't die—but I thought she was going to. It was terrible. My very worst nightmare about being a nurse. I gave a woman the wrong dose of medication, and she went into a coma. Luckily, my supervisor realized what was happening and called a STAT. That's an emergency situation when about ten doctors come running at once. They were able to stabilize the patient and reverse the effects of the overdose. But it could have been fatal." Lucy shuddered, remembering that day. "I couldn't deal with it at first. After years of school and tests, and months of training, I just gave up. I thought, well if I could screw up that big, I shouldn't be a nurse. That proves it."

"But you didn't give up, right?" Zoey said. "I mean, you must have gone back since you are a nurse now."

"I took some time to sort things out. Little by little, I learned to forgive myself and remember that everyone makes mistakes. That's part of learning and gathering experience. Other people encouraged me to try again. Even Charlie," she told Zoey, who looked surprised. "He knew I really loved it and wanted to be a nurse more than anything. I'm good at it, too," she added. "The thing is, you can't just lie down and give up every time you fail. You have to get up and keep going. If you stick with it, before you know it, you're good. Now I'm considered one of the old-timers, and I'm training the student nurses. I would have helped you, too, to learn what to do in the diner. I wasn't going to just throw you out there, sink or swim," she added quickly.

"You were going to help me? I didn't know that."

"Of course I was. I'd train you and get you rolling. And Charlie was going to be on his best behavior," she quickly added. "If you hated it, nobody was going to make you stay. I'm sorry you didn't realize that when we talked the other night. I should have explained all that."

"I'm sorry, too," Zoey said quickly. She turned to Lucy, her dark eyes wide. "Do you think I could still try? I'd try it if you were going to help me."

Maybe she was making a little progress here, Lucy thought. Maybe it wasn't such a great idea to move Zoey to yet another household. Maybe this one was helping her.

But now she wasn't so sure it would work out. There was Rita to deal with. And Charlie.

"Listen, I can't make any guarantees, but I'm going to try to work it out," Lucy said. "I have to talk to Mrs. Schuman and to Charlie again."

"Oh, just forget it," Zoey said quickly. "It's okay. Whatever."

She was so anxious, so insecure. Lucy's heart went out to her. She took the girl's chin in her hand and smiled into her eyes. "Hey, slow down, pal. I'll do my best for you. Okay?"

Zoey nodded and gave Lucy a hesitant smile. "Okay. . . . Thank you."

"It's all right. We can only do what we can do in this world. You just have to try your best and leave the rest to heaven above. The angels watching over us," Lucy murmured. She had stood up and without thinking, coaxed Zoey to slip down under the covers and settle into bed.

She tucked the blankets in and smoothed her hand over Zoey's forehead then quickly kissed her cheek. "Good night, honey. Don't worry about anything. It will all work out. Have a good sleep, okay?"

"Good night, Lucy," Zoey whispered. She seemed surprised at Lucy's show of affection, but this time didn't shrink away.

It was too late to call Rita Schuman, Lucy thought as she headed downstairs again. She would call her in the morning.

LUCY'S SHIFT THE NEXT DAY STARTED AT FIVE A.M., AND SOME friends in her unit insisted she join them for an impromptu birthday party during her break. The floor was so busy the rest of the day that the first chance she even had to think about Mrs. Schuman was late afternoon, as she was leaving the hospital for the day.

She took a deep, steadying breath and tapped in the social worker's number on her cell phone. *This woman is going to think I have a personality disorder, constantly flip-flopping and changing my plan. That alone might disqualify me from taking care of Zoey. But here goes.*

Rita Schuman greeted her, sounding surprised. "Hi, Lucy. What's up? Is everything okay?"

"Everything's fine. We had a nice time last night decorating our Christmas tree. Zoey had pizza with us and helped hang the ornaments. I think she really enjoyed herself."

"That's good. Sounds as if she really does feel better."

"She's just about completely recovered. Even Charlie noticed that her color has come back. The thing is," Lucy said, "Zoey changed her mind about trying the waitressing job in the diner. She wants to try it now. I told her I would help her and show her what to do, and that seemed to make the difference. I didn't tell her you were close to finding a new family though," Lucy added. "Is there any chance she could stay with us a little longer?"

"Well, that's a surprise," Rita replied. "But I guess it's a good thing. I just found out that the placement I was working on isn't going to work out after all. The mother in the family just heard she has a health issue she has to take care of, so it's not a good time for them to take in any more children."

"Oh, that's too bad. I hope it's nothing serious," Lucy said sincerely. "Does that mean Zoey will be staying with us awhile longer?"

"I really don't have any other likely prospects right now for placement. Would that be all right with you and your husband? I had the sense that you were only available to take care of her until she felt well again."

"That's not really the situation anymore. . . . We're happy to have her . . . until you can find a new foster home. However long that takes, we're happy to have her."

You can take your time, Lucy wanted to add.

"Good. I'm relieved to hear that. It's difficult to make a placement during the holidays. But I'll keep working on it and keep you posted. I think it's fine if Zoey wants to start a job and feels up to it. She has some working papers on file. I'll send you a copy. I'll also call her later to talk about staying with your family awhile longer."

"I'm sure she'll be glad to hear from you." Lucy knew it was important for Zoey to stay in close touch with Rita. The social worker was the only truly stable figure in the girl's life right now. She was sure Zoey confided things to Rita that she wouldn't tell anyone else.

"There's something else we ought to talk about," Rita said. "The other day I just gave you the basics about Zoey's school experience. I mainly told you how she feels about school, but there's more to it. Zoey has high intelligence, but she may have a learning disability. Because she's moved around to so many schools, she's never been properly tested or gotten much help. So she'll probably be all right with a waitressing job, but it could be difficult for her."

"I understand," Lucy said. "We'll be patient with her."

They said good-bye and Lucy put her phone away. She was relieved that things had worked out, at least this much. Maybe the girl would stay until the holidays. That was only two weeks from now. Lucy could guess that Zoey did not have many good Christmas memories. It was probably a sad time for her, thinking about her mother and grandmother, who were gone, and how she was separated from her brother. The girl had been through so much. It was hard for Lucy to even imagine what she might be feeling at the holidays.

Lucy really hoped that Zoey would be with them for Christmas and that, for this year at least, they could fill her battered heart with good memories.

CHAPTER SIX

"I'M GLAD I TOOK THE VAN. ALL THAT STUFF WOULD HAVE never fit in my car." Betty came into the shop and hung up her down jacket. She had just made a quick sweep around town, gathering donations for the food pantry. "Everyone is so generous. It's amazing."

"Why don't you get Santa to help you?" Molly asked. "I don't see why you have to do all that grunt work yourself."

"I didn't realize it would be so much. And that's not even all the places who have called me back. I'll have to go out again over the weekend to get the rest." Betty felt tired but happy, too. She put on some water for tea. "I guess I can bring the stuff home with me tonight and stick it in the garage. I'll just leave my car here and bring the van back tomorrow."

"That should work out. We don't have anything cooking tonight," Molly said.

It was late afternoon on Friday, a brief downtime for them,

since they weren't booked for any parties that night. They had completed all their preparations for the three weekend events. They had two on Saturday: a big outdoor skating party in the afternoon, and a small intimate party at a private home that Sonia and Betty were handling without Molly. On Sunday afternoon, they would serve an elegant brunch at the old Warwick estate, Lilac Hall.

Betty wasn't sure how she had managed to make calls for the food pantry on top of her real work. But somehow she had done it. Just as she'd promised Nathan, Betty had worked her list of friends and acquaintances through the town of Cape Light and beyond. Practically everyone she spoke with had come through in some way with donations of goods or funds to help restock the food pantry and put on the party. Several shop owners set out collection bins in their storefronts for canned goods or gifts. Others put jars for money near the cash register. All of them seemed to be calling her at once.

"That reminds me. Santa called. He left a message." Molly leaned over and handed Betty a sticky note. It read, *Nathan Daley called. Try home number.* The time of the phone call and number were written below.

Betty could tell Molly didn't really like Nathan that much. Or she would have asked more questions about him. And she wouldn't have kept calling him Santa in that somewhat sarcastic tone.

But Betty didn't care what Molly thought. Besides, there was nothing to think, she reminded herself. She and Nathan were barely acquaintances, getting to know each other working on this project together. After his surprise appearance at the shop on Monday, they had exchanged a few phone calls and e-mails. Nothing personal.

Did she want it to get more personal? Oh, dear . . . she wasn't sure. She knew she liked him. She enjoyed talking to him. He was interesting and amusing. But maybe that was all there was to it. She had met enough men to know that you really don't know—until you know.

"So, when is the big party for the food pantry?" Molly asked. "You put us down for some food, of course," she added.

"Yes, I did," Betty confirmed. "But I'm not sure yet when they're holding it. And they don't know where yet either."

"Sounds very organized. Just don't let anyone know you're a partner here, okay?" Molly teased her. She was leafing through the big black ledger that held a record of all the scheduled events, a page or two devoted to each. Betty had designed the book, and it was now indispensable. Every time a new client signed up, they slipped the page into its proper place and had one spot to keep all important information and any special notes. The groom was highly allergic to nuts, for instance. Molly scribbled a bit on a page, then turned to look at the next party.

The phone rang and Betty answered it. "Willoughby Fine Foods, may I help you?"

"I think you've already helped me," Nathan's voice greeted her. "My sources tell me that you've collected a truckload of donations."

"It's actually a van," Betty corrected him. "But it is full. Who told you that?" she asked him curiously.

"I have my sources. They told me I picked the right woman for the job, too."

She laughed at him, ignoring the compliment. "The elves again, I should have guessed."

"Actually, it was Reverend Ben. I was just on the phone with him. He spotted you around town. He's offered the Fellowship Hall at the church for the party. I think that's a good place—plenty of room and the church has a big kitchen."

Betty belonged to the same church but didn't attend often. She had never been a joiner, always more focused on her work. She knew that Nathan was an active member at church, though, and gathered he had a strong faith. That was a trait in a man she might have scoffed at when she was younger. But though she didn't share it, she did admire it at this stage of life.

"How can I help you now?" he asked. "What should I do? I think you've already done too much loading and lifting on your own."

That's just what Molly had told her. But it wasn't Nathan's fault. Betty knew she tended to have a "do-it-all" personality and was bad at asking for help. Nathan made it easy for her to ask, though.

"There is a lot of stuff in the van right now," she told him. "Food to restock the pantry and gifts and decorations for the party. I was going to bring it all home tonight and put it in my garage. Is there someplace else to store it so we don't have to move it twice?"

"That's a good question. We can't bring it to the pantry. It's a mess over there. The church wouldn't work either. They don't have much storage room. Why don't you just bring it all to my house and I'll stick it somewhere. Can you come by tonight? I'll make you dinner," he added.

"Um . . . sure. That sounds great." Betty was surprised and pleased by the impromptu invitation. She had toyed with the idea of asking Nathan to come to her house to help unload the van, but she hadn't wanted to seem like some damsel in distress.

This was better. This was different. She had rarely had a man make her dinner, and never one who seemed so casual about it. If they did it at all, it was usually a big drama.

"Not if it's any trouble for you," she said. "I can just come by with the stuff and we can unload it. You don't have to go to any trouble."

"It's no trouble. That's the least I can do to thank you for all your hard work."

Betty was convinced. And she was curious to see where he lived. They set a time, and Nathan gave her his address and some directions.

Molly had wandered into the office but came out just as Betty was ending the phone call.

"So, was that Santa, checking in?"

"Yes, it was Santa, and he's invited me for dinner tonight. He's going to keep all that stuff at his house until we have someplace to bring it."

"He's making you dinner? Interesting," Molly said with a sly smile. "Let me guess the menu—"

"No more Santa jokes, please?" Betty asked. "It's getting a little stale."

"Sorry, but it's hard to resist. So where does this guy live? And I'm resisting some great jokes about the North Pole."

Betty shook her head. There was no stopping her sometimes, was there? She picked up her note with the address and directions. "He lives on North Creek Road."

"Fancy address. That's by the water, not far from the Warwick estate." Molly peered over her shoulder. "Maybe he's an eccentric millionaire who likes to dress up and play Santa Claus?"

"He must be really eccentric if he has me running around collecting donations when he could just write a check for the whole deal."

"He might not be a millionaire, but he sure seems an odd duck to me," Molly said.

"He is different," Betty agreed. But in a good way, she thought. Refreshing. Original. Genuine.

"So a date with Santa Claus. How does it feel?" Molly continued to tease her.

"It feels fine. He's very interesting to talk to," Betty said lightly. "But I don't think having dinner there under these circumstances is really a date. At least, I'm not thinking of it that way."

That was true, too. Betty didn't want to jump to any conclusions.

"Glad to hear it. Don't get me wrong. He seems very attractive and good-hearted. And he's definitely . . . unusual. But I don't think he's a guy who will give you a long-term relationship. I don't really think he's your type," Molly said.

Betty wasn't sure what her "type" was anymore. And dating her "type" all these years hadn't gotten her very far, had it? But before she could debate the point, Molly deftly changed the subject. "So, how's it going with Alex?"

"It's going fine. We went to the movies last night. A romantic comedy sort of thing. It was fun."

"That sounds about right." Molly looked up from the party ledger and smiled. "I'm glad to hear things are coming along. Did he ask you out for New Year's Eve yet?"

"What do you mean 'yet'?"

New Year's Eve had become Betty's least-favorite holiday. She rarely had a date and hated to go to parties by herself on that night. This year, she was considering lying to all her friends and saying she had an invitation out of town, then hiding out at home alone and going to bed early. Then again, Alex might ask her out. The thought did cross her mind. It certainly seemed possible, but she wasn't going to count on it.

Molly seemed to think it was a sure thing. "Oh, he will. I just have a feeling. Trust me on this one." She closed the ledger and put it aside. "When are you due at Nathan's house?"

"About six." Betty checked her watch. "I'd better get going. I need to stop off at my house first."

Molly gave her a look but didn't say anything. She had probably guessed that Betty was going to change her sweater and put on some makeup before heading over to Nathan's house.

"I need to pick up a few donations there," Betty said simply.

"Don't stay out too late. We have a big day tomorrow," Molly reminded her.

She sounded like an overprotective mother, Betty thought,

well-meaning but not quite approving of her daughter's date. Betty gave her a wave and headed out.

After a pit stop at home, where she quickly changed into a new black cowl-neck sweater and dressier earrings, Betty started off toward Nathan's house. She turned onto Beach Road, in the direction of the old Warwick estate, Lilac Hall. There were some magnificent old homes on this road, just visible through the bare winter trees.

The road was dark and empty. Out here, you would hardly know Christmas was coming, Betty thought. In her neighborhood and down in the village, the decorated houses and stores heralded the season everywhere you turned. Betty knew her own Christmas spirit was still lagging, despite her efforts to be more positive. She hadn't done any Christmas shopping yet and hadn't even put up her tree.

"Maybe dinner with Santa will help," she quipped to herself. "If that doesn't do it, the condition must be serious."

Betty saw the landmarks Nathan mentioned and looked for the turn. It was on the water side of the road, the higher-priced real estate, and she found herself steering the van through high wrought-iron gates set in a stone wall. She wondered if she had made a mistake, but the directions had been very clear and so had the number on the mailbox at the side of the road.

She drove down the long, narrow road slowly. She couldn't even see a house, though she did spot some lights through the trees up ahead.

She and Molly had been joking, but . . . maybe it was true that this man *was* an eccentric millionaire. She wished Molly was with her right now. Would she be so disapproving and snippy about Nathan if she could see where he lived?

Betty drove up a long curved driveway and finally reached the house. It was an old stone mansion with a large portico and entranceway. It looked entirely dark—and spooky.

She hesitated in the van, wondering if she should get out. Why weren't there any lights on in there? Was he trying to save on energy costs?

Her cell phone rang. She checked the number. It was Nathan. "Hi, there. I made it. I'm right out front," she told him, glancing at the dark house again.

He laughed at her. "You can't be, Betty. You just flew past my front door. I live in the cottage, about halfway down the entry road. You must be parked in front of the big mansion. There's no one in there now."

"I thought it looked sort of empty," she admitted. "I'll be right there," she added, feeling foolish.

She drove back down the road, more slowly this time, and finally spotted a small cottage set off from the road in a circle of tall trees. It was such a pretty little house, she wasn't sure how she had missed it the first time. *I was too overwhelmed with the notion that he lived in some big spooky mansion,* she realized. But this place was even better. Much more inviting. Much more Nathan's style.

It looked like something out of a fairy tale with a sloping, peaked roof and gingerbread trim. Smoke rose from the brick chimney, and a thick pine wreath decorated the front door.

She pulled the van up to the front and got out. Nathan was waiting in the doorway for her, the room behind him cast in an inviting golden light, the windows glowing warmly. The smell of wood smoke and pine mingled in the frosty air.

"Come in, come in. It's getting cold out there." He shepherded her inside and helped her off with her coat.

While he hung up her things on an antique coatrack, Betty had a chance to look around. The cottage was even more charming inside, with a low-beamed ceiling and an open floor plan. The decor was comfortable, somewhat messy but clean, and strictly masculine with a worn leather armchair and couch and a kilim-patterned area rug in front of the fireplace. Bookshelves and piles of books were everywhere.

A beat-up rolltop desk stood in one corner by a window, piled with papers and more books. A notebook computer peeked out. On the other side of the door she spotted a dining area with a round oak table set for two. Beyond that, there was a small kitchen with two large pots on the stove.

"Something smells good in here. I would have found you once I got hungry enough."

Nathan laughed and led her to the living room. "I hope you like Italian food? I'm sorry, I forgot to ask. I made some pasta and meat sauce. I must admit, it's a little intimidating, cooking for a professional."

"Don't be intimidated by me, please. That chili the other day was really my best effort."

"If you say so. But you'll have to be honest about my dinner. I'm interested in an expert review."

They sat by the fire, Betty on the couch and Nathan in the armchair. He opened a bottle of red wine and had already put out some hors d'oeuvres—olives and tangy cheese and slices of French bread.

A big brown dog came out from some hiding place and stuck its muzzle in Betty's lap.

"Come on, Rosie. Leave Betty alone. She might not like dogs. You didn't even ask."

"Don't worry, I love dogs. She's a very pretty girl, too." Betty took the dog's big head in her hands and scratched her behind the ears, earning an instant look of doggy devotion.

The dog acted like a puppy, but Betty could see a little graying in her whiskers and chin. She wasn't that young but still energetic.

"She reminds me of a brown Labrador we had when my son was little. Brian named the dog Elmo, after the character on *Sesame*

Street. Elmo was a sweetheart." She glanced up at Nathan and grinned. "A great consolation after the divorce."

I got the dog, she added silently. *My husband ended up with our son.*

"Dogs can be very comforting, no doubt about that. How long were you married?" he asked.

"Eleven years. Ted, my ex-husband, traveled a lot for his job. And when he was home on the weekends, I was working hard, trying to build my real estate business. I guess we just grew apart." The yawning gap between them leaving plenty of room for another woman to swoop in, Betty was about to say. But she didn't want to sound maudlin or even still angry at her ex. That was ancient history now. She was well over it and had realized long ago that there was blame enough to go around. The failure of their marriage hadn't entirely been Ted's fault.

"That was so long ago," she said. "Time just flies by. I can hardly keep track anymore."

"The years seem to go faster and faster as you get older," Nathan agreed. "Inside, I don't feel older at all. Know what I mean?"

"I do," she said sincerely. "I'm facing a big birthday soon. . . ." She was embarrassed to say the number, though she was sure he could guess. "But I don't feel *that* age. I mean, what are you supposed to feel like when you're fifty?"

Great, Betty. You finally meet a man you're really interested in and you have to go blabbing your real age, right out of the box? What is wrong with you?

"Excuse me?" Nathan looked confused, pretending he hadn't heard her correctly. "The big *four—o*? I can't believe that. You don't look a day over . . . twenty-nine."

He was teasing, of course. He had heard the right number and was just trying to make her feel better. Betty felt heat flood her cheeks. He was overly flattering, to be sure. But it helped.

"Right, let's get on to another topic, shall we?" she said. He gazed at her with gleeful blue eyes, which didn't help much. "Were you ever married, Nathan?"

"I was. We were divorced about five years ago. It was a fairly amicable parting," he said, though Betty noticed a look of sadness flash over his expression. "Not really messy, like some people."

"Any kids? That's when it gets complicated," Betty said knowingly.

"I don't have children," he replied.

She found that surprising. He seemed to like kids so much and get along with them so well, she would have guessed he had some of his own. She wanted to know more about his marriage, but he didn't seem inclined to say more.

"So, how were you able to collect a van-load of donations in such a short time?" he asked. "I've rounded up some stuff, but it barely fills that narrow little area behind the seat of my truck."

Betty shrugged. "It wasn't hard. I just made a few calls and sent out some e-mails. You'd be surprised how many people you know in town when you really sit down and think about it. There was some cash, and checks, too. I had them made out to the food pantry."

She reached into her purse and handed him a thick envelope. Nathan tilted his head back and peeked inside. "Whoa, look at this. You really are . . . unbelievable." He shook his head. "It was my lucky day when I ran into you, Betty Bowman. A lucky day for the pantry and everyone who depends on it."

His admiration and gratitude made her feel wonderful. As if she had done something very special and worthwhile.

It was *her* lucky day when she ran into Nathan, she thought. He had given her the chance to do this good deed, to use her energy and smarts—and her business connections around town—to help a lot of families. That really was a gift. Even if nothing but friendship ever came of this relationship.

Betty downplayed the compliment. "People were very willing to give once they heard the story. I didn't even have to say much."

"But whatever you did say must have been brilliant," he insisted.

"I'm a good salesperson when I need to be," she admitted. "Let's just say that this time, I used my superpowers for good."

"And how very super they are," he agreed, laughing.

Betty knew she was a good saleswoman. The talent came naturally to her, polished by years in the real estate game. But she truly felt she hadn't done that much; it wasn't just false modesty. But Nathan seemed so impressed. There was no talking him out of it.

Rosie had planted herself right next to Betty and leaned against her leg. She lifted her head for more petting and sighed. "Even my dog is in awe of you," Nathan told her.

"Oh . . . she looks pretty easy to impress," Betty said. His quiet laugh warmed her inside.

They talked a little more about the donations and what more would be needed for the party, then Nathan checked the food on the stove and announced that everything was ready. He led Betty to the table and pulled out her chair with a flourish. "You sit here. I'll be right back."

He headed to the kitchen and soon returned with a big bowl of salad, a basket of crusty bread, and two appetizing dishes of pasta with sauce.

"This is delicious," she said, taking a small bite. "You'll have to give us the recipe."

"I can give you the jar label, to be perfectly honest," he admitted with a laugh. "But I do doctor it up my own special way. That part is a secret."

Betty had to smile. He had a lot of secrets. He was Santa Claus, right?

They sat in silence for a few moments, just enjoying the food. Betty felt so relaxed in his company, she didn't feel the pressure to talk. But one question still nagged at her. "So, Nathan, I've been wondering, how did you get started being a Rent-a-Santa? I was wondering what you do in the off-season," she added casually. She really wanted to know what he did for a living. That couldn't possibly be all, could it?

"People do wonder about that. Especially at this time of year. It does take up most of my time right now. And it is an odd vocation," he agreed. "But I do have a day job, as we say in show business. I'm a freelance writer most of the time. In fact, I donned my first Santa suit doing research for an article, aptly titled, 'Confessions of a Department Store Santa.' And the rest, madam, is history."

"That's how you got started? How interesting." Betty sat back, secretly pleased to hear that he did have a real job, one that greatly impressed her. She already knew he was smart and creative and very good with words. Then there were all the books around here. She might have guessed. "That experience must have made a big impression on you."

"It did. I was amazed that I liked it so much. I was pretty good at it, too. I liked doing it for kids in hospitals and at charity parties. But I take some paying jobs, too," he admitted. "I know it's hard to believe, looking at this luxurious home, but most writers don't make that much money."

Betty laughed. "Maybe not, but not too many people can earn any money at all writing. You must be very talented."

"Thanks, but . . . you haven't read my writing yet," he reminded her.

"I'd like to. Will you show me some? How about that Santa article? Now you've made me curious."

He shook his head modestly. "You don't have to bother. Maybe some other time, I'll make you a copy."

"I want to read it," Betty insisted. "I really do. Do you have a copy around here? I'll take it home and give it back to you."

They had finished dinner, and Nathan was just starting to clear the table. Betty got up to help him, carrying in their dishes.

"I've got an idea. Why don't you sit in the living room and relax while I stack this stuff up? I'll give you the article and you can read it now."

"Okay." Betty was pleased and surprised by the offer.

She followed him to the living room and he sat her in the big leather chair, adjusting the floor lamp over her shoulder. "Here you go, the chair of honor."

Then he walked over to his desk and searched around a few minutes, moving stacks of papers and opening desk drawers. He finally reached up and pulled a big cardboard pocket folder from a top shelf. He wiped it off with a stray paper napkin from the coffee table.

"It's a little dusty. My work is not that much in demand."

Probably because you hide it away in this little cottage, Betty wanted to say.

She took the messy folder with both hands and held it in her lap. It was so worn-out, Betty hoped the whole thing wouldn't just explode in her lap. "I'm sure there are some undiscovered masterpieces in here. Why don't you go back to the kitchen and let me decide?"

She waited until she heard Nathan moving around the kitchen. Then she opened the folder and pulled out a thick stack of clippings. Some were from magazines and others from newspapers and some were just typed pages, yellowed on the edges.

"Confessions of a Department Store Santa" was right on the top. It had been published in the *Boston Globe* Sunday magazine section, about five years ago, she noticed. As she read the printed words, she heard Nathan's voice; his style was so natural and authentic. His personality shone through in every line.

The article was not only funny and clever, but also full of insight and compassion. Nathan observed how the Christmas marketing machine brainwashes kids to want all kinds of things that look so good on TV but end up being disappointments moments after they are unwrapped. Kids had no qualms asking for every toy advertised on TV—and could even be a little greedy, he noticed as an undercover Santa. But what they truly wanted most of all were the things money can't buy—more time with their parents, asking Santa to make someone in their family who is sick feel better again, or to stop drinking or being so angry. Or to come home.

His simple, honest observations and real-life stories touched her heart. He was a powerful writer. Betty knew that she would never look at a costumed Santa the same way again.

Betty placed the article back on the pile and gazed at the fire awhile. The logs had burned down, and the burning embers cast the room in golden shadows. She heard Nathan in the kitchen, still washing up the pots and pans, whistling a little. He was definitely an unusual man.

She leafed through the other articles in the stack of clips. Many were based on his firsthand experiences—his monthlong attempt to reproduce Henry David Thoreau's famous year at Walden Pond, an essay about driving cross-country, a night in a homeless shelter. There were also interviews, one with the mystery writer Robert B. Parker, and another with the New England Patriots' quarterback Tom Brady. At the very bottom she came to a short, one-page article that had been published in a parenting magazine. It was titled "Losing Leah." Betty began to read it and soon realized it was a first-person account by a father who had lost his only child. Once again, she heard Nathan's voice in the very personal narrative. Her breath caught in her throat, halfway down the page.

But Nathan said he didn't have any children.

Not never, she realized. He just said he doesn't have any now.

She couldn't read on, feeling as if she had seen something very private, something he wasn't ready to reveal to her.

She had been so distracted by finding the article, she didn't notice that the kitchen had gone quiet, and Nathan was walking back into the living room with a tray that held coffee and a dish of cookies. She quickly stacked the pages together again, making it appear as if she hadn't reached that last one yet. She looked up to find him standing near the chair, looking down at her.

"You're so quiet out here, Betty. Did my writing put you to sleep?"

"Anything but," she told him honestly. "I loved the undercover Santa article—and I read a few others," she admitted. "You're very talented. You have a real knack for making a person feel as if they're right there, on the scene of whatever you're describing. But you see so much more than I would . . . and have so much more insight into these everyday situations," she tried to explain. "I'm sorry. . . . I'm not really explaining this very well, am I?"

"You're doing great. I'm amazed you can have so much to say after reading just a few pages." He sat down nearby and smiled at her. "Writing is a lonely profession. I find I need a lot of peace and quiet to do my work. I don't really hear much from readers. I hear reactions from editors, of course, but most of them are cranky and rushed. A lot of the time I feel as if I'm sending my writing out into outer space. It's nice to hear someone's real reaction."

He was very modest. She liked that quality. Betty realized she would be happy to read all of his writing and talk to him about it, given the chance.

But it was getting late and she had a big weekend of work ahead of her.

"Well, thank you for letting me read your work. I would love to see more of it sometime. What are you working on now?" she said, handing the folder back.

He placed the folder on the coffee table and took a seat on the couch, across from her. "Oh . . . this and that. I have a pretty ordinary article due soon on unusual family traditions for the holidays.

Then I'm just making notes and doing research for other ideas. Nothing specific right now. I have a novel I've been fooling around with for years, but I can never seem to get much traction on it. Every time I try to go back and finish it, I end up rewriting the whole darn thing and I'm back to square one again."

"I bet your novel is pretty good if it's anything like these articles," Betty said. "At the risk of sounding like some self-help, armchair psychologist, it sounds like plain old fear of success to me."

He didn't seem at all offended by her diagnosis. "You might be right. I'll have to think about that. Right now helping the pantry is my main focus. I have absolutely no fear of success there. Not with Betty Bowman on the job. That would be impossible."

Betty was reminded of the real reason for her visit. Funny how little they'd talked about the party. "We really should talk about the event," she said. "It's getting late and I need to go soon. A big work weekend," she explained.

"Right, let's try to figure this out," he agreed. "I don't want to keep you too late."

Betty took a big pad out of her purse, where she had made a quick inventory of the donations she had received so far. They talked about party details, the number of people that might come, and the food needed.

"You're so organized," Nathan commented. "Take a look at my system." He nodded at his messy desk. "It's amazing I get anything done."

"We all have our personal styles," she said with a small smile. She slipped the pad back in her purse, feeling satisfied that things would come together on time for the event. "Well, I guess that's it. I'd better go."

"Right. I'd better empty out the van first, though. We almost forgot about that."

"Oh . . . right. The van." Betty had forgotten about it, too. She felt so silly. Where was her mind tonight?

"I can help you. It won't take long." She jumped up, slipped her shoes back on, and grabbed her coat.

Nathan put on a down vest and gloves. Rosie got excited, too, seeing the humans about to go out. She ran to the door and wagged her tail wildly.

"Yes, you can come outside awhile," Nathan told the dog. "But don't go far. I don't feel like chasing you through the woods all night."

The dog gave him a serious look, sitting at complete attention. He opened the door and she flew out.

"Ladies first," he said, holding the door open for Betty. She smiled as she walked past him out into the frosty night air. It was very dark outside the cottage, except for a small porch light. There seemed to be a million stars twinkling in the velvety dark sky. She tipped her head back to look at them.

"It's a lovely night. Not too cold," she said.

"Yes, it would be nice to take a walk in the woods," Nathan said. "But I guess you don't have time."

She would have loved to take a walk in the woods right now with him. But she didn't dare.

Something was happening here. She wasn't quite sure what it was . . . or where it was leading her. She looked at her watch and sighed. "I'd love to, but I really have to get going."

"That's okay. I have to work tomorrow, too," he said.

Dressing up as Santa, he meant. Maybe at some parties . . . or at the mall?

That thought brought Betty back to earth. Nathan had already started unloading the van, carrying everything up to his porch. Betty started to help him.

"You don't have to do anything, Betty. I can handle this. You just supervise. I feel guilty making you do so much."

"I can supervise *and* help. Don't worry. The catering business is a lot of lugging and loading. It keeps me in shape."

He glanced at her, his arms full of boxes. "I won't argue with that."

The way he looked at her made her blush, and Betty was thankful it was so dark he couldn't see.

The van was unloaded quickly. Nathan slammed the doors closed and turned to her. "Well, I guess that's it."

"For now, anyway. I'll probably have another load by Monday," she predicted. "Thanks for dinner. It was great."

"Thank you for coming. And for reading my work," he added.

"Thank you for showing it to me," she said sincerely.

They just stood looking at each other for what seemed to Betty a very long moment. She knew she should turn to get into the van, but she couldn't step away. Was he going to kiss her good night? It wasn't that sort of relationship . . . was it?

Finally, he leaned over and gently hugged her for a moment.

"Drive safely. I'll talk to you soon," he said in a gentle tone.

"Okay . . . good night." Betty felt a little dazed by the small show of affection. She quickly turned and got into the van.

Rosie suddenly ran out of the woods and came to Nathan's side, panting and wagging her tail. Betty was sorry now she hadn't said good-bye to her. She was a sweet old girl.

He grabbed the dog's collar and waved to Betty with his other hand as she drove away.

They made a perfect picture, she thought, Nathan and his dog, standing in front of the little cottage. She held it in her mind, all the way down the dark road home. She still felt his embrace, the nearness of him, their closeness filling her senses for just a moment. A friendly hug that could have easily been more.

The night had turned out very differently from what she'd expected. Betty didn't know what to think about him now. Or what she wanted this relationship to be.

LUCY COULDN'T POSSIBLY THINK OF A WORSE TIME TO START ZOEY at the Clam Box than Saturday morning. Talk about tossing someone in at the deep end. But there was no help for it. She had already worn out her supervisor's patience, asking for special favors while Zoey had been sick, and this second request was pushing it. But she did get three days in a row to train the girl—Saturday, Sunday, and Monday. Lucy hoped that would do it.

Lucy had found Zoey a uniform and bought her a pair of suitable sneakers. Zoey came downstairs dressed for work and looking miserable.

"This uniform is horrible. I look like a supergeek!" she moaned. "How did you ever stand wearing this for so long?"

"Oh, I don't think it's so bad. You should have seen these T-shirts Charlie had us wearing for a while. They had a big picture of a dancing clam. Now, that was a fashion disaster," Lucy said with a laugh.

"Puh-leeze." Zoey rolled her eyes and quickly ate some cereal. "Let's not even go there."

"Yes, let's not," Lucy agreed. "You look really cute," she assured Zoey. "You just need to put your hair up in a ponytail or something."

Zoey fixed her hair in the car while they drove into town. They reached the diner before eight. There were plenty of customers, but the Saturday morning rush hadn't quite hit yet.

Trudy was rushing from table to table and also tending the counter customers. Charlie was behind the counter, too, but mostly working at the grill. He glanced over his shoulder as Lucy and Zoey came in.

"Well, well. You finally made it. I hope you both got your beauty sleep."

"I told you we would be in by eight, Charlie." Lucy stashed her purse under the counter. "It's still a quarter to."

Charlie didn't reply, just flipped over two fried eggs, then deftly slipped them onto a plate alongside an order of bacon and two slices of toasted rye. "Fried egg platter. Rye dry," he called out. He glanced at Zoey, who had taken off her jacket, but didn't know what else to do. "Get it? That was toasted rye bread with nothing on it."

Zoey gazed back at him. She looked very nervous; her eyes were wide and she seemed to have lost her voice.

Charlie scowled at Lucy. "Do something with her, will you? She can't just stand around all day."

Zoey practically jumped at his harsh tone. Lucy bustled her away. "He just gets nervous when he's behind the grill and there's a crowd. It doesn't last long."

"Him getting nervous—or the crowd?" Zoey asked.

"Good question. A little of each, I'd say," Lucy replied. She took out two order pads and two sharp pencils. "You stick with me awhile and help me wait on my tables. We won't give you a station yet."

"Good," Zoey said with relief as she followed Lucy out onto the floor. "I'm not so sure this was a good idea after all."

"Don't worry. It will be fine. Just watch what I do," Lucy said calmly.

A couple with two children walked through the door and gazed around for a table.

"Sit anywhere, folks. I think that booth by the window is empty," Lucy greeted them.

As the family headed toward the table, Lucy took two menus from the stack near the door and two children's menus, which were printed on place mats that also served as coloring pages.

"When little kids come in, give them these. And we have packs of crayons over there. Keeps them busy for about . . . three minutes."

Zoey nodded, a serious expression on her face, as if she were memorizing everything Lucy said. Lucy handed her the menus and told her to give them out at the table. She went over to another table where the family looked as if they had been waiting awhile and took their order.

Zoey met her there. "That man with the red baseball cap? He asked me for more coffee."

"Okay. The coffeemaker is behind the counter at the very far side. See it?" She pointed to the machine. "Just bring the pot over, very carefully, and fill his cup."

That was an easy assignment. Lucy watched out of the corner of her eye to see how Zoey managed the task. The girl found the pot, carried it carefully, and then began to pour the coffee for the customer, who was talking in a loud voice to another man who sat across from him.

"Whoa, there! Is that regular coffee? I said *de-caf.* You want to kill me with that stuff? I'll get a heart attack."

Lucy saw Zoey's eyes narrow as she turned and headed back with the coffeepot.

"What an idiot," Zoey mumbled as she walked by Lucy.

"Yeah, he is," Lucy agreed. "But just bring him his coffee. Ours is not to reason why," she reminded her trainee.

Zoey sighed dramatically and returned to the table with the pot of decaf. Lucy watched from a distance. She didn't want to be right on top of the kid all day. She'd never get any confidence that way.

"Here you are, decaffeinated coffee." Zoey's tone was a bit sarcastic, but the man was so intent on his conversation, he didn't even glance at her.

Zoey leaned over to pour the coffee, and the man suddenly

seemed to notice her. "Did you bring the right coffee this time? You're sure now?"

"Yeah, I did. . . . Just chill." Zoey made a face and started pouring the coffee.

But her customer was not convinced. He reached out and pulled his cup away to make sure. It was too late. The hot coffee kept falling, now without a cup beneath to catch it.

"You idiot! For crying out loud . . ." He jumped up as if the diner were on fire. "Are you trying to kill me or something?"

Zoey shrank back, cowering as if the man might hit her. "Why did you move your stupid cup? That's not my fault!"

"Hey, I didn't come here to take smart talk from a waitress. Where's the manager? I want to see the manager," he insisted

Lucy ran over and started cleaning up the coffee with a towel. The man was red in the face and looked totally incensed, though Lucy noticed that the spilled coffee hadn't even touched him. Most of it trickled down off the table onto the floor.

"I am so sorry, sir," Lucy said, making sympathetic little sounds. "Here, let me take your check. This is on the house. Did you get coffee anywhere on that nice sweatshirt?" she asked, though the dark green sweatshirt decorated with a picture of a deer with massive antlers would have been improved by a stain or two, she thought.

He looked down at his large stomach, about to complain, but couldn't find a drop. "I think she got a little on my new boots" he said instead.

Lucy and the man's friend both looked down at the boots.

"That's just some mud or car oil," his friend said helpfully. "That's not coffee."

Lucy looked up and smiled. "I think you're right."

Charlie had come out from behind the counter to see what all the fuss was about. "What's going on here?" he asked sternly.

"We had a little spill," Lucy explained. "It's all cleaned up. But I'm buying these nice folks breakfast."

She graced the two men with her sweetest smile. By their softening expressions, she could tell she was getting away with it.

Charlie frowned. "I can guess how that happened." He looked around for Zoey, and Lucy did, too. The girl had retreated to the coffee station and remained there. Trudy was chatting with her, hopefully telling her not to pay any attention to the hotheaded customer.

But Zoey looked shaken, and Lucy felt sorry for her. She walked over to commiserate.

"That was unfortunate, getting such a big grouch the first time out. People usually don't overreact like that, even if you drop their whole order."

"He moved his cup right while I was pouring. What was I supposed to do?"

"I believe you. I saw him." Of course, an experienced waitress waits until all the action at the table stops before pouring coffee, but Lucy would explain that later. She patted Zoey's arm reassuringly. "Don't worry. It will get better."

"I told you I couldn't do this. Who wants to be a stupid waitress anyway? Wear this dumb uniform . . . get yelled at by stupid men wearing moose-head sweatshirts?"

Lucy sighed. The girl did have a point. Lucy had come to the same conclusion about waitressing herself. Only it had taken her almost twenty years, not twenty minutes.

That was the problem when you didn't even have a high school diploma. Maybe this experience would open Zoey's eyes to how limited her opportunities would be if she didn't go back to school. ,

"Just give it another try—an hour or two? If you still hate it, I'll take you home, no questions asked," Lucy promised. Zoey didn't answer but after a moment sighed and nodded her head.

"Hey, was that a moose? I thought it was just a big buck," Lucy said as she cleared the table. "It was ugly, no question. I'd be tempted to pour coffee on that sweatshirt on purpose," she said, making Zoey laugh.

Zoey stuck by Lucy as she made the rounds of her tables. Lucy didn't let her do much more than give out menus or clear for a while. A few hours later she advanced her to serving the orders when Charlie called them out at the service bar. She saw Charlie bark at the girl once or twice as she was collecting the food. Lucy sighed. She and Charlie had already discussed this—how he was supposed to be patient and encouraging. But Charlie didn't do patient and encouraging very well. The best Lucy could hope for was Charlie holding on to his temper.

The morning rush flew by. Zoey continued to make mistakes, mixing up orders, getting rattled and distracted when customers would call out to her as she passed by—"More coffee, please?" "More water?" "Some ketchup over here, miss?"

Lucy could see she had trouble focusing. She was easily distracted. Was that part of the learning problem Rita Schuman had mentioned? Lucy didn't want to bring it up with Zoey. She knew the girl would be self-conscious about it. Instead, she tried to gently address it on her own with a few small tips, the things every waitress had to keep in mind to keep organized.

"When it's busy like this, everyone is going to shout and wave at you, as if you were a taxi in the middle of Times Square. Just keep your cool and focus," Lucy coached her. "You're one person and you can only do one thing at a time, right?"

"Sometimes, not even that much," Zoey said glumly.

"Chin up, pal. It's just your first day. Your first meal, for goodness' sake."

"You're doing great, honey," Trudy agreed, as she whizzed by. "Just having another pair of legs out there is a blessing, believe me."

Lucy silently thanked the other waitress. Trudy was so good-hearted; she could see Zoey struggling and knew exactly what to say.

"How do you feel? Still want to go home?" Lucy asked.

Zoey thought about it a moment. "I'm okay for now, I guess."

Lucy spotted Reverend Ben coming in the door and looking around for a table. He was the perfect customer for Zoey to wait on for her first solo flight, Lucy thought. She knew Reverend Ben would be patient with the fledgling waitress. He might even undo some of the trauma from the man with the spilled coffee.

"Hello, Reverend Ben. Your favorite table in the back is empty," Lucy greeted him. She picked up a menu and gave it to Zoey. "This is Zoey, our new waitress."

"Hello, Zoey, nice to meet you. Shall I sit back there?" he asked politely.

Zoey nodded, looking a bit nervous. "Just follow me, please," she said. She led Reverend Ben to his table and handed him the menu. "The specials are on the board. Can I get you something to drink?"

"Some hot tea with lemon would be nice," Ben replied. He smiled at the girl and opened his menu.

"I'll be right back," Zoey promised. Then she ran off to make the tea.

So far, so good, Lucy thought. She walked over to Reverend Ben's table and turned so Zoey couldn't hear her.

"That's the girl I told you about, Reverend. The one who's staying with us awhile," she said quietly.

"I thought that must be her. She's recovered from her illness, I see."

"Yes, she's feeling fine now. We thought it would be good for her to have something to do outside the house. She's dropped out of school and won't go back," Lucy added.

"I see. Good idea to find her a job. So you're working here, just to help her?"

"For a few days. I changed my schedule to the night shift until Tuesday."

"You're working two jobs, to help her? That's very good of you, Lucy."

Lucy shrugged. "It's just a few days. I don't mind. She's a little nervous. She was serving some coffee this morning and a very rude customer managed to spill it on himself, then acted as if it were her fault."

"I'll be sure to give her lots of positive reinforcement," Reverend Ben promised. "How long will she be staying with you?"

"I don't know. Her caseworker is looking for a permanent placement but said these things move slowly around the holidays. I hope she'll stay through Christmas," Lucy added.

"It will be good for her to be with your family," Reverend Ben said. "But I hope this isn't hard on you, Lucy. In these situations, guardians get attached. It can be painful when the children move on."

"I know," Lucy said quietly. "But I can't worry about that. I don't think I can help her much if I keep worrying about myself."

Reverend Ben gave her a serious look, an admiring look, too, she thought. "That's very true," he said.

Lucy felt he understood. Should she be more distant, more detached? Then how would she really be helping Zoey? The girl needed affection, trust, kindness. Could you give a person those things at a cool distance? Lucy didn't think so. She wouldn't know how.

It was still going to hurt, no matter how she cut it.

Zoey returned with the tea, then took Ben's order and gave it to Charlie. Lucy drifted off to wait on other tables, keeping her eye on Zoey. But Zoey did very well, getting the soup and turkey sandwich and bringing them to Reverend Ben without any mishaps.

By the time Reverend Ben was finishing his pie and asking for the check, Lucy knew it had been a successful first outing.

"Good-bye, Lucy," the Reverend said as he was leaving. He turned to Zoey and smiled. "And thank you very much for the excellent service."

After he left, Zoey cleared the table. "Wow, what a nice guy! Look at the tip he left me."

Lucy was also impressed by Reverend Ben's generosity. She could see it made Zoey think that maybe she wasn't half bad at this job—and that was making all the difference.

IT WAS ALL HANDS ON DECK FOR THE CREW AT WILLOUGHBY FINE Foods. Betty had arrived at the shop at eight sharp on Saturday morning to find Molly, Sonia, and three other helpers already busy at work, prepping and packing the foods for the parties scheduled that weekend. Other part-time employees, who were only called during a big rush, would be out setting up and serving. Betty knew it was going to be one of those days.

She and Molly were so busy that morning they barely had time to exchange greetings. At midday, when the van was sent out to the first event and there was finally a lull in the action, Molly collapsed on a stool at the counter and let out a long sigh.

"One down, two to go. Every time I think I'm beat, I just think of all that Christmas shopping I still have to do," she confessed with a laugh. "Three girls, who all send me wish lists of clothes off the Internet. And there's still little Betty to worry about."

Molly had four girls altogether. Matt's daughter, Amanda, who was the same age as Molly's oldest daughter from her first marriage, Lauren. And there was Lauren's younger sister, Jill, and finally, the little girl who Molly and Matt had together, whom Molly had named after Betty.

"I haven't bought a thing either," Betty confessed. She poured

Molly a cup of coffee and got one for herself, as well. "I don't even know when I'll have a spare minute to do it."

"Well, it's going to get worse around here before it gets better," Molly warned. "Next weekend will be even busier. It's the very last weekend before Christmas. We have a party Friday night, two on Saturday night, and the four on Sunday. And that's not even counting the food pantry event," Molly added. "But we're just donating food to them right? We don't have to be there."

"We don't have to be there. But I did plan on going."

"We can just set up a buffet. Won't the volunteers do the rest?"

"But I am a volunteer," Betty explained. "I've spent hours on this event, and I want to see how it comes out."

Molly shrugged. "Okay. If it's that important to you."

She sounded agreeable enough, but Betty could tell her friend was annoyed. Molly simply didn't understand how Betty could take time off on one of their busiest days of the year. Betty was a partner and didn't really need Molly's approval—but Molly was also her best friend. She didn't want to let her down.

"I really want to be there. I don't have to show up at the beginning, but I've put so much time into this project, I just want to see how it turns out."

"I understand," Molly said. "I've heard that being one of Santa's elves is like organized crime. It's hard to get out once you sign on."

"Molly, you're terrible," Betty said, but she couldn't help laughing.

"Speaking of Santa, how was your date last night?"

Oh, here we go. Betty struggled to sound indifferent, though she felt anything but. "It wasn't a date, just a friendly get-together. We talked about the party, ate spaghetti. He's an interesting person," she added. "He's actually a writer. That's how he got involved with the Santa business. He was doing research for an article."

Molly seemed only mildly impressed by this explanation. "A writer? . . . Well, that's almost a real job."

Betty didn't comment. She didn't need to defend Nathan to Molly. She had a feeling that Molly actually liked Nathan and thought he was an interesting, even admirable person. She just didn't like the idea of Betty getting involved with him. Molly preferred Alex Becker in the role of Betty's romantic partner, and her next question proved it.

"I guess it's hard to find time to see Alex, with all these weekends booked up with work."

"We're getting together Sunday night," Betty reported. "If I'm not totally exhausted. We have the Village Garden Club party at Lilac Hall on Sunday afternoon. That one will be a doozy."

"I know it," Molly agreed. "Those ladies are never satisfied with anything we do. But for some reason, they keep hiring us."

Betty didn't bring up either man again, and she and Molly were soon on their way out the door and into the festivity fray. It was good to have the distraction of such intense work, Betty thought. Life was just getting too confusing.

ZOEY WASN'T WILD ABOUT WAITRESSING. BUT SHE LIKED MAKING money. When Charlie came out of the kitchen and told her that she had a half-hour break, Zoey felt the wad of dollar bills in the pocket of her uniform and grabbed her jacket off the coatrack.

"Hey, where you going?" Charlie called after her. "Are you taking off on us again?"

She thought his tone was half-joking and the other half, hoping. "I'm just going down the street to the variety store. I'll be right back," she promised.

"Okay. Don't get lost now," he warned her.

Zoey didn't answer. If she kept up with the waitressing awhile, she would have enough money to get away on her own again. She certainly didn't get enough tips for that this morning. Most of the customers—except for that minister guy—had been pretty stingy, she thought.

But she did have enough to get her cell phone working again, and that was the very first thing she wanted to do. She soon found the cards, which were on display behind the cash register. Zoey bought one for her phone, then found a pay phone on the street and registered the card number. She waited a few minutes, window-shopping on Main Street. The shop windows were all decorated for Christmas and full of things to buy. In the window of a gift shop, an electric train circled a miniature Christmas village. Zoey peered at the other items on display, china teacups and flowered platters and fancy Christmas ornaments. She was glad she had a little money. She wanted to buy Lucy a Christmas present. Lucy was so nice to her, Zoey sometimes thought it had to be an act. Nobody could be that nice naturally. Besides, Zoey didn't understand why Lucy would like her so much or go to so much trouble to help her. There had been a teacher or two who had treated her that way. But after a while, they either got bored or tired of trying; they had all sort of drifted away. It wasn't smart to depend on this sort of kindness, she had learned. It never lasted very long.

She checked the clock in front of the bank. She still had a few minutes before she was due back at the diner. She pulled out her phone to see if the service was on. It was working again, and she quickly dialed her voice mail, to check messages. As she expected, the box was full. She had only been able to call her best friend, Caitlin, once or twice from the Bates house. Otherwise, she had been totally out of touch with her friends. She typed in her code, and the messages began to play. The first two were from Caitlin. The next was a voice she dreaded to hear.

"Hey, it's me, your own sweet Kurt. Where you been hiding,

girl? Caitlin says she doesn't know, but I think she's lying. Don't worry. I'll get it out of her. You know I have my ways." His voice hadn't changed. It was flat, chilling. "It wasn't nice, the way you ran out on me, Zoey. I didn't like that. Think you can hide from me? Get real. You're not smart enough. Simple fact: I'm going to find you, Zoey. And you're going to be very sorry you ever tried to leave me."

Zoey pressed down on the red button, ending the call. Her hands were shaking so hard, she nearly dropped the phone. She checked the record of incoming calls and saw that one number again and again. Kurt, her old boyfriend. It looked as if he'd been calling her for days. Why didn't he just give up? What did she have to do to get away from him?

She swallowed hard and jammed the phone in her pocket. She should have changed her number, but since the phone wasn't working it hadn't seemed to matter. Could he really find her? Zoey worried that he could. Even if Caitlin didn't tell, Zoey knew Kurt would try to scare her friend, but Caitlin was tough enough to stand up to him. Zoey hoped so anyway.

She crept back into the diner, feeling shaky. Charlie was standing behind the counter, talking to a cop who sat there drinking coffee. Zoey guessed this had to be Charlie's friend Tucker, the one he was always talking about.

"Well, you made it," Charlie remarked, glancing at her. "Only five minutes late, too. I was going to send Tucker out looking for you, but he was still working on his donut."

Zoey didn't answer. Just picked up her apron and order book.

"Hey, you okay? You look a little pale," Charlie said. "Lucy said you shouldn't stay here too long on your first day. I can take you home in about an hour," he added.

"I'm okay," Zoey said. She started clearing off a table.

The door over the diner entrance jangled, and Zoey nearly

jumped out of her skin. It was just a mother with two little kids, but her stomach had lurched as if she were coming down on a roller coaster. She had expected to see Kurt standing there, that satisfied smirk on his face as he cornered her.

Maybe Kurt won't even recognize me in this dorky waitress getup, she thought. But that was just stupid wishful thinking. He definitely would. He wouldn't rest until he found her—and made good on all his ugly threats.

AFTER WORKING FROM EIGHT UNTIL TWO AT THE DINER, LUCY had driven over to the hospital and worked a full shift there, too. She finally got home around midnight, feeling so tired she could hardly make it from the garage to the side door.

Her hours were so scattered that no one in the family waited up for her anymore. She couldn't blame them. They hardly knew when she was coming or going. She was surprised to see a light on in the kitchen and find Zoey sitting at the table, reading a magazine.

Zoey looked up when Lucy came in and *almost* smiled at her. "Hey, Lucy. Charlie wasn't sure what time you were coming back. He went to bed."

"He gets up early to open tomorrow," Lucy said. Had Zoey waited up for her to come home? Lucy suspected she had but didn't want to ask. She knew it would only embarrass Zoey, and the girl would likely deny it anyway.

"You should be in bed, too, young lady," Lucy said instead. "You're still getting over your flu, and there's a big breakfast crowd on Sunday. Especially after church gets out."

Lucy didn't like missing church, but Zoey still needed her coaching and moral support. She had to keep her promise. Besides, Charlie needed her help at the diner this weekend, anyway. Trudy was taking the morning off and there was no one to cover for her.

"Do you want some tea or something?" Zoey asked. "I can make it for you."

Lucy was surprised by the offer. "I ate at the hospital, but a little mint tea would be nice. How did everything go after I left? Did you do okay?"

"No major disasters. I got some good tips, too. I stayed until four. Trudy dropped me off."

"That's great," Lucy said, sitting down at the table. But she noticed that Zoey seemed nervous. On edge. Lucy wondered if there had been some problem with Charlie that Zoey wasn't telling her about.

Zoey brought two mugs of tea to the table and then two spoons and the sugar bowl. "Here you go—and I didn't give you a bath in it either," Zoey said.

"Nicely done," Lucy complimented her. "Spilling that coffee was just nerves."

"Thanks for helping me, Lucy . . . and for not yelling at me. And for making me try again," she added.

"I didn't do much. You just needed someone to push you back in the ring. Waitressing is harder than it looks. I respect the job. But you don't have to be a waitress your whole life. For a long time, I thought I did. Then one day, I decided I had to try for something better."

"Becoming a nurse, you mean? Didn't you have to go to college for that?"

Lucy sipped her tea. "Sure I did. I didn't even have my four-year degree. I was almost forty years old my first semester. I was the oldest student in all my classes. I felt a little self-conscious, sitting there," she admitted. "But I just kept reminding myself why I was there. To be a nurse. That's what really mattered."

"Forty? I thought you went when you were young, like right out of high school."

"Oh, no. Charlie and I met in high school, and we married right after. I daydreamed about having a career, but going to college seemed out of the question. I didn't think I was smart enough. Then I had my kids and forgot about it for a while. But I finally got the bug again, and I just couldn't let it go. I had to talk Charlie into it, too. Now I think he's glad I went. He's proud of me—in his own way," she added. "You have to try the thing you think you cannot do. Just think how it went for you today. This morning you were terrified. You wanted to run right out of that diner and never go back. And tonight, you're counting your tips and you know you can do it."

"I guess," Zoey answered doubtfully. "But school isn't the same. Not for me. I'd never be able to be a nurse. Or do anything like that. You have to be really smart to go to college."

"Zoey, honey, if you don't finish high school, you're going to spend the rest of your life getting yelled at by dumb guys wearing moose-head sweatshirts. You're a bright girl. Is that what you want for yourself?"

"No, not really. Who would want that?" Zoey looked down at her fingernails and picked at a cuticle. "But I have this . . . this learning problem. School is really hard for me. You know that kid who's always sitting in the back of the room and never knows what's going on? That's me. I just didn't want to be that kid anymore," she said honestly.

Lucy patted her hand. "I know. Mrs. Schuman told me a little about that. You probably have some learning issue, and no one's ever really worked with you. But you can get help for that, too. Special classes. I'll talk to Rita about it if you're willing to try."

Zoey didn't respond.

"Can I talk to Rita about this?" Lucy asked quietly. She wondered if she was pushing too hard. Zoey was just opening up to her. Maybe this was too much, too fast. She might pull away again.

But Lucy felt an urgency to help her now. Zoey wouldn't be

here for much longer. Something about the girl touched her heart. Maybe she saw herself in Zoey in some way. Even though her own life had been far easier, Lucy recognized Zoey's insecurities and her fear of failure. Or maybe she was just missing having a daughter who would wait up and make her a cup of tea at night, Lucy thought with a small smile. Either way, she knew she had to help the girl as much as she could while she was still here.

"I'll think about it," Zoey told her. She offered a wan smile. Lucy smiled back, wishing she could give her a hug.

"Fair enough. Now we both need to go to bed," she told the girl.

And I'll say a prayer for you, Zoey, Lucy added silently, *asking heaven above to help you find your way. Not to give up on yourself, but to use all the gifts God has given you, and to find the courage and strength to make your best effort in life.*

Chapter Seven

Betty's alarm clock sounded on Monday morning at the usual time. She rolled over, sorely tempted to hit the snooze button. The marathon of parties over the weekend had been tiring. But she willed herself to get out of bed, and after a quick shower and some coffee, she started the first chore at the top of her list. Cleaning her son's former bedroom—which was now the guest room but still bore a shadow resemblance to his high-school lair. There were some of his old books on the shelves and even a few sports trophies she could never bear to part with. He had been the star of his high school track team and had won a lot of medals and awards. There were only a few left on the shelves but just handling them brought back memories of cheering him on at track meets or picking him up at practice. Those were special times, though she hadn't realized it back then.

The mere thought of having Brian all to herself on Christmas Day and visiting for a few days afterward was more than a little overwhelming. Betty was both excited and nervous about it. She couldn't think about it for too long a time and kept pushing it aside in her mind. It was easier to think about work or even about the food pantry party. But the days were counting down. Her boy would soon be here. She not only had to prepare his room, she knew she had to prepare her heart. This was an important visit, her last chance to be with him before he married. She knew they had a lot to catch up on and a few bridges to repair.

Betty had bought a new bedspread and curtains but needed to move out all the miscellaneous junk that had gravitated to the unused room, then vacuum and dust. It was too late for any touch-up painting, but she planned to wash the windows and the woodwork.

And those were only her plans for the morning. Luckily, she had gotten home early from her date with Alex and there were no sports contests involved. Alex had taken her out to dinner, and they had spent a quiet evening at a seafood restaurant in Essex, a casual but elegant place on the water. It was just what she had needed. After her long hours at the noisy, crowded Christmas parties, she had enjoyed spending time with him.

At one point, Betty thought she might have been talking too much about the volunteer work she had been doing for the food pantry, but Alex seemed interested and asked a lot of questions. She couldn't help it if that was on her mind right now.

The party would take place on Sunday, and this week was the last big push. Michael and Eve Piper, who ran the pantry, were very encouraged, Nathan had told her. They had gone from utter despair to total gratitude. Just about everything needed for the Christmas party had been donated, and they had made good progress toward restocking their shelves.

Betty had more ideas for them, fund-raising strategies for after the holidays. Sponsoring a 5K run in the spring could be a great fund-raiser, she thought, and everyone who came out for the race, runners and spectators, could be asked to bring some canned food, a box of cereal, or some other donation. She had made a few notes and planned to talk to Nathan about it.

She thought he would like the idea; he had told her that he was a runner. Of course, he couldn't wear his Santa suit to that one, she reflected, but a red T-shirt and some running shorts would look pretty good on him.

She and Nathan planned to meet again in the late afternoon. They were going to use some of the cash and gift-card donations to buy more toys for the party. Betty hadn't roamed around a toy store at Christmastime—or anytime for that matter—in years. She was definitely looking forward to it. After all, how many people get to go toy shopping with Santa, she wondered, pushing the vacuum cleaner into high gear.

BETTY WAS SUPPOSED TO MEET NATHAN IN FRONT OF THE TOY store at five but arrived at the mall at two. She had a long list of gifts to buy and figured she needed at least three hours to even make a dent.

The stores were not that crowded, considering there were only eleven days left to shop. Betty didn't usually leave it until this late, but this year her holiday mood had been missing. These last few days, though, she was feeling more and more in the spirit. She suspected it had something to do with her volunteer work for the pantry. And maybe with working so closely with Santa, too.

Eager to check some items off her list, Betty began choosing gifts for her family and friends. Sets of silver bangles for Molly's older girls and a ballerina outfit for little Betty. She bought Molly a cashmere sweater and a matching silk scarf, then found a book on sailing for Matt. There were more gifts to buy for her father and brothers and their families. None of her relatives lived nearby, but she would certainly be able to give Brian his gift in person this year. He had mentioned that he had just lost a good camera and his insurance wouldn't replace it. Betty seized the opportunity to buy him a new digital model that also took video, which she had carefully researched online. He would be needing a good camera now, she reasoned, for all the events that surrounded the wedding.

Feeling quite satisfied by her progress, she strolled up the main aisle of the mall, shopping bags dangling from each arm. She spotted the North Pole village that was set up in the middle of the mall, with its fantasy ice castles and giant candy cane sculptures. There was even some fake snow and extra-loud, extra-cheerful Christmas music.

Betty spotted a long line of toddlers waiting patiently—and not so patiently—to meet Santa. She walked closer, drawn by their excitement. Then she looked up and there he was, sitting in a big chair right in front of his workshop, which looked something like a snow-covered log cabin.

Santa smiled as he bent his head to hear a little girl's secret wish. She cupped her hands around her mouth and whispered in his ear. He nodded, looking very serious. Betty could see it was Nathan behind the silky beard and bushy white brows. He was working here. She hadn't even thought of that when he had picked it as a meeting place.

Though she had seen him play Santa at the Rotary Party, this was different. This was in public, and he was completely unaware that she was looking on from the sidelines. She watched awhile longer as the girl slipped off his lap and another child approached, a little boy with a wary expression on his face. But he was smiling just a few seconds later, after Nathan had told him something that cheered him up.

It wasn't the most important job in the world, certainly not one that garnered much respect or pay. But Betty had come to see the role of Santa much differently these past weeks. It was like any other job, just an outline, an empty space and empty suit, actually. The worth of it depended on the person filling the costume. Nathan brought a great deal to the job. He gave the kids a part of himself and made the moment something magical, she thought.

Betty slipped back into the crowd. For some reason, she didn't want him to know that she had seen him working. She headed down another aisle and continued to shop.

At five o'clock sharp, Betty stood in front of Fun Works, the big toy store. She had stashed all her shopping bags in her car, so her arms would be free to carry the next load.

Nathan soon appeared, dressed in one of his usual outfits—his leather jacket, a dark burgundy sweater, jeans, and running shoes. He spotted her in the crowd and their gazes met. She smiled back, feeling completely happy and, for one brief moment, as if everything around them had disappeared.

Then the world rushed back again.

Betty took a breath and focused on the big window display. What was that all about? She must be having some sort of low-blood-sugar, mall reaction. She often got a little loopy when she was out shopping too long.

"Here are the lists, one for you and one for me." Nathan took two folded sheets from his jacket pocket and handed her one. "Ready to do this thing?"

"Ready."

Together, she and Nathan entered the huge toy store, each of them trying to look more determined than the other.

"Okay, then. Let's each get a basket. Synchronize your watches . . . last one to the cash register buys dinner. Wait, I'm buying dinner," he corrected himself. "Last one to finish has to wrap everything."

They were going out to dinner after this? He'd never mentioned that.

"You're on, pal." Betty grabbed her cart and raced to the first aisle. The sign above read Board Games. She was sure there were a few of those on the list, which was written in a neat, square masculine hand. Since Nathan listened for hours on end to children telling him what they wanted for Christmas, he had the inside scoop on the most popular, longed-for toys and games. Betty didn't recognize the names of most of the items, but that didn't mean anything. Nathan was definitely the expert in this department; she was just the number one Santa helper today.

She suddenly realized, *Now I know how Mrs. Claus feels.*

Betty kept filling her shopping cart, bringing it to the front of the store, then grabbing another. She had filled four carts before her list was done. Nathan had filled the same number and was finished before she was. Granted, some of the toys were large and practically filled a cart on their own, but between them, they had grabbed a mountain of toys. Betty couldn't begin to imagine the cost.

She was so distracted packing up the bounty, she barely noticed when Nathan paid the bill. She wondered if the donations would be enough to cover the cost, then wondered if Nathan was spending his own money to make up the difference. She had a feeling he was, but she felt it was too nosy to ask.

It took several trips with three shopping carts to get all of their bags out of the store. Two of the employees helped, and Nathan gave them each a tip.

The back of Nathan's truck was loaded. Betty's car was parked nearby and when he walked her over, it was the same story. She could hardly fit herself into the driver's seat.

"Are you okay in there?" he asked. "Can you see through the rear window?"

"I'll be all right. We're not going far. I made a little space so I could see out the back," she told him. The entire experience suddenly seemed very amusing to her. "I know it's hard to park, Nathan. But next time, I think you ought to just bring the sleigh."

"You're right," he said with a grin. "It would hold more. But I hate cleaning up after the reindeer. The mall security here is pretty strict about that."

Betty shook her head. They had decided to have dinner first and worry about what to do with the toys later. Nathan had asked her to meet him at the Lobster Trap, a seafood restaurant in Essex, which he claimed was one of his favorites.

Betty knew the place, an oldie-but-goody built out on a dock. It was extremely casual with a simple menu on a big chalkboard and plain white paper covering the tables. Betty had always liked it, though she hadn't been there in a long time.

She pulled up and parked. Nathan was right behind her and parked nearby. He met her as she got out of her car. "Want to take a walk on the dock first? I could use some fresh air."

"Good idea," Betty said. She, too, needed a minute to unwind from their whirlwind shopping spree.

They walked along the dock side by side. Nathan had his hands jammed in his pockets and a striped muffler slung around his throat. Betty's boot heel caught on a nail and she nearly stumbled, but he quickly reached out to steady her. She thought for a moment he was going to take her hand, but he soon let go and they resumed their parallel stroll.

She didn't speak and neither did he. There didn't seem to be any need to talk. The sun had set, but a fading light kept the darkness at bay. On the eastern horizon, she could already see stars and a sliver of silver moon, while along the western horizon the sun's final rays glazed the edges of blue-gray clouds with a violet hue.

Betty gazed out over the calm water and tall, waving marsh grass. She felt miles away from the bustling mall with its false cheer, Muzak, and overwhelming choices and goods for sale. This place was serene and real. And grounding. She could see why it was one of Nathan's favorites. It definitely suited him.

They stood at the very end of the dock a moment, watching and listening. A flock of birds rose from the reeds, filling the air with a rushing sound of wings. An amazing sight, especially in the winter—especially at twilight. Betty felt her breath catch in her throat as her gaze followed their graceful arc through the sky. They soon disappeared, headed for goodness-knew-where.

Filled with surprise and awe, Betty turned to Nathan. "That was beautiful."

"Yes, it was. Birds are so lucky to be able to fly away like that whenever the impulse strikes. They don't even realize it."

His tone was wistful, maybe even sad, she thought. She had never heard him sound like that before. He was always so positive and optimistic. She glanced at him, wondering what he was thinking about. It was impossible to tell. She really didn't know him all that well, she realized.

They returned to the restaurant, and Nathan helped her off with her coat. The place was practically empty, and they were soon seated at a table near the window. Nathan smiled at her from across the table as they checked the chalkboard menu. He seemed back to his typical good humor.

They ordered quickly, then sat back and relaxed. "We got a lot done this afternoon, Betty. I think we're just about set. Thanks for your help—yet again. I know I couldn't have done all this without you."

"You would have managed. And I'm not the only one who's been working. A big event like this takes a village, as they say."

"Yes, it does. And we're lucky the people who live in our village are so generous. So, what did you do today besides buy out a toy store with me? Were you at the catering shop all day?"

Betty shook her head. "No, thank goodness. Molly and I were working all weekend. We had three parties, back-to-back. So we decided to give each other the day off. We have another killer weekend coming up. We don't want to burn out before Christmas."

"Three parties. Wow, that's a heavy schedule." He glanced at her with a serious look. "I know you've taken a lot of time from your work the past two weeks to help me. If you can't come on Sunday, everyone will understand. We all know what a great contribution you've made."

"Thanks for being so understanding, but I'll definitely be there. At some point," she clarified. "We have a lot going on that day, and I have to drive around and supervise. But after all this work, I can't miss the pantry party. Besides, I need to see how everyone likes my chili recipe."

Betty's turkey chili was among the dishes Willoughby's Fine Foods was donating to the party. Nathan had put in a special request, and Betty had been secretly flattered.

"Oh, you have to come for your big chili debut. You don't want to miss that," he agreed with a gentle smile. "You're an unusual person, Betty," he said sincerely. "I'm not sure I've ever met anybody quite like you. You can charm everyone, organize anything, and do it all without being pushy. You're smart, full of energy and common sense, and so . . . so . . ." His voice trailed off, leaving her hanging on the edge of her seat. "So easy to be with."

Betty didn't know what to say. She wasn't sure where all these accolades were coming from or what they added up to. Was he declaring his feelings for her? Or was it his gentle way of telling her just the opposite? That he liked and admired her a lot—as a great friend.

"Well . . . thanks very much," she said slowly. "I think you're pretty special, too."

"Because I'm a grown man who runs around dressed up like Santa—and likes it?" His tone was humorous, but she could see a serious question in his eyes.

"No, not just that, though I must say that is a unique trait." Betty searched for the right words, but it was hard to say why she found him so interesting and why something about him just touched her heart.

Before she could speak the waitress returned and set down their dinners—two broiled fishermen's platters and baked potatoes. A lot of questions followed about side dishes and condiments and whether more water and rolls were needed. By the time their privacy was restored, Betty felt the moment had passed.

She took a bite of her dinner and decided to retreat to neutral ground. "I can't believe there's less than two weeks to Christmas. At least I got a little shopping done today—things on my own list," she explained.

"That was productive. I'm in the mall all week, and I can't seem to find the time. I guess I'll make a mad dash at the last minute. Maybe I'll keep the suit on. I'll get better service."

"I bet you will," Betty agreed. "What are you doing for the holidays? Do you travel anywhere to see family?"

"I have a sister in Vermont, but she's going to Canada this year to visit her husband's relatives. I'll just stick around here and relax. On Christmas Day, I usually go visit my friends, Michael and Eve Piper. They have a big get-together, family and friends. It's noisy but fun."

"That's pretty much what I do. I go to Molly's house for a big party on Christmas Eve," Betty said.

"I have to work that night. No parties for me." His tone was serious and made her laugh. "What do you do on Christmas Day? You don't spend the day alone, do you?" He seemed concerned about that and, for a moment, she thought he would ask her to come with him to the Pipers' house.

"Actually, this year I have something very special planned for Christmas Day. My son, Brian, is coming. He's going to stay with me a few days, which is a real treat. It's been almost a year since I've seen him, and that was a very short visit."

"Where does he live?" Nathan asked with interest.

"In Chicago. He's an attorney. I really wished he had settled closer but that's where he went to school and one of his professors recommended him to a big firm. He seems happy there. That's the most important thing."

"Very true," Nathan agreed. "Sounds like he's in his early twenties?"

"Twenty-six. It's hard for me to believe he's a grown man, even though he's just gotten engaged. I haven't met his fiancée yet, but her family lives around here so they've both come back for Christmas and he's going to introduce us."

Nathan's blue eyes grew wide. "That's exciting. Congratulations!"

"Thanks, I guess. I'm excited to meet her and to see him, of course. I'm a little nervous, too," she admitted.

"That's only natural. You've been living apart from him since he went to college? Even if you call and e-mail a lot, it's not quite the same. Sounds as if he has his own life now."

"Yes, that's part of it. But we didn't have an ideal relationship after my divorce," she confided. Betty paused, wondering if she should disclose these private matters to him. Was it asking too much of him to hear her out? Would her story burden—or worse—bore him?

But Nathan seemed interested and concerned. He leaned forward and gave her his full attention. "Was Brian angry about the divorce?" he asked.

Betty nodded. "He was just eleven or so. On the brink of his teenage years. A bad time for the family to split up . . . but is there ever a good time?" She shook her head. "Ted and I tried to make it easier for him. I think Brian always knew we both loved him very much. At first, he lived with me and stayed at his father's house on weekends. But eventually, he asked if he could live there. His father had remarried and had a new baby. Brian's stepmother, Linda, was always home, a full-time wife and Super-Mom." Betty rolled her eyes. "Which I definitely was not. I was running a business, trying to support him and save for his college."

"Understandably," Nathan said. "We all have to make choices. I'm sure you were just trying to do your best—what you thought was best for him."

"Yes, I was." She sighed, surprised that she was relating this story and so easily. She didn't talk about this side of her relationship with her son much, and few people, even close friends, knew her true feelings or regrets. But somehow it was easy to tell Nathan. She met his gaze—not judging, simply listening and understanding. She felt she could trust him and more than that, she wanted to tell him. She wanted him to know this private part of her, the one she kept hidden from the rest of the world.

"It was hard to know the right thing to do. I've always second-guessed myself," she admitted. "I agreed to let him live there. But it hurt. It hurt a lot. I got to see him weeknights and every other weekend. I still wonder if I did the right thing—or whether Brian was just testing me, to see how much I cared. I sometimes think I should have refused to let him go. It was almost like admitting I wasn't a very good mother," she said finally.

Nathan gazed at her with a gentle smile. "You put your son's happiness above your own. You believed that choice would make him happy and be best for him. I'd say that obviously makes you a good mother."

Betty tried to smile a little, too. "I've tried to think of it that way. I'm just never sure if I'm rationalizing and fooling myself. But it's true. It hurt me to let him go like that. I missed him like crazy. I always wanted him back home with me. We've never really talked about it, though I was thinking that we should when he comes this time."

"And anticipating that confrontation has got you worried?"

Betty nodded. "I'd say so. Then I get mad at myself, because I really just want to enjoy seeing him. I mean, it's Christmas."

"I understand. But isn't it ironic how the holidays bring up all this stuff we've buried? Like a big wave, dragging up a load of seaweed and tossing it out on the beach. Christmas is a good time to sort this stuff out. Christmas is a time for looking back with love and forgiveness in our hearts, and looking forward with hope," he told her. "Your son is a grown man now. He understands things differently. If he's anything like his mother, I think you can have a good talk with him and feel even closer afterward. It will take some effort, but it will be worth it, Betty."

She nodded, feeling too emotional to speak. "Thanks for listening. And thanks for the wise advice," she said finally. "I like what you just said about Christmas. Is that a quote from a book or something?"

"From an article. . . . One that isn't entirely written yet. But my deadline's getting closer and so is Christmas," he confessed with a laugh. "So it's got to get done pretty soon."

Betty knew she should have guessed. "It sounds good. I can't wait to read it."

"Maybe I'll give you a preview. You can give me a critique."

Betty was honored that he thought so well of her opinion. "I'd be happy to read it, though I doubt I'll find any shortcomings," she said. "I thoroughly enjoyed the articles you showed me the other night at your house."

She suddenly recalled the essay she had found about losing a child. She wanted to ask him about his past, too. Especially about that piece, which seemed to be drawn from personal experience. Now she wondered if that's what it was really about. She had glanced at it so quickly. Maybe she'd been mistaken. Maybe she had just assumed he always wrote autobiographical pieces, but perhaps he had just taken someone else's story and used that point of view to make it more powerful?

She couldn't know for sure without asking, and it didn't seem like the right time.

After the dinner was cleared, Nathan paid the check and they headed outside again. They lingered in front of the restaurant, talking about what to do next with all the toys. They decided it was most efficient to bring all the gifts to the church. The sexton, Carl Tulley, had cleaned out a closet for them just the day before, so the bounty could be stored there and wrapped before the party on Sunday. Their schedules were different, though. Betty knew she wouldn't see Nathan when she stopped at the church in the morning.

"Reverend Ben and Carl Tulley will help you," Nathan told her. "I'll call the Reverend tonight and give him a heads-up."

Nathan walked her to her car. She felt as if their talk over dinner had drawn them closer, but she also felt self-conscious around him, too. She had revealed a lot about herself tonight. She usually wasn't like that. Not this early in any relationship. But something about Nathan made it easy to confide these things. He was an exceptionally good listener.

"Thanks again for dinner. And for listening to me about my son."

"No need to thank me." It was so dark, she could barely see the expression on his face. But his eyes were bright and gently shining down at her. He rested his hands on her shoulders in a reassuring touch. "Don't worry. I think it's going to be fine."

Then he hugged her good-bye again, holding her just a little closer and tighter, she thought. And maybe a few moments longer than the last time? He pressed his cheek—and maybe even his lips in a soft kiss—against her hair. Or was she just imagining that? Betty wasn't sure once he finally let go.

All the way home, she wondered about it.

* * *

LUCY WASN'T SURE HOW SHE HAD MANAGED TO WORK AT THE diner all weekend and again on Monday until after the lunch rush, then drive up to Southport for her shift at the hospital. But somehow, to help Zoey, she did. In her own thoughts, though, she sometimes heard an echo of Charlie's questions: *Why are you so interested in this kid, Lucy? Why do you feel you need to go out of your way so much to help a total stranger?*

Lucy wasn't sure entirely. At first, it had seemed the right thing to do and she'd been touched by the child's plight. Once she had gotten to know her, she could see that the girl had so much good in her, so much potential. And it would all go to waste if someone didn't step in and help her. And of course, she cared about Zoey now. Her feelings were involved, which somehow made the matter more complicated and simpler at the same time.

During her break on Monday night she mulled over this question. It wasn't really late, and it seemed a good time to check in with Rita Schuman, even though Lucy had to call the social worker at home. Lucy had promised to tell Rita how Zoey was doing at her new job.

"I'm just calling to let you know how Zoey is doing with the waitressing," Lucy said when Rita picked up. "She started on Saturday, so today was her third full day working."

"And how's it going? Does she like it?" Rita asked.

"She didn't seem to at first. She got a very surly customer right at the start, and I thought she was going to walk out," Lucy confessed. "But we got over that hump and it's been pretty smooth sailing since. I don't think she's crazy about the profession, but she does like the tips. And she hasn't complained at all."

"That's good, very good." Rita sounded pleased and a bit

surprised, too. "Waitressing is hard work. But without a high school diploma, her job choices are very limited."

"I've talked to her about that," Lucy replied. "In fact, we talked a little about Zoey going back to school and trying that special program you mentioned. She didn't say she would do it. Far from it, actually. But she agreed to let me ask you about it and get the information for her."

"I'd be happy to drop that off and answer any questions," Rita said. "I think that's real progress, Lucy. She's been very turned off to any effort in that direction. She seems to be doing very well with you, and in a short time, too."

"Thanks," Lucy said. "I've really enjoyed having her stay with us. How is the placement search going?" Lucy tried to keep her tone light, but she heard a note of anxiety seep through. She really wanted Zoey to stay through Christmas. It wasn't even two weeks away.

"I'm still looking, though I haven't found anything yet," Rita reported.

"How quickly would Zoey need to leave if you did find a home for her?"

"Fairly quickly."

The answer made Lucy's heart sink. "I was wondering if you could just stop looking for a while," she said honestly. "I mean, just until after Christmas. It would be nice if Zoey could spend the holiday with us."

"I'm sure that would be a good experience for her, though there are always pluses and minuses. It might be easier for everyone if I found a permanent placement tomorrow. The longer Zoey stays with you, the harder it will be for her to go," the social worker said. "But I'm sure you've considered that."

"Yes . . . I have," Lucy replied quietly. She did think of that question from time to time, but the answer always came back the same: *Do your best right now and deal with the future when you get there.*

"As for her staying on through Christmas, I can't make any promises. I have to keep looking for a placement." Rita paused. "Unless you and your husband apply as foster parents. Is that what you're thinking about?"

"No . . . we're not thinking about that." The answer was painful for Lucy. "Temporary guardianship is all we can do."

"That's fine. I was just wondering," Rita replied.

Lucy noticed that her break was almost over, and she quickly wrapped up the call. She was left with an odd feeling after the phone conversation, her mind circling the question about taking Zoey in permanently. No, they were not thinking of doing that, was an accurate answer. But still, not entirely true.

Sometimes she did fantasize about keeping Zoey with them and how that would be. But that was just daydreaming. She knew Charlie would never agree, so she didn't even bother bringing it up. And that was nothing she needed to confide to the social worker, who probably had already guessed the situation.

Lucy was back to her day schedule on Tuesday. She came home around five and started dinner. It was one of the few nights this week they were all eating together, and she needed everyone to stick around for a few minutes afterward, and she didn't want any arguments about homework or important TV shows.

When the time came however, of course there were a few.

"Is this going to take very long? I have a lot of homework." C.J. stood in the kitchen doorway, ready to bolt.

"Not long at all. Just take your seat again, please. The sooner we get started, the sooner we'll be done," Lucy told her oldest son.

They had just finished dinner. Charlie and Jamie were still at the table, and Zoey was helping her clear the dishes.

"Reverend Ben dropped off the pages for the Advent candle-lighting ceremony today," Lucy explained. "I know we have nearly a week to prepare, but we do need to practice our parts. And honestly, I don't know when we'll all be together like this again before Sunday. So here's the reading." She took the pages down from the kitchen bulletin board, where she had pinned them up for safe-keeping.

"Reverend Ben said that we each need to take a part. He marked them with numbers, but we'd better put our names down next to the lines, then read it out loud and see how it sounds."

"I'll get a pen," Jamie said helpfully. He jumped up and checked the kitchen drawer where Lucy stashed pens, pencils, and other odds and ends.

"Guess I'll head upstairs," Zoey said.

"You need to stay," Lucy told her. "Aren't you going to read with us on Sunday?"

Zoey looked surprised. "Do I have to? I mean, I've never even been to your church. I thought this was just for . . . for you guys."

Before Lucy could answer, Charlie jumped in. "Of course you don't. This is for the family. And there's only four parts, so there's no lines for you," he pointed out quickly. He glanced at Lucy with a challenging look.

"Um, right. No problem," Zoey said, standing up again. "I didn't want to do it anyway. I hate getting up in front of people."

Lucy heard the tight, trembling tone in her voice, and she was so angry at Charlie she could hardly speak. She reached out again and gently touched Zoey's arm. "No, you stay. Just sit right here. We'll figure this out," she insisted.

She looked straight at Charlie. How could he have embarrassed Zoey like that and hurt her feelings? Didn't he have any heart at all? Didn't he have any common sense? The girl needed to feel included now, not rejected by them. Lucy hung on to her temper, knowing that if she blew up at her husband now, in front of Zoey, it would embarrass her even more.

C.J. let out a long, frustrated breath and squirmed in his chair. "She can have my lines. I don't care. I'll just hang out and light the matches or something."

Lucy glanced at him. He barely spoke to Zoey, but she figured that was mostly due to adolescent self-consciousness, not because he didn't like her. This offer was a small but meaningful gesture for him, she thought.

C.J. looked at Zoey. "We can split it up. I don't like to read in front of a whole bunch of people either. I know it's church and all, but . . . I think it's sort of dumb."

Lucy's eyes widened but she didn't scold him. He had reached out to Zoey and touched some common ground. Now Zoey could see that everyone felt a little anxious being in the spotlight; it wasn't just her. Maybe that would put her a bit more at ease.

Jamie had returned to the table with a pencil and now took the sheets from Lucy's hand and looked them over. "There are plenty of lines for five people," he said a few moments later. "Let's just split it up this way." He started writing on the pages before anyone could object. "D for Dad, M for Mom, J for me, C for C.J., and Z for Zoey. . . ." He quickly marked the pages then counted. "It's pretty even, I think. Though, I ended up with an extra line."

"You deserve it for that brainstorm, honey." Lucy took the sheets and checked his solution. "Perfect," she announced. "We each have our lines, and the three kids will each light a candle. Is that okay with you, Charlie?"

He sat at the head of the table, his arms crossed over his chest. "Seems you have it all worked out. What does it matter what I say?"

Lucy ignored him and rushed ahead. "Okay, let's pass the pages around and take turns reading our parts out loud. Just one time."

Charlie went first. He read his lines, then Lucy read, followed by the boys. Zoey was last. Lucy could see that she was nervous when C.J. handed her the pages, even though it was only the family listening to her.

She read her verse in a shaky, hesitant voice, speaking too quickly and much too softly. When she hit a word that was difficult to pronounce, she stammered and got annoyed at herself.

She tossed the paper down. "I can't do this. . . . It's okay. You don't need me there."

"Yes, we do need you. We want you to do it with us," Lucy insisted. She checked the word that Zoey stumbled on. "That word is a weird one, 'un-be-knownst.' It's old-fashioned. You don't pronounce the k," she added quietly.

Zoey nodded and reread the last part of her verse—a tiny bit smoother on the second try.

"Much better," Lucy said.

"Don't worry, we have time to practice," Jamie told her. "I have some weird words in my part, too."

"Are we done now?" C.J. asked. "I have to study."

Lucy nodded. "Yes, we're all finished. You go on up."

"I'm finished, too," Charlie said in an angry tone. He got up and stalked toward the family room. Lucy had a feeling she hadn't heard the end of this argument.

Jamie went to do homework in his room, and Lucy started cleaning up the kitchen from dinner. Zoey stayed to help her.

"Do you really want me to do that church thing with you?" Zoey asked. "I mean, I know you do, but Charlie doesn't."

"Don't mind him. He just doesn't like surprises," Lucy said, which was partly true. She glanced at Zoey as she covered a dish of leftovers with a piece of plastic wrap. "I want you to do it and so do the boys. So that makes three against one."

Zoey looked grateful for her answer. "But I don't have anything to wear," she pointed out. "I mean, nothing churchy enough. Can I borrow a sweater or something?"

Lucy hadn't thought about that. It was true. Lucy had bought her a few items of clothing, but mostly things to wear around the house. As for the clothes Zoey had brought with her, "not churchy enough" was an understatement. It was going to take more than a borrowed sweater to have her looking appropriate.

"I've got an idea. I think we just have to go shopping for something new," Lucy said gleefully.

"You mean, like, to the mall or something?"

"Yes, to the mall. I think we can find some nice things there for you. You don't want to wear my old stuff. It'll be swimming on you and the styles are very . . . mom-ish."

"You dress okay, Lucy," Zoey said. "I mean, aside from the uniforms. You don't dress too mom-ish."

Not *too* mom-ish? That was some comfort. "Thanks, but that's what we'll do. Maybe we can even go for a manicure," she added in a whisper. "Would you like that?"

Zoey's eyes lit up. "That would be great. My nails look horrendous," she said sincerely. "I have some money from my tips. I can pay for myself."

"Don't worry about that. It's an early Christmas present." Lucy forced a bright note into her words, but they only served to remind her that Zoey might not even be with them on the holiday. *At least I'm able to give her a nice gift before she goes,* Lucy thought. *And spending time together will be a gift to me.*

Her plans with Zoey put Lucy in a good mood for the rest of the evening. Once the kids were all upstairs, she joined Charlie in the family room, toting along a big basket of laundry that needed to be folded. Lucy sat on the couch and pulled out a towel. Charlie was watching the news channel. She couldn't tell if his dark scowl had been brought on by the world situation, or the one in his own kitchen an hour ago.

He wasted no time in answering that question.

"Why did you go and do that, Lucy? That girl doesn't belong up on the altar with us. She's not family," he insisted. "And she knows it, as well as anybody."

"We signed on to be her temporary guardians," Lucy reminded him. "She's part of our family until the social worker calls and says she has to move on to her permanent placement."

"Everyone in church is going to talk about her. They'll be asking questions we have no answers for."

"What's the difference? We'll just say she had no place to go and she's staying with us for a while. Period. End of story."

"Easy for you to say. I don't think it's right. This candle-lighting thing is for families. Reverend Ben won't like it," he added.

"I already checked with Reverend Ben. I called him while I was making dinner. He thinks it's fine. 'A very nice idea.' Those were his words exactly," Lucy countered.

"Really? I don't agree. I don't get the point. I think it will do more harm than good. It will give her false hopes. And big expectations. Did you think about that at all?"

Lucy had to admit, so far she hadn't thought too much about that side of the question. It was more or less the same point Rita Schuman had raised. Lucy wondered now if she thought she was being kind but actually setting the girl up for a fall. Was it wrong to treat Zoey as part of the family for the short time she was here? Would that do more harm than good in the long run?

She glanced at Charlie, unable to meet his eye. "You have a point," she admitted. "But I know her a lot better than you do, Charlie. I know a little of what she's been through and what she's trying to deal with now. I think Zoey needs to feel that people care about her, that she has a place in the world and counts for something. Not that she's invisible, or a nuisance—as if nobody wants her," Lucy tried to explain. "Sure, it's going to be hard for her when she goes. But it's going to be hard either way—whether we make her feel included or we push her away and hold her at a distance from us. I think that in the long run, it's better to pull her in, to let her know we care about her, even if she can't stay forever."

"Okay, okay, I get your point. It's not the way I see it but . . . well, she's not going to be here for very long, so what's the point of arguing about it?" Charlie let out a long, frustrated sigh. "I'm going to bed," he said. "Got to get up early tomorrow."

Lucy nodded, then pulled a pair of jeans from the laundry pile and folded them into a neat square. "Good night, Charlie," she replied evenly.

"Good night," he said with another long sigh as he marched out of the room.

She felt some satisfaction in knowing Zoey would read with them on Sunday, no matter what Charlie thought. But even though she had won the battle, she knew she had not won the war. Zoey would soon leave them.

Could Charlie ever be persuaded to be a permanent guardian? Was that a mountain she could ever scale? Lucy wondered. She had seen a few small signs of his growing acceptance of Zoey. He had even noted that she was catching on to her new job quickly and might make a pretty good waitress someday. Underneath all his arguing and his gruff manner, her husband was essentially a good man. But before they could take Zoey into their home permanently, Charlie had to take her into his heart. And Lucy wasn't sure if that would ever happen.

LUCY PICKED ZOEY UP AT THE DINER ON THURSDAY NIGHT WHEN she got back to Cape Light after working at the hospital. They decided to go straight to the mall and have a bite to eat in the food court after they finished shopping.

Zoey didn't show her excitement in an obvious way, but Lucy could tell she was happy.

Lucy felt happy, too. She had been looking forward to this. When she told Charlie about her plans, she had expected an argument, but he just shook his head. "You'll do what you want no matter what I say. Just watch what you spend, okay? One outfit for church, so she doesn't totally embarrass us."

Lucy had agreed but, of course, planned on buying Zoey much more than one outfit—if they could find some clothing acceptable to both of them. She could hardly wait to see Zoey in a dress—a nice dress, one that wasn't too tight, too short, or purposely torn to shreds.

"So, where should we go?" Lucy asked as they walked down the first row of stores. "That store has some cute things." She pointed to a window. Zoey checked out the display, but her expression looked bleak.

"I don't think so . . . too expensive," she said quickly. Lucy suspected that Zoey also considered the styles too prim and preppy. "I know a good place. It's just down this way. Follow me," Zoey said.

Lucy quickened her pace to keep up, and they soon arrived at a store that did look more Zoey's style. Lucy was wary. "I don't know, honey. It might be more reasonable, but will you find anything right for church in here? We are going to stand up at the altar," she reminded Zoey.

"Don't worry. I'll put something decent together. I know I have to look serious. I just don't want to look like queen of the geeks."

Lucy nodded. "Okay, let's see what they have."

Loud rock music assaulted Lucy's ears from every direction. She could hardly hear herself think. How could anyone shop in this environment?

Meanwhile, Zoey was instantly excited, as animated as Lucy had ever seen her. She skipped from rack to rack, pulling out hangers, putting things back, and slinging other items over her arm.

Lucy followed a few steps behind. She didn't offer any comment on the choices—one of which was neon purple—but was secretly wondering what she had gotten herself into. She suddenly realized. She'd been having some lovely daydream about helping Zoey choose clothes—tailored, classic styles. Which were the complete opposite of Zoey's actual taste. She had never expected a place—or clothing—like this. If they returned home with some wild outfit, Lucy knew she would never hear the end of it from Charlie.

Zoey went into a dressing room and Lucy waited outside. When the girl didn't come out for a very long time, Lucy leaned over and whispered through the curtain, "How are you doing in there? Any luck?" She didn't really know if she wanted a yes or a no for an answer.

"Just a sec. I think I found something."

Lucy held her breath.

Zoey finally emerged, wearing a sleeveless dress with a black background and a smattering of multicolored dots, hot pink, light blue, and yellow. It was bright but not too bright, Lucy thought. It wasn't too short or too tight. And the scoop neck and high waist were practically modest.

"What do you think?" Zoey asked hesitantly.

"I think that's really nice." Lucy stepped back to get a better look, unable to hide the surprise in her voice.

It certainly wasn't the dress Lucy would have picked out. But it was a pretty dress and Zoey looked cute in it. "It's just your style," Lucy added. "You look very pretty."

Zoey seemed pleased by her compliments. "And I can wear this on top if you think going sleeveless isn't right for church." She slipped on a black sweater that had long sides that sort of wrapped around and tied in front. "What do you think? Is it too much?"

"I think it's very stylish," Lucy said honestly. "You have very good taste, Zoey." *When you're trying to look churchy, that is.*

"Thanks." Zoey smiled at her.

"So, what else did you find? We can get more than one outfit," Lucy told her, feeling encouraged. "How about some new sweaters and jeans? Or something for every day?"

"I thought we were just getting clothes for Sunday. You don't need to get me anything else. Honest."

"It's Christmas, Zoey," Lucy reminded her. When it seemed that Zoey wasn't convinced, Lucy said, "Listen, you just show me some things that you like. Maybe Santa will surprise you."

Zoey rolled her eyes a little, but Lucy could see she was going to take the bait. It took a little more convincing, but what teenage girl doesn't like to shop for clothes?

Pretty soon, Zoey was giving her a guided tour of her favorite store, and then they went on to two others, including a shoe store, where she tried on a pair of "totally awesome boots."

Lucy made a few notes on a little piece of paper, so she would remember it all. She certainly couldn't buy everything on Zoey's wish list, but she wanted to make a solid dent.

Along with the dress and sweater, they bought two long-sleeved tops, a pair of jeans, and some dressy flats to wear on Sunday.

After making a round of the stores, they headed to the food court. "I'm starved," Lucy said. "Shopping works up a real appetite."

"How true," Zoey agreed. "I think I'll get a taco at that Tex-Mex window. It has the shortest line."

"Sounds good to me." Lucy followed her and they got on line. Lucy stared at the menu, trying to figure out which entree had the least calories. She loved Mexican food, but she was watching her diet these days, trying to save her carbs and fat grams for all the treats at Christmas.

A group of noisy teenagers walked up to a line nearby, in front of a Pizza Express counter. Lucy didn't notice them at first, but they were making so much noise, she finally turned to glance their way. There were girls and boys together, acting goofy and loud.

They didn't really look like nice kids, Lucy thought. Of course, she was judging from their clothes and the things they were shouting at each other, which included some pretty foul language. Zoey was looking at the group of teens, too. Then she suddenly turned and stared straight ahead, her body stiff. The man at the counter asked her what she wanted, and she didn't answer.

She turned to Lucy instead. "I have to go to the ladies' room. I'll be right back."

Lucy was confused. "Do you want me to order something for you?"

"No . . . don't do that. I'm not hungry. I don't feel well," she said quickly, backing away. "I'll meet you at the car."

Then she turned and ran off toward the mall exit, a short distance away.

Lucy followed her. She glanced over her shoulder at the rowdy group, wondering if they had anything to do with this strange behavior. She finally caught up with Zoey just outside the mall.

Zoey turned, looking as if she thought Lucy might be mad at her. "I'm sorry I left you like that. . . . I really needed some air."

Lucy gently touched her arm and searched her eyes. "Are you okay? Do you feel dizzy or anything?" Maybe she was having a relapse of her lung infection.

"I'm okay," Zoey assured her. She glanced over her shoulder at the mall and still seemed spooked by something. "Can we go back now? I'm really tired."

"Sure. Let's go," Lucy said as they headed into the parking lot. "I love burritos, but I didn't need the calories," she said lightly.

Once they got in the car and were driving back to Cape Light, Zoey seemed to relax. "Thanks for the clothes, Lucy," she said quietly.

"I love the dress and the wrap sweater. I'm going to pay you back for everything. Out of my waitressing money."

"That's okay, Zoey. I told you before, don't worry about it. Consider them early Christmas presents. Besides, we are taking care of you right now. I want to make sure you have everything you need."

Zoey didn't say anything. She just stared out the window.

They drove along in silence for a while before Lucy said, "Listen, did something about those kids in the food court bother you?"

"What kids?"

"That group of teenagers who got on the line next to us. The ones who were so noisy and obnoxious." Lucy turned and looked at her, trying to see her expression in the dark. "Do you know them from your old school or something?"

Zoey quickly shook her head. "I don't think so. I mean, I hardly noticed them. They were just . . . you know, a bunch of kids hanging out, I guess."

"I guess," Lucy agreed. Something in Zoey's words didn't ring true, but Lucy didn't know how to pursue it, or if she should even bother.

CHAPTER EIGHT

⌒

ON SUNDAY MORNING, LUCY JUMPED OUT OF BED BEFORE her alarm rang and woke the entire household. They couldn't be late for church today. Everyone had to get dressed up and look especially nice and well-groomed. Which was sometimes a challenge for her boys, but she had already picked out their outfits—khaki pants, crewneck sweaters, and dress shirts underneath.

C.J. looked alarmed at her choice for him. "Is that a joke? I'll look like a total dork."

"No joke," Lucy told him. "Would you rather have your father pick out your outfit?"

Her son rolled his eyes and fell back on his bed, as if he had been struck over the head.

They both knew what Charlie's first choice would be—a navy blue suit that C.J.'s grandmother had bought him. Which made him look a lot like a miniature Charlie.

"The undertaker suit? . . . No thanks. I'll do the sweater."

"I thought you'd see my point."

Jamie was easier. He wasn't at an age when boys cared much about their clothes—or even noticed if the clothes were clean or colors matched.

For herself, Lucy chose a brown tweed suit that had tones of gold and spicy amber. With a silk blouse underneath, the outfit complemented her red hair and fair coloring. She wore gold earrings and a diamond heart necklace Charlie had given her several Christmases back. As she left the bedroom, she noticed that Charlie was wearing his best charcoal gray suit. He looked very handsome in it, she thought, except for the red tie with the candy cane print. Lucy thought that was a little tacky but overall, he looked nice and she didn't want to start an argument with him this morning. He hadn't said another word about Zoey doing the reading either.

They had all had one more practice, reading their parts together, but Lucy had rehearsed with Zoey a few times in her room. Lucy was now convinced that Zoey had some sort of learning disability—dyslexia maybe?—that had never been properly diagnosed or addressed. If only she would go back to school again, Lucy thought, this time she would get the help she needed.

Lucy checked on the boys and was pleased to see they were almost ready.

Zoey had her door closed, and Lucy called up to her. "Zoey? How are you doing, honey? We have to leave soon. Need any help?"

"I'm good. I'll be right down," she shouted back.

Lucy went downstairs, feeling a little anxious. What if Zoey had decided at the last minute that she didn't like the dress they'd chosen and put on one of her old favorites instead? The shredded denim miniskirt and black fishnet stockings came to mind. Lucy shuddered at the thought.

The others soon came down and joined her in the kitchen,

quickly eating bowls of cereal. Charlie sipped his coffee, being extra careful of his tie. "Where's the girl? Isn't she coming?"

Lucy glanced at him. She could tell he was hoping that Zoey was backing out at the last minute. "She'll be right down."

"Here I am." Zoey stood in the kitchen doorway. She wore her new dress, the wrap sweater, and low black flats with her long hair pushed back from her face with a wide band.

She paused, a self-conscious expression on her face. Everyone turned to look at her. Lucy blinked. She didn't even recognize the child for a moment.

"Wow! You look like a model," Jamie nearly shouted, practically spilling his cereal.

C.J. swallowed hard and looked back at his breakfast. Lucy could see he agreed.

Even Charlie sat with his mouth agape. "For goodness' sakes . . . I hardly recognized you. You ought to wear your hair back like that more. I can see your face," he said briskly.

That was the closest to a compliment Charlie was going to get, Lucy knew. But she could tell he was impressed.

"You look beautiful. You do look like a model," Lucy said. She walked over to Zoey and cupped her cheek with her hand. "And your hair does look very pretty pulled back like that."

"Stop saying that. I do not look like a model. No way," Zoey complained quietly. But Lucy could see she enjoyed the compliment.

Lucy just smiled at her, feeling happy that—just for today—this beautiful girl was part of their family.

Lucy was a bit nervous for the candle-lighting ceremony. She didn't often get up at church and stand in front of the entire congregation. She was glad that they had practiced a few times. It all went by in the blink of an eye and went very smoothly. Even Zoey read her part well, though she kept her head down the entire time and practically whispered.

Lucy felt so relieved afterward, the rest of the service was a bit of a blur. Reverend Ben was suddenly standing at the back of the sanctuary, saying a final blessing. Then the choir sang their last closing hymn. Zoey leaned closer. "It's over now, right?"

"Yes, it's done. We can go. Right after this hymn," Lucy whispered back.

The congregation left the pews, and Lucy steered Zoey to the line that filed past the Reverend. "Let's just say hello to Reverend Ben," Lucy told her. "You remember him from the diner, right?"

"Sure I do. He was the first person I waited on. He comes in a lot, too."

Reverend Ben did like the food at the diner. Or maybe it was just the chance to meet up with members of his congregation and friends in town and relax with them outside of the church setting. She couldn't count the times he had invited her to sit with him for some coffee, and he ended up listening to her worries and offering sage advice.

"Good morning, Reverend," Lucy said when it was their turn to greet him. "Thank you for inviting us to light the Advent candles this morning."

"Thank you for taking part in the service, Lucy. You all did a splendid job up there." His gaze turned to Zoey. "And thank you very much, Zoey. It's nice of you to come to worship today and help Lucy and her family."

Zoey smiled and shrugged. "It was fun. Sort of. I got some new clothes out of the deal."

He laughed. "You look very lovely, both of you." He included Lucy with a glance. "Are you coming to the party this afternoon, for the food pantry? It starts at three and I think they could still use a few more volunteers."

"Yes, we are. Charlie is donating some chowder and clam rolls— and some money. The boys are going to help me bring it over later."

"I'll see you later then. Have a good day."

"I'd like to help, too," Zoey said as they walked away. "But I promised Charlie I'd work this afternoon. I don't think he'll let me go with you."

"Don't worry. I'll speak to him about it." Lucy put her arm around Zoey's shoulder and gave her a quick hug. "Trudy will be there, and I'm sure the diner will be very slow this afternoon. Everyone in town is going to be over here at the church," she said with a grin.

BETTY HAD WANTED TO HELP SET UP FOR THE FOOD PANTRY'S Christmas party, but it was a workday for her, which had started at eight in the morning, and was one of the busiest days of the year. The catering company had four parties to run, two in Cape Light, one in Essex, and one in Hamilton. Even though Molly had agreed that Betty could take a few hours off for the church party, Betty felt too guilty about leaving her and Sonia to oversee the madness on their own.

She didn't feel good about it at three o'clock and not even at four. By five o'clock, with one party finished and another at the halfway point, she felt ready to go. But it wasn't until nearly six that she actually made it to the church and walked into the Fellowship Hall.

Her eyes opened in sheer wonder at the way the space had been transformed. Decorations covered the walls and windows, and large glittering stars hung from the ceiling. The overhead lights had been dimmed and softly sparkling Christmas lights added to the festive mood.

There were so many guests and volunteers that the long buffet tables had been set up in the long hallway that led to the church office and sanctuary. But, even with the food in another room, the hall was filled with adults and children.

Everyone seemed so happy, in such a joyful mood. Sheet music had been handed around, and most of the guests were singing

"Deck the Halls." Reverend Ben's wife, Carolyn, sat at a piano near the Christmas tree, playing the lively tune.

Emily Warwick, her old friend from high school—and the woman who had held the mayor's seat for the longest term in the town's long history—beckoned her over. "Betty, come and sing with us." Emily stood beside her husband, Dan, who was holding their little girl Jane up so she could see the song sheet. Emily gave Betty a quick hug. "Everyone's been looking for you," Emily whispered. "They all want to thank you."

"I didn't do that much," Betty whispered back. "It took a lot of people to put this together."

Emily grinned. "You weren't nearly as modest in high school. That must be a trait of maturity."

Betty laughed. "I guess so. Time does make us humble, doesn't it?"

"If we're lucky," Emily whispered back. She held her song sheet so Betty could see it, and they sang side by side.

Betty suddenly realized that the elusive Christmas spirit she had been lacking all these weeks had finally come to her. She smiled as she sang out loud, feeling almost silly.

Then her gaze found the one person she had been looking for— he was already dressed in his red velvet suit and long white beard. Decked out in full Santa attire, Nathan came out from behind the Christmas tree just as the group finished singing the carol.

The kids—especially the little ones—screamed with excitement. Jane Forbes practically jumped out of her father's arms and ran to see Santa.

Emily chased after her. "See you later, Betty," she called over her shoulder.

"Hello, everyone," Nathan called out. "Thanks for inviting me to your party. I can only stay a few minutes but I do have some presents for all the children who are here. Why don't you all come a bit closer and sit down on the floor near me?"

Any child who had been hanging back now raced up closer to Santa. Betty was glad that she stood out of the way. It was practically a stampede.

There were so many children and so many gifts—most bought by her and Nathan on their shopping spree. Santa needed a few helpers to distribute the bounty. Reverend Ben, dressed in a bright red vest over a white shirt and black pants, helped give out presents. He looked a little Santa-like, too, Betty thought, with his long beard and gold-rimmed glasses. Even his reddish-brown hair had gone mostly gray over the recent years. Another couple helped, too. Betty recognized Michael and Eve Piper, who ran the pantry. They both looked very happy, giving radiant smiles as they handed each child a gift.

Standing near the tree, looking on eagerly, Betty noticed Digger Hegman and his daughter Grace. Digger, who was in his eighties and had always worn a long white beard, also looked like another version of Santa—or at least a very tall elf.

The Hegmans had given Betty a very large cash donation toward the party and toward restocking the pantry, with strict orders that she keep their generosity a secret. Betty had been shocked at the sum. Grace ran a small antique shop in town, the Bramble, and lived above the store with her father, who had once been a fisherman. They appeared to be comfortable but by no means wealthy. Now she knew differently. There was a nest egg somewhere in that tiny, cluttered shop, that was for sure.

Betty tried to catch Nathan's eye. But he was focused on the long line of children who came up to him, one by one.

Finally, all the gifts were given out and all the carols sung and the last gingerbread man eaten. Parents rounded up their children and headed for home. Only a handful of volunteers lingered, taking down the decorations and sweeping up wrapping paper and ribbons. Santa had disappeared behind the Christmas tree and then, into some private hideaway—like a classroom downstairs, Betty guessed—to transform himself back into good old Nathan Daley.

As Betty waited for him to reappear, she grabbed a trash bag and joined the cleaning effort.

"There you are," Nathan greeted her, sounding as if he had been waiting all afternoon to see her. Betty was stuffing wrapping paper into the bag and turned at the sound of his voice. "Don't tell me you came just in time to clean up?"

"I got here during the carols. I guess you didn't see me." Betty smiled into his eyes. She had the strangest urge to give him a hug hello but held herself back. It was just so good to be with him again. She felt both happy and peaceful inside at the same time.

He took the trash bag out of her hand. "Put that down. You've done enough. I want you to meet some friends of mine."

Before Betty could argue with him, he pulled her over to a group that was standing nearby. The only person she recognized at first was Reverend Ben. Then the couple the Reverend was speaking with turned, and Betty guessed they were the Pipers, whom she had never actually met in person. "Michael, Eve . . . this is Betty Bowman. Otherwise known around town as Super-Fund-Raiser," Nathan said.

Betty felt her cheeks color at the exuberant compliment.

"We've been looking forward to meeting you, Betty. Nathan's told us so much about you." Eve extended her hand and shook Betty's, then impulsively gave her a hug. "Thank you so much for everything you did. We could never have held this event without your help."

"The donations are still coming in. Whenever we ask how they found out about us or who asked them to donate, practically everyone says 'Betty Bowman,'" Michael reported.

"She's amazing, isn't she?" Nathan beamed at her and slung his arm around her shoulder.

Betty felt her breath catch and couldn't answer for a moment.

"I just know a lot of people in town," she tried to explain. "Most are happy to support a good cause. You just have to ask."

"Well, thank you for asking them on our behalf," Eve said.

"Betty has some really great ideas for fund-raising," Nathan said. "Events you could hold in the spring, to keep the support coming in."

"That would be a big help," Eve said. "Let's get together to talk sometime. We'd love to have you and Nathan over for dinner after the holidays."

Betty smiled graciously but felt a jolt. Did the Pipers think that she and Nathan were a couple? Betty felt a little awkward—but couldn't say that she objected to the idea.

Hold on, Betty. Just chill. Don't make a big deal out of this, she coached herself.

"I'd love to get together. You can call the catering shop anytime," she said.

"Great, we will," Michael said. "And have a very Merry Christmas, Betty," he added.

"You, too," Betty replied.

"We will now," Eve assured her. "Bless you, Betty. See you soon."

Others were walking over to say good-bye to the Pipers and Reverend Ben. Betty was suddenly alone with Nathan again. The party was just about cleaned up. Tables and chairs were being folded up and the floor swept clean with wide brooms.

"Come with me. I need to pack up," Nathan told her. They walked down the hallway and went into the church conference room, which was filled with leftover wrapping paper and ribbon. Betty spotted Nathan's Santa suit in a heap on the table. He lifted it carefully and put it on a hanger, then slipped it into a garment bag.

She picked up the beard and held it to her face. "Ho-ho-ho. How do I look?"

"Your delivery could use some work. But you look very pretty.

No help needed in that department." He smiled at her briefly but sounded almost sad about his observation.

Betty handed the beard to him. He did seem a little low-key tonight, she thought. Not quite in his usual, upbeat mood. "You must be tired. All these parties and performing."

"I am a bit burnt out. But it's almost over. This was the big one."

"Five more days until Christmas," she observed. "Then you're off for eleven months. Even schoolteachers don't have it that good."

"No, they don't. And freelance writers don't have it good at all," he added. "I'm really behind with my work. This year seems worse than usual, for some reason. I'm going to chain myself to the desk on December twenty-sixth and stay there until the first thaw."

Betty didn't like the sound of that. Did that mean she wouldn't see him again until . . . the spring?

Calm down. He's just venting. That doesn't have anything to do with you.

"Sounds pretty gruesome," Betty said, trying to keep her reply on the light side. "If you need a few meals left on your doorstep, just let me know. There are always some tasty leftovers hanging around the shop."

"I'll keep that in mind. There are some leftovers in my office, too, but even the dog won't go near those," Nathan said with a quick grin. He turned away, packing up his boots and wide black belt in a knapsack. Despite their banter, Betty had an odd feeling he wasn't being entirely honest with her.

When he was all packed, he slipped on his leather jacket and they headed outside. Nathan left his bags in his truck, which was parked in the lot behind the church, and then walked Betty to her car, which was on the far side of the green. There had been so many cars in the lot when she arrived, she hadn't been able to find a space.

They walked across the green side by side, not touching at all. Betty thought Nathan might put his arm around her shoulders again, as he had at the party, but he walked along with his hands in his pockets, seeming deep in thought. The village green faced the harbor and the open water was a lovely sight at night, despite the cold wind. It felt good to get outside, into the brisk air and the quiet night.

She thought of the night they met, when Nathan fixed the van for her. That seemed so long ago for some reason, though it had been just a month. But they had spent a lot of time together since and had been in close touch with calls and e-mails about the party nearly every day. Now that the party was over, she wondered where their relationship would go.

He might have been wondering the same thing, she thought. He seemed in such a thoughtful, even serious mood.

"Well, here I am," she said, when they reached her car.

"I'm glad you were able to stop by for a little while. I know how busy you were today," Nathan said.

"I wanted to come sooner, but I couldn't get away," she confessed. "At least I got to see Santa, the highlight."

"Santa is okay. But I think the way people in this town came together and pitched in to get the pantry back on its feet again is the best part," he said. "It wasn't Santa who made that happen, Betty. It was mostly you."

Then he leaned down and kissed her, gently holding her around the waist. Betty was surprised at first, then kissed him back. The feeling of his lips on hers was indescribably wonderful and, for a moment, time stopped and she felt lost in the sensations of his nearness.

When he gently pulled away, she felt a little dazed. The sparkling stars above seemed to be spinning in space. He held her for a moment and pressed his cheek to her hair.

Then he stepped back and smiled. "I'm not sure when I'm going to see you again," he said quietly. He sighed. "I have all this work and . . . well, it's just hard right now. You have a great Christmas and a great visit with your son, okay?"

Betty nodded. She felt as though he was trying to tell her something. There was some message hidden between the lines here, but she couldn't quite figure it out yet.

"Yes, I will. You have a great Christmas, too," she said quickly. He just nodded. "I'll call you."

Betty didn't say anything. She felt a cold knot of dread in her stomach at those words.

"Good night, Nathan. Merry Christmas," she said again. She forced a smile and got into her car, then started the engine and drove away.

She saw him in her rearview mirror, still standing there, watching her car disappear. He looked so sad, so forlorn. Maybe he just gave so much of himself at this time of year that it emptied him out, and he didn't have anyone close to take care of him. To help him fill the well again. Was that what this "I'll call you" business was all about? He was just tired and worn out right now?

Would he really call her or was that actually a good-bye kiss for some reason that she couldn't quite figure out. *Maybe he's just not into you, Betty,* chided a little voice.

Oh, shut up. He's definitely into me. That is clearly not the problem.

Maybe he likes me so much, he's just scared himself. Men were like that. She knew better than most women how that part of the story went.

Betty sighed. She wished she didn't care so much, but she knew she did.

She had bought Nathan a present and had been hoping he would mention getting together again sometime before New Year's Day. She couldn't give it to him now. He seemed to have drawn some sort of line between them tonight, and she didn't want to cross it. She didn't want to look foolish.

She checked her watch. It was only seven thirty. She was due to meet Alex at eight for a late dinner in town, at the Beanery. She didn't really feel like going out tonight. She was very tired and all stirred up about Nathan. But she knew it was too late to cancel on Alex. That wouldn't be right. He had made a generous donation to the food pantry. He had even wanted to volunteer at the party but had to be at the hospital this afternoon.

And to be perfectly honest with herself, it was some comfort to realize that Alex was still waiting for her. He was a great guy and she liked him a lot. Maybe she didn't feel that special chemistry she had with Nathan. But Betty wondered now how seriously she should take that element. It certainly wasn't that reliable a factor, was it?

Alex was the type of man she was used to dating, who shared her tastes and interests—unlike Nathan, who was unconventional, even eccentric, and always surprised her. But Alex was reliable and consistent. When he said he was going to call her, he called. That counted for a lot.

It seemed Molly's prediction was right, though Betty hated to admit it. Nathan was attractive, but he didn't seem interested in the kind of relationship she wanted, something steady and long-term. Not just pure, inexplicable . . . magic.

THE GOOD FEELINGS FROM CHURCH AND HELPING AT THE FOOD pantry party stayed with Lucy into the evening. After dinner, Lucy decided to start her Christmas baking. She always made three kinds of cookies—chocolate chip, molasses spice, and something her family called "Swedish Butter Bombs." Lucy did have some Swedish heritage, and the recipe had come down from her grand-mother on her mother's side.

The first step was creaming the butter with some sugar. Lucy was focused on that task when Zoey wandered into the kitchen.

She had long since changed from her polka-dot dress into blue jeans and a sweater, but still wore her hair back in the wide band.

"What are you doing, Lucy? Cooking something?"

"I'm making cookies for Christmas. Want to help me?" Lucy asked hopefully. "The boys used to help me back when they were younger, but they're only interested in eating the finished product now."

Zoey laughed. "Why am I not surprised? I've never really baked Christmas cookies. Maybe once with my grandma?" Zoey said, trying to remember. "You'll have to tell me what to do."

"You can grab an apron if you like, in that drawer." Lucy pointed to a drawer near the stove. "I always wear an apron, even if I have on grungy clothes. It sort of centers me. You do need to focus a little more for baking. It's not like cooking dinner. You need to follow the recipe more carefully or it can come out wrong."

Zoey nodded with a serious look. "You'd better just let me stir stuff up then."

"Don't be silly. It's not rocket science. It's still only cookies. Here, crack these eggs and put the yolks in this little bowl and the whites in this container."

Lucy could soon tell Zoey didn't even know how to separate an egg, and showed her how.

Once Zoey had gotten the knack, Lucy said, "You've never said much about your real family, Zoey. You must be thinking about them a little, now that Christmas is coming."

"I do think about my grandmother. She was really nice. My brother and I lived with her after my mother got sick. But she got sick, too, and we went to live with my aunt . . . and then that didn't work out either. And then my mom . . ." Zoey stopped, unable to finish the sentence. "I miss my brother, Kevin," she said finally.

Lucy sighed. "It's too bad you and your brother had to live with different foster families. That must have been very hard."

Zoey shrugged. "It was. At first. Then you sort of get used to it. We used to talk on the phone sometimes. I tried to call him a while ago, before I came here, and he never called back. Maybe he didn't get the message or something. I'm not even sure I know where he is."

Zoey had gone into her "tough kid—I don't really care" mode, but Lucy knew by now that that was when the girl cared the most and felt the worst about her life. Lucy's heart went out to her. Her own boys fought like tigers at times, but she couldn't imagine them being split up and unable to see each other or even stay in touch by phone.

"Hey, I have an idea. I could find out from Rita where Kevin is living and take you to see him soon. Would you like that?"

Zoey had been beating the egg yolks and now looked up. "Could you do that? I didn't even know that was allowed."

Her answer gave Lucy's heart another pang. "I can't see why not. If that's the rule, then it's really dumb. We'll have to figure out some way around it," Lucy insisted. "I'll talk to Rita and find out for you."

"That would be great. I'd love to just hang with him awhile." Zoey handed Lucy the egg yolks, and Lucy showed her how to measure the tablespoon of vanilla extract and stir it up again.

"What kind of cookies are we making?" Zoey asked.

"Swedish Butter Bombs," Lucy announced with a small smile. "A family tradition."

"Butter Bombs? Cool."

"The real name is too hard to pronounce in Swedish, so that's what we call them. Okay, this is sort of the hard part, double-sifting the flour," Lucy explained. "You want to get it real fluffy, so the cookies aren't dense."

She showed Zoey how to sift the flour on a baking sheet and put it carefully into the measuring cup with a spatula. "Voilà! Then we mix that into the butter and sugar, a little at a time—"

Zoey blinked. "I thought you said this wasn't hard? It seems hard to me."

"Don't worry. It will be worth it. We'll do macaroons next. That's a total no-brainer, only two ingredients."

"More my speed," Zoey said, handing Lucy the measuring cup again.

"So . . . since we're talking about foster families, you never really told me why you ran away, Zoey. Were you just unhappy there?"

Zoey put a dirty bowl in the sink. "It wasn't the family," she said finally. "They weren't really nice, like you, but they weren't horrible. The thing was, I had this boyfriend. But I didn't like him anymore. I tried to break up and he wouldn't let me. He said some things that . . . that scared me."

Lucy put aside the cookie batter and turned to face her. "You were afraid he was going to hurt you, you mean?"

Zoey nodded bleakly.

"Did he ever hurt you while you were dating?"

Zoey sighed and looked away. "Well, we would argue a lot and he had a really bad temper. But he didn't hurt me. Not really."

Lucy wasn't sure she was telling the entire truth. What did "not really" mean? But she didn't want to bother now getting into the fine points. This was serious, any way you looked at it.

"Did you tell your foster parents about him?"

"There were a lot of kids living in that house—their own kids and three of us extra kids. They got sort of excited and angry if you got in trouble at school or had a problem. Maybe I should have told Rita. I don't know . . . I was afraid I'd just get put back in the system," Zoey admitted. "So I ran away. After I had a fight with him about breaking up. I figured it was better to be on my own and decide things for myself than go with some other family that might be even worse."

"What happened to this boy? Are you still in touch with him?"

"I don't want to be. But he keeps calling my cell phone. For a while, it was out of service. Then I turned it back on last week, with my waitressing money, and I found all his creepy messages. He said he's going to find me. He's not giving up."

Lucy got a chill. "That's against the law, threatening someone like that. Or it should be," she added quickly. She really didn't know what the laws were in these cases. But she was going to find out. First thing tomorrow.

"We'll get you a new phone number right away," she promised. "That shouldn't be too hard. But you need to tell us if you hear from him again, especially if he says he's found out where you are. Does anybody know you ended up in Cape Light—any of your other friends?"

"Just one of my girlfriends, Caitlin. She's my best friend. I talk to her and text like, all the time. But she'd never tell him," Zoey added quickly.

Lucy wasn't so sure about that. News had a way of leaking out when you were that age.

The important thing now was to keep Zoey safe. Until somebody could catch up with this boy and straighten him out. She would have to leave that to Rita.

"Can you tell me this boy's name, Zoey? It's important."

Zoey swallowed hard and looked away. "What's the difference? I don't think he'll really bother me. He just likes to look tough and say stuff."

Like those kids in the mall, Lucy suddenly realized. That's the way they were acting, talking loud and tough. Lucy realized now that Zoey must have recognized one or two of them and didn't want them to see her.

"I wish you would tell me," Lucy said quietly. "It will be easier to help you if we knew his name. I know you're afraid, but we can protect you. You don't have to worry."

"I just can't, okay?" Zoey spun away, nearly shouting at her. "It doesn't matter. I think he's seeing someone else now. Just stop asking me all these questions, okay? I shouldn't have told you anything. What a jerk I am."

She pulled off her apron and ran out of the kitchen. Lucy heard her quick steps on the stairs, the first flight and then the second, up to her room.

Lucy wished she could tell Zoey that she could hide out here forever, that they would always take care of her. But Lucy knew she wasn't free to make those promises. And that was not a good feeling.

Once the cookies were in the oven, Lucy dialed Rita Schuman's number. It was nearly ten o'clock, but Lucy thought the situation was important enough to call the social worker at home.

"I'm sorry to bother you so late," Lucy began. "But there's something I think you should know about."

Lucy quickly related the talk she'd had with Zoey. "I'm afraid this boy might find out that Zoey is here in Cape Light with us. At least one of her friends back in Gloucester knows, and even though Zoey thinks that girl won't tell anyone . . . well, you know how kids are."

"Yes, I do. This is serious. I'm glad that you called me. Did she tell you the boy's name? What school he goes to? Anything like that?"

"I asked her a few times, but she won't say. She's afraid. You know how these things work."

Lucy heard Rita sigh with concern. "I'll make some inquiries at her old school and try to find out who this kid is. We'll have to let the police know. We might need her cell phone for evidence, if she didn't erase the calls. Let me look into it tomorrow, and I'll call you."

"Yes, please. Let me know what happens," Lucy said quickly. This was turning into a much bigger situation than she had expected. The police were getting involved now. But it had to be done. Zoey had to be protected. Lucy would never forgive herself if something happened to her, and she had just stood by and made light of it.

"Um, one more thing," Lucy added quickly. "I was wondering about the steps we would take to apply for permanent custody. I mean, since you haven't found a foster family yet, could we still apply?"

"We haven't found a family. You and your husband could apply if you want to. There would be an interview, an application, and references. There's not much more involved than you've already been through to be temporary guardians," she added. "But what about your husband, Lucy? I got the sense that he was not in favor of that level of commitment. Has he changed his mind?"

Lucy didn't answer right away. She bit down on her lip a second. "I don't know," she said honestly. "I have to talk to him about it again. Zoey has been here for a month now. The boys really like her. She feels like part of the family."

"She seems to be having a good experience with your family," Rita said. "I think you've done very well with her, and I would recommend you if you did apply."

Lucy felt good hearing that. Rita's opinion meant a lot her.

"Something else came up tonight. Before I heard about the boyfriend," Lucy explained. "Zoey would really love to visit her brother, Kevin. I would be happy to take her to him, wherever he is now. Could we figure that out for her? I was hoping they could get together soon, for Christmas. He's the only real family she has left, and it's a shame they've been separated."

"I think it would be good for them to visit, Lucy. I should have thought of that myself. I'll look into that tomorrow, too, and try to make some arrangements. Give me a few days on that one. I'll get back to you."

Lucy hung up the phone just as the oven buzzer rang for the cookies. She pulled out the first pan of Butter Bombs. They were golden brown and looked scrumptious, though they still needed to be rolled in confectioners' sugar. She would put on the final touch, then call the kids down for a taste test.

Maybe Zoey would have cooled off by then, too. She hoped so. For a while there, they'd had such a nice time baking together. Lucy had caught a glimpse of how it could be if Zoey were to live with them permanently.

The high hurdle was Charlie. Wasn't he always?

Charlie's attitude had softened, though not nearly enough. Lucy would start to think he was warming up to the girl, then he would suddenly put down his paper and say, "When is she going to leave anyway? Isn't it time?"

Could she persuade Charlie to make the girl part of their family? Was it worth the argument? Lucy wasn't sure that even if she won, it would be the right way to go forward with this decision. A person needed to open his heart to a child in order to parent that child.

She wouldn't want to take Zoey in if Charlie was going to resent her. It wouldn't be fair to Zoey. If Charlie was going to agree, it couldn't be to placate his wife. It had to come from him, for his own reasons. And right now, Lucy couldn't see what those could be.

CHAPTER NINE

～

"—So all I have left to pick up is the iPod. I should have just grabbed one when I was at Computer Barn last week, but they were out of blue. Lauren has to have a blue one. And then I have to find a briefcase for Matt. I bought one online, but the leather looked a lot nicer in the picture. . . ." Molly was reviewing her Christmas shopping list out loud. Betty didn't mind. She wasn't listening that closely, and Molly didn't seem to notice.

They were in the shop, making appetizers for the last wave of holiday parties. Betty was preparing big batches of hummus in the food processor, blending the chopped chickpeas with lemon, olive oil, tahini, and spices.

"Betty . . . you don't want to turn that into chickpea soup, right?" Molly's voice broke through her wandering thoughts. Betty released the button and stopped the machine. "I'll fix it, don't worry," she said, peering into the processor.

"Is something the matter? You don't seem yourself today."

Molly gazed at her with concern. "Are you still worried about Brian's visit?"

"It's not that. I'm excited about seeing him. He and Tina are coming into Logan tonight. He'll be with his future in-laws until Christmas Day. But he's going to call me, just to let me know he's gotten in all right."

"It's all good," Molly said. "You're going to have a great time with him."

"I think so," Betty agreed. She opened another can of chickpeas and drained the liquid into the sink. The truth was, talking to Nathan had helped put the situation into perspective. He had reminded her that Brian was an adult now and they could talk together, like adults, about their past. Betty had really appreciated that advice. She wanted to thank him again for helping her—if she ever heard from him again.

"I guess I'm just tired," she told Molly. "We've been working like mad- women, and then there was the fund-raising for the pantry."

"I bet you're glad that's over with." Molly shook her head. She was making spinach pies, handling the delicate phyllo dough.

"Yeah, I am. It's a relief," Betty said quietly.

It was a relief to be done with the party preparations and all the fund-raising. But no relief at all to be suddenly cut off from Nathan. It was Wednesday, three days since she had last seen him, but it seemed much longer, especially after being in touch with him so much while they worked on the party. The steady stream of e-mails and phone calls had suddenly dried up. It was a bit of a shock, Betty realized.

"Well, we only have three more events to do and the food deliveries on Christmas Eve," Molly reminded her. "Then our slate is clear. That will be a relief for me," she added. "Except for worrying about my own Christmas Eve party."

"You always do a beautiful job, Molly. You could do that one in your sleep."

"I'm so tired this year, I may have to." She smoothed a layer of spinach filling over the dough and started to cover it with another layer of phyllo.

"I'll cover the food deliveries that day, don't worry. I think you should just stay home all day and take care of your own party."

"Would you do that for me, Betty? That would be great," Molly said. "That would really take a load off my mind."

"It's nothing. Don't even mention it. I know I spent a lot of time the last two weeks working on that pantry party, and you never gave me any grief. So, thanks."

"You're welcome. But I did give you some grief," Molly admitted with a mischievous grin. "You're letting me off too easy. I hope they appreciated all the effort you put in. Especially Santa. Did he thank you?"

Betty nodded quickly. "Yes, he thanked me several times. Everyone did."

"And—?"

"And what?" Betty asked innocently, though she knew what Molly was getting at.

"Did he ask you out? Are you going to see him again?"

"Um . . . no. Nothing like that. He has a lot of work right now. Some big deadline he has to catch up on." Betty tried to sound vague and offhand, though inside her heart ached. "I don't think I'll see Nathan for a while. I mean, we're just friends."

Molly seemed satisfied. "So you've told me. But I was getting a different impression there for a while. And how's it going with Alex? Did he ask you out for New Year's Eve yet?"

Betty looked up at her. "Yes, he did. It's been hard to get together, with both our schedules being so crazy. We had a date last week, but he had to run over to the hospital for an emergency,"

Betty explained. "But I did see him Sunday night, and he mentioned New Year's Eve. Nothing specific, just that he'd like to spend it with me."

"That's an excellent sign," Molly said encouragingly.

Betty had to agree that it was. Too bad she didn't like Alex more. She would have definitely been happy at the progress.

"You're going, right?" Molly pinned her with a look.

Betty met her gaze and looked away. "I think so. But I'm not sure yet what's going on with Brian. How long he'll be staying and when I'll meet his fiancée. Alex said that was fine. I just need to let him know when I figure it out."

"That's sweet. I guess he doesn't want to ask anyone else if you won't go," Molly pointed out. Betty hadn't thought of that, but maybe it was true.

"I'll figure it out. I like Alex. He's a great guy. But right now I'm really thinking of Brian. He's the only man I'm focused on."

"As it should be," Molly agreed. She turned back to the spinach pie and brushed melted butter on the top crust, the finishing touch before slipping the trays into the hot oven.

Betty turned on the food processor again, pulsing more carefully this time so the beans wouldn't turn to mush.

She wished she could talk openly to Molly about Nathan. But she already knew her friend's opinion of him and doubted Molly could offer an objective take on why he suddenly seemed to be running for the hills. Besides, Molly was clearly lobbying for Alex and would only remind Betty that she knew from the start Nathan was not the reliable, consistent type.

Betty realized now that maybe she should have seen this coming. Men scared themselves silly when they started to have feelings. That was par for the course. She had thought about calling Nathan several times over the past few days, but knew that would be too pushy. Too . . . needy. He had talked about work demands, but maybe he was just trying to tell her that he needed some time alone. Some space. What was wrong with that? He didn't owe her any explanations.

Things will sort themselves, one way or the other, Betty told herself. She liked Nathan but if nothing more happened between them, she would survive. She had definitely been through this with men before.

Her distraction over Nathan seemed to have robbed her of her holiday spirit the last few days. Betty was annoyed about that, too. She didn't want to be in some sort of romantic funk when her son arrived. That was just . . . unacceptable.

She decided to focus on the one truly bright spot of her holidays, seeing Brian. She would put aside distracting thoughts of both Nathan and Alex. What she had told Molly was true. There was only one man she wanted to focus her attention on now—her dear boy.

LUCY FELT LUCKY TO FIND A PARKING SPOT RIGHT IN FRONT OF the Clam Box. It was about six o'clock, but most of the shops were still open for last-minute Christmas shopping, and the village was bustling, as if it were a Saturday afternoon. Lucy had worked at the hospital until five and had stopped at the diner to pick up Zoey and take her home. Charlie usually brought her home around this time or a little earlier, but he needed to stay late and close up.

Lucy was so tired, she didn't feel like cooking. She decided to bring something home from the Clam Box tonight. Even though the kids rolled their eyes when they saw the familiar takeout tins, it was convenient for a working mom when her husband owned a diner.

When she got inside she was glad to see that the diner was almost empty. Zoey was waiting on a table with a father and two children, but they were almost finished. The check was already on the table.

"Hi, Zoey. Ready to go?" Lucy asked.

"Almost. I have to wait for Trudy to get back from her break. She just went down the street to pick up a gift at the toy store."

"No problem. I need to bring some food home for dinner. That will take a few minutes anyway. I'll put the order in with Charlie. What should I get for you—or are you sick of looking at this food by now?"

Zoey rolled her eyes. "I'll just have a salad. With a side of fries."

Lucy blinked. "That's a joke, right?"

Zoey's expression was perfectly serious. "I've decided to be a vegetarian. I read about it in a magazine."

"Right." Lucy shook her head and picked up an order pad from the counter. Maybe she could get Zoey to drink a glass of milk or eat a hard-boiled egg with that meal, she thought as she marked down their choices.

Lucy took the slip back to the kitchen and looked around for Charlie. He stood at the big stainless steel stove, looking a lot like a juggling act as he cooked two sizzling hamburgers on the grill side and fixed an order of meat loaf and a side of mashed potatoes. Someone else must have called in for takeout.

"Hi, Charlie. How's it going?" She gave her husband a quick kiss on the cheek. He smiled for a second but didn't kiss her back.

"Okay, I guess. The mixer broke down on me, right in the potatoes. I hope it's just a part, and the motor didn't burn out."

A new motor would be a big bill; even Lucy knew that. "Yes, let's hope. Why do these things always happen right around the holidays?" she said with a sigh. "That reminds me, I need an order of your famous meat loaf for Jamie, and C.J. wants two BLTs." Lucy winced at her older son's order. She should have her nursing license revoked. But it was the holidays. Everyone ate badly. She would get them back on track next week, she promised herself.

Charlie glanced at her. "I guess those boys like their old man's cooking."

"I guess so," Lucy agreed. She was just about to ask for her own dinner, and Zoey's salad and fries, when the sound of crashing glass and two voices arguing in the dining room fractured the air.

It sounded like Zoey was having a fight with a customer.

Lucy turned and raced through the kitchen's swinging doors. Charlie was right behind her.

Lucy reached the dining room and stopped dead in her tracks. A tough-looking boy—tall with a dark buzz-cut and a hooded sweatshirt under a black leather jacket—stood shouting and cursing at Zoey. His face was red with anger and a blue tattoo on his cheek looked like a hideous scar. He grabbed Zoey's arm, trying to drag her out of the diner. When she fought back, he grabbed her ponytail.

Zoey was screaming and struggling. "Let go of me! I hate you! Let me go!"

She used her free hand to throw anything she could grab at him—dishes, silverware, a sugar container, a metal creamer full of milk.

"Charlie, help her. Please, do something!" Lucy screamed, and ran toward the fighting couple. But Charlie got there first. He ran up behind the boy, twisted his arm behind his back, and easily pulled him away. "You stinking piece of trash, let go of her!" He shoved the boy toward the door and pushed him outside. "Get out of here while you can still walk. If I ever see your face again, you'll be arrested so fast your stupid fat head will spin. And don't you ever go near that girl again, got it?"

The boy stared at him for a long moment, rubbing the arm

Charlie had twisted. "Chill, old man. I get your point." Then he gave Zoey one last look. "You're not getting away so easy. I'll be back, Zoey. Count on it."

Charlie slammed the door in his face. Then he went straight to the phone by the cash register. "Is she okay? Give her some ice or something," he shouted at Lucy.

Zoey sat crumpled in a chair, her head pressed against her arms as she sobbed. Lucy rubbed her back to soothe her, but Zoey wouldn't look up.

Lucy's own heart was still racing. What a monster that boy was. They were lucky he was so brazen and walked right in here. What if he had cornered Zoey alone somewhere? Lucy didn't even want to think about it.

"It's okay, honey. It's all over. He went away. Charlie is calling the police."

"No! No police!" Zoey suddenly looked up with a desperate expression. "If the police pick him up, he'll get even madder at me. He found me. He said he would. I can't believe this. I can't stay here anymore. He'll come back. . . ."

Lucy heard Charlie talking to Tucker on the phone. "Yeah, some punk. Must have been about sixteen, seventeen years old. Leather jacket, about my height, dark hair. He had a big blue tattoo on his face. Hard to miss that. I just kicked him out. No, I didn't see any car. . . . Wait, I'll ask her. . . ."

Charlie turned to them. "Who is that guy anyway? Some boyfriend or something?"

"For about five minutes," Zoey said, her voice bitter. "Now he's going to ruin my entire life. His name is Kurt Schmitt."

Charlie gave Tucker the information. "All right. You can talk to her. Come on over. I've got to close up. This place is a mess."

Charlie hung up and walked over to Lucy and Zoey. "Tucker called the patrol cars around town with the description. Says they'll pick the punk up if they find him in town. He needs to make a report. He's coming over to talk to Zoey."

His gaze fell on Zoey, and she looked down at her lap. She seemed ashamed of what had happened.

Lucy put her arm protectively around Zoey's shoulder. "I think we need to go home now. Tucker can come over or call us." She looked down at Zoey and urged her to get up. "Come on, honey, let's go."

The girl seemed worn out and let Lucy lead her through the broken dishes to the door.

"Just like always, leave me with the mess," Charlie grumbled, his hands on his hips. "Now we've got to worry about some thug kid taking revenge on my place. I bet he comes back with some of his hoodlum friends and vandalizes me."

Just like Charlie, more worried about the diner than people, was Lucy's first thought. But then she realized: Charlie was as shaken up as she was. For all his faults, Charlie would never let anyone hurt a child. He had gone after Kurt, like a lion protecting its young. And now, he was retreating into his usual cranky behavior in an effort to get things back to normal.

"Trudy will be back soon and she'll help you clean up," Lucy said. "And Tucker will keep an eye on the place."

"Maybe so. But it's just one more thing to worry about," Charlie said as she and Zoey reached the door. "See what I mean, Lucy?" He didn't say more, but Lucy knew what he meant: That he had predicted that Zoey would bring trouble into their life.

"Oh, hush," Lucy said. "We'll talk about this later."

Lucy didn't want to wait for the boys' food either. She decided to stop at a drive-thru, and bustled Zoey out of the diner and into her car.

She glanced at Zoey as they pulled away and headed down Main Street. Zoey seemed so sad, back to square one. Lucy knew Zoey had understood Charlie's parting words. She wasn't dumb. Lucy felt bad that she'd had to hear that, on top of everything.

"I'm sorry he came around and busted up the dishes and every-thing," Zoey said. "He's such a jerk. Tell Charlie I'll pay for that stuff. Out of my check this week."

"It's not your fault, Zoey. You don't have to pay for a thing."

Zoey stared out the window. "He's going to come back. I know the way he is," she said quietly. "I know you like your friend Tucker, the cop. But Kurt is smart, smarter than Tucker."

Lucy slowed the car and pulled over. She turned to Zoey and gave the girl her full attention. "Okay, he found you. But we were there to keep you safe, Zoey. You need to remember that," Lucy stressed. "I hate to think about what might have happened if you were on your own. So don't get any ideas now about running away. There are ways to deal with people like Kurt, ways that will keep him away from you forever. But you have to trust me to help you. You can't run away again. That would be the worst thing to do. I know that you must be thinking about that now, but you can't do it. Do you promise to stay and let me help you?"

Zoey stared at her in surprise, and Lucy could see that she had struck a nerve, maybe even guessed the girl's thoughts.

"Okay," Zoey said at last. "I'll stick around. Maybe he'll give up." She shrugged and traced some fog on the window with her fingertip. "Maybe Charlie scared him. I thought I'd seen Charlie mad, but that was something else. That was like pit-bull territory."

"Yeah, it was," Lucy agreed. She started the car again and pulled onto the road. If there had ever been an upside to Charlie's anger, this had to be it. She hoped Zoey had told her the truth and would keep her word. If she ran away again, no telling what would happen to her.

THE NEXT MORNING LUCY SET OFF TO MEET RITA SCHUMAN. The night before, when Lucy called and told her about the incident in the diner, Rita suggested that they get together the next day to talk about Zoey's situation and her future.

Meeting at the Clam Box was out of the question. Lucy wanted to talk to Rita away from both Zoey and Charlie. Rita had to make a home visit in Rowley, so they agreed to meet at the Dolce Vita Café in Ipswich, a little coffeehouse that served cappuccino and Italian pastries. Ipswich was only a few miles north of Cape Light on the coast of Cape Ann, but far enough away for some privacy.

"It's too bad you weren't able to get the police over there faster," Rita now said, sipping her espresso. "You could have detained him and had him arrested."

"Maybe," Lucy said. "Guys like that never stay in jail very long, and then they come back and do more harm. How can we help Zoey? How do we protect her? I'm sure she's thinking of running away again. I spoke to her about it—very firmly. I tried to convince her that she has to stay with us, for her own good."

"You said the right thing, Lucy. I'll talk to her about it, too. She can appear before a judge and apply for an order of protection, and this Kurt would be arrested if he came within a certain distance of her."

"Does an order of protection really work?" Lucy asked skeptically.

"It's really just a deterrent. Nothing is one hundred percent foolproof, unfortunately."

It seemed to depend on how persistent this boy was, how obsessed with chasing Zoey—all factors that no one could be certain of. It was all so trying and worrisome.

"I'll ask her about it," Lucy said. "But I think I know what she's going to say. She doesn't have a lot of faith in the legal system."

"I'll talk it over with her, too," Rita promised.

"I guess we'll just have to take care of her, watch over her, until this kid gives up and goes away," Lucy added.

Rita put down her espresso cup. "Did you speak to your husband about applying for guardianship?"

"Not yet," Lucy admitted. "We've been very busy. We haven't had a chance to talk about it." *And I haven't been able to get up the nerve,* she added silently. This latest episode was not going to make Charlie feel more positive about the idea, either. In fact, if he'd had any inclination at all toward keeping Zoey with them, this incident would probably change that.

From Lucy's point of view, the situation really changed things, too. She couldn't abandon Zoey now. Not when the girl's actual safety was at stake. Lucy just wouldn't do it. No matter what Charlie said.

When Lucy got home from work that night, Zoey and the boys were watching a video in the family room. Lucy guessed it was one of those silly comedies, with a lot of "boy" humor. Jamie was laughing so hard, he could barely catch his breath. When Zoey wasn't saying, "Ugh . . . gross!" Lucy heard her laughing, too. That was a welcome sound.

Charlie sat at the kitchen table, paying bills, the table covered with his calculator and paperwork, even though he had a desk at home and another in the diner and could have easily done it in a more private space. He needed to grunt and sigh as he wrote out the checks, ask Lucy questions about charges on credit cards, and generally make a drama out of the process.

Lucy knew this was not a good time to bring up any serious topics. Bill-paying always put him in a foul mood, but she had to talk to him about Zoey and couldn't wait for a better moment.

Lucy heated a pot of soup and brought a bowl to the table. She cleared a little spot and sat down. "Charlie, can I speak to you about something? I know you're busy, but this is important."

He peered at her over the edge of his reading glasses. He was tapping numbers into the calculator and held up his index finger. "One second . . . this water bill is out of control. We need to tell the kids to take shorter showers. Especially the mermaid you've got living on the third floor," he added, meaning Zoey, of course.

She did take a lot of long showers, always washing her hair. But that was a teenage girl thing. They lived in the bathroom.

"I'll talk to Zoey and the boys about that. We all need to use less water—for the environment." Charlie grunted at that. He wasn't worried about the environment; he was thinking of his checkbook. "I met with Zoey's social worker today," Lucy began. "It's not too late for us to apply to be Zoey's permanent guardians. They haven't found a family for her, and Rita thinks that Zoey is doing very well with us. She's come a long way in just a month, don't you think?"

Charlie shook his head and yanked off his glasses. "Please, Lucy. You know how I feel about it. What about that kid who nearly tore my place apart? Is that what I'd have to look forward to if she stays here?"

"That just goes to prove how much Zoey needs us. We can help her, Charlie. We can put her on the right track. We would never have let her get involved with a boy like that. Don't you see? She hasn't had anyone looking out for her. She's a good kid under all the makeup and hair dye. She's a hard worker, too, you have to admit that."

Charlie nodded. "She does work hard. She gets the job done and doesn't complain. But is that a reason to adopt her? Do I have to adopt Trudy now, too?"

Lucy sighed. Were they going to get anywhere with this conversation when he answered her like that?

Charlie sat back and folded his arms over his chest. He stared at the ceiling, appealing to some unseen force in the ceiling fan for patience.

"She just needs a chance, Charlie. I think you see that. She needs to be around people who will help her have more confidence and self-esteem. I think we've already helped her. Rita thinks so, too. I'm almost certain that Zoey has a learning disability and has never gotten proper help for it. That's why she dropped out of school. If we could help her with that, she would at least finish high school, maybe even go on to college someday. Anyone can see she's very bright."

"Send her to college? We have two boys, our own flesh and blood, to send to college. Remember them? Jamie's the young one and C.J. is the big guy."

"Charlie, there's no need to be so sarcastic."

"Well, lately I wonder if you do remember your own children. You're so focused on that girl. You do put her first, Lucy. You have to admit it."

Lucy sighed and stirred the soup around. It was cool enough to eat, but her appetite had suddenly vanished. Had she been neglecting the boys and favoring Zoey?

"I have been giving her a lot of time," Lucy admitted, "but she's needed my help. I don't think the boys have been deprived any."

Charlie shook his head, looking as if he wanted to disagree with her on that point, but instead he stuck to his original argument. "The thing is, Lucy, you want me to start worrying about and taking care of a complete stranger. I know the state gives something toward the support of the child, but we both know we would exceed that. This isn't just about feelings, Lucy. It's about real-life, practical considerations."

It was hard to argue with Charlie's point. It was fine to say Zoey needed a chance and needed help to finish school and go to college. But all this support was not just emotional. It was financial, as well. Just taking her to the mall had made a dent in Lucy's budget, though she had loved every minute of it.

"I'm sorry for her, too," Charlie continued in a kinder tone. "I know I've given you grief, but I think we did the right thing, keeping her here a few weeks. Helping her get back on her feet. But I'm not in it for the long haul, Lucy. I can look down that road and see it's not for me. We can't fix all the problems in the world. It's hard enough taking care of this family, without taking on some troubled girl. I told you she would bring trouble with her, didn't I? And she did. I thought that would have opened your eyes."

Lucy considered his words and even recognized that there was a lot of truth to what he was saying. His concerns were valid. She knew that. But there was more to life than worrying about expenses and budgets and who will pay for what. More even than worrying about what kind of trouble Zoey might bring. Lucy couldn't quite explain it. She just knew in her heart that there was a deeper truth here than Charlie's.

"It opened my eyes to the fact that she needs us even more," Lucy said. "I can't close my heart to this girl, Charlie, and I don't believe that you can do it so easily, either. You act as though you don't care about her, but you jumped right in and protected her without hesitation. That boy could have had a weapon—a knife or worse. You didn't think twice about it."

Charlie suddenly looked embarrassed. As though she had caught him caring about Zoey.

"I heard her screaming and I knew I had to stop it. Anybody would have done the same," he muttered. "And I was worried about the diner," he added. "Of course I didn't want to see her hurt by that bum. But that doesn't mean I want to adopt her and take on her problems. In fact, it just proves my point. That girl brings trouble. She doesn't mean to. Doesn't want to. But she does. A leopard can't change its spots, Lucy. No matter how much you want it to—or how many shopping trips you take to the mall."

His final cutting remark put Lucy over the edge. "You're right.

A leopard can't change its spots. Just like you can't change, Charlie. I'm tired of always trying to persuade you to be something you're not. I understand about money issues. I'm not saying that isn't a consideration. But it makes me sad to see that you can't open your heart to this girl." She shook her head. "I can't say I'm surprised. I've known you too long."

"Sorry to be such a disappointment to you," he said grimly. "She can stay until Christmas. After that, I think she should go. I don't care where either," he added.

Lucy let out a long sigh. She carried the bowl of soup to the sink and left it there.

Then she turned to look at her husband. "Okay. If that's your answer, I guess that's all there is to say. But I promised her I'd help her and keep her safe. I can't see sending her back to a sad, hopeless kind of life again. It doesn't seem right. I promised her I'd help her, and I intend to keep my promise. With you or without you."

Charlie sat back. "What do you mean by that? Is that some sort of threat?"

"It's not a threat. I'm just telling you how I feel. I don't know how or why Zoey came into our lives, but I believe God sent her to our family for a reason. I'm going to help her. Even if you don't want to. I'll do it on my own. I don't know what my alternatives are right now. But I'm going to find out."

He let out a long breath, then scratched his forehead. She could tell he didn't know what to say to her.

She decided there was nothing left for her to say either. They had reached some sort of impasse and Lucy felt frightened. What would she do? She wasn't even sure. But somehow, she would keep her word to Zoey. She was sure of that.

This wasn't the end of the debate with Charlie either. But it wasn't the time to argue anymore. She just wanted to get through

Christmas and not ruin the holiday for her boys and for Zoey. Just three more days. A few days wouldn't make a difference.

CHARLIE LEFT EARLY FOR THE DINER THE NEXT MORNING. LUCY was still sleeping—actually, pretending to be sleeping so that she didn't have to speak to him. Soon after he left, she got the boys and Zoey up and started her day. She only had the morning off but wanted to make some headway with her to-do list. There were about a million chores she needed to take care of to prepare for the Christmas Day family party they were having at their house. It would be mostly her family but a few of Charlie's relatives, too.

She drove into town with Zoey at eight thirty and dropped her off at the diner, then headed over to the post office, which had the long, slow line she'd expected. Lucy was prepared with her travel mug of coffee and a notepad to work on her list.

She had just left the post office and was heading down Main Street when she saw Reverend Ben walking toward her.

"Hello, Lucy. You're out early today."

"I have a little time before I start work today. I wanted to get a few things done on my list."

"Our to-do lists. What would we do without them? Do you have time for some coffee? I hate to be a turncoat, but I was just about to stop at the Beanery." He smiled at her, his kind blue eyes sparkling behind his glasses as he mentioned the Clam Box's main competition.

"I'd love to stop into the Beanery with you, Reverend," Lucy said with a mischievous grin. "Just don't tell Charlie." *He's mad enough at me already,* she nearly added.

They walked together a short distance down the street and entered the café. They were soon seated at a table safely away from the window, Lucy noticed with relief. Walking into the Beanery was like landing on a different planet for Lucy. The place was an alternate universe to the Clam Box. It was shadowy inside—no fluorescents—a long narrow café with storefront windows covered with hanging plants. A tin ceiling and a bare wooden floor added to the vintage décor. Walls the color of pumpkin soup were covered with art, original pieces on display by local artists. The cappuccino machine filled the air with a hissing, steaming sound that blended with soft jazz.

"I wonder if Zoey's ever come in here," Lucy said to Ben after the waitress took their order. "She's never mentioned it. But I bet she has. I bet she liked it."

"How is she doing? She's waited on me at the diner a few times. She seems to have gotten the knack of it very quickly."

"She's a good waitress and a hard worker. Even Charlie has to admit that," Lucy replied.

"He's always looking for a good waitress," Reverend Ben said. "But how long will she stay?" he asked gently. "Has her caseworker found her a new foster home?"

"No, they haven't found a placement yet. Actually, I asked Zoey's social worker if she could slow down a little and let Zoey stay with us for the holidays."

"I see," Ben said. "Well, it looks as if you got your wish."

Their waitress brought the order and quickly served them—a cappuccino and a croissant for Reverend Ben, and an espresso and a bran muffin for Lucy.

Lucy stirred a packet of sugar into her tiny cup. "What I've really wished for," she confessed, "is that we could keep her with us. But Charlie doesn't want to. He seemed about to change his mind a few days ago," she added. "But something happened. . . . This boy that Zoey used to see—a really bad kid—he came into the diner and made a scene. He grabbed Zoey, really hurt her, and tried to drag her out—"

"Really? How awful." Reverend Ben looked shocked. "Did you call the police?"

"There wasn't time. Charlie grabbed the kid and threw him out. I think the boy was scared off, but you can never tell. And now Charlie's got cold feet about letting Zoey live with us." Lucy shook her head sadly. "I'm really upset about it, Reverend. That little girl needs us. She needs to be with people who care about her, who'll take a real interest. You can see how far she's come just in the short time she's been here. Even Charlie will admit that. But . . . he doesn't want the responsibility of taking care of another child. He says we already have two of our own. He keeps calling her a . . . a stranger," Lucy added, as if it was hard to say the word. "She's not a stranger to me. Not anymore," she finished quietly.

"Lucy . . . I'm sorry you're so upset. I didn't realize you and Charlie had come to such a gridlock about this."

"Gridlock, that's what it is," Lucy agreed. "We talked again last night and we just . . . just hit a wall. But I can't give up on her, Reverend. I cannot just go along with my husband to keep the peace this time. I feel as if I've promised that girl that I'd help her and protect her. And I mean to do that." She stared at him, not knowing what else to say. "What should I do? How can I make Charlie change his mind?"

"I don't know that you can," Reverend Ben said honestly. "It sounds as if a change of heart is what's really needed. And that has to come from within Charlie. You can't force him to agree to be Zoey's guardian. That scenario will never work out."

"Yes, I know that. I thought he was getting there, too, but now we're back to square one."

"Don't give up, Lucy. Charlie might still come around to your point of view. Difficult as he may be, Charlie loves you. I've got no doubts about that. And your commitment to this girl is strong. What you do, not what you say, might persuade him. You can only do your best. Then leave the rest to God."

Lucy smiled. "That's what I told Zoey. Well, something like that. I've said some prayers about this, Reverend," she confided, "and I realized that I just want what's best for Zoey. That's the most important thing."

"Absolutely," he agreed. "Though I think you need to consider that the best thing for her in the long run may not be to stay with you, Lucy. As painful as that possibility seems right now, moving on to another home might be in her best interest."

"Yes, I know that." Lucy nodded, feeling suddenly like she might cry. She had considered that possibility of course. But it was hard to talk about it openly.

Reverend Ben reached over and patted her hand. "I don't think you'll need to wait too long for your answer."

"Probably not," Lucy agreed. "For the next few days, I'm just going to focus on giving Zoey—and the rest of the family—a good Christmas. We can share that with her at least."

Ben nodded thoughtfully. "That's a good plan, Lucy. I'll say a prayer for all of you," he promised.

They were soon done with their coffee. Reverend Ben insisted on taking the bill, and Lucy left the tip. Out on the street again, Reverend Ben gave Lucy a gentle hug good-bye as they parted.

"Don't give up hope," he said.

"I won't," she promised.

Lucy felt a little shaken by their honest conversation, but it had been good to open her heart to someone. She was lucky to have run into him this morning, she decided. It had helped her get her thoughts and emotions in order so that she could carry on and do what she had to do. She had meant it when she told Reverend Ben that she was just going to put this all aside for a few days and focus on Christmas. She knew he was right. It would all sort itself out one way or the other. There was not much more she could do.

It was the day before Christmas, and Lucy was thrilled to be home. She had earned some seniority at the hospital over the past few years, and this was the first year she was able to make up time the week after Christmas in order to have days off on both Christmas Eve and Christmas Day.

She was having a full house on Christmas Day and needed the entire day before to prepare for her company. At least she had done her shopping and wasn't racing around at the last minute. But there was still food shopping, cleaning, and cooking to do—not to mention making the house look extra nice and festive.

It was hard to be in the holiday mood with everything so unsettled about Zoey. Lucy had resolved to put those problems out of her mind for a day or so, but that was easier said than done.

Zoey had gone to work at the diner early that morning, and Lucy worried every minute that the girl was out of her sight. She was sure that Zoey, too, was worrying about Kurt coming back. She had to be.

Lucy had tried to take Reverend Ben's advice and pray about the situation. She wasn't sure it had helped her much. She had asked God to protect Zoey and help her find her way. That seemed to be the main thing here. She had prayed He would open Charlie's heart. And she prayed for the wisdom and peace of mind to accept the situation if Zoey had to leave them after all. But above all, she asked God to help Zoey. To make the right things happen for her. Whatever that turned out to be. Lucy didn't presume to know best. She only knew what was in her heart.

Later that day, Lucy was making good progress working down

her list. She stood wrapping a few more presents on the kitchen table before starting on some cooking for tomorrow's big Christmas dinner. The diner had closed after lunch, and Charlie had dropped Zoey off at the house, then headed to the mall for his Christmas shopping. He was the King of the Last-Minute Shoppers, and Lucy knew that he might not be back until late that night.

The boys were home from school early today, too, and playing one of Jamie's video games. Now she had a whole week of that to look forward to, Lucy reflected. Zoey had taken some gift wrap and tape up to her room earlier, to wrap the gifts she had bought for the family.

The phone rang. She expected it was either Charlie, calling to ask about a size, or her mother, checking in again about how many folding chairs Lucy needed to borrow. She picked up the phone quickly.

"Hello, Lucy? It's Rita. I'm glad I caught you in. I have some news for you."

Lucy braced herself. Was this about Zoey's permanent placement? Had Rita found a family? Lucy couldn't think of any worse news to hear just before Christmas.

"I wanted you to know that Kurt, Zoey's former boyfriend, has been arrested. He was caught red-handed stealing a car. I just got a call from the police department in Gloucester. He's been suspected of other burglaries, and stolen goods were found in the apartment where he was staying. Looks like there will be a lot of legal action against him, putting him away for a long time."

Lucy felt so relieved, her body sagged against the table. "That *is* good news. This is much better than having Zoey bring charges against him that might not stick."

"I think so, too," Rita agreed. "He's considered a flight risk, so I don't think he'll be out on bail," she added. "I have some other news for you. I've been in touch with the family that's been taking care of Zoey's brother. They're very open to the idea of the siblings having a visit. They said that you can contact them directly to make plans. Zoey's brother has asked about her, too. They're happy to bring the kids together."

"That's great. Who should I call?" Lucy asked eagerly. She pulled out a pen and paper and took down the necessary information. She could hardly wait to tell Zoey the news. "You've given us a great Christmas present, Rita. And all I got for you was a box of chocolates."

"No problem, I'll take it. You can never have too much chocolate. Send Zoey my love and best wishes for Christmas."

"I will," Lucy said. She wished Rita a merry Christmas and quickly hung up the phone. Then she headed up to Zoey's room.

A visit with Zoey's brother was an important gift, Lucy realized. Something more meaningful than a nice sweater or a pair of stylish boots. But maybe she needed to keep it a surprise until she was sure it would all work out. The girl had had enough disappointment.

In the meantime, she could definitely share the other good news.

She knocked on Zoey's door. "It's Lucy. Can I come in? I have to tell you something."

"Sure, it's open."

Lucy stepped into the room. It looked pretty tidy, she thought, except for the bed, where Zoey sat cross-legged, wrapping gifts.

"Rita Schuman just called. She had some big news. The police arrested Kurt today. They charged him with car theft—and found all sorts of stolen goods where he was living. Rita says he's going to jail for a long time. He can't bother you anymore, Zoey."

Zoey stared at her. "Are you sure? I mean, it's not like they just *think* he did those things?"

"They caught him red-handed, stealing a car," Lucy reported. "Rita said it looks like he might not even be let out on bail."

"Oh, wow. That is something." Zoey let out a long breath, then covered her face with her hands. "I hope he does stay in jail. I hope he rots there. He was so horrible to me. . . ."

She was sobbing. Lucy sat down on the bed next to her and put an arm around Zoey's shoulders, comforting her. "Shhh . . . it's okay now. He's never coming back to hurt you."

Finally, the girl lifted her head, and Lucy saw a trembling smile. She brushed Zoey's hair off her face and smiled back. "There now. Take a breath. You're fine."

Lucy hadn't even heard Charlie come in or up the stairs. He suddenly stood in Zoey's doorway, looking at them. "What's going on in here? What's the matter now?"

"Nothing is wrong, Charlie. That boy who was bothering Zoey has been arrested. He was caught stealing a car. It looks like he's going to be in jail a long time."

Charlie didn't have much reaction at first. Then he looked truly relieved. "That is good news. I'm going to call Tucker. He doesn't have to watch the diner so closely."

"No, I guess not."

"Well, thank goodness I only have to go shopping once a year," Charlie went on. "The stores were insane. I'm going to take a nap. I can't believe tomorrow is Christmas already."

The tone in her husband's voice and the way he shook his head, as if he was utterly surprised by the holiday's arrival, made Lucy laugh. Or maybe that was just sheer relief bubbling up now that the dark cloud shadowing their Christmas had passed.

Lucy stayed with Zoey a few minutes more, making sure she had calmed down. When she finally went back downstairs, she felt as if a great weight had been lifted from her heart. She no longer had to fear for Zoey's safety. But she also felt better about the custody issue. It no longer seemed to be a tipping point in her marriage. She and Charlie were still in a gridlock about it, but this news had given them a little breathing room, she thought. A little space to work things out.

MOLLY AND MATT'S CHRISTMAS EVE PARTY WASN'T OFFICIALLY starting until seven o'clock, but Betty arrived early to help with the preparations. Molly and her family lived just outside of town in an area of new homes. Some people might call their house a McMansion. Those people were probably jealous, Betty thought. It was spacious and comfortable, with all the extras and beautifully decorated, too. Molly had known some difficult years, living in an apartment over a store in town. She had worked hard for this dream house, and Betty thought her friend deserved it.

Amanda, Molly's stepdaughter, met Betty at the front door. "Merry Christmas, Betty. Good to see you." Amanda leaned over and gave Betty a hug.

"It's good to see you," Betty said. "You look so beautiful! When did you get home from school?"

"Just last night. I wanted to get home sooner, but I had too many finals and papers to write."

"Yeah, I hate that, too," Betty teased her. She slipped off her long wool coat, and Amanda took it from her. Amanda was so grown up now, a real young woman. She was in her second year of college, a music major at the University of Vermont. Molly's oldest daughter, Lauren, was in the same year, but attended Boston University down in the city. Molly's younger daughter from her first marriage, Jill, was in her senior year of high school and would be off to college next fall.

No wonder Molly was such a workaholic, Betty reflected. Even though Matt was a doctor, it was hard to have two children in college and one on the way these days. Not to mention little Betty, who was going to be four years old next week.

Amanda led the way to the back of the house. "Molly is in the kitchen. I think she's waiting for you."

Was there a slight tone of warning in Amanda's voice? Betty wouldn't doubt it. Molly was a party professional, who handled huge weddings and even corporate events with ease. But for some inexplicable reason, entertaining her family threw her into a complete tizzy, no matter how many times she did it.

Betty made her way back to the kitchen, admiring the decorations throughout the house. A large Christmas tree stood in a corner of the living room not far from the big stone fireplace. It was a tall tree, soaring up to nearly the top of the room's cathedral ceiling and trimmed in white and gold this year. The mantel and shelves were decked with loops of fresh pine garlands and bunches of variegated holly tied with white satin bows. The tables were covered with rich, cream-colored linen cloths and lace-edged napkins. White roses twined in pine branches made up the centerpieces, and glowing white tapers provided the lighting. Everything looked natural and simple, yet elegant.

"Molly, the house looks beautiful." Betty gave her friend a hug as she stepped into the big kitchen. "I love the white roses with the pine. They look just like those pieces at the Historical Society Christmas Tea we did last week."

"I shamelessly copied them. I was going for a Victorian Christmas look anyway, I guess."

Molly had already set out some platters of appetizers on the big kitchen island that she used for a worktable. Betty could see that the dishes needed some garnish and sauces.

"Want me to work on these?" she asked.

"Would you, please? They're all going to be rushing in any second now. I should have let that cheese sit out. It's not going to have any flavor. And these crab puffs never defrosted. I hope they cook okay . . ."

Betty turned and grabbed Molly by the shoulders. "Look into my eyes. Repeat after me. . . . 'I am a professional, a much sought-after caterer. I always give a great party. This is just my family. It will be great. It will be perfect. Everyone will have a good time . . . It's Christmas, for goodness' sake.'"

Molly just laughed. "Okay, I get the point. You have permission to smack me if I start to go crazy again."

"Will do," Betty promised. She took her own apron from her big tote bag and slipped it on over her outfit, a long velvet skirt and a shimmering satin top. Molly's parties were a little formal, and Betty enjoyed dressing up.

Betty was wondering where the rest of Molly's family was hiding, when Molly's youngest daughter raced into the room. She looked like a beautiful little doll that had somehow come alive, Betty thought, with long dark shiny curls, blue eyes, and dimples—a miniature of her mother. She was wearing a red velvet dress with a white satin collar, lacy tights, and black patent leather shoes.

She ran to Molly and grabbed her around the legs. "Tell Lauren to go away. She's being mean."

"She's just trying to make you pretty, for the party," Molly explained.

"She did a good job, too," Betty said. "What a pretty dress. You look like a little girl in a picture book."

"Let's see how long it lasts. I'm predicting an hour," Molly said under her breath.

Lauren came in next, carrying a hairbrush, followed by Jill. They were also dressed up and looking very glamorous and grown up.

"She won't let me finish her hair. I wanted to make a braid," Lauren told her mother, obviously talking about her little sister.

"I think we're going to have to settle for the wild, curly look tonight," Molly told Lauren.

"Maybe we can sneak that velvet hair band on her later," Betty said.

Molly had so far raised three other girls, so she knew when to pick her battles. Lauren, however, was determined to get her little sister looking picture-perfect. "You'd better let me fix your hair—or Santa won't come."

The little girl suddenly stopped her fussing, and it only took a moment or two of coaxing for Lauren to lead her away again by the hand.

"Betty's all excited. She's at the perfect age for Santa Claus—old enough to understand it and still young enough to believe. I put our house on the list for the Santa from the fire department," Molly added in a whisper. "The volunteers drive around tonight and give out gifts. Janie will love it, too," she added, mentioning Emily's little girl who would also be at the party.

Betty was placing lemon wedges around a bowl of shrimp cocktail. "The town still does that? We used to have him come for Brian."

Betty's thoughts raced. Would she see Nathan tonight after all? She had not heard a word from him since last Sunday and had not given in to the temptation to call. Now that Christmas had arrived, she felt a bit melancholy, wishing she could at least wish him a good holiday. She still had his gift, because there had been no chance to give it to him. And maybe there never would be, she realized.

Matt, Molly's husband, came into the kitchen and greeted Betty with a hug.

"Betty! Good to see you. Thanks for helping Molly. She always says she wants me to help, but then she won't let me do anything in here."

Molly rolled her eyes. "These men . . . can't live with 'em, can't teach 'em how to peel an onion."

"I can peel an onion," Matt insisted cheerfully.

"I think we have that covered. Can you put this tray on the dining room table? Then come back. We have more stuff to take out," she ordered him.

"Will do." He turned with the tray of appetizers as he left the room. "Oh, Alex just called. He's on his way to visit his daughter, but he's going to drop by for a few minutes."

Molly cast a glance in Betty's direction. "Christmas Eve is just full of surprises."

"Yes, it is," Betty agreed. The doorbell rang then, saving her from more conversation about Alex. She heard more guests arrive and could tell that Molly's brother Sam and his family had arrived.

Molly's sister-in-law Jessica came back to the kitchen, carrying a tray of Christmas cookies. "Hi, Betty. Where should I put these?"

"Just put it on the counter. I'll take care of it. . . . Wow, these cookies are beautiful. We could use you in the shop," Betty teased her.

"These were a labor of love. A once-a-year effort," Jessica explained.

Sam came in carrying their little girl, Lily Rose, who would be a year old in February. She looked very sleepy with her head resting on her father's shoulder. "Hey, Betty. Merry Christmas," Sam said with a big grin. Sam had the trademark Morgan good looks, complete with the same dimples, dark hair, and blue eyes as his younger sister, Molly. In fact, so did the baby.

"Merry Christmas, Sam," Betty replied. "She looks just like you. But I guess you already know that." Betty laughed. "Where are the boys?" Sam and Jessica had two older boys, Darrell and Tyler.

"They're still unloading our car. We had so many presents. . . ."

Sam leaned closer so Jessica couldn't hear. "And with such a full car, we couldn't pick up Jessica's mother."

Betty held back a smile. Sam had never gotten along with Lillian Warwick very well, even after all these years. But he tried. She did hear that Lillian's marriage last February to her longtime friend, Ezra Elliot, had softened her edges. But she had yet to see it with her own eyes.

The doorbell sounded again and Betty heard the next wave of guests enter—Emily Warwick, Jessica's older sister and her husband, Dan, and their little Janie. Then Betty heard the unmistakable, aristocratic voice of Lillian Warwick rising above the din.

". . . yes, you may take my coat, young lady, but please do not drag it along the floor. That's a fur coat, not a dust mop."

Did Lillian still have that vintage, moth-eaten mink? Betty shook her head and grinned. "Lillian, calm yourself," Ezra admonished her, his voice calm and amused. "We're hardly in the door. Wait a moment. Is that what I think it is?"

"Ezra? . . . What in the world . . . ?"

Betty heard the group laughing and peeked out just in time to see Dr. Elliot catching his wife of ten months under the mistletoe. He gave her a sweet, solid kiss, which actually made her blush and left her flustered.

"For goodness' sake," Lillian stammered, moving away from the offending decoration as quickly as she could. "Wasn't that silly."

"Wasn't it?" Ezra agreed, straightening his bow tie. "We are still officially honeymooners, Lily."

"So you keep reminding me." She sighed, then settled herself in a big armchair near the hearth. Ezra took her hand and laughed. Betty noticed that Lillian did give him a sentimental look just then. It was true. Marriage had softened her—a bit.

Emily and Dan were still taking off coats while the young

people carted in bags of presents and set them around the tree. Molly was in the middle of everything, directing traffic. In the midst of the confusion a fire truck siren cut through the family chaos.

"What in the world is that?" Matt asked theatrically. He swung open the door. "Hey, look who's coming. Is that Santa Claus?"

Everyone watched as the two little girls—Betty and Jane—ran to the door. Jane still had her coat on, and Dan bent down quickly to zip it up again. "Look, Jane. He's going to stop right in front of Aunt Molly's house. Shall we go out and see what he wants?"

"Maybe he needs directions," Jane said sagely.

"If he does, he'd be the only man I know who would stop to ask for them, sweetie," Molly told her. "I think he knows where he is. And I think he might have presents for you and for Betty."

Matt had put Betty's coat on and along with Dan, they took the little girls out to see Santa.

Betty followed Molly outside and stood near the porch rail, waiting. Betty felt her heartbeat quicken as she strained to see. If it was Nathan out there, what should she do? Wave from here and hope he recognized her? Run down to talk to him? Was that too obvious? He hadn't been in touch in nearly a week now. Shouldn't she be angry at him—or something?

It was dark and Santa was at the very back of the long truck. Betty thought she recognized the suit and beard, but when Santa hopped off the back of the truck and leaned down to talk to the girls, she could see, even at such a distance that it wasn't Nathan hiding under all that red velvet. Her hopes crashed. Her heart sank like a stone in deep water.

False alarm. She wasn't going to get to see Nathan tonight after all.

The two men each held their little girls by the hand and stood back as the crisp night air was filled with the sound of sleigh bells again and the fire truck horn sounded, just for good measure. Then Santa jumped back on and the truck pulled away.

Betty followed the rest of the group inside. She was grateful for the cold night air. It had cleared her head—and even kept her from getting a little teary-eyed out there.

Betty was in the living room, talking with Emily and Dan, when Alex arrived. Betty saw him in the doorway, looking around. Then his gaze found her and he smiled.

He walked straight to her. "Merry Christmas, Betty." He leaned over and dropped a kiss on her cheek.

"Merry Christmas, Alex," she said. She felt glad to see him. She had been enjoying herself but still felt a bit lonely, being the only single adult there. Even Amanda and Lauren had invited their boyfriends over and were having their own party in the family room.

Betty introduced him to Emily and Dan, and they soon got into a conversation about the food pantry, and Emily started praising Betty for all the fund-raising she'd done.

"You don't have to convince me. She did a great job for them. I was very proud." Alex put his arm around her shoulders in an affectionate hug. Betty felt herself tense, though she kept smiling. He seemed to be telling the world—or at least, everyone at the party—that they were a real couple and he had a right to be proud of her.

She couldn't help thinking of the end of the food pantry party when Nathan had put his arm around her the very same way while talking to the Pipers. For some reason, that gesture had felt more natural to her. More . . . authentic? Maybe because they had worked together on the project, it had all felt right with Nathan.

But she and Nathan were not a couple. Anything but. This week of silence should have been enough to convince anyone of that.

Dan and Alex started talking about sailing, one of Dan's favorite subjects. As the two men drifted off to refresh their drinks,

Emily pulled Betty aside. "He's great. Where have you been hiding him?"

"I haven't been hiding him anywhere. We just started dating a few weeks ago. Molly introduced us."

"Good pick. I'll have to congratulate her." Emily chose a crab puff from a tray and popped it in her mouth.

"If you must. But we're still in the 'we'll see' stage, if you ask me," Betty explained.

"Oh, I don't know. You two look good together. Sometimes you can tell how these things are going to turn out."

Betty didn't know what to say. Emily had known her for a very long time. If she thought this was a serious relationship . . . well, maybe it was going in that direction. *Maybe I'm going to be the last one to know,* Betty thought.

Alex was expected at his own family party, which was being held at his daughter's house in Essex. But he didn't seem in a great rush to get there. He loyally stuck to Betty's side, even following her when she went to help Molly in the kitchen.

When it was finally time for him to go, Betty had mixed feelings. Part of her wanted him to stay and keep her company, and the other part felt relieved.

She walked him to the mud room behind the kitchen, where Molly had set up a coatrack. He took down his coat, then said, "I have something for you, a little Christmas gift." There was a small shopping bag near his coat, and he handed it to her. Betty recognized the wrapping from an exclusive, expensive store.

"I have something for you, too, Alex. But I didn't bring it with me. I didn't know you were going to be here. Maybe we should save the gifts and open them together?"

"That's okay. I can wait for mine. You go ahead. I want to see if you like it."

Betty thought that was very sweet. But now she felt a certain pressure as she undid the fancy bow and ripped off the paper. What if she didn't like it? He'd obviously gone to some trouble and spent a lot of money, too. She was just going to have to act excited and pleased—no matter what was in there.

Finally, the box was unwrapped. Betty's eyes widened in awe. She didn't have to playact at all. She was totally surprised and thrilled.

"Alex, I love this perfume. How did you guess?"

He had bought her a bottle of her favorite perfume, a scent so expensive she'd only had one tiny atomizer of it her entire life.

"You mentioned it once to me, don't you remember? We were in a restaurant, and you said that some woman nearby was wearing your favorite perfume. I couldn't remember the name exactly, but I called Molly. She obviously gave me the right information."

Molly. Of course. Betty knew she should have guessed.

Still, it was really lovely of him to think of that and go to the trouble of finding out the right name. He really wanted to buy her something that would please her, something that was her own taste. Not his taste, like some men did.

She leaned over and gave Alex a hug, still holding her perfume in one hand. "Thank you. I love it. That was so sweet of you, Alex. Honestly."

He hugged her back then gave her a kiss. Betty closed her eyes and kissed him back.

Then she heard sounds in the kitchen and suddenly felt self-conscious.

She pulled away a bit, but he wouldn't let her go. "I wish you could come with me tonight. I've told my daughter all about you. She really wants to meet you."

Betty was surprised by his impromptu invitation. Surprised and . . . not at all tempted.

"I'd love to meet her, too," she said quickly. "But I really can't leave, Alex. I wouldn't feel right." She slipped out of his hold, putting a little distance between them.

"Oh, I think Molly and Matt would understand. But that's okay. Another time. But soon," he added. "Any progress on New Year's Eve?"

"I spoke to Brian when he got in Wednesday night, but we didn't talk about New Year's Eve yet. He's staying with his future in-laws until tomorrow. But I promise I'll ask him right away and get back to you."

"Don't worry about it. It's not like I'm going to ask anyone else. I understand if you need to spend the time with him, Betty. I do." He slipped on his long tan overcoat and a fine silk scarf. The coat looked so soft and silky. Definitely cashmere, Betty thought. "I was thinking of dinner at the country club. I know they have live music and dancing," Alex continued. "Why don't you ask your son and his fiancée to go out with us? I'd love to meet them."

"That sounds like a great way to ring in the new year," she replied, feeling more uncertain than she sounded. "I'll talk to Brian and see what he thinks."

Alex seemed pleased with that answer. He leaned over and gave her one more quick peck on the cheek. "Well, I'm off. I'm glad I was able to spend some time with you tonight, Betty," he said sincerely. "Have a merry Christmas and have a great time with your son."

"You have a great Christmas, too. Thanks again for the perfume."

"My pleasure. It's a lovely scent. I look forward to enjoying that gift myself," he confessed with a smile.

Betty hung back as she watched him leave the house. He had given her more than a bottle of perfume tonight. Alex had given her a lot to think about.

* * *

AFTER THE BIG NEWS ABOUT KURT, ZOEY HAD PRETTY MUCH stuck by Lucy's side, helping her prepare for Christmas Day, all afternoon and into the night.

The hours had flown by much faster for Lucy, having Zoey to help her and talk to. And the chores had seemed much easier. As they set out china and checked for spots on the crystal glasses, Lucy suddenly realized that it was well past eleven. In fact, close to midnight.

"These have a few spots." Zoey carefully placed a few wineglasses on a tray. "Should I rinse them off in the kitchen?"

Lucy took the tray from her. "You go to bed. You've helped me enough. I'll finish in here."

"I guess I am a little tired. But when are you going to bed? You have all that company coming tomorrow," Zoey reminded her. "And all that cooking to do."

Lucy shook her head. "Moms don't need as much sleep. You'll see when you're older."

"Some moms," Zoey corrected her. "Other ones never get out of bed."

She was thinking of her own mother, Lucy realized. She kept forgetting how hard the holidays must be for Zoey. Even though she was in a nice, "normal" house now, she still had all her dark memories to deal with.

"Hey, there is one more thing you can help me with," Lucy suddenly remembered. She took Zoey by the hand and led her into the living room. The room was dark except for the lights on the tree. "I love the way the tree looks in the dark like this," Lucy confided. "When I was a little girl I could sit for hours, just looking at it."

"It does look cool. Is that what you wanted me to see?" Zoey stood in the middle of the room, gazing up at the tree.

"Not exactly . . ." Lucy checked a small, painted wooden box on the fireplace mantel. The box, a souvenir from her mother's trip to Italy, stood empty most of the year. But at Christmastime Lucy used it for a special hiding place. Now she lifted the lid and took out a little pack of tissue paper, which held the missing figure from the crèche scene Jamie had set up under the tree.

"Here you go. Jamie usually does this job. But I wanted you to do it this year," she told Zoey. She handed her the packet and watched as Zoey unwrapped it. Inside she found a tiny plaster figure, the baby Jesus, wrapped in swaddling clothes.

"Oh . . . cute." Zoey turned the baby over in her hand. "What do I do with it?"

"Just put the baby in the cradle. Down there, inside the manger."

Zoey stared at the figure in her hand. Lucy thought she was going to respond with a smart remark, but a moment later she bent down and carefully put the figure in its place.

She paused, then shifted the other figures around a bit so they looked even more like they were all focused on the cradle. "Is that right?" she asked Lucy as she stood up.

"Perfect. Now it's complete. It's really Christmas."

"Yeah, I guess so." Zoey pointed to the clock on the mantel. "Look, it's even midnight."

"So it is." Lucy hadn't meant to time the task so perfectly. Some things were just meant to be.

"Our family put up a Christmas tree sometimes," Zoey said. "But we never had a manger and a baby. It looks like a miniature world under there. The way all the figures are standing around in the straw. It looks like a stage where a play is going on. Sort of magical," she said quietly.

"Yes, it does. That's the perfect way of describing it." Lucy put her hand on Zoey's shoulder and gave her a quick kiss on the cheek.

"Thanks for helping me today. I never had so much help with a holiday before."

"No big deal," Zoey said in a faltering voice. "I wish . . . well . . ." Her voice trailed off.

Lucy could guess Zoey's wish. Or at least she believed she could. Maybe because Lucy shared the same wish.

Just before Lucy finally shut off the lights on the Christmas tree, she sent up a quick final prayer. That unlike the baby born on Christmas night, without any real shelter or roof above its head, Zoey would find a real home with them.

BETTY LEFT MOLLY'S PARTY A LITTLE AFTER MIDNIGHT. SHE would have stayed even longer to help clean up, but she needed to get up bright and early the next day and prepare for Brian's homecoming.

A shopping bag of gifts sat on the seat beside her, among the boxes the special perfume Alex had given her. There was also a shopping bag on the floor that held her gift for Nathan. She had found a beautiful leather portfolio that seemed perfect for keeping his articles. Much better than the worn-out cardboard folder he was using now. Betty had bought it on impulse, not even knowing if she would have the courage to give it to him. Now she kept eyeing the box as she drove along the dark road that headed back to the village.

A moment later, as she approached the turn to Nathan's cottage, she suddenly found herself steering down North Creek Road, and driving through the big iron gates on the deserted estate.

She felt a little crazy. And wondered what she was doing there. If Nathan saw her, she knew she would feel embarrassed.

But she drove right up to the cottage and stopped the car just a short distance away.

His truck was there but the cottage was dark.

He was probably sleeping. Or still out working, riding around in his sleigh, she thought with a small smile.

It was now or never, she told herself. She took a breath and drove the car up to the cottage then parked. She had come this far. There was no turning back.

She grabbed the gift, got out of the car, and ran up the porch steps as if she were being chased. She dropped the box by the door, in a place that he couldn't miss, and then ran back to her car again.

Okay, I've broken the sacred rules of dating, Betty thought as she drove off. *I've probably scared him away for good, showing him how much I care. I'll give him one more chance. Then I give up and it's Alex all the way.*

CHAPTER TEN

❧

"*L*OOK AT ALL THIS STUFF. . . . I CAN'T BELIEVE IT. OH . . . I love this shirt. Thank you so much!" Zoey sat in a pile of torn wrapping paper with boxes all around her. Her eyes were bright and her smile as wide as Lucy had ever seen it. Even the ponytail on top of her head seemed especially perky this morning. But after all, it was Christmas, Lucy reflected.

"I can't believe it, either," Charlie said drily. "Lucy, you must have bought half the mall."

"Not quite . . ." But almost. It had been fun to shop for Zoey. Lucy had enjoyed choosing "girl stuff," and she also knew how very little Zoey had of her own. She needed just about everything.

The boys had finished opening their gifts and seemed very happy with their presents. Jamie had gotten more video games and accessories, some books and clothes, and a new skateboard. C.J. had gotten a new phone, clothes, and sports equipment. Lucy and Charlie didn't get as many gifts as the kids, but Lucy was very happy with the things her family had picked out for her. A mug that read "World's Best Mom" from Jamie, and a pretty plaid wool scarf from his older brother.

Charlie had made a grand gesture with an expensive designer purse she had been eyeing and a pair of gold earrings. She knew he was trying to make it up to her for their impasse about Zoey. And she was also sure he knew that what she wanted most this year, money couldn't buy.

Zoey had gotten the most gifts of all. Both boys and Charlie had also bought surprises for her. She seemed to love everything and unwrapped the boxes very slowly.

She had bought gifts for them as well, small, carefully chosen items. A calendar for Jamie with his favorite video game characters, a sports book for C.J., and for Charlie, an expensive oven glove, made from a special material that was practically indestructible. Lucy knew that Zoey must have bought it at a specialty store somewhere and guessed that Trudy had taken her shopping in secret one day.

Charlie couldn't hide his excitement about the oven glove. He tried it on and showed everybody, explaining how he could stick his hand right in the broiler fire and not get a mark.

"Thank you, Zoey. Thanks very much. I always wanted one of these," he told her sincerely.

Zoey gave Lucy two gifts. Each touched her in a special way. The first one Lucy opened was a beautiful ornament for the Christmas tree, an angel to add to her collection. It was made out of papier mâché with a chinalike face and feathery golden wings. It was fairly large and swooped sideways, holding a long golden trumpet. Lucy put it up on the tree immediately, right in the very middle. She knew it would always remind her of Zoey.

The second gift was the collage Zoey had been working on when she first came to stay with them. Zoey had even put it in a frame.

"You don't have to hang it up if you don't want to," Zoey said as Lucy unwrapped it.

"Of course, I'm going to hang it up. I'm going to hang it right here, in the living room." Lucy held the collage up to the wall, covering the antique map of Cape Light Harbor that already hung there. "I'm tired of this old map. We needed something new. This is perfect."

Charlie stared at the collage wide-eyed. "Wow . . . that is something. Looks like a picture in a modern art museum."

Lucy couldn't tell if he liked it or not. But at least he was trying to be nice.

"That's awesome, Zoey. You made it?" Jamie asked.

"It's pretty cool," C.J. agreed as Lucy passed the framed piece around. "I like the drawings in between the cut-out stuff. Neat."

"It's okay. I've made better ones, probably. But thanks." Zoey looked down shyly, taking in the praise. She seemed quietly proud and for once, stopped finding fault with her handiwork. Finally, it was Zoey's turn to open the one remaining gift in her pile. "Last one," she said.

"Thank goodness for that," Charlie mumbled.

She tore the paper off the big box and flipped off the lid. "The boots! You got me those totally hot boots? Oh Lucy, I love them!" Zoey sprang out of her seat and caught hold of Lucy's neck. She gave her a quick hug. Then she turned to Charlie and hugged him, too. "Thank you, Charlie. I know Lucy picked everything out, but I know it's from you, too."

Charlie stiffly patted Zoey's back, not quite hugging her back. "That's all right. You . . . You enjoy them."

He looked back at Lucy with surprise. Lucy grinned at him. She had this funny feeling he was starting to soften up just a little about Zoey.

After a special Christmas morning breakfast with scrambled

eggs, bacon, and loads of leftover cake and cookies, Lucy hustled everyone to get ready for church.

Zoey seemed hesitant, though. "I can stick around here and clean up," she offered.

"Stay home and clean up? Don't be silly. It's Christmas. Everyone goes to church on Christmas." Lucy put her arm around Zoey's shoulders and steered her from the kitchen to the living room. "It's a very nice service. The choir sings carols . . . you'll like it," she promised.

She quickly bent over and handed Zoey a pile of her gifts. "And you can wear your new boots."

Lucy wasn't quite sure which point persuaded her. Or if Zoey was just coming along to be agreeable, but she took hold of the boxes and headed upstairs. Lucy was glad. She liked to have her whole family in church on Christmas morning.

BETTY'S CAREERS HAD ALWAYS REQUIRED WORKING ON SUNDAYS. In real estate, Sunday was the busiest day of the week, and in catering, Sunday was a big day for parties almost year-round. For this reason, and perhaps others, she reflected, she'd never gone to church much. She had taken Brian to Sunday school when he was young, but aside from Easter and Christmas, she rarely attended services herself.

Even though she expected Brian at her house later in the day, she was determined to get up early and get to church this morning. She always enjoyed the Christmas service, and lately she had become more interested in things going on at church, like the fund-raiser for the food pantry. She had decided that she wanted to get involved in more volunteer work. That was her New Year's resolution. It wasn't because of Nathan, she told herself. That wasn't it at all. She had been thinking about this for a while. Though Nathan might suspect less than idealistic motives if they met up volunteering— which would probably be the only way she would get to see him at this rate.

Or maybe here, at church. If she could find him in the crowd. Molly's brother Sam was a deacon and greeted her at the door. "Merry Christmas, Betty," he said, handing her a program. "I think Molly saved a seat for you," he added, showing her the row.

Betty made her way to the pew where Molly and her family made room for her. The service was just about to start, the choir gathering at the back of the sanctuary.

Betty looked around at the sea of familiar faces. She saw so many people she recognized, including Nathan's friends, the Pipers. Eve Piper caught her eye and gave a little wave. Betty waved back. But she didn't see Nathan nearby.

The choir strode in, their long red robes floating around them as they sang "Come All Ye Faithful." Reverend Ben followed in his long white cassock, and took his place at the front of the church before banks of red and white poinsettias. A Christmas tree stood to one side of the altar near the podium, and a crèche had been set up opposite the Advent candles.

Betty sat back, enjoying the music and the prayers. Then Reverend Ben came to the podium for the morning's scripture. "Today's reading is from the second chapter of the Gospel according to Luke, verses fifteen to twenty." He adjusted his glasses and looked down at the large Bible on the lectern. "'When the angels went away from them into heaven, the shepherds said to one another, Let us go over to Bethlehem and see this thing that has happened, which the Lord has made known to us. And they went with haste, and found Mary and Joseph, and the babe lying in a manger. And when they saw it they made known the saying which had been told them concerning this Child; and all who heard it wondered at what the shepherds told them. But Mary kept all these things, pondering them in her heart. And the shepherds returned, glorifying and praising God for all they had heard and seen, as it had been told them.'"

He looked out at the congregation, then put the good book aside. "I just can't help it. After all these years of waking up on Christmas morning, I still feel that same thrill. Perhaps not quite the same as when I ran downstairs to the Christmas tree to see what toys and goodies Santa had left me," he explained, causing many to softly chuckle. "But a feeling of excitement that we all get when we hear that a new life has come into the world. When we learn that friends or kin have been blessed with a new baby. Doesn't that always bring a smile and a warm feeling bubbling up in your heart? So much promise. So much to look forward to.

"That's why, to me, Christmas is a time to look forward with hope and with renewed faith. Renewed by the gift of new life, the birth of our Savior. There is nothing so challenging, so daunting to us, no burden so heavy to our soul, that it cannot be lifted by this news. We celebrate the birth of the baby Jesus, and we are encouraged to lift up our sight with renewed hope and faith and look forward with excitement and optimism. With courage and trust in the future God has in store for us.

"But Christmas is also a time to look back. To relish our memories, our good deeds, our kind acts, the generosity we've shown to family and friends and strangers. And also, more importantly perhaps, to reflect on our actions and examine our hearts. Just like the joyful but nervous expectant parents prepare the baby's nursery—making everything clean and new—we too must also prepare our hearts for the new baby who will arrive and be nurtured there.

"How do we do this? The answer is simple . . . but not so easily done. Just as God the Father sent this child as a messenger of forgiveness, we must look back and make amends to all whom we've harmed. We need to let go of all the anger and grudges and grievances we cling to. That's how we clear out the cobwebs, how we scrub the floor, how we clean the windows so that the pure golden light can stream through today, on Christmas morning.

"And isn't Christmas itself like a window? A good friend, a member of this congregation, pointed this out to me just the other day," Reverend Ben noted. Betty knew who it was, too. She sat up suddenly alert, listening even more intently. "He said, 'You can think of Christmas like a window. We must look back with forgiveness and look forward with hope and joy.'" Reverend Ben paused and gazed out at his audience. How quiet the church was, Betty noticed. Even the fussing children seemed suddenly still.

"I leave you with that image to think about. That beautiful, shining window in a newborn's nursery. Let us try with all our heart to be worthy of this gift of new life. Today, on Christmas morning, let's give thanks for the new babe born in our midst, this precious miracle. And let's look back with mercy and compassion to clean our hearts and cleanse our souls . . . and look forward with hope, love, and faith."

The sermon ended, Reverend Ben returned to his seat. The church was silent and still for a moment. Betty felt very moved by his words. Not just because he had included Nathan's idea, but because of the wisdom and spiritual nourishment the words offered.

Did she hold grudges against people? She thought of herself as a forgiving person, but had she really forgiven her ex-husband for the way he had hurt her during their marriage? Betty knew in her heart that she had never resolved that anger. She had often felt she had earned the right to remain angry with him for the rest of her life. But Reverend Ben was really saying that carrying around that grudge, that cobweb, that dirty smudge on the window of her soul, was hurting her more than it was hurting Ted. And she could never look to the future with true clarity as long as her vision was blocked by this old grievance.

The time had come for members of the congregation to stand

and share any blessings they had experienced or any burdens they were carrying. A few people asked for prayers for family members who were sick or out of work. One or two shared happy occasions, like the birth of a child. Reverend Ben pointed to someone at the back of the church. "Yes, Nathan?"

Betty felt her heart beat a little faster as she turned and caught sight of him. So that's where he had been hiding. Directly behind her.

"I'd just like to thank everyone who helped out or donated to the fund-raiser last Sunday for the Three Village Food Pantry," Nathan said. "The party was a big success. Families received gifts and groceries, and every child left with at least one great toy. They were all very appreciative and asked me to thank you all for helping them have a good Christmas." Nathan paused and looked down a moment. "I know everyone involved worked hard, but I'd especially like to thank one person, Betty Bowman. Without her efforts, we wouldn't have gotten very far."

Finally Nathan looked straight at her. Their gaze met for a brief instant. She saw his mouth turn up a bit. Not quite a smile but almost. Betty couldn't help it; she smiled back without reservation.

When the service ended, Betty filed out with the rest of the congregation. She looked around for Nathan but didn't see him anywhere in the sanctuary. The church was very crowded and it was slow going down the side aisle to the back of the church. She went out to the narthex, missing the line of congregants greeting Reverend Ben. She didn't spot Nathan outside the sanctuary either, and wondered if he had ducked out of church a few minutes early. She had been almost certain he would thank her in person for the gift she left on his doorstep last night.

She headed out to her car, glancing around for his pickup truck in the lot. Maybe he would call later to thank her and wish her a merry Christmas?

Or maybe not, Betty, she chided herself. *One definition of insanity is doing the same thing over and over again and expecting a different result. You've tried with Nathan, so stop banging your head against a wall and expecting it to feel good.*

Besides, she needed to get back home right away, she reminded herself. Brian was coming at two o'clock and she still had a few things to do.

Betty got back to the house at noon and did her last-minute dinner preparations, putting a filet mignon roast in the oven along with the oven-roasted herb potatoes she knew her son would adore. There were string beans and a salad with pears, blue cheese, and walnuts. They would start with the appetizers from the shop, only the most gourmet choices. Brian hadn't really eaten a meal at her house since she had gotten involved in the catering business, and she was determined to pull out all the stops. She hadn't been much of a cook when he was growing up, but perhaps she had caught up a bit now and would impress him.

Betty was so anxious to see him, she knew she was overdoing it. Checking the table a million times and tilting the roses in the crystal vase this way and that. She was fussing with the logs in the fireplace, trying to build a bigger fire when she saw her son coming up the walkway.

She stood up, took a deep breath, then yanked off her apron and headed for the front door. She pulled the door open before he could lift the brass knocker.

"Brian, I'm so glad to see you." She slung her arms around him in a big hug.

"Hi, Mom. Merry Christmas!"

"Merry Christmas to you. Come in, come in. Let me take your bag."

She had forgotten how tall he was. "You look wonderful—so handsome and healthy," she told him. "The Midwest agrees with you." He was a good-looking young man and had always looked a lot like his father. But now Betty saw more of herself in his features—around his eyes and even in his smile.

"You look great, too, Mom. I like your hair like that."

"Thanks, hon. I let it grow out a little. I don't know why. One last fling for my golden tresses, I guess."

Betty led the way into the living room and to the big armchair near the fire. "Here, sit right there. It's very comfortable. It goes back if you want to put your feet up."

"I'm all right, Mom. Slow down," he said with a gentle laugh. Brian took her hands in his and smiled into her eyes. "You don't have to wait on me. I'm going to be here a long time. You'll get sick of having me around."

"I'll never get sick of that, Critter," Betty said, teasing him with his old childhood nickname. "Never in a million years."

They made some small talk about Brian's trip east and he told her a bit about his fiancée's family. They lived in Concord in a grand old house and, from the sound of it, were quite well-off.

"I can't wait to meet Tina," Betty said. "She's a teacher, right?"

"That's right. She teaches special education at an elementary school. She's a good teacher, too. Very patient and warm with the kids. She's a sweetheart. You'll love her."

"She sounds like a great girl," Betty said honestly. Brian had been telling her about Tina for the past year now, ever since they started dating. They seemed to share the same interests and enjoyed life in Chicago, taking in the restaurants, sporting events, museums, and jazz clubs.

"It's funny that you met halfway across the country, and it turns out that her family lives in Concord. She was living just a couple of hours from you, all these years."

"It's true," Brian said. "I guess one of the things that drew us together was the fact that we had both grown up around here and shared a love of New England. We just spoke the same language or something. We could always talk to each other really easily, just as friends. I always felt so relaxed and happy around her. It's not that we never disagree about things. We do. But we've been on the same wavelength from day one."

"Any wedding plans yet?" Betty asked curiously. "I want to help any way I can. I don't want to seem intrusive," she quickly added. "But I am in the business. I can offer some good advice—and some amazing food."

Traditionally the bride's family planned the wedding. But Betty knew that she wouldn't be human if she didn't want some input in her son's wedding.

"I know, Mom. Tina's parents know that, too. The only thing we're sure of so far is that we'll have the wedding around here. Both of our families are here, and a lot of close friends, too. We've made good friends in Chicago, but they'll have to come east, I guess."

"Oh, good," Betty said. "That feels right somehow."

"Tina's parents are throwing a party for us," Brian went on. "They were having friends over for New Year's Eve and the list just started growing, so they're calling it an engagement party now. They want you to be there, too, of course. They're going to call you but they asked me to tell you about it first. Do you have any plans for New Year's Eve?"

Betty was shocked by her son's question. "What could be more important than your engagement party? Of course I'm coming. What a nice idea. They sound like lovely people."

"They really are," he assured her. "I already feel comfortable with them. Oh . . . Dad will be coming with Linda and the kids. They've already accepted."

Betty kept smiling, unfazed. Of course her ex-husband, his second wife, and his new family would be there. She had fully expected that. She still thought of Linda as Ted's new wife, though they had now been married almost as long as she and Ted had. They had two children, a girl and boy. Linda had always been a stay-at-home mom, a model homemaker, tennis, and golf partner. A great hostess, too, Betty had heard, throwing fabulous parties for Ted's business clients.

Betty had been none of those things as a wife. She had been more career-minded and, at the time, thought that Ted was happy to have a wife who was his equal in the business world, influential around town, and even earning a higher salary. Boy, did she ever call that one wrong.

She did believe that after all this time, she had put all that behind her. But for some reason, every time she had to face them at social occasions like this—usually centering around Brian—she felt all the old wounds aching again. It was so dumb and pointless.

"If you're not comfortable about this, Mom, honestly, you don't have to come. Tina and I will understand. You can meet her folks some other time. Maybe we can go out to dinner, just the five of us," Brian suggested.

Had her reverie been that obvious? Betty felt embarrassed. She leaned over and patted his hand. "I'm fine with it. Totally. But I'd love to go out to dinner with them anyway. Let's try to figure it out."

"Great. That would be fun," Brian said.

"Reverend Ben gave a good sermon in church today. I've been thinking about it," Betty told him. "He said that we might think of Christmas as a window—a good place to stop a moment and look at our lives. Look back with forgiveness and look forward with hope."

"That's a nice way of putting it," Brian said. "I like that idea."

"He actually got the idea from a friend of mine who's a writer," Betty explained. "He's a very perceptive, thoughtful person." Then she stopped herself, reluctant to say anything more about Nathan. Her son knew her too well. She knew she would give her true feelings away.

"What I'm trying to say, Brian, is that I've decided to put aside all my grudges against your father. Those you've seen and those you've never seen," she added, knowing that she had always been adept at hiding her feelings for Brian's sake. "I'm going to look back and forgive and look forward in hope. Toward your wedding and your new life. I don't want you and Tina to be burdened with any stress about the past at this very happy time. Or at any time in your marriage. Not coming from me, anyway."

Brian slowly smiled at her. "Thank you for saying that, Mom. I think Tina was a little worried about you and Dad. These brides-to-be hear a lot of stories," he explained. "I know you went through a lot way back when. I know Dad could have been . . . kinder to you," he said honestly. "Now that I'm getting married myself, I can see that. It's big of you to put that all aside for our sake. But that's the kind of person you are. I always knew that. Even when I was too young to really understand it very well."

Betty couldn't help it; she blinked back a few tears. "Thanks for saying that. I did try."

He gave her a quick hug. "We have a lot to catch up on, don't we?"

She nodded and dabbed her eyes with a paper napkin. "Here, have a crab cake . . . don't forget the sauce," she reminded him. "I made that myself. I'm a pretty good cook now."

He sat back, smiling at her. "So I've heard."

LUCY AND CHARLIE'S CHRISTMAS DAY PARTY HAD BEEN A BIG success. Once all the guests had left, Lucy felt herself deflate like a leaky balloon. Charlie and the boys crept upstairs to bed. Once again it was just Lucy and Zoey, staying up late, taking care of all the cleanup that a big holiday party entailed.

"You can go up if you want, Zoey. I'll finish this," Lucy said.

"That's all right. I had too much chocolate cake. I'm totally wired. I wouldn't fall asleep."

Ever since the good news had come last night, Zoey had been in a very good mood, with and without chocolate cake, Lucy noticed.

"It was cool to meet your family. I pictured your mother different, but your sister looks just like you. Except that her hair's a little darker."

"Everybody says that. I'm the pretty one," Lucy added with a grin. "Didn't you notice?"

"I noticed that they were all really nice. Guess that's where you got it from."

"That's how it usually goes," Lucy observed.

"Are you going to work at the hospital tomorrow?" Zoey asked as she loaded some glasses into the dishwasher.

"Not until the afternoon shift. I'm looking forward to sleeping in a little. But I wondered if you wanted to take a ride with me in the morning."

"Want to go back to the mall? I bet there are some awesome sales."

Lucy laughed. "Aren't you sick of the mall? I guess not," she added, seeing Zoey's expression. "I had someplace else in mind. But you might want to stop in a store for a present."

"A present? For who?"

"Remember when you told me that you wanted to see your brother? I asked Rita about it. It took a while, but she put me in touch with his foster family and they said that we can visit him tomorrow."

Lucy watched Zoey's face carefully, unsure of what her reaction would be. Zoey put down the towel she was holding. For a moment she stood very still. Then she turned to Lucy. "Is he still in Gloucester? Why didn't he ever call me?"

"He was moved to another family—they live in Plymouth—soon after you guys last spoke. He's been through a big transition there," Lucy tried to explain. "That's what his foster mother told me. But he's really excited to see you, Zoey. I hope you're not angry with him. You want to see him, don't you?"

It had never occurred to Lucy that Zoey might refuse, but now she realized it was possible.

Zoey might be angry—or maybe just afraid to open herself to more pain by making contact only to lose touch again.

"His foster parents want to meet you," Lucy continued. "They sound very nice. Like good, caring people."

Zoey's eyes narrowed. She looked at Lucy warily. "Are you bringing me so they can check me out or something? To see if they want to take me, too?"

"No, no . . . not at all. I mean, I did wonder why the two of you were split up and if you could be with your brother now. But Rita has already looked into that. This family would love to have you, too, honey. But they can't take any more children right now. This is just a trip to visit your brother. That's all."

Zoey looked relieved . . . and finally, happy. "That will be great. I've been thinking of Kevin a lot lately, wondering if he was having a good Christmas. I guess you've been so good to me, giving me so many gifts and all, it made me feel a little guilty," she admitted. "I'm going buy him something really nice before we go," she decided. "We can stop at some stores, right?"

"Absolutely. But I think his real present will be seeing you, Zoey."

"For me, too," she said. "I mean, I loved all the stuff you and Charlie gave me. But this is . . . different. Thanks. Thanks a lot."

She leaned over and gave Lucy a quick hug around her waist then ran out of the room.

"Good night, Lucy," she said quickly.

"Good night, Zoey. Merry Christmas again."

* * *

BETTY WAS EXHAUSTED AFTER HER CHRISTMAS DAY WITH BRIAN. But it was a good kind of tired, a sweet, contented feeling. They had eaten all the good food she'd cooked and talked for hours, taking out old photos and telling stories. There were so many things in the house he wanted to show Tina, he told her. Betty was secretly glad she'd hung on to his old sports trophies and hadn't totally redecorated his room. It was good to know that her son wanted to show his future wife the house he grew up in, at least for part of his childhood. It told Betty he had good memories of his time here. She did, too. He was still the most important person to her in all the world, and it was wonderful to reminisce and renew their relationship.

She hadn't thought about anything but her son since the minute he had stepped in the door.

But now, late at night, as she put the kitchen in order, she noticed the message light blinking on the phone. She checked the list of calls and saw Nathan's number. She stood for a moment, unsure of whether she actually wanted to listen to this message.

Curiosity won out. She played back the message, finding herself glad to hear his voice again. "Hi, Betty. It's Nathan. I saw you at church, but there was such a crowd. I'm sorry we didn't get to say hello."

Forget the crowd. Try your famous Santa disappearing act, Betty nearly said aloud to the machine.

"I just want to wish you a merry Christmas and thank you for the thoughtful gift. I hope you're having a great visit with your son. I know how much you've been looking forward to it. I know what I'll be doing for the rest of the week—and after. I've got these horrible deadlines, one after the other. I don't know when I'll be able to lead a normal life again. But I hope to see you soon, Betty. . . . Take care."

Betty sat back and swallowed the lump lodged in her throat. She was not going to cry over this. There was absolutely no reason. She knew a brush-off when she heard one, and that message was a classic.

What did I do wrong? she wondered. *Nothing*, she told herself. *It's not you. It's him.*

And that's the truth this time.

He was just another relationship-phobic man, hiding it under that baggy red suit and cute smile. Well, she had learned her lesson. At least Alex was more dependable, more stable—and he wasn't running from her.

When Brian had told her she could bring a date to his future in-laws' New Year's Eve party, a few possibilities had flashed through Betty's mind. She could invite Alex. He would be a great escort. Everyone would be very impressed, especially her ex. But the party was also the perfect excuse to wriggle out of the tentative plans with Alex. And to invite Nathan, instead.

But Nathan was crossed off her list now. There was no way she could invite him or even call him back. He didn't want her to. He had made that very clear.

Just like Santa Claus, it seemed he needed to disappear right after Christmas.

THE DAY AFTER CHRISTMAS, LIFE RESUMED *ALMOST* AS USUAL AT the Bates house. Charlie went off to the diner at the crack of dawn, and the boys slept in. Lucy and Zoey got up at a reasonable hour and then headed off to visit Zoey's brother, who was living in Plymouth, a town at the very start of Cape Cod. They stopped on the way at a big department store so Zoey could bring Kevin a gift.

She wasn't sure what to buy him, torn between a sweatshirt with a surfing decal on the back and a computer game. Lucy loaned her some money so she could buy both. She could tell Zoey was anxious. She hardly talked during the drive and when she did, her words came out in a rush.

"I bet he looks different," she said suddenly. "Taller, I mean. Boys grow a lot at that age."

"Sometimes," Lucy said. Kevin was about five years younger than Zoey, so Lucy figured he was around ten. "When was that last time you two were together?"

"More than a year ago. I remember because I didn't see him for Christmas last year. We just talked over the phone."

"I see." Even though the ride was long and Lucy had a lot of housework waiting at home, she was reminded once more that she was doing the right thing. A good thing, for Zoey.

They arrived at the town of Plymouth, a favorite stop for tourists with all its historical sites. The village was beautifully decorated for Christmas and the streets full of visitors. "This place looks nice," Zoey said, gazing through the window as they drove down a main street.

"This is where the Pilgrims landed," Lucy explained. "The first year, they lived on their ship, the *Mayflower*. See, there's the monument in that park, and you can go on a replica of the ship over there." Lucy pointed as they drove near the harbor. "Maybe we could go sometime, with your brother."

"Oh . . . okay. I'd go see it, I guess." Zoey shrugged then looked out the window again.

Lucy realized too late that the offhand comment assumed Zoey would remain living with them—or at least, stay in touch after she was placed with another family. Lucy didn't want to raise false hopes or disappoint her. She was determined that no matter what happened, she would find a way to keep a relationship with Zoey, to be a person in her life who truly cared and watched out for her. Maybe that would have to be enough for both of them, Lucy thought with a sigh.

Zoey read the directions aloud, and they soon found the house where Kevin was living. It was in a pretty neighborhood where rows of modest, older homes stood side by side. The house was decorated with lights and a wreath. Lucy saw a big swing set in the backyard and a sled and a row of snow boots on the porch.

The front door swung open as they came up the walk. A woman stood smiling at them. "Lucy? Zoey? Good to see you. We've been waiting."

Standing just behind her, a boy with dark hair peeked out. He looked at them warily, then a huge smile spread across his face. With his dark hair and eyes and gangling build, the resemblance to Zoey was unmistakable.

"Hey Lizard Lips—you made it," he shouted. "Still pretty ugly, I see."

"Not as ugly as you, thank goodness," Zoey shouted back happily. He ran up to her, wrapped his arms around her waist, and buried his head in her jacket. Zoey hugged him back fiercely.

"You stink, Lizard," he said, stepping back.

"So do you. What happened to your hair? You look bald."

"I got a crew cut. I like it. It's pretty bad." Lucy knew that really meant good. "You still don't know anything. Come inside. I'll show you my room."

Zoey glanced back at Lucy a moment, but she happily waved her on. Kevin pulled Zoey the rest of the way inside, and they disappeared into the house.

"Hi, there. I'm Mona Crawford. You must be Lucy." The woman who had come out with Kevin extended her hand. She was shorter than Lucy and a bit plump. She had a very pretty face, Lucy thought, with thick brown chin-length hair. She wore a big textured sweater and a long skirt with tall brown boots.

Something about her seemed warm and friendly. Lucy liked her immediately. Mona led Lucy into the house, a center-hall colonial with large rooms on either side of a big foyer. Lucy could see immediately that this house was not destined to be a showcase of period decorating, though it seemed to hold all the sought-after architectural detail—ornate molding, pocket doors, and beautiful plank wooden floors.

But the decorating scheme seemed to be totally family- and child-oriented—with a row of hooks by the door for coats and schoolbags, a low table loaded with books and games in the sitting room, and the floor strewn with shoes.

"We're still picking up after Christmas," Mona explained. "The kids had a blast. I think they're all a little worn out."

"How many children do you have?" Lucy asked.

"My husband and I have two of our own, and then we've taken in three now from the foster system. We really did want a big family, and there are so many kids that need good homes out there."

The Crawfords were clearly special people. If only a home like this could be found for Zoey, Lucy thought. But it was a sad fact that most foster homes did not provide such a nurturing environment, and Zoey probably wouldn't be as lucky as her brother, Kevin.

The two women sat in the living room, and Mona brought in some tea and a plate of cookies. "How long has Zoey been with you now?" Mona asked.

"Oh, not that long. Since Thanksgiving," Lucy told her. "I'd like to be her permanent guardian, but . . . well, my husband isn't ready for the commitment."

Mona nodded. "I understand. It's a very personal decision. It works for us, but it's not for everybody. We'd love to take Zoey and reunite the kids," she went on. "But we just don't have the space. Zoey would be the only girl and especially at that age, she needs her privacy."

"She really does," Lucy agreed. "We're lucky to have a spare room for her, with her own bathroom." She felt guilty, as if she wasn't stepping up, doing her part.

Mona seemed to sense Lucy's feelings and smiled gently at her. "It's great that you asked Rita to find Kevin so we could bring the two kids together. It's important that they stay in touch and don't lose track of each other."

"It means a lot to Zoey. I know she misses him. There's really not too much we can do for her. I mean, meaningful things. I can give her a nice room to sleep in, or buy her some new clothes. But staying close to her brother is even more important."

"You've done a lot, Lucy," Mona assured her. "I know how Kevin was when he came to live here. I'm sure Zoey was in the same state, or even worse. I can see there's already a good bond between the two of you."

"I wish I could do more," Lucy said honestly. "But . . . it's hard."

The conversation moved on to lighter topics, comparing how they both spent Christmas, and discussing the sights in Plymouth.

Mona showed her a picture of all her children together, along with her and her husband—it was a stair-step row of boys who all looked different but somehow jelled as a family. Love was really the glue that held it all together, Lucy thought. The family had gone on vacation last summer, a camping trip in Maine. Kevin was holding up a live lobster, waving it over everyone's head. It was a perfect portrait of a happy family.

"Where is everyone?" Lucy asked suddenly. "It seems sort of quiet in here."

"My husband took the three big ones bowling, and the youngest went to a movie with a friend. We wanted Kevin to have some uninterrupted time with Zoey. It can get a little rowdy in here. We were afraid the rest of them might upstage the reunion."

"That was very thoughtful of you," Lucy said.

"Let's go and see what they're up to," Mona suggested. "Maybe they'd like a snack."

Lucy followed Mona upstairs to Kevin's room, which he apparently shared with one of his foster brothers. Lucy saw a set of bunk beds and two desks.

Zoey and Kevin were sitting on the floor, playing a board game. "How are you guys doing up here? Having fun?" Lucy asked.

"I'm beating her. As usual," Kevin bragged.

"I'm letting him win. I don't want to hurt his feelings," Zoey explained. Though Lucy could tell from her tone and expression that was just an excuse. She really was losing to him.

When the game was done, they came downstairs and Mona served some fruit, cheese, and crackers. Finally, it was time to go. Zoey and Kevin hugged good-bye in the foyer. Lucy saw Zoey close her eyes a moment, patting her brother's back. He was already wearing the sweatshirt she had bought him.

"Good-bye, Lizard," Kevin said sadly.

"I'll see you again soon," Zoey promised. "You can call me. My phone is working again. And I'll call you. At least once a week, okay?"

"Okay." He smiled for a second and stepped away. Mona put her arm around his shoulders in a comforting gesture.

Lucy put her arm around Zoey's shoulders, too. She seemed forlorn, reluctant to part from her brother.

"I'll make sure of it," Mona promised Zoey. "Good-bye, dear. Good luck. Both of you."

Zoey didn't say much on the way home. A visit like that was a double-edged, bittersweet situation, Lucy knew. There had to be a letdown afterward.

"Tell me something," Lucy asked her finally. "How did you get that nickname Kevin calls you? What is it . . . Lizard Lips?"

Zoey smiled for a second. "Yeah, the little punk calls me that. He made it up just to annoy me. He used to have this pet lizard, a gecko or something. It scared me, and I would scream and run away if he brought it like, anywhere near me. And also, my real name . . . my real name isn't Zoey," she said quietly. "It's Elizabeth. So my family used to call me Liz."

"Yes, I know, but I won't tell Jamie or C.J. about that," Lucy promised. "We don't want it to catch on back home, right?"

Zoey shook her head. "No, we definitely don't."

Lucy was glad to see her brighten again for a moment. But realized she'd done it again.

She had said "back home," as if Zoey belonged there and would stay forever. That wasn't right. She had to stop talking that way. But it was hard. And getting harder every day.

LUCY STOPPED AT THE DINER THAT NIGHT ON HER WAY HOME from work. She knew that Zoey was at home and thought it was a good time to talk to Charlie. She wanted to make one more try at persuading him. She knew what he would say, but she couldn't let it go. Not after seeing Zoey with her brother this morning and talking to Mona Crawford.

The place was empty; even Trudy was not at work tonight. Lucy didn't know why Charlie opened up the day after Christmas. It was just force of habit, she figured, and he got like a restless tiger around the house when he wasn't working.

She walked up to the counter and saw him cleaning the grill with a metal brush. The grill had to be hot for a good scrubbing, and Lucy noticed that Charlie was wearing the special heat-protecting glove that Zoey had given him. The mere sight of it gave her a little courage.

"Hi, Charlie. How's it going? Did you have any customers tonight?"

"It was pretty quiet. I had some time to work on the mixer. I need to head down to the restaurant machinery place in Needham for a part. I don't know when that's going to happen."

"It wouldn't kill you to get out of the diner for a few hours. Jimmy can cover for you," she noted, mentioning their part-time cook. "He told me he wants more hours."

Charlie put the wire brush aside and pulled off the glove. "This glove thing is great. I don't know how I've managed without it."

"It was very thoughtful of Zoey to find that for you."

"Yes, it was. There's more to that girl than meets the eye," he admitted. "How did it go in Plymouth? Did she like seeing her brother?"

"They had a wonderful reunion. They really missed each other."

Charlie wiped down the counter with a cloth. "That was nice of you to take her down there. I have to hand it to you, Lucy."

Lucy was surprised by his comment. He usually didn't notice these things. "I still don't know if it really did any good. Zoey seemed sad afterward. She has so much on her shoulders, Charlie. So much baggage." Lucy had never admitted this to Charlie before, fearing he would use it as another point against applying for custody. But it was true. There was no sense denying it.

"Yes, she does. That girl's been through a lot. But she's not nearly so snippy and smart-mouthed as she used to be. I think it's helped to live with a normal family. I think she's coming along."

Charlie was actually saying a few good things about Zoey. Not that Lucy would have described their family as "normal," but she sensed an opportunity to push her case.

"She is coming along. I think we've helped her," Lucy said. "I think we can help even more. You know how I feel. Are you thinking you might agree that we could become her foster family?"

"Oh now . . ." Charlie ducked his head and started wiping a different section of the counter. "Don't put words in my mouth, Lucy. I didn't say that."

"I know. But I'm asking. I think you know that she's a good kid, and she just needs a chance. Would you reconsider? Would you think about letting her stay with us?"

He sighed. "I'm willing to see how it goes," he said slowly. "When do we have to know?"

"Rita said Zoey could be moved anytime now. She held off working on the placement until the holidays were over, but she's probably started looking for a family again. I really think we need to make a decision, Charlie. We could miss the boat here."

She knew this was a boat her husband would be willing to miss, to wave at with relief from the shoreline. But she also sensed he was considering hopping aboard.

"Oh, Lucy . . . I'm thinking. Honestly. The girl is growing on me," he said finally. "But this isn't my final answer. I still need some more time."

"I understand," Lucy replied. "Just don't take too long."

Charlie's answer was vague, but Lucy felt encouraged. She got up and grabbed the broom, happy to help clean up and close down. As Lucy swept a path around the diner, she let herself hope that things with Zoey just might work out after all. She thought back to her conversation with Reverend Ben and wondered if he was right. Maybe her own commitment to helping Zoey had finally penetrated Charlie's heart.

Chapter Eleven

⌒

Betty spent the Monday after Christmas with Brian. They visited Molly in the shop, ate lunch at the Clam Box, then walked through the village, stopping at some of Brian's favorite old haunts. Brian was meeting an old friend from high school for coffee, so Betty left him in town in the late afternoon and walked home.

She was taking Brian and Tina to dinner that evening. It would be her first meeting with her future daughter-in-law. The reservation was early, and Betty had a lot to do to get ready—a major overhaul, she'd call it. But there was something she needed to do before she left for the evening. She was glad Brian was out so she had some privacy.

She dialed Alex's phone and he quickly picked up, sounding happy to hear from her. "Betty, I was just thinking of calling you. How is your son's visit going? Are you having a good time?"

"It's great to have him here. Everything's going very well." She took a breath and pushed on, to the main point of her call. "I did want to get back to you about New Year's Eve, though. Brian's future in-laws are having an engagement party on New Year's Eve, and of course, I have to go. I'm sorry, but that means I won't be able to see you, Alex."

"Oh . . . that's all right. I understand. This is important." He sounded disappointed, and Betty felt bad about that.

"Maybe I can meet him some other time then, before he goes back to Chicago."

"Maybe," Betty said hesitantly. "Alex . . . I have to be honest with you. I've been thinking about our relationship. I've really enjoyed getting to know you these past few weeks and spending time together. Your attention has been very . . . flattering," she added.

Oh, this was so hard. No matter how many times she had to say it.

She heard him sigh. "It's all right, Betty. I think I know what you're trying to say."

"You do?"

"Yes, I do. I had a sense that we weren't quite on the same page when I saw you on Christmas Eve. You seemed . . . distracted."

"Did I? I'm sorry—"

"It's okay. No need to apologize. These things either work out or they don't. We've both been here before, right?" he said philosophically.

"Right. You are a terrific guy," she said honestly. "A real catch."

He laughed. "Thanks. I feel the same about you, Betty. You have a happy new year."

"You too, Alex," Betty said quietly.

She hung up, suddenly wondering if she had made a horrible mistake. A single woman her age didn't meet a man like Alex every day. He was good-looking, successful, smart, and kind. Molly was going to pop her cork when Betty told her that she'd dumped him.

But the truth remained. Alex might be a catch, but not the one she wanted in her net. It was unfair to keep encouraging him. The upcoming engagement party had just made everything clear to her. If she had invited Alex to be her escort, it would have sent a certain message—that she felt the same about him as he did about her. Which she did not. He deserved to be with someone who could return his feelings.

I did the right thing, Betty decided. Not the easy thing, but the right thing.

She had been so busy with Brian that she hadn't thought about Nathan much these last two days. Now she felt a twinge. She hadn't known him very long—about the same amount of time she'd known Alex—but with Nathan it just worked. That was the marvelous, mysterious thing about a genuine attraction. And that's why it was still hard to realize it was over.

There wasn't much time left to get ready for dinner. Betty ran upstairs to shower and change. She wasn't even sure yet what she was going to wear. She wanted to look her best for this special occasion but didn't want to look overdressed or too formal. Most of all, she wanted Tina to like her.

Betty had insisted that she was taking the couple out and had made all the arrangements, choosing an old but elegant restaurant on the water in Newburyport, known for wonderful food and a quiet atmosphere. Tina's parents weren't available to join them, which was just as well, Betty thought. Meeting her son's fiancée and his future in-laws at once might have been overwhelming, and she was nervous enough to meet Tina. She really wanted to get to know her future daughter-in-law. As she and Brian left the house, she sent up a little prayer that the evening would go smoothly and everyone would get along.

Tina was already at the restaurant. Brian spotted her immediately in the waiting area. Betty knew he saw her just from the way his entire face lit up. They raced toward each other and kissed hello.

She was just as Betty imagined from her pictures, petite with dark brown hair and big gray-blue eyes. She had beautiful skin and a heart-shaped face. She was as pretty as a model, Betty thought, and very sophisticated-looking, in a dark blue wool dress and black heels.

"Tina, this is my mom," Brian said, introducing them.

"Mrs. Bowman, I'm so excited to meet you." Brian's fiancée extended her hand, then leaned over and gave Betty a real hug.

"It's Betty . . . and I'm thrilled to meet you," Betty said honestly.

Betty knew in an instant that her prayers had been answered. Tina was not only beautiful but sweet, bright, and very down-to-earth. Betty was charmed by her warmth and her cheerful personality.

They all had a lot to talk about since Tina had grown up in the area, and there was, of course, talk about the wedding, too. Betty asked Tina about her teaching and was impressed by Tina's knowledge and her obvious love for children. She would someday be a wonderful mother, Betty thought, and that was a lovely thing to look forward to.

"So you two seem pretty settled in Chicago," Betty said. "Any chance that you'll ever move back east?"

"You never know. Maybe someday. Anything can happen." Brian reached out and took Tina's hand.

Betty knew that Tina's father was an estate attorney with a very successful practice. There was certainly a chance that Brian could join his firm someday. But for now, she could understand why her son wanted to strike out on his own, in his own territory. There was time enough for these things to unfold.

When dinner was over Betty paid the check, brushing off her son's protests. "I hardly get to see you, dear. And this is such a special occasion. Please, it has to be my treat. Don't argue with your mother," she teased him.

"All right. Thanks, Mom. That was great."

"It was perfect, Betty. Thank you," Tina added.

It was perfect, Betty thought. *And so are you, dear,* she wanted to add. She suddenly realized she had not only been nervous about Brian's fiancée liking her, but she had been worried about what type of girl he'd chosen. *What if I didn't like her or I thought she wasn't the right person for him?*

As they left the restaurant and Brian walked Tina to her car, Betty practically sighed aloud with relief and gratitude. She liked this girl and would soon learn to love her. Just as her son did. That was a blessing.

"She's just wonderful, Brian," Betty said as she started her car. "She's so bright and charming. I can't tell you how happy I am that you've met such a wonderful girl."

"I think so. But it's good to hear you say it, too." Brian smiled at her in the dark and she suddenly realized how much her opinion mattered to him.

"I think she's just terrific," Betty assured him. "It was hard for me to imagine a girl good enough for you," she said honestly. "But you've made a wonderful choice."

"Oh, I had a good idea what to look for," he said. "Someone just like you, Mom."

"Thanks, honey. That's very sweet of you to say. But . . . was I really a good mother? You can tell me honestly. We're both adults now."

"Of course you were." Brian seemed surprised by the question. "Where is this coming from?"

"Oh, I don't know. I've had some time to think, waiting for your visit. Especially since you got engaged. It made me . . . think about the past a lot. I was looking back and thinking that I really worked too much when you were young. I wasn't there for you enough. Was I so focused on my job that you felt neglected?" She rushed on before he could answer her. "I guess I felt sort of driven. Especially after your father left. It helped me to work, to feel productive. . . . And I wanted to make a good living to support you and save for your education. Especially when your father remarried and had more children," she added.

"I understand that, Mom. I really do."

"Do you? Well, maybe now you do," she conceded. "But back then, I'm afraid that in some ways, I didn't pay enough attention to you. The little things—being there when you got home from school. Baking cookies. When you asked to go live with your father and his new family, it hurt me very much," she admitted. "But I agreed, because I thought it was what you really wanted, to live with a big family. I missed you a lot. But I just wanted to do what was best for you, whatever made you happy. It wasn't because I didn't want you with me," she said firmly. "I'm not sure you ever understood that."

"I never felt that you didn't want me with you," Brian replied. "When I got home from school sometimes I did feel a little lonely. But I was busy, too, with sports and my friends. I think it taught me to be more self-reliant. And it wasn't like we were ever out of touch. You called me about a thousand times a day." His reminder coaxed a small smile.

"I did call you a lot, didn't I? You're lucky that was before cell phones. Then I really would have embarrassed you."

Her son laughed. "Let's not even go there."

They had arrived home, and Betty pulled the car into the driveway. Brian sat facing straight ahead, and she wondered if she had said too much. Had she just ruined their wonderful evening?

She was ready to get out of the car, but her son looked at her, seeming reluctant to end their conversation.

"I never knew you felt that way, Mom. I have to admit, I was just a kid and I wasn't thinking about your feelings. Looking back, I guess I was mad at the both of you for breaking up our family."

"That was only natural, Brian. Of course you felt that way," Betty said quietly.

"There was more going on at Dad's new house, with the baby, and it just seemed like more fun. And Dad did push the idea every chance he got," Brian added. "Maybe he was trying to prove something to you, but I didn't see it that way at the time."

"Yes, I know. You were stuck in the middle. We were fighting over you. That wasn't fair to you."

"Or to you," Brian added. "I can see now that Dad could have been kinder to you. And I—I wanted to please him. I knew that you loved me, no matter what. Maybe that's why it was easier to leave your house and live with him," he explained. "I guess that sounds a little convoluted . . . but I just realized it now when we were talking. I knew that you loved me no matter what choice I made. I guess I was never as sure of Dad's love."

Betty felt a lump in her throat and couldn't speak. She had never thought of it that way either. "And I always will love you, no matter what," she promised him. "I'll always be here for you—and for Tina."

"I love you, too, Mom. You're one in a million." Brian leaned over and gave her a long hug. When he leaned back he said, "I'm really glad we had this talk."

"I'm glad, too," Betty said honestly. "It was time. You're starting a new phase of your life. But having a son get married is a new page in my life, too."

THE GOOD FEELINGS FROM THE NIGHT BEFORE CARRIED BETTY right into the next day. She felt a weight had been lifted. Her heart was at ease, knowing her son had chosen a wonderful wife. And she was also glad that she had seized the moment to talk about the past. She felt ready now to face the New Year and the big party Friday night at the Carvers' house.

Brian needed to work in the afternoon on a brief that arrived via e-mail. He had his laptop with him, of course. Betty set him up in her home office and then headed out for a walk to the village. It was a crisp, clear day with bright winter sunlight reflecting off the newly fallen snow.

The air was so cold and sharp, it almost hurt to take a deep breath. But she was happy to get the exercise. She had been eating too many rich foods and missing her workout at the gym. She had promised herself she would be in great shape for her birthday in February, and that big five-o deadline wasn't very far off now.

She had never imagined she would be facing this milestone alone. She had always believed she would be in a serious relationship by now, if not remarried. But that's how life goes, Betty reflected. You just never know until you get there.

Still, she was determined to have a good new year and a good birthday anyway. She knew she had a lot to be thankful for and a lot to look forward to. She had been blessed in so many ways. She had to focus on what was right in her life right now, not what it lacked.

Betty walked down Main Street, not really having a destination in mind. She decided to drop by the shop and check in on Molly. Molly had been wonderful about letting her have the entire week off to visit with Brian, even though her own daughters were home now, too, for their school break. "But I see the girls all the time. You never get to spend time with Brian. You take the entire week, Betty, and don't argue with me," Molly had ordered her.

It was definitely a slow time in the catering business, except for one or two New Year's parties on the schedule. Sonia, their best helper, was also taking time off this week because her little boy was home from school, so Molly was really stuck there all alone. Betty thought she might appreciate going home a few hours early today. With Brian working, there was no reason why she couldn't give her partner a break.

Molly was happy to see her and just as happy to hear that Betty would mind the shop for a few hours. "Thanks, Betty. You're a pal. So, are you ready for the big party Friday night? What are you going to wear?"

Betty had told Molly about the engagement party—and also about turning down Alex's invitation. Molly had looked a little disappointed but hadn't said much about it. Betty had a feeling that after a short period of recuperation, Molly would be back with another eligible bachelor in Betty's age range.

"I have this black velvet dress with a draped neckline. I've only worn it once and I could perk it up with some dangly diamond earrings."

"Perfect." Molly nodded in approval.

"I hope it still fits when it comes back from the cleaners. The holidays haven't done my hips any favors."

"Just grab a pair of Spanx and go for it," Molly urged her. "And I want a full report on Saturday." She hugged Betty tight and gave her a quick kiss on the cheek.

"Do I have a choice?" Betty teased. "Don't worry. I'll call you and give you the scoop."

Molly's blue eyes widened. "You'd better." Then she smiled and scooted out the door.

After Molly left, Betty decided it was a good time to look over their accounts. During the holidays, funds flew in and out of their bank account and their bookkeeping got a little wild. Best to start the new year with that area in order, too, she thought.

She had been working in the office for a while when she heard the bell on the shop door sound. She stepped out to the shop and saw a woman walk in, her face partly hidden by a big bouquet of flowers. When she put the bouquet down, Betty quickly recognized her. It was Eve Piper, who ran the food pantry.

"Hi, Eve," Betty greeted her. "Are you planning another party so soon?"

"Not yet, though we did love your food." Eve smiled and held out the flowers. "I'm glad I found you here. These are for you."

"For me?" Betty was surprised but took the bouquet, a mixed bunch with roses, snapdragons, colorful mums, and leafy greens. "These are beautiful . . . but why are you giving me flowers?"

"Michael and I wanted to thank you again for all your help with the Christmas party. We're sending out letters to all the businesses and people who donated, of course. But we wanted to do something special for you."

"That's sweet of you, but I really didn't do that much. That party was all Nathan's doing. I was just . . . just Santa's helper," she said, though she felt a little twinge at the silly joke.

"That's funny, he says the same about you."

Betty didn't answer at first. It was hard to talk about Nathan, especially with his friend.

"How's he doing?" Betty asked at last, careful to keep her voice casual. She put the flowers down on the counter. "I haven't seen him in a while. He told me he's stuck in his house. He has this big deadline or something. And he won't be out until spring?"

"He is stuck in his house," Eve agreed, giving her a curious look. "But it's not because of a deadline."

"Oh? That's what he told me." That news made Betty feel even worse. Now she knew she had gotten the brush-off.

Eve looked a little puzzled. "I guess Michael and I had the impression that you and Nathan were . . . well, closer. I mean, from the way he talks about you."

Betty took a breath and stared down at the flowers. "We're friends. Or we were. I really don't know what's going on with him now."

"I see." Eve nodded, her expression thoughtful.

"Is he okay? Is something wrong?" Betty asked quickly.

"Nathan needs his friends now," Eve said. "He needs our help. I think that you could help him, Betty. I know he cares for you."

"What's wrong? How can I help him?"

"It's a hard time for Nathan," Eve began. "Christmas brings back a lot of memories. He . . . retreats. From everyone. This year seems worse than ever," she added. "Did you know that he lost a child?"

Betty nodded. "I know a little about it. He didn't really tell me, though. He let me read some of his articles once, and I saw an essay he wrote about the subject. I wasn't even sure it was autobiographical. We never got to talk about it."

"His daughter, Leah, died about five years ago. A sudden, severe infection. Nathan and his wife tried to stay together after but, as it often happens, the grief was too much and the tragedy broke up their marriage."

"How sad. He lost everything at once," Betty said.

"Yes, he did. It all happened around Christmastime. He tries to distract himself, with all his charity work, especially around the holidays. But after the holidays, it's even harder. This year he didn't even come over on Christmas Day. He made some excuse the night before. But we knew the real reason. And we haven't heard from him since then. We're very worried about him."

"I am, too," Betty said quietly. All this time, she was feeling hurt, rejected—when it wasn't about her at all. Nathan needed her help and she hadn't even seen that. She felt very selfish and self-centered.

"Have you and Michael gone to his house?" Betty asked.

"We've tried. But he won't open the door. I told Reverend Ben," Eve added. "But Nathan won't see him either."

"Do you think he'd see me?" Betty asked.

"I don't know," Eve said honestly. "It's worth a try. We would have told you sooner, but we just thought you knew."

"I understand. No need to apologize." Betty reached out and touched Eve's hand.

I should have guessed there was something more, just by the tone of his voice on the phone, she thought. She was mad at herself for writing Nathan off. She could have called him back, just to say hello and see how he was doing with his work. That's what a friend would have done. But she had let her ego get in the way and made it all into some silly game.

"What are you going to do?" Eve asked her.

Betty met her glance for a moment, then picked up the bouquet. "I'm going to put these beautiful flowers in some water," she said, heading to the kitchen. "Then I'm going to close early and go over there."

Eve looked relieved. "I was hoping you would say that. Will you let us know how things turn out?" She took out a card and left it on the worktable. "Here are our numbers, the pantry and the house."

"Yes, I'll let you know," Betty promised. "And thank you for coming over here today. I wasn't even supposed to be here. Wasn't that lucky?"

Eve smiled. "I'm not sure luck had that much to do with it. God has His ways of working these things out. I have a feeling he picked you out for this job, too."

TEN MINUTES LATER, BETTY CLOSED THE SHOP, JUMPED IN HER car, and drove to Nathan's cottage. She pulled up front and parked behind his truck. It was not quite dark, but the temperature had dropped well below freezing. There was no light in any of the windows and no smoke rising from the chimney.

She walked up to the door and knocked, at first in a reasonable way. And then harder and even harder, nearly rattling the old door on its hinges. "Nathan, I know you're in there. Open up," she called out to him.

She didn't hear a sound inside and wondered if he was sleeping. She walked the length of the porch and tried to peek through a window, but she couldn't see a thing.

She walked back to the front door and called in a loud voice. "Nathan? Please just come to the door. I'm not going away until I speak to you. . . . If you don't come to the door, I'm going to come through one of these windows. I mean it."

Betty paused, checking the window frame and wondering if she could even make good on her threat. That would be a new one, even for her—feeling so desperate to see a man, she broke into his house.

She approached the far window on the porch, which opened into the living room. There was a screen on the window but no storm window. The screen looked easy to remove, she thought. The shade and curtains were drawn, but she could see the top sash and tried to figure out if it was locked. She was pondering these questions, about to work on the screen, when she heard a dog barking. She quickly turned to see Rosie bounding out of the woods.

Nathan followed a few steps behind. He stared at her but didn't smile. She wondered if he had heard her tirade at his front door.

"Just hold perfectly still. She thinks you're breaking in." His voice was serious, but Betty could tell from his eyes he was teasing her.

"I am breaking in. Or about to," she confessed. "What is she going to do—lick me to death?"

Proving Betty's point, Rosie jumped up to greet Betty, stretching up to lick her face.

"Down, you silly hound." Nathan came up on the porch and tugged at the big dog's collar. Then he looked at Betty. For a long moment his eyes seemed to devour her. Then he quickly looked away.

"Well, here I am. You've seen me. I'm alive and well. Mission completed," he said in a flat tone.

"You're alive," she agreed. "But you look pretty awful."

"Thanks. I've been working on that."

He did look like a mess, his beard overgrown and his hair all mussed and matted.

"So you have been working on something," she said pointedly.

He glanced at her and shook his head. "I'm sorry I lied to you, Betty. I didn't know what to say."

"I understand now. I saw Eve today. She told me what happened to you. The night I was here and I read your writing . . . I saw an article about your daughter, Nathan. I didn't know what to say. I wanted to ask you about it but . . . I thought maybe that was too private. Maybe I should have said something though."

"What difference would that have made?" He sighed and looked down at his boots. "It's cold out here. You want to come in a minute?"

Betty nodded. She was shivering.

Nathan opened his front door and they went inside. He shed his jacket and turned on a few low lights. The place was a mess. He swept aside a pile of newspapers so she could sit on the couch.

Betty took a seat but kept her jacket on. "Don't worry, I won't stay long."

"You don't want to catch anything, you mean?"

"I don't want to bother you . . . too much." She sat back and opened her down jacket. "You say it wouldn't have made any difference. I think it would have. I would have had some idea of what you're going through. I thought you just . . . just didn't want to see me anymore, and I didn't understand why. Was it because I was going out with Alex Becker?"

Alex had called her once when she and Nathan were together. She knew that Nathan had noticed.

"I knew you were seeing somebody. I didn't know if it was serious or not," he admitted. "The real reason I dropped out on you is because I'm such a mess. Betty, I'm not the guy for you. I'm just . . . not in your league. I mean, just look at you. And look at me."

"I am looking at you," Betty said quietly. "You need a shower and a shave but otherwise, I have no complaints."

"You know what I mean. You should be with a guy who's more your type—successful and together. You don't belong with a none-too-successful freelance journalist, who sidelines as a part-time Santa. That's not good enough for you, Betty."

"Really? I think I should be the one to decide that," she said firmly. "And you should have told me all this before I sent Dr. Becker packing."

He tried to look unaffected by that news, but Betty saw an encouraging flicker in his eyes.

"Look, Nathan . . . let's just put all this dating stuff aside. I'm here first as a friend. I care for you. I want to be there for you." She reached forward and took his hand, feeling relieved when he didn't pull away. "Losing a child . . . that's the worst thing anyone could go through. I can't even imagine it. But we—I mean, *all* your friends—we understand that you're hurting. So don't shut us out. Please. We want to help you through this. This isn't a time to be alone."

"I know. But I can't help that. I just feel like . . . like I failed her. I couldn't protect her. It's such a helpless, frustrating feeling. I know, rationally, it wasn't my fault. Leah caught a virus that turned into an infection, and there was no medication that would knock it out. It just . . . took over her body. Logically, that wasn't my fault. But it still feels that way. I was her father. I should have figured out some way to keep her safe." He let out a long breath and stared down at his hands. "Every year at this time, I go through this all over again. . . . I can't let it go."

Betty knew she could never imagine his despair. She wasn't sure what to say to him.

"I don't know how anyone gets over that kind of loss," she said at last. "But what about that line from your article about Christmas—that Christmas is like a window? Reverend Ben even quoted it in his sermon."

Nathan shrugged. "I told him about it. I had to ask him a question about some bit of scripture I might put in there." He sighed and ran his hand through his scruffy hair. "What does that have to do with this?"

"You have to look back and forgive yourself. You have to look back with love . . . and love yourself and accept that you did everything you could to save her. It wasn't up to you at all, Nathan. Don't you see? We can never understand a tragedy like that. But you can't blame yourself for it either. God doesn't blame you," she said finally. "Do you think you know better than He does?"

He stared at her, then let out a long sigh. He stood up suddenly and walked over to the fireplace, then knelt down and started building a fire.

She could tell he didn't want to talk anymore. She decided it was time to go. She wasn't sure she had helped him at all. But at least she'd tried. Eve and Michael would be relieved to hear that he was physically all right, she thought. Maybe now he would let them visit, too.

She suddenly remembered her son was at her house and she hadn't even called him. She stood up. "I'd better get going. Brian must be wondering what happened to me."

"How is Brian? How is your visit going?"

"It's been great," Betty said. "We had a good talk last night. You were right. He is an adult now. He does see things differently."

Nathan nodded, looking pleased. "I'm glad that went all right. . . . Well, thanks for going out of your way like this. I feel like you're always doing things for me, Betty. You're always helping me. Maybe someday I can make it up to you."

There was a hopeful note, she thought. She decided to pounce on it. What did she have to lose?

"There is a way you can help me, Nathan," Betty said. "Not someday either. If you really want to pay me back, you can help me this Friday night."

She wasn't sure where she found the courage to toss out that challenge to him. Once the words had come out, she wondered if it had been a terrible—and even insensitive—idea. Or was it a good idea? A little jolt to shake him up and call him back to the land of the living?

"Friday night—New Year's Eve? What kind of help do you need on New Year's Eve?" He rose and looked at her curiously, wiping the fireplace soot from his hands with a towel.

"I've been invited to a party to celebrate Brian and Tina's engagement. It's Friday night, down in Concord, and I don't have a date . . . and I'm really not looking forward to going alone."

She had prepared herself to face that fate bravely, without any qualms. Until she saw him again, Betty realized. And now she couldn't stop thinking about how much better it would be to have Nathan at her side.

"A party? You want me to go to a party with you?" He asked the question as if she had been speaking a foreign language and he wasn't sure he trusted his translation.

"Yes, I do. And it's a fancy one, I expect. I'm going to wear a black velvet dress and diamond earrings," she warned him. "You'd need to wear a suit. . . . Do you own one? I mean, one that's not red velvet?"

"I think I have one somewhere," he said vaguely.

Betty was tempted to laugh but forced a straight face. "Well, if you were sincere about your offer, I need your help. I'm afraid to face all those people and my annoying ex-husband and his extremely perfect wife," she confessed. "I need . . . backup."

Nathan rubbed his bearded chin. She could see he was thinking about it but not persuaded. "You'll be fine. Those in-laws will love you. And your ex-husband will wonder why he ever asked for a divorce."

"I'm sure that's true," she countered. "But . . . then I'll be wishing I had a friend to witness these social victories."

And someone to hug me at midnight, she nearly added, *when everyone else is grabbing their significant other.* He was the perfect man for that job, too.

"Will you just think about it?" Betty asked him. "I wouldn't ask you if I didn't really need the favor."

He gave her a quizzical look. "You won't be ashamed to bring a department-store Santa with you?"

"I would be proud," Betty said. "I've come to see that it's a very important job. And you'll have the most interesting job in the crowd, that's for sure."

Before he could argue further, she turned and walked to the front door. "You need to pick me up at six. I'll be waiting. And remember, I'm the only *nearly* fifty-year-old woman who still believes in Santa. Don't let me down."

"I HAVE TO WORK TOMORROW, BUT I SHOULD GET HOME AROUND eight," Lucy told her family. They were having dinner on Thursday night. "We'll get some pizza and watch the New Year's Eve shows on TV."

"The boys want to go bowling tomorrow," Charlie said. "I'll close the diner early and take them."

Charlie rarely closed early, even on a holiday. Lucy was glad he was taking some time off to do something special with the kids.

He glanced at Zoey. "Do you like to bowl, Zoey? You can come with us."

Lucy was surprised by Charlie's invitation. Zoey looked surprised, too. "I tried it once or twice. I'm not very good at it."

"Neither am I," Jamie said. "You can be on my team."

That did seem to make sense in a strange way. Lucy had to smile.

"Oh, there's nothing to it. You just stand there and throw the ball. We'll show you how," Charlie told her. He took the bowl of string beans and added more to his plate.

The phone rang and Lucy leaned over to see who was calling. They had such little time together, she didn't like to interrupt dinner with telephone calls.

But it was Rita Schuman, she noticed, so she quickly picked it up. "Hi, Rita, what's up?" Lucy stepped away from the table, into the dining room.

"I just wanted you to know, there's more news about Kurt Schmitt. The police and the district attorney's office are building a case and trying to tie him to a string of home robberies now. They want to question Zoey about what she saw and heard during that relationship."

"Question her? You mean, as a witness?"

"Yes, as a witness. She wouldn't be implicated in his wrongdoing. It's nothing like that. But they need more testimony to make the charges stick."

This was serious, Lucy thought. She glanced over at Zoey. They had all thought this situation had gone away. But it was back again, uglier than ever.

"I'll talk to her about it," Lucy said. "What if she doesn't want to give her testimony?"

"If they want it enough, they'll get a judge to write a subpoena. I think it's best if she goes in willingly. The police will ask her questions and take a statement. It shouldn't take that long. She may never be called to court. It may never even go to court if there's enough evidence against him," Rita pointed out. "This is one way she can help put him behind bars, where he belongs. Have Zoey call me later. I'll talk to her about it."

"Yes, of course."

Lucy glanced into the kitchen. Her family had finished dinner and had started to clean up the kitchen. Charlie and Zoey at least. The boys were throwing smashed-up paper napkins at each other and making explosion sounds. Zoey got into the fray and squirted C.J. with the hose from the sink. They were all acting goofy but having a lot of fun. Even Charlie didn't try to stop them.

She hated to drag a dark cloud over the household again with this news. But there was nothing she could do. This hurdle had to be faced.

"What was that all about?" Charlie asked when she came back in the kitchen.

"I'll tell you later," Lucy said quietly. "Hey, guys, if you're not going to help, just move along. I thought you were going to watch a movie tonight? Better start it, it's getting late."

She was glad to see that when the boys left, Zoey stayed in the kitchen. She had taken the sponge mop from the broom closet and began wiping up the water on the kitchen floor.

Lucy put her hand on Zoey's shoulder. "Let's do that later. Sit down a second. I have to talk to you." Zoey looked alarmed but sat down.

Charlie looked worried, too, and came over to the table. "What's this all about, Lucy?" he said before Zoey could.

Lucy related the news from Rita Schuman.

"I can't go to court and talk against Kurt." Zoey's expression had changed from alarm to sheer terror. "Are you crazy? What if he doesn't go to jail, or he gets out early or something? He'll kill me."

Lucy put her hand on Zoey's, trying to calm her down. "Zoey, honey, that's not going to happen. He's going to be put away. For a long time. But the police need your help. They need to make sure their case against this guy is airtight."

"Of course the police are going to say that. Like it's a TV show or something. But you don't know how it works. Guys like Kurt get away with stuff all the time. Kurt's not going to end up in jail. He's going to get released—and come after me—before you even know it. You people are so blind."

They hadn't seen this side of Zoey in a long time, her snide, smart-mouthed personality.

Lucy was taken aback but not really surprised. Zoey was frightened, like a cat backed into a corner. She had to lash out.

"Okay, young lady. That's enough," Charlie cut in. "We're trying to help you out. That's all we're doing here. No need to talk like that to Lucy."

Zoey glanced at him a second, then stared down at the table. Lucy felt her drifting away from them. Retreating to some dark, private place.

"Zoey, the thing is, if you don't go willingly to talk to the police, they'll order you to come, and if you don't go even then, well . . . you'll be in a lot of trouble. It's better to just go and get it over with. I know it's scary. But we'll be there with you. And Rita will probably come, too. Maybe we'll even find a lawyer."

Zoey looked up at her. At least she looked as if she was listening again, Lucy thought.

"A lawyer? Do you know how much a lawyer costs?" Charlie said sharply. "Who's going to pay for that?"

"I am," Lucy answered without even looking at him.

"Great," Charlie said. "There goes our retirement fund."

Zoey covered her face with her hands and burst out crying. "I'm so sorry. . . . I don't know what to do. Why does this stuff always happen to me?"

"It's not your fault, honey." Lucy sat down next to Zoey and rubbed her back. "And it's not such a big deal—just a mess we have to clean up for once and for all. It's going to be okay, I promise. We'll get through this and just put it all behind you."

She glanced up at Charlie for a moment. He seemed about to say something, then turned and left the room.

That night, Lucy slept with one ear open. She was afraid Zoey might try to run away while everyone was sleeping.

Charlie rolled over and put a hand on her shoulder. "What's the matter? Can't you sleep?"

"I thought I heard a noise. It was nothing. . . . Charlie, what if Zoey decides to run away again? She's so afraid to give testimony against that boy."

"Yeah, I know. It's not a pretty situation, is it? What can we do? We're doing all we can for her. If it's not one thing, it's another with that girl."

"Charlie—" Lucy began to protest.

"I like her, Lucy," he went on. "I can't say that I don't. But she has problems, and we can't solve everything for her. Right now, the truth is, I'm sorry we ever got involved."

Lucy felt tears fill her eyes. She rolled to her side so Charlie wouldn't see her cry.

She knew there was some truth to what Charlie said. They could only do so much for Zoey. They couldn't keep her under lock and key. She felt sorry, too, in a way, that they had gotten so involved in Zoey's life. If she hadn't, it wouldn't hurt so much, Lucy knew. She couldn't do anything about that either. That's the way it was when you opened your heart to someone, anyone—even a stray cat or dog. There was always the risk of heartache and regret. But what would life be without taking that risk—without making those connections? Without giving of your own self to someone in need?

Lucy wished she could give the girl even more—a stable, permanent home with their family. But she could see that this last twist in Zoey's story had set them back. Maybe irrevocably.

Chapter Twelve

~

BETTY WAS DRESSED AND READY FOR THE NEW YEAR'S Eve party well before six. She sat in the living room waiting for Nathan, distracting herself with a magazine. But she couldn't sit still and crossed over to the window every once in a while to look outside for his truck. She was glad Brian had gone down to Concord earlier to help Tina's family prepare for the gathering.

She had told Brian she might bring a date to the party, but she wasn't sure. Brian didn't ask any questions, though the look in his eyes said it all. Wasn't this occasion too important to be left so open-ended? And it was New Year's Eve besides, when everyone seemed to be paired off like geese.

The clock on the mantel chimed the hour. It was definitely six. She waited a few more minutes, returning to the magazine but barely seeing a word of print. She could hear every sound in the empty house. The waiting was unnerving. She rose from her chair with a sigh and decided it was time to go.

Nathan wasn't coming. If he was just running late, wouldn't he have called? Yes, he would have, and now she just had to face the harsh truth and get going herself, or she would be late for her son's big night.

Betty caught a glimpse of her reflection in the hallway mirror. She'd had her hair done, had a manicure, and had taken special pains with her makeup. She hoped she wasn't going to start crying now and make a big mess.

She wasn't really mad at Nathan. She'd given him a choice, understanding that he was in a bad place right now. But if she ended up getting raccoon eyes tonight on top of everything . . . well, then she'd really be annoyed with him.

Betty sniffed and dabbed at the corners of her eyes with a tissue. A sharp knock sounded on the door and she turned, not quite letting herself believe it was Nathan. Her neighbors were having a party. Maybe they were just coming by to borrow something.

She pulled open the door, trying hard not to get her hopes up.

But there he stood, looking so handsome she hardly recognized him. He'd had a haircut and a shave and seemed so polished and groomed, he practically . . . glowed.

He smiled at her and ducked his head. "What a look. Did you give up on me?"

"Actually . . . yes, I did."

"Professional hazard. Santa always has to keep 'em guessing."

"Very funny," she said. She did feel a little mad at him, she realized. But when he met her glance and smiled into her eyes, she felt her heart fill up with gladness and a sweet peaceful feeling, so that there was no room for any other emotion.

"I got the suit," he reported, stepping back for Betty's appraisal. "The salesman helped me pick out the shirt and tie."

Betty looked him over from head to toe. The well-cut navy blue suit had been matched with a light blue shirt and a burgundy silk patterned tie.

"That salesman has good taste," she said decidedly. "And you look pretty good in real clothes."

"Thanks. So do you." She felt herself practically blush as he looked over her outfit, a black velvet gown that draped gracefully to the floor. She had added only hanging diamond drop earrings and a necklace with a single teardrop diamond pendant.

"It's not too much, is it?" she asked nervously. She had wondered about this dress when she put it on. She didn't want to be overdressed and embarrass her son.

"You'll be the most beautiful woman there. But I already knew that."

Betty just smiled. His compliment did make her feel beautiful and confident. Ready to take on any challenges the night might bring.

"I knew there was a good reason I invited you," she said quietly.

Nathan just laughed. "Shall we go? I think we'll just make it in time." He took her coat and held it out so that she could slip it on. Betty grabbed her small silk handbag and they left the house.

They drove out of town and soon reached the highway, heading south toward Concord. On the ride down Nathan told her that since her visit he had spoken to both the Pipers and Reverend Ben, and had even made it to his desk for a few hours.

Betty found that news encouraging. Nathan's tone was light, but Betty sensed how hard it truly was to surface from his deep well of sadness. Which made her appreciate his presence even more.

The drive passed quickly and they soon found themselves in Concord, a beautiful village about forty minutes outside of Boston.

"I haven't been here in ages," Nathan said as they drove through the village center and passed the famous Concord Inn.

The Carvers lived in a grand old colonial with a long, columned porch across the facade. The house was set on a large plot of sloping property, and they drove up a circular driveway to the front entrance. With a wreath and a glowing candle in every window, the house looked to Betty like a painting on a Christmas card.

"Wow," Nathan said quietly. "Quite a house."

Betty glanced in the front windows as Nathan found a parking spot. "And it looks like quite a party."

They entered the front door and were greeted in the large foyer by waitstaff, who took their coats and handed them each a glass of champagne.

As they made their way to the crowded living room and Betty looked for the happy couple, she couldn't help feeling nervous.

Nathan must have sensed it. He took her hand and tucked it around his arm. "They're going to love you, Betty. Don't worry."

She smiled up at him, realizing again that she'd made the right choice.

Brian suddenly appeared at her side. "Hey, Mom. There you are. Right on time."

Betty gave her son a quick kiss on the cheek, then turned to Nathan. "Brian, I'd like to introduce you to my friend Nathan."

"Great to meet you, Brian. Congratulations." Nathan smiled warmly as he shook Brian's hand. "I've heard a lot about you and your wonderful fiancée."

"Where is Tina?" Betty asked, looking around.

"Over there, with her parents. They're dying to meet you, Mom." Brian led Betty over to the Carvers. They were a very attractive couple, Betty thought. Tina's father was tall, with dark hair touched with silver. Her mother was petite, like Tina, and had the same large dark eyes and cameo features. She wore a long, elegant champagne-colored satin dress.

"You must be Brian's mother. We're so happy to meet you." Mrs. Carver greeted Betty with a warm smile, then leaned over and kissed her cheek. "I'm Samantha, and this is my husband, Doug. Welcome."

Doug leaned forward and eagerly shook her hand. "Thanks so much for coming. It's such a happy occasion. What an amazing way to celebrate the New Year."

"Absolutely," Betty agreed. "I couldn't be happier."

"Brian's told us so much about you, I feel as if we're already good friends," Samantha said.

Tina's mother had such a warm way about her, Betty liked her already. "I know we will be," Betty promised.

Betty had been so focused on the Carvers, she'd totally forgotten to introduce Nathan. She glanced at him and could see he didn't mind. His smile told her he was even a bit amused. "Oh . . . my goodness. You must be wondering about this handsome man standing here so patiently."

"I'm her bodyguard," Nathan said seriously. "The catering business can get dangerous. All those secret recipes."

The Carvers glanced at each other, then laughed.

Betty shook her head but had to laugh, too. "This is Nathan Daley, my . . . my friend. He's a writer."

Doug Carver leaned over, looking very interested. "Your name sounds familiar. Didn't you interview Robert Parker a while back?" he asked, mentioning the famous Boston-based mystery writer. Nathan nodded, but before he could answer, Samantha was saying, "You must meet a lot of interesting people. Have you interviewed any famous actors?"

There were more questions and more recognition of articles Nathan had written for the *Boston Globe* and national magazines.

Betty suddenly felt as if she were with a celebrity. How ironic, since her only qualm about dating him had been this situation exactly— when sooner or later at a cocktail party, people ask what you do for a living. Why had she wasted so much time worrying about that? Betty was suddenly reminded of a famous comment by Mark Twain: "Some of the worst things in my life never happened."

Tina and Brian came by, and there were more happy introductions and some talk about the wedding. When the couple drifted off to greet more guests, Samantha turned to Betty and sighed.

"It's hard to believe my little girl is getting married. Seems like it was only yesterday when she was running outside to play or needed help with her homework."

"Oh, I know what you mean. It's gone so fast. Too fast." Betty turned to her with a wistful smile. "But I know that Brian couldn't have found a lovelier girl. Tina's just terrific. He's very, very lucky."

"Thank you, Betty. We feel the same way about Brian. You must be very proud of him."

"I am," Betty admitted, glancing over at the happy couple. "I really am."

Samantha Carver was soon drawn away by other guests. Betty felt relieved to retreat out of the spotlight for a few moments. Waiters and waitresses passed hors d'oeuvres on silver platters and tall crystal glasses of champagne. On the far side of the room, a four-piece band played jazz standards, and a space had been cleared in the room for dancing.

Nathan, who had been talking to Doug Carver, returned to her side. "Sorry to leave you for so long. He wanted to hear all about the famous athletes I've interviewed. He's a big sports fan."

"Looks like he's one of your fans now, too," Betty teased him.

Nathan just smiled. "How are you holding up? Are those comfortable shoes?" He glanced down at her sleek black silk heels.

"Very, thank you. Why do you ask?"

"Well, they're lovely shoes but they don't look very comfortable. I mean, if someone wanted to ask you to dance."

"Let someone ask me and he'll find out," Betty replied.

Moments later, they were out on the small dance floor alongside several other couples.

Betty couldn't recognize the song—though she knew it was a famous one—partly because she was distracted by Nathan's nearness. They danced together, his hand on her waist and her hand around his shoulder. He was a very good dancer, and Betty felt relaxed and happy in his arms. There was something about being with him that felt so familiar and at the same time so exciting. Was it the same for him? she wondered.

The music stopped. She tipped her head back to look up at Nathan's face and try to read his expression. He smiled down at her and seemed about to say something when they both suddenly became aware of somebody nearby.

Betty turned to see her ex-husband, Ted, standing right beside her. "Hello, Betty. May I have this dance?" he asked politely.

"Ted . . . Why . . . When did you get here?" Betty had looked for him and his wife. She had been both relieved not to see them— and concerned for Brian. She knew he wanted his father there.

"Just a few minutes ago," Ted replied. "We were stuck on the highway behind a fender bender. So, may I have this dance?" he added, glancing at Nathan this time.

Nathan met her eyes a moment, as if to say, *Is this the guy? He's even more of a jerk than I thought.*

Betty looked back, saying, *Yes, I know. But I'd better dance with him. It's just easier that way.*

Nathan slowly parted from Betty and stepped back. "Enjoy."

"Thanks. I'll take her for a quick spin and bring her back, safe and sound."

Betty nearly rolled her eyes at his condescending tone. The way he talked about her, as if he were borrowing a lawn mower. She was so glad they weren't married anymore.

Ted took his place and Betty placed her hand on his shoulder, feeling stiff and awkward.

"You look great, Betty," he said sincerely. "The catering business must agree with you. Or something does," he added, glancing again at Nathan.

"The business is doing well," Betty said, wanting to keep the conversation impersonal. "We've been very lucky. How about you? How's everything? How's your family?" She'd nearly said *new* family, but caught herself just in time.

"Everyone is great. The kids are growing up so quickly. And now our little Brian is getting married. Can you believe it?"

Betty knew what he meant. Here was some common ground between them. "No, I can't," she said honestly. "I'm still in shock. They want to get married this coming summer. That will give me at least a few months to get used to the idea."

"I don't know if that will be long enough for me. But I guess we weren't much older when we got married, were we?"

"We were younger, Ted. I wasn't even finished with college," she reminded him.

"Yes, I remember now." He was silent a moment. Betty shuffled her feet, trying to follow him. He'd never been a very good dancer. "We were young, too young maybe to make that decision," he admitted. "We may not have been a great success at being married, but we did a great job raising our boy. I'm very proud of him."

"So am I," Betty agreed. "And you were a good father," she added, feeling magnanimous.

"You were a very good mother," he said, surprising her. "You always put Brian's happiness first. I hope he appreciates that."

"He does," Betty said. "We've had some good talks. He's a real adult now, Ted. He's ready to start his own life, hard as that might be for us to believe. He's going to do fine."

"And he'll always have us there in the wings, to help him out if he hits a rough spot."

"Not if. More like when," she said knowingly. There were always challenges and rough spots in any life. Despite the fact that his family had broken up, Brian knew he still had two loving parents who would always help him.

"So who's your date?" Ted asked. "I don't think he liked the way I cut in," he added with a chuckle.

Betty had to agree. Nathan had been a gentleman about it, but it had definitely rubbed him the wrong way. "His name is Nathan Daley. He's a friend."

"A friend? Really?" Ted sounded like he didn't quite believe that. "What does he do for a living?"

"He's a writer. He's written a lot of articles for the *Globe* and magazines."

Ted glanced down at her, looking impressed. "A writer? Interesting. . . . So he's just a friend? It looks more serious than that." His voice had that "I've known you a long time, Betty" tone that usually irritated her. Mostly because he had known her a long time and was often right with his suspicions. This time, however, she didn't feel irritated at all.

"We only met about a month ago," she said. "But I guess it does feel serious—or as if it could be."

"I hope it works out for you," Ted told her. "You deserve to be happy, Betty. And I hope he deserves you."

"Thank you, Ted," she said simply.

The song soon ended, and they parted with more kind words. This was another encounter Betty had been dreading, but she had vaulted that bar with ease, she thought.

All in all, this was easily turning out to be the best New Year's Eve outing she could remember. And it wasn't even nine o'clock.

LUCY GOT HOME FROM THE HOSPITAL A LITTLE BEFORE NINE. Charlie had called her fifteen minutes earlier to say that the bowling was a big success, and he was on his way home with the kids and the pizza.

She came through the front door and walked back to the kitchen, turning lights on as she went through the dark rooms. She pulled off her jacket, thinking she should make a salad. She and Zoey were the only ones who would eat it, but at least something green would be on the table. She wondered if Zoey had liked bowling. Charlie hadn't said one way or the other. Well, at least she'd tried and probably had some fun with the boys. As Lucy started setting the table, she heard Charlie and the kids coming in the side door.

"Hi, guys. How did the bowling go?" Lucy called out to them.

"Just fine. It was pretty crowded there," Charlie reported as he walked in.

"Did Zoey like it?" Lucy asked, turning to glance at him.

"Zoey? She didn't come with us. She told me she was tired and wanted to stay home." Charlie put the pizza boxes down on the stove and gave Lucy a puzzled look.

"Really? The house was dark when I came in." And so quiet and empty feeling. A wave of unease washed over Lucy, but she tried to stay calm. "Maybe she's upstairs, having a nap. I'll go see."

Lucy left the kitchen and headed to the staircase. "Zoey? Are you up there?" she called. She paused, listening for an answer as she climbed the first flight. "We're all home now. We're about to have dinner."

She stood on the second-floor landing, looking up. The door to

Zoey's room was open, but the room was dark. Lucy felt a knot of dread in her stomach. She started up the steps toward the dark room. "Zoey?" she called softly. "Are you sleeping?"

Finally, she reached the doorway. The curtains and shades had been left open, and pale light from the street streamed in through the windows. The bed was empty. So was the bathroom.

Lucy turned on the small lamp on the bedside table. The room looked empty, deserted. Some pictures Zoey had hung on the walls were gone—along with all her makeup and the hair clips that were always scattered on the dresser top. Lucy felt sick to her stomach, but she forced herself to open a few drawers in the dresser and pull open the closet door.

Empty. All of Zoey's things were gone.

Lucy sat down heavily on the bed. She pressed her hand to her head, feeling as if she had gone into shock. "Charlie? Charlie, come up here. She's gone. She's left. She's run away. . . ."

Charlie must have been curious and followed her, she realized. He appeared in the doorway seconds after her sad, desperate call. He stood in the doorway and looked around the room. She could see that he understood the scene in an instant. Or maybe he was just more willing to believe that Zoey would do such a thing.

"Looks like she's taken off," he said. "Any note?"

"I didn't see one. But I wasn't really looking." She rose and searched the room again. But there was nothing.

"She told me she was tired and didn't feel like bowling. So I just let her stay home. I never suspected a thing. Honest, Lucy."

Did Charlie think she would blame him for Zoey disappearing? She didn't blame him. Not for leaving Zoey home alone this afternoon. "I would have done the same thing," she told him. "But are you sure she didn't mention anything? Do you think that boy got to her somehow?"

"I don't see how. He's not out on bail. Unless he called her and scared her? Are they allowed to have phone calls?"

Lucy shook her head. "I don't know. We should have been more careful. Zoey was terrified of having to testify against him. That was the thing." She glanced at her watch. "I wonder when she left. What time did you leave for the bowling alley?"

"Oh, I guess it was about four o'clock by the time we got going."

"She's had almost six hours. We'd better call the police and Rita Schuman. We'd better get out there and start looking. Maybe we can find her." Lucy felt a sudden spurt of energy and headed downstairs again.

In the kitchen, the boys sat at the kitchen table, drinking glasses of iced tea and helping themselves to the pizza. "Where's Zoey? Is she sick again?" C.J. asked.

Lucy stopped in her tracks. It was hard to tell them. "It looks like Zoey has left," Lucy said. "Your dad and I are going to call the police. Then we're going out to look for her."

"She left? Why did she leave? You mean, like forever?" Jamie seemed very upset.

Lucy walked over and rested her hand on his shoulder. "I know it's hard to understand, honey. But Zoey wasn't really running away from us. She's afraid of someone she used to know. She's afraid he might hurt her and we can't protect her. But we can. She just has to trust us."

"Can I come with you to look for her?" Jamie asked. "We should take pictures of her with us," he added. "To show people."

"Yes, we should. Great idea, Jamie." Lucy knew she would have thought of that if she hadn't been so unnerved and upset. "I think I printed out a few from Christmas Day. Go look on my desk."

"I want to go, too. I know where kids hang out. I could really help you," C.J. said.

"Yes, you could," Charlie agreed. He had just walked into the kitchen and looked at Lucy, as if waiting for instructions.

"Why don't you call Tucker and I'll start off," she said. "Jamie can come with me and then you can go out with C.J. I'll look around town first, then go to the bus and train stations in Essex and Hamilton. Or the mall."

The task suddenly seemed overwhelming. Where should she look? Where would Zoey go? She could have hitched a ride and be up in Maine by now. Was searching for her a futile effort?

Lucy wondered if Charlie was going to say just that. But he didn't. He looked surprisingly upset and concerned. "Okay. Let's keep in touch by cell phone."

Jamie returned with two photos of Zoey, taken on Christmas Day. She looked so pretty and happy, Lucy thought. She didn't look like a girl who wanted to run away. Why did she do that, when things were going so well for her here?

Charlie took a photo, then leaned over and gave Lucy a kiss on the cheek. "Drive carefully. It is New Year's Eve," he reminded her.

"Yes, it is," Lucy replied, pulling out her car keys. Some way to start the New Year. Lucy and Jamie jumped in Lucy's car and headed back to the village. Lucy realized that she had never called Rita Schuman and quickly pulled out her cell phone. She had Jamie dial the number and then used her handless headset to talk.

"Rita, I'm sorry to bother you. But I came home a little while ago from work and it looks like Zoey has . . . has . . . left us. All her belongings are gone." Lucy found it hard to say the words; her throat felt as if it were closing up.

"Oh dear, that is bad news. When do you think she left the house? Do you have any idea?"

Lucy explained how Zoey was supposed to go bowling but decided to stay home at the last minute. "Charlie left the house a little past four and I came home just before nine. So she's had a few hours' jump on us," Lucy said sadly. "Charlie's called the local police, and we're giving them pictures."

"Did she have much money with her?" Rita asked.

"She has some—money she earned at the diner. I'm not sure how much. But she spent a lot on Christmas gifts and clothes for herself."

"Okay. Sounds like she doesn't have a lot of funds—not enough to buy a plane ticket somewhere."

Lucy hadn't even considered a plane ticket. That was yet another worry. "Oh, I feel so awful," she confessed. "I can't believe this is happening."

"It's not your fault, Lucy. Zoey has done this before. This is her way of coping with problems. She's scared about testifying against Kurt Schmitt. This was the only solution she could come up with."

"I'll never forgive myself if something happens to her."

"I think she'll be all right. I think we'll find her," Rita said, her tone reassuring. "I'll call you in a few hours and, of course, you'll call me with any news."

"Of course I will," Lucy promised before ending the call.

She had almost forgotten that Jamie was with her, sitting beside her in the front seat. He stared at her in the darkness, looking worried and unhappy. "What did Mrs. Schuman say?"

"She thinks Zoey will be all right and that we'll find her," she said, repeating the caseworker's assurances—though Lucy herself didn't entirely believe them.

"Maybe if we had really adopted Zoey, she wouldn't have been so scared and she wouldn't have run away," Jamie said.

Lucy felt a lump in her throat. "I don't know, Jamie. Maybe," she said quietly.

She'd had the same thought ever since discovering Zoey was gone. But she hadn't found the courage to say it out loud.

* * *

JUST BEFORE MIDNIGHT, DOUG AND SAMANTHA CARVER STOOD by the musicians, Tina and Brian beside them. Doug took the microphone. "I've been told it's just about time to ring out the old and ring in the new," he began. "On behalf of our family, I want to thank you all for coming tonight and helping us celebrate Tina and Brian's engagement. We wish you all a wonderful New Year, full of health, happiness, and every blessing." He glanced at the mantel clock. "It's time. Everybody count with me. Ten . . . nine . . . eight . . ."

Nathan and Betty had been dancing, and now stood side by side, counting aloud together. Nathan took her hand when they hit "five." At "three" he turned to face her and gazed straight into her eyes with a smile. At "two" his smile widened.

Betty smiled back and held her breath. They both shouted "One!" with the rest of the guests and then, "Happy New Year!" Nathan put his arms around her and whispered the words again.

"Happy New Year, Betty," he said right before he kissed her.

She held him close, closed her eyes and kissed him back. A deep, sweet kiss that carried her away on a wave of pure emotion. For a moment she lost all sense of time and place. Even the racket of noisemakers tooting and rattling all around them and the band playing "Auld Lang Syne" above the fray was totally silenced for a brief, magical moment.

They parted a bit, though Nathan still held her in a loose embrace. Betty felt a little stunned and breathless, but blissfully happy.

"Are you all right?" he asked her.

"Couldn't be better," she promised with a smile. "How about you?"

"I couldn't be better either," he replied. "Thank you for inviting me to come here with you, Betty. You asked me to do you a favor by being your date. But it seems, once again, it's gotten all turned around and you've done something wonderful for me."

"Made you break down and buy a real suit, you mean? You would have gotten around to that sooner or later," she teased him.

"Possibly. But I didn't mean that. You pulled me out of my cave of gloom. The very last thing I wanted to do tonight was come to this party. I just didn't think I could do it. But every time I pictured you waiting to see if I'd show up . . . well, I couldn't let you down." He reached up and cupped her cheek with his hand. "I knew the minute I met you that you were someone very special. Someone who could change my life. You know, even Santa has a wish list. And you're the answer to all of my wishes . . . and all my prayers."

Betty felt a catch in her throat. "I knew you were special, too," she told him, "from the first moment I saw you. It just took me a while to see that you were the one. If ever I had to describe the man who would be right for me, I couldn't have invented you—free-lance writer and professional Santa. But that's the way it works sometimes. You just never know, do you?"

"No, you don't. But I know one thing for sure. Now that I've found you, you won't get away from me easily." He held her close again, and Betty closed her eyes, laughing softly.

As if she would ever want to be with anyone else, ever. She couldn't imagine it now. The New Year had started—her fiftieth—along with a new and unexpected chapter in her life, she realized. One that looked to be the happiest she'd had in a long time.

LUCY PULLED INTO THE DRIVEWAY OF HER HOUSE AT HALF PAST one in the morning. Jamie was asleep in the passenger seat next to her. She gently shook his shoulder. "We're home, honey. Time to go inside."

He opened his eyes and blinked, then got out of the car without saying a word. At one point, he'd gotten so despondent, the truth of the situation finally hitting home to him, that he had burst out crying. Lucy had started crying, too. She just felt so heartsick.

The house was dark but the light over the front door was still on. Charlie's truck was parked at the top of the driveway, and she wondered when he and C.J. had given up and come home. When they went inside, Jamie went straight upstairs. Lucy went back to the kitchen and made herself a cup of tea. She was exhausted but wound up and wasn't sure she could sleep.

She was sitting at the table, sipping her tea, when Charlie came in, wearing his bathrobe.

"You're home," he said quietly. "That's good. I was getting worried. You told me you were on your way a while ago."

"I made one more sweep in Beverly. There's an all-night diner there and some fast-food places."

"We didn't get home too long ago," Charlie said, sitting down. "C.J. knew some places that kids hang out, clubs where Zoey might have snuck herself in, even though she's a minor. We showed her picture around, too." He was quiet for a long moment. "I'm sorry, Lucy. I know this girl means a lot to you, and I'm sorry about the way this turned out."

Lucy glanced at him. She believed that he was sincere, not just wrapping up an "I told you so" in kinder words.

"Well . . . it's not over yet," Lucy said, dredging up a last shred of hope. "Maybe she'll turn around and come back. Maybe once she's out there a few hours, she'll realize that this solution doesn't work for her anymore, and there's a better way—here with us."

He sighed. "Maybe, but I doubt it. She was with us for a few weeks, Lucy. But she's been living the other way for years. It takes a lot longer for people to change."

"I thought she changed a lot. Even you said she's come a long way, Charlie. Don't you remember saying that to me just the other day?"

Lucy didn't mean to sound angry at him. It was very late, and they were both exhausted. But why did he have to persist with these comments about Zoey that were unfair and untrue?

"I do remember saying that," he admitted. "But maybe that was just an act. Or maybe she just couldn't change deep inside, where it really matters. New clothes don't change a person, Lucy," he reminded her. "It was bound to happen sooner or later. Maybe Zoey just needed a place to recharge her batteries for a few weeks. She made out pretty well here, with all the things you bought her. But I don't believe she ever meant to stay. I think she liked us. Especially you. I'm sure she's never met anyone in her life who was as sweet and kind to her as you were," he added in a gentler tone. "Not even her own mother, I bet you. But she just never learned how to live with that, how to reciprocate. That's just the kind of girl she is. I know how hard you tried, but you can't change someone like that. Now we know that for sure," he said finally.

Lucy wanted to interrupt her husband's long speech, but she was too choked up to get a word out. She was feeling very angry— angry at Charlie . . . and even Zoey. And at the entire situation. "Zoey wasn't using us," she finally replied. "She's just scared. Don't you get it? She didn't believe we would protect her. We should have taken full custody. She would have felt secure if we'd made a real commitment to her. She still feels she can't trust anyone to help her, that she has to do everything for herself."

He stood up and walked around the table behind her. He rested his hand on her shoulder and dropped a kiss on her hair. "You tried your best, Lucy. You've got a heart of gold, anybody can see that. Some people take advantage. That's all I'm trying to say." He sighed. "I'm going to bed. Come up soon and get some sleep, okay?"

Lucy nodded, feeling teary all over again. "I'll be up soon," she promised.

She sat and listened to Charlie's footsteps going up the stairs.

We didn't wish each other a Happy New Year, she realized. Well, that would be hypocritical, wouldn't it? She felt anything but happy right now. She felt as if her heart were simply breaking. She felt she'd promised Zoey she would help her and failed miserably— and she didn't know how to make things right again.

Lucy sent up a silent prayer, as she had all night while driving around, asking God to watch over Zoey and keep her safe from harm, wherever she might be.

The pews were as empty the first Sunday after the holidays as they had been full the week before. That was the wax and wane of church attendance that Reverend Ben knew well. He had come to think of his congregation's churchgoing as a tide, washing in and out of the sanctuary to its own natural rhythm, closely in sync with the seasons. The holidays pulled them in, and it was part of his job, as he saw it, to keep them coming back, even on the ebb tide.

He was not surprised then on the first Sunday of the New Year to see so few faces staring back at him from the pews. The sparse audience actually made it easier for him to recognize his congregants and make a few observations.

As he opened the service with the usual greeting and made the weekly announcements, he noticed Betty Bowman and Nathan Daley seated together toward the front of the church and looking very much like a couple. It was just something in their body language, the way they sat so comfortably together, the way they looked at each other. He already knew how Betty had visited Nathan last week and persuaded him to emerge from his self-imposed isolation. It looked as if her kind and loving attentions had worked wonders. Nathan had helped Betty, too, he thought. She had rarely looked lovelier or happier. The way Nathan had encouraged her to do good work in the community had opened a new door for Betty—and a new path that could lead toward new meaning and purpose. Ben had already seen that. He said a quick prayer that they would continue to help each other and that their relationship would flourish.

At the back of the church, he noticed Lucy Bates coming in late with her son, Jamie. She found a seat in one of the last rows, sat down, and shrugged off her jacket. She didn't look right, he thought. Her lovely red hair was pulled back in a simple, haphazard style and she wasn't even wearing lipstick. It wasn't at all the way she usually dressed for church. She looked tired, too, and Ben wondered if she had a cold or was just overworked from the holidays. Most of all, she looked sad. He could see that in her face, even at a distance. He could only guess the cause of her unhappiness and decided to look for her later and see if she wanted to talk about anything.

When it came time in the service for the congregation to share their joys and concerns, Ben's suspicions about Lucy were confirmed. She was one of the first to raise her hand.

"I'd like to ask for everyone's prayers for Zoey, the young girl who's been staying with us these last few weeks," Lucy began. "She's been to church with us once or twice. Perhaps some of you remember her. . . . We came home on New Year's Eve and discovered that she left the house and took all her belongings. We've been working with the police and her counselor and looking everywhere, trying to find her. We just pray that she's all right and will come back soon."

Poor Lucy, Ben thought. She felt so much for the girl, had invested so much of herself in their brief relationship. No wonder she looked so sad.

"That's very distressing news, Lucy. We'll all pray for her safety and speedy return."

Ben offered up the prayers of thanks and concern and continued with the service. Later, as he stood at the back of the sanctuary, greeting those who waited to see him, he scanned the line for Lucy, but she wasn't there. He did see her gathering her belongings and moving toward a side door. In an artful—and experienced—maneuver, he backed up into the narthex between his chats with other congregants, managing to cross paths with her. Perhaps she'd been trying to avoid him, but maybe she just felt too depleted to seek his help. He felt he had to reach out to her and take his chances.

"Lucy, I'm very sorry to hear about Zoey. Is there anything we can do?"

Lucy sighed and shook her head. "I don't think so, Reverend. We've done just about everything we could do over the past few days. Charlie and I have both been driving around, looking everywhere. I even posted flyers in the village and other towns nearby, asking if anyone's seen her. And I took an ad out in the local newspapers, with a reward. Maybe we'll get some calls. The police are looking, too, but they have so many other things to do. Looking for a runaway is probably not a big priority."

"Why did she leave, Lucy? Do you have any idea? Did she leave any sort of note?"

"Oh, we know why she left." Lucy told him about Kurt, and Zoey being asked to give the police a statement. "Zoey was afraid that he wouldn't go to jail, that he would find her and hurt her. We tried to convince her that we'd protect her, but she didn't believe us, I guess," Lucy finished.

"It's complicated, isn't it?" Ben reached out and patted her hand. "I can see that you had a deep attachment to Zoey. I'm sure this is very painful for you."

"It is," Lucy admitted in a shaky voice. "We're all pretty upset. Even Charlie is, though he hates to admit it. He says that it was bound to happen, and she was just probably using us. But I know, deep in his heart, he liked her and he's worried. It's just easier for him to turn his back and write her off."

"And you're just the opposite," Reverend Ben said. It was hard for him to find the right words to comfort her. "Don't give up. Let's pray for her safety and God's help in finding her. Maybe she'll have a change of heart and come back on her own."

"That's what I've been praying for," Lucy replied. "Charlie has sort of given up looking. He says she's a smart girl and we won't find her if she doesn't want to be found. I'm starting to think he's right," she admitted.

Though Charlie had a talent for seeing the glass half-empty, Reverend Ben had to acknowledge that this time, Lucy's husband had a point. "Well, let's just hope that if she's smart enough not to be found, she's smart enough to keep herself safe," he said. That thought seemed to make Lucy feel a little better, he noticed.

Her son Jamie suddenly appeared beside them, eating what appeared to be a large apple muffin. Jamie had already been into the coffee hour spread and back, Reverend Ben realized.

"Jamie, no eating outside the Fellowship Hall, you know that," Lucy reminded him.

Jamie complied by popping the rest of the muffin into his mouth and just about swallowing it whole. "Sorry, Mom, I forgot," he mumbled.

Lucy finally had to smile as her son gulped the cake down in one lump. "Boys, they are something else."

Reverend Ben laughingly agreed. He only hoped that her own sons would be some consolation for Lucy if there was an unhappy ending to Zoey's story.

* * *

IT WAS THE FIRST MONDAY MORNING OF THE NEW YEAR, AND the diner was a madhouse, just as Charlie had expected. Except that he was down one waitress, and Trudy, who would never win any prizes for speedy service, seemed to be moving even slower than usual. Charlie had to practically bite his tongue to keep from yelling at her every five minutes. The only thing that kept him from losing his temper entirely was the thought that if she quit, he might as well shut the door and put up the GONE CLAMMING sign. For good.

He'd called Jimmy, the other cook, about two hours ago and woke the man out of a sound sleep. If Jimmy handled the kitchen, Charlie figured he could go out into the dining room as needed and pick up the slack from Trudy.

Jimmy had happily agreed to come in; he needed the extra hours. But he also moved like an arthritic turtle, and Charlie kept checking the clock, waiting for the man to arrive while running between the grill and serving the most annoyed of Trudy's customers in the dining room.

"I'm sorry, Charlie. I've only got two hands and two feet," Trudy grumbled as she rushed by, breakfast orders for her tables in each hand.

"Yeah, so I've noticed."

"Why don't you call Lucy? Maybe she'll come over and help out."

Charlie answered her with a dark look. "Lucy can't come to the rescue today. So let's just try to keep this place running, shall we?"

More like, he couldn't ask Lucy for the favor. Every since Zoey ran off, he had been feeling as if Lucy blamed him, as if it were all his fault. Which, of course, it wasn't. So he had not taken an instant liking to the girl, had not jumped at the chance to sign on as her guardian. Would any of that have changed the unhappy ending of this story? He doubted it.

But try to tell Lucy that. She just wouldn't listen to reason where this girl was concerned. Charlie was tired of trying to talk any sense into her. Now it was just a case of wait and see. Sure, he cared about the kid and hoped she would land on her feet. But she was one smart cookie. He had a feeling Zoey could watch out for herself. Though the world wasn't a very nice place, and she was a young girl, on her own. . . .

Charlie swept his dark thoughts aside. Zoey had done this to herself. He wasn't going to feel guilty over the situation. He had a business to run. He couldn't worry about this stuff all day.

The dining room seemed under control. At least for the moment. Charlie stomped back into the kitchen and got back to work. He was making the Monday night dinner special, meat loaf, and had already dumped most of the ingredients into the big mixer.

He flipped on the switch, wondering again about Jimmy's arrival, when he heard a hideous grinding sound—the sound of machinery going completely out of whack—along with the distinct smell of hot metal and burning rubber.

He quickly flipped the switch off, then tossed his rubber spatula across the room in a fit of rage. It hit a hanging pot and struck it like a gong.

"For pity's sake!" he screamed. "What else is going to go wrong today? Huh? Is the place going to blow up on me or something?" Charlie yanked the plug, pulled out the bowl of ground beef and fixings, and attacked it with a long metal spoon. "Why is my life so miserable? Can anyone tell me that?"

"Hey, boss . . . something wrong?"

Charlie looked over at the back door and saw Jimmy coming in.

"Finally. What did you do, walk here from Rockport?"

"Why would I walk, Charlie? It's cold out. I have a car." Jimmy gazed at Charlie curiously as he put on his apron. Jimmy did not get sarcasm. Lucky thing, Charlie realized, or else he might have quit long ago.

"Never mind." Charlie sighed. He looked down at the meat and tossed aside the spoon. "You finish that up when you get a chance. It's tonight's special, the meat loaf."

"Sure. No problem," Jimmy said amiably.

Charlie pulled off his apron and washed his hands. "I'm going out. The mixer broke down again, and I can't fix it. I already tried twice. I'm going to bring it over to Needham, to the restaurant equipment place."

"When will you be back?" Charlie heard the note of anxiety in Jimmy's voice but chose to ignore it. It was definitely unusual for him to leave during the day like this.

"I don't know. Later," Charlie said curtly, taking his jacket from a hook by the back door. Then he wrapped the cord around the machine and grabbed it off the counter. "I'll call you later, Jim," he added in a kinder tone. "You'll be all right. Tell Trudy I'm going, will you? And try to watch that all the customers don't walk out on us. She's slow as molasses today."

"Okay, Charlie. Will do," Jimmy said loyally.

Charlie glanced at him. He was a good guy. The place would probably burn to the ground . . . but Jimmy was all right.

Charlie lugged the machine outside and hoisted it into the truck bed, wedging it between boxes of canned goods, so it wouldn't slide around. Then he jumped into the driver's seat and headed out of town, toward the highway. He felt as if he had been driving all weekend, looking for Zoey, up and down the same roads, cruising around the same towns, feeling like a total fool when he showed that picture of her around.

Now here he was, on the road again. At least this time he had a destination and a purpose, and something productive would come of his trouble. It felt good to get out of the diner, into the fresh air. Sometimes the place just seemed to suffocate him, though it was also so much his environment that he couldn't survive very long away from it. Lucy teased him about his needing the diner the way a fish needed water. He couldn't deny it.

Charlie drove along for nearly an hour, listening to sports talk radio. He noticed the needle on his gas gauge getting low and felt a grumbling in his stomach. He hated to eat at truck stops, but figured he could gas up and find something to eat that wouldn't kill him.

He spotted the sign for fuel and made the turnoff, then searched the big lot for a parking spot. He left the truck, figuring no one would walk off with a big piece of kitchen equipment.

Good riddance if they did. Maybe his insurance would cover the loss and he could buy a brand-new machine.

The food service area looked like a big family restaurant with tables and booths and stools at a counter. Charlie noticed a sign for take-out orders at the end of the counter and walked over.

"Can I help you, sir?" a waitress asked.

"Just a coffee, to go," he said. "Milk and one sugar, that's all."

"Okay, sir. I'll be right back." She smiled, scrawled the order, and disappeared.

He stepped back and stuck his hands in his pockets. A revolving glass cabinet, filled with cakes and pies, stood nearby and he turned to check it out, half-tempted by the cherry pie.

He suddenly stopped and blinked. Then he leaned over to peer around the cake display. A teenage girl sat at the far end of the counter. He couldn't see her face but something about her build and just the way she sat, reading a magazine and sipping a mug of tea, seemed painfully familiar. Her dark hair was bunched up at the back of her head and when he squinted his eyes and focused on the hairdo, he found telltale streaks of blue and red.

It was her all right. *Well, I'll be a monkey's uncle,* Charlie swore silently. He felt his hands go all clammy, and his heart pounded in his chest, as if he had just chugged down an entire pot of coffee.

His first impulse was to call out her name. But somehow, he couldn't quite get the words out. He felt sort of choked up, he realized. He started to walk over to confront her. Then suddenly, he stopped, hearing a familiar little voice inside him.

Slow down, Charlie. Think about what you're doing for a minute here.

Look at her, she's okay. Sitting around, reading a magazine. Fine as you please. She's not some fragile flower. She doesn't need you and Lucy to survive. It was a lucky break for you when she ran off. Now you aren't stuck with this kid and all her baggage. Who's ever going to know you saw her here? No one. Not if you don't tell.

Just let her go. Let her disappear forever.

Charlie let out a long breath and slipped behind the cake display, so Zoey wouldn't see him. Where was that waitress with his coffee?

He ought to just go. Forget the darned coffee. No sense in lingering here, he decided.

Charlie headed for the exit, walking slowly and quietly. But still, he couldn't help glancing back just one last time. Maybe just to make sure his eyes hadn't been playing tricks on him and that the girl he'd spotted was really Zoey. Or maybe, just because he wanted one last look at her.

Just as he turned for that last look he noticed a guy about his age sidling up to Zoey. The guy was probably a trucker, from the looks of his jacket with an emblem on the sleeve. Charlie saw him look Zoey over, as if checking out the revolving cake cabinet. Then he sat down right next to her, even though the entire row of seats stood empty.

Charlie hung back, waiting to see what would happen. Though he had a good idea already.

The stranger didn't take long starting a conversation. First, asking her to pass the sugar and then the milk container. Then talking about the weather and asking her where she was headed. Charlie felt himself starting to steam up. He crossed his arms over his chest and let out a long breath. He walked a few steps closer again, listening intently.

"I'm going in that direction if you want a ride. That's right on my way. No trouble for me at all," he heard the truck driver say. The waitress came by and dropped Zoey's check. The stranger beside her quickly picked it up. "This is on me," he told her.

Charlie could see Zoey looked confused and even scared. "Don't do that. I can pay it," she said.

"That's all right, sweetie. Hey, if you ride with me, I'll pay for all the food. Whatever you like."

"That's okay. I can pay," Zoey insisted. She stood up and tried to take the check from his hand, but he pulled it just out of her reach and laughed. "You're cute," he said. "Come on. Let me give you a lift. We could have fun."

Zoey didn't answer. But she didn't walk away either, Charlie noticed. She just stood there and stared at the stranger, hugging her backpack to her chest.

Charlie couldn't take it anymore. He suddenly stepped forward, standing right between the two of them. "How about me? Am I cute?" he asked the trucker.

The man gave Charlie a puzzled look.

Zoey stared at him, too. "Charlie . . . what are you doing here?"

"Oh, you know this guy?" the trucker asked.

"Yeah, I do," she answered, her gaze fixed on Charlie.

"Yeah, she does, you jerk," Charlie shouted back. "I'm her—" He realized he was about to say "father." But at the last second, he stopped himself. He actually did feel like her father, he realized with a jolt.

"What's it to you, buddy?" he asked the trucker instead. "You should be ashamed of yourself—sitting here, flirting with a girl half your age. She's only fifteen years old. Did you know that? Why I could have you arrested—"

"Hey, mister, slow down. I was just offering the girl a ride. She said she'd been hitchhiking. That's dangerous—"

"Yeah, it's dangerous. That's why I'm taking her home. Right now," Charlie shouted back.

"Taking me home? What are you talking about?" Zoey suddenly whirled on Charlie. "Is that a joke? I don't have a home."

"You come with me and stop talking back so much," Charlie grumbled, taking a firm hold of her arm.

As he led her out of the restaurant, a waitress called after him. "Sir . . . ? What about your coffee?"

Charlie looked over his shoulder. "What about it? It's probably ice-cold by now. What did you do, go down to Brazil to pick the beans?"

Zoey looked at him with shock, then laughed out loud.

"Well, I'm glad one of us is laughing," he said once they were outside the restaurant. "What were you thinking, talking to a man like that? Couldn't you see he was up to no good? I thought you had more common sense than that."

Zoey lifted her chin and stared right back him. "Okay, Charlie. You did your good deed for the day. Now just let me go. I'll go on my way, you go on yours. Just pretend you never saw me. I'll do the same."

She'd read his mind, he thought. Pretty good. He had to hand her that.

"I'd love to, Sassy Mouth. As a matter of fact, that was my first idea when I saw you," he confessed. "But it doesn't work like that. You've been living under our roof for over a month. Then you take off without a word. We were worried sick about you. We drove all over the county, looking for you, putting up flyers, handing out your photograph. . . ."

He could see Zoey's expression slowly changing, her narrowed eyes growing wider and wider with surprise. He could see that she couldn't quite believe anyone had made such an effort for her.

"Yeah, that's right. I've been wearing down my tires, looking for you. Lucy is beside herself. She's sick over it."

That last sentence hit a nerve. Zoey stared down at the ground, suddenly looking contrite. "I'm sorry I hurt Lucy's feelings. She's so nice . . . she's the sweetest person I've ever met."

"You're darned right she is. I don't even deserve to be married to her," he added candidly.

"No, you don't," Zoey agreed.

Charlie gave her a look. "Lucy has a heart of gold. She'll go the limit for a person who needs her help, no questions asked. People take advantage of her. I've seen it before. Are you one of those? Is that what you are?"

Zoey bit her lip. "I didn't mean to hurt anyone. I like Lucy . . . I miss her," she admitted.

"Well, she's taken a liking to you. She loves you like her own child. Do you deserve that kind of love? Or are you going to just answer all that goodness by hurting her feelings and disappointing her? She trusted you. But you didn't trust her," he pointed out.

Zoey stared at him and sighed. He could see that she was torn, trying to choose between the freedom she had in hand or the promise of security—and its limitations.

"I didn't want to have to testify against Kurt. It didn't have anything to do with Lucy. Or even you, for that matter," Zoey said finally.

"We know that. We know you're afraid of that punk, and we're going to keep him away from you. You've got to believe us about that, Zoey." He paused and met her gaze. "You've got a place in our family—if you want it. But you have to trust us to take care of you. And we have to be able to trust you."

He watched and waited for some sign. She stood very still, hugging the pathetic little pack to her chest. She bit her lip again, but didn't answer, and Charlie thought he might scream with frustration.

"Hey, I can't drag you back by that ponytail. You've got to come willingly. I know you're scared. But if you stay with us, we're going to keep you safe. Heck, this is the second time I've protected you, you realize that? I'm turning into a regular, personal bodyguard." Charlie was surprised at the realization himself.

Zoey suddenly looked curious. "Do you just like to be a tough guy, Charlie? Or do you like me more than you let on?"

"What kind of question is that? Of course I like you. Why would I be standing here arguing with you all this time? You've got a smart mouth sometimes, honey. But you're tough. I admire that. You've been through a lot and you're a smart girl. You could straighten yourself out and do all right. You could have a good life," he added in a gentler tone. "But you've got to let us help you. Don't be so . . . so thickheaded. It doesn't help you much in life, believe me."

"So you want to help me now, too? Whoa. That is news. Let me process."

Charlie didn't answer at first. He didn't entirely understand her but thought they were moving in the right direction. "Yeah, I do want to help you. Now once and for all, will you come with me? I

don't have all day. I have to drop my mixer at the restaurant equipment place. The service window closes at three."

Zoey let out a long breath. "Well, in that case, I guess we'd better get going."

Charlie felt an amazing wave of pure relief, so strong it nearly
knocked him off his feet. He stared at Zoey a second, then started
off back to his truck, feeling a little weak in the knees. He couldn't
quite believe he had not only found her but persuaded her to come
back with him. Even when she sat in the truck cab on the seat right
next to him, he could not quite believe she was really there.

He started up the truck, then pulled out his phone. "We'd better call Lucy. She's going to be mad at me for not calling her the
moment I spotted you."

He punched in Lucy's cell phone number, and Lucy picked up
almost at once. She greeted him in a huff. "Charlie, where are you?
Trudy called me in a panic and I had to run over to the diner to
help her. I have to leave for work in a few minutes. I can't stay here
all day. What were you thinking, walking out like that—?"

"Hey, slow down, Lucy. Stop yelling at me. I'll tell you where
I've been if you give me a second. Guess who's sitting right here in
the truck. . . ." He handed the phone over to Zoey and felt his
smile get so wide, his face hurt. Oh, he wished he could see the
look on Lucy's face when she heard Zoey's voice.

"Lucy? It's me . . . Zoey," she said, her voice apologetic.

Charlie heard Lucy on the other end of the phone, her reaction
was so loud and emotional. "Zoey? Is that really you? I can't believe
it. . . . Are you all right, honey? We were all so worried about
you. . . ." Then he heard Lucy start crying, her words dissolving
into sobs.

Zoey sighed. "She's crying," she reported softly.

He glanced at the girl. "So are you."

Zoey looked over at him. "So are you," she sniffed.

"Me? What—are you kidding?" Charlie rubbed his eye with the back of his hand. "I just got some dust in my eye, that's all."

Zoey gave him a look but didn't reply, turning back to her phone call with Lucy. "We're on our way back, Lucy," Zoey explained. "But Charlie has to drop off his kitchen machine in Needham."

Zoey listened for a moment, then handed the phone to Charlie. "She wants to talk to you."

"Charlie, you turn around and come right home this instant," he heard his wife say.

Charlie laughed. "Okay, okay. We'll be right back. But who's going to do all the mixing until that machine is fixed, huh?"

"Drive safely," Lucy said. "I'll be waiting right here."

He hung up, glanced over at Zoey, and laughed. "That's Lucy for you. I should be the hero of the day. But I just can't do anything right, can I?"

"Oh, I don't know, Charlie. You're not so bad," Zoey replied, looking out the window. "I'll put in a good word for you."

"Well, thanks, Zoey. You're not so bad yourself. In fact, you're a pretty great kid," he added in a more thoughtful, affectionate tone. "Isn't it funny how things work out? I popped my cork this morning and ran out of the diner with that broken mixer, like it was a life-or-death situation. But if I didn't get so fired up, I would have never caught up with you. And that would have been a real shame."

"I guess it was meant to be," Zoey said, turning in her seat to look at him again.

"I guess so. Lucy will probably say there was the hand of God in this." He shook his head and grinned. "And this time, I don't know that I'd disagree with her."

* * *

ABOUT AN HOUR LATER, CHARLIE FOLLOWED ZOEY INTO THE diner. Lucy rushed up to greet them, hugging Zoey close and bursting into tears all over again. The boys were there, too, and took their turns hugging her and teasing her. Even Trudy gave Zoey a hug and playfully held out an apron. "Boy, did I miss you on the floor. Are you sure you don't want to work with me tonight?"

"Not tonight, Trudy," Lucy answered. "We're going home."

Lucy glanced at Charlie and he nodded. "That's right. What the heck. This is a big day. I'm closing up. Everybody has the night off," he announced.

"With pay?" Jimmy asked from behind the counter.

Charlie hesitated, feeling his jaw tighten.

"That's right. With pay," Lucy answered for him. "See you at home, Charlie. I'll take the kids," she called out happily.

"Okay, I'll be right there," he promised. After Trudy and Jimmy left, Charlie locked up without even cleaning the place. That was a first for him, too. Seems today was a rare day. Funny how you never knew what was coming your way when you got up in the morning, he reflected.

When he got home, he smelled something good cooking in the kitchen. Lucy greeted him, happier than he'd seen her in weeks, and he felt a familiar tightness in his chest slowly begin to dissolve. "Dinner's almost ready," she told him. "The kids are upstairs, doing homework. Zoey's in her room, putting her things away."

Charlie followed Lucy back to the kitchen and sat down at the table. She was making spaghetti and meatballs, one of his favorites. Lucy made the dish better than he did, though he wasn't sure he had ever admitted that to her.

"So, quite a day," Lucy said, turning to him as she stirred the pot of sauce. "I called Rita Schuman from the car on the way home. She was absolutely thrilled. She's coming over later to talk to Zoey."

"That sounds like a good idea," Charlie said.

"Zoey told me how you found her in the truck stop. She told me all about it, how that man was pressuring her to go with him and you just walked up and scared him off."

"It wasn't that dramatic, Lucy," Charlie said, though he did feel a puff of pride. "We had some words. Dirty slime bucket," he grumbled. "Did she tell you that she didn't want to come back with me at first? But I persuaded her."

"Yes, she did tell me that part." Lucy nodded and turned to him. She gave him a grateful look that just about melted his heart. "Thank you, Charlie. Truly and absolutely, from the bottom of my heart. This is the best thing you've ever done for me. You never have to buy me another gift . . . or sit through a play or a symphony . . . or take out the garbage."

"Whoa, now," he said, laughing. "Let's not get carried away. I might remember all this stuff and take you up on it."

"I mean it. Bringing Zoey back here safe and sound was the answer to my prayers."

He heard Lucy's voice tremble and knew she was going to cry again. He stood up and put his arms around her. "Hey there, Lu-lu. There's nothing to cry about. The kid is snug as a bug in a rug. She didn't need too much persuading to come back. When I mentioned you, that sort of clinched it," he explained. "But she can be a sassy little cat. A real spitfire." He laughed, remembering some of Zoey's smart-aleck answers. "We'll have our hands full with that girl, don't fool yourself. She's going to take some special handling."

Lucy looked up at him. "Does that mean you're willing to keep her here—permanently?"

Charlie nodded. "Yeah. She didn't tell you that part? We worked it all out, me and Zoey. We're all square. I told her we would stick by her with this legal situation and we'd keep her safe, no matter what. But she's got to trust us and treat us straight."

Lucy dabbed her eyes with a paper napkin and nodded. "You said the right thing." She sighed and smiled. "When Rita Schuman comes, can we tell her we're ready to apply as foster parents?"

"I'll tell her myself," he promised. "I know I've been difficult about this, Lucy. Maybe too practical and even a little suspicious of the girl. But you were right. My eyes were open, but my heart was closed. I had to open my heart to her and now . . . well, I feel like she's one of our own. I wouldn't let her go anywhere else."

"Thank you, Charlie," Lucy said simply. "Thank you for this. I'll never forget it."

"You don't have to say that. I'm the one who should be thanking you, Lucy. You show me how to be a better man."

Lucy put her arms around him and they kissed. She rested her head on his shoulder a moment, and he felt as if she had pinned a medal on his chest. "I think we should both be counting our blessings right now and thanking heaven that she's back safe and sound."

"Amen to that, dear," Charlie said quietly.

EPILOGUE

~

"SHE WAS DESPERATE. I DIDN'T KNOW WHAT TO SAY." BETTY glanced over at Nathan, feeling guilty.

"That's all right. We'll catch the movie some other time. I'm sure it will be out on DVD soon."

She noticed that he wasn't smiling. They had plans to drive up to Newburyport, to see a movie and have dinner. The film was at a small art theater and would only be showing over the weekend. Nathan had been talking about it all week. But at the last minute, Molly had called with an emergency. She and Matt had to attend a big fund-raiser for the hospital, and their sitter had canceled at the very last minute. The older girls were both back at college, and Jill was away at a basketball tournament. And Molly's mother was down in Florida, and Sam and Jessica had taken their kids skiing. The list went on and on.

"I tried everyone," Molly promised. "From age eleven to eighty. I wouldn't call if it wasn't an absolute emergency. Could you possibly please come over and watch little Betty for us? Otherwise, Matt will have to go by himself, and I won't get to wear my new dress, and I just had my hair done—"

"Okay. Calm down, I get the idea. You spent a fortune primping and you don't want to be left at home, watching SpongeBob videos."

"What a pal," Molly had exclaimed in relief. "I owe you for this one. Big-time."

"You don't have to stay," Betty told Nathan as they pulled up to Molly's house. "You can just drop me off, go see the movie, and come back later."

Nathan sighed. She could tell he was considering the idea. "We'll see. Let's just play it by ear. I think there's a good Hitchcock movie on TV. Maybe little Betty will go to sleep early."

"Let's just hope," Betty said as they walked up to the front door. She hit the bell and waited. The house was quiet and dark except for a few lights on upstairs. She guessed that Matt and Molly were still dressing.

Finally, the door opened. Molly stood there clutching a bathrobe around her neck, though her hair and makeup were perfect. "Come in, come in. Sorry to make you wait. I just have to put my dress on."

Betty stepped into the foyer. It was so dark, she could hardly see.

Suddenly the lights glared and people jumped out from every corner.

"Surprise!" they all yelled at her.

"What in the world . . . !" She turned to Molly, who was laughing, and then to Nathan, who was smiling from ear to ear.

"Happy birthday, Betty. I guess you were surprised," he said, kissing her soundly.

"Was I ever . . ." She gasped, catching her breath. "How in the world did you pull this off?"

"It wasn't as hard as you think, hon. You're getting old. Not so sharp anymore," Molly teased.

Betty socked her in the arm. "This is all your doing, I'll bet."

"Actually it was Santa's idea," Molly said, slanting her head in Nathan's direction. She leaned closer so that only Betty could hear her. "You were right about him, pal. I have to give you credit. He's a diamond in the rough, that one."

Betty beamed. "I told you so." But before she could say more, she was quickly surrounded by friends, wishing her well and teasing her about her astonished reaction.

Emily held out a digital camera, showing her pictures of the big moment. "Look at this one. You look like you're in shock."

"Don't make fun, Emily. You're next," she reminded her old high-school chum. "You're all lucky I didn't have a heart attack."

"We know you're tougher than that," Emily said, giving her a hug.

So many friends and people she knew from business and the church surrounded her, Betty felt like a movie star.

"We have one more surprise for you," Molly said, taking her hand. "This one just arrived, special delivery."

She led Betty toward the kitchen, and Betty imagined that Molly had cooked up some exotic dish and their helpers were bringing it over from the shop.

But when Betty reached the kitchen, she stopped in her tracks and just stared. "Brian . . . and Tina? What are you guys doing here?"

"It's your birthday, Mom. Did you think we'd miss it?"

"Oh my goodness . . ." Betty started crying. "This is just too much." Nathan was beside her in a flash. He put his arm around her shoulders and she buried her face on his chest, until she could get control of herself again.

"Here, take my hanky," he offered.

"That's all right. I already wiped my eye' sweater," she confessed.

Nathan just laughed and let her go, and she greete⌐ his fiancée with hugs. "You guys didn't have to come all ⌐ for me," she insisted.

"We wanted to. We wanted to celebrate with you," Tina said.

"Oh, that's so sweet of you, dear. I'm so happy you're here." Betty smiled at her and then looked over at her son, who stood next to Nathan. And then at Molly and Matt, who also stood nearby.

"You all know how much I was dreading turning fifty," Betty told them "But I must say, if I knew it was going to be this good, I would have done it a lot sooner."

It was a wonderful party, with warm company, high spirits, and Molly's terrific food. Betty blew out the candles on her cake with one big puff, wishing hard. The happy hours went by in a flash and before Betty knew it, she and Nathan were back in the car, heading home with a pile of gifts in the backseat.

"So, did you enjoy your party?" Nathan asked.

"I had a great time. I didn't really want a big party for this birthday, but thank you for ignoring my wishes and charging ahead anyway."

Nathan laughed. "Well, Molly had a little to do with that part. But as long as you're happy."

"I am happy," she assured him. So much in her life had been resolved, Betty reflected. Her relationship with her son, her solitary state. She had never really been afraid to be alone, but she was definitely happier being with someone she truly cared for.

She took his hand as they pulled up to her house. "I think my happiness has a lot to do with you," she said softly.

"I hope you'll always feel that way." He turned and glanced toward the back of the car. "You have a load of gifts back there," he noted. "But I didn't give you one yet."

"Oh, you don't need to give me a gift, Nathan. You just gave me a beautiful party. That's enough of a present."

"Of course I have to give you a gift. I never got you anything for Christmas," he reminded her. "And then there's Valentine's Day coming up. So it had to be something really special," he explained. "It's just that it's in this tiny box." He took a small blue velvet box out of his jacket pocket. "I didn't want to put it in with the rest of the gifts. I was afraid it would get lost."

Betty eyed the box and then looked at him. She felt suddenly breathless. He handed it over to her, smiling softly in the dark. "This is for you. Happy birthday, Beautiful."

She took the box, noticing her hands were actually shaking. Was this what she thought it was? She tried not to get her hopes up. It didn't have to be a ring box. It could be holding any sort of jewelry. Earrings maybe . . . or a pendant.

"Don't you want to open it?"

She took a deep breath and felt him watching her intently. She slowly opened the box and peered inside. A beautiful dark blue stone—a square-cut blue sapphire—glittered in an elegant gold band.

"Oh, Nathan . . . this is so beautiful." She looked up at him, speechless.

"Do you like it? I know that we only met a few months ago. Some people might not think that was long enough to know for sure. But I think I knew from the first time I saw you. You were the one for me. The only one. I love you with all my heart. I would be the happiest man on earth if you'd have me. Will you marry me, Betty?" he asked, staring into her eyes.

"Marry you? . . . Of course I will. Oh, Nathan . . . I love you so much." Betty flung herself into his arms and held him close. "I never thought I could feel like this again," she confessed. "But I think love is even better now when you're our age. I appreciate it more. . . . I appreciate you more. I couldn't think of anything that would make me happier than to spend the next fifty years of my life with you."

Nathan laughed softly. "Is that all you'll give me? It would never be long enough with you. We are truly blessed," he whispered against her hair.

Betty didn't have to answer. She looked back at her past, feeling healed and resolved over all that had gone before. And looked ahead now to the rest of her life beside this remarkable man, feeling complete and unexpected joy. They had so much to be grateful for.